I was six years old when my parents told me that there was a small, dark jewel inside my skull, learning to be me.

Microscopic spiders had woven a fine golden web through my brain, so that the jewel's teacher could listen to the whisper of my thoughts. The jewel itself eavesdropped on my senses, and read the chemical messages carried in my bloodstream; it saw, heard, smelt, tasted and felt the world exactly as I did, while the teacher monitored its thoughts and compared them with my own. Whenever the jewel's thoughts were *wrong*, the teacher – faster than thought – rebuilt the jewel slightly, altering it this way and that, seeking out the changes that would make its thoughts correct.

Why? So that when I could no longer be me, the jewel could do it for me.

I thought: if hearing that makes *me* feel strange and giddy, how must it make *the jewel* feel? Exactly the same, I reasoned; it doesn't know it's the jewel, and it too wonders how the jewel must feel, it too reasons: 'Exactly the same, it doesn't know it's the jewel, and it too wonders how the jewel must feel . . .'

And it too wonders –

(I knew, because I wondered)

– it too wonders whether it's the real me, or whether in fact it's only the jewel that's learning to be me.

Greg Egan lives in Perth, Western Australia. He alternates programming contracts with stretches of full-time writing, and his short fiction has twice won Best Story of the Year in *Interzone* magazine.

AXIOMATIC

Greg Egan

MILLENNIUM

Orion Paperbacks
A Millennium Book
First published in Great Britain by Millennium in 1995
This paperback edition published in 1996 by Orion Books Ltd,
Orion House, 5 Upper St Martin's Lane, London WC2H 9EA

A CIP catalogue record for this book is available
from the British Library.

ISBN: 1 85798 309 2

Typeset at The Spartan Press Ltd,
Lymington, Hants

Printed and bound in Great Britain by
Clays Ltd, St Ives plc

Thanks to Caroline Oakley, Deborah Beale, Anthony Cheetham, Peter Robinson, David Pringle, Lee Montgomerie, Gardner Dozois, Sheila Williams, Jonathan Strahan, Jeremy Byrne, Richard Scriven, Steve Pasechnick, Dirk Strasser, Stephen Higgins, Kristine Kathryn Rusch, Lucy Sussex, Steve Paulsen, Andrew Whitmore and Bruce Gillespie.

CONTENTS

ACKNOWLEDGEMENTS

'The Cutie' was first published in *Interzone #29*, May/June
   1989.

'The Caress' was first published in *Isaac Asimov's Science
   Fiction Magazine*, January 1990.

'Eugene' was first published in *Interzone #36*, June 1990.

'Learning to Be Me' was first published in *Interzone #37*, July
   1990.

'The Safe-Deposit Box' was first published in *Isaac Asimov's
   Science Fiction Magazine*, September 1990.

'Axiomatic' was first published in *Interzone #41*, November
   1990.

'The Moral Virologist' was first published in *Pulphouse #8*,
   Summer 1990.

'Blood Sisters' was first published in *Interzone #44*, February
   1991.

'The Moat' was first published in *Aurealis #3*, March 1991.

'The Infinite Assassin' was first published in *Interzone #48*,
   June 1991.

'Appropriate Love' was first published in *Interzone #50*,
   August 1991.

'Into Darkness' was first published in *Isaac Asimov's Science
   Fiction Magazine*, January 1992.

'The Hundred-Light-Year Diary' was first published in *Interzone #55*, January 1992.

'Closer' was first published in *Eidolon #9*, Winter 1992.

'Unstable Orbits in the Space of Lies' was first published in *Interzone #61*, July 1992.

'The Walk' was first published in *Isaac Asimov's Science Fiction Magazine*, December 1992.

'Seeing' is a previously unpublished story.

'A Kidnapping' is a previously unpublished story.

THE INFINITE ASSASSIN

One thing never changes: when some mutant junkie on S starts shuffling reality, it's always me they send into the whirlpool to put things right.

Why? They tell me I'm stable. Reliable. Dependable. After each debriefing, The Company's psychologists (complete strangers, every time) shake their heads in astonishment at their printouts, and tell me that I'm exactly the same person as when 'I' went in.

The number of parallel worlds is uncountably infinite – infinite like the real numbers, not merely like the integers – making it difficult to quantify these things without elaborate mathematical definitions, but roughly speaking, it seems that I'm unusually invariant: more alike from world to world than most people are. How alike? In how many worlds? Enough to be useful. Enough to do the job.

How The Company knew this, how they found me, I've never been told. I was recruited at the age of nineteen. Bribed. Trained. Brainwashed, I suppose. Sometimes I wonder if my stability has anything to do with *me*; maybe the real constant is the way I've been prepared. Maybe an infinite number of different people, put through the same process, would all emerge the same. Have all emerged the same. I don't know.

Detectors scattered across the planet have sensed the

faint beginnings of the whirlpool, and pinned down the centre to within a few kilometres, but that's the most accurate fix I can expect by this means. Each version of The Company shares its technology freely with the others, to ensure a uniformly optimal response, but even in the best of all possible worlds, the detectors are too large, and too delicate, to carry in closer for a more precise reading.

A helicopter deposits me on wasteland at the southern edge of the Leightown ghetto. I've never been here before, but the boarded-up shopfronts and grey tower blocks ahead are utterly familiar. Every large city in the world (in every world I know) has a place like this, created by a policy that's usually referred to as *differential enforcement*. Using or possessing S is strictly illegal, and the penalty in most countries is (mostly) summary execution, but the powers that be would rather have the users concentrated in designated areas than risk having them scattered amongst the community at large. So, if you're caught with S in a nice clean suburb, they'll blow a hole in your skull on the spot, but here, there's no chance of that. Here, there are no cops at all.

I head north. It's just after four a.m., but savagely hot, and once I move out of the buffer zone, the streets are crowded. People are coming and going from nightclubs, liquor stores, pawn shops, gambling houses, brothels. Power for street lighting has been cut off from this part of the city, but someone civic-minded has replaced the normal bulbs with self-contained tritium/phosphor globes, spilling a cool, pale light like radioactive milk. There's a popular misconception that most S users do nothing but dream, twenty-four hours a day, but that's ludicrous; not only do they need to eat, drink and earn money like everyone else, but few would waste the drug on the time when their alter egos are themselves asleep.

Intelligence says there's some kind of whirlpool cult

in Leightown, who may try to interfere with my work. I've been warned of such groups before, but it's never come to anything; the slightest shift in reality is usually all it takes to make such an aberration vanish. The Company, the ghettos, are the stable responses to S; everything else seems to be highly conditional. Still, I shouldn't be complacent. Even if these cults can have no significant impact on the mission as a whole, no doubt they *have* killed some versions of me in the past, and I don't want it to be my turn, this time. I know that an infinite number of versions of me would survive – some whose only difference from me would be *that they had survived* – so perhaps I ought to be entirely untroubled by the thought of death.

But I'm not.

Wardrobe have dressed me with scrupulous care, in a Fat Single Mothers Must Die World Tour souvenir reflection hologram T-shirt, the right style of jeans, the right model running shoes. Paradoxically, S users tend to be slavish adherents to 'local' fashion, as opposed to that of their dreams; perhaps it's a matter of wanting to partition their sleeping and waking lives. For now, I'm in perfect camouflage, but I don't expect that to last; as the whirlpool picks up speed, sweeping different parts of the ghetto into different histories, changes in style will be one of the most sensitive markers. If my clothes don't look out of place before too long, I'll know I'm headed in the wrong direction.

A tall, bald man with a shrunken human thumb dangling from one ear lobe collides with me as he runs out of a bar. As we separate, he turns on me, screaming taunts and obscenities. I respond cautiously; he may have friends in the crowd, and I don't have time to waste getting into that kind of trouble. I don't escalate things by replying, but I take care to appear confident, without seeming arrogant or disdainful. This balancing act pays off. Insulting me with impunity for thirty seconds apparently satisfies his pride, and he walks away smirking.

As I move on, though, I can't help wondering how many versions of me didn't get out of it so easily.

I pick up speed to compensate for the delay.

Someone catches up with me, and starts walking beside me. 'Hey, I liked the way you handled that. Subtle. Manipulative. Pragmatic. Full marks.' A woman in her late twenties, with short, metallic-blue hair.

'Fuck off. I'm not interested.'

'In what?'

'In anything.'

She shakes her head. 'Not true. You're new around here, and you're looking for something. Or someone. Maybe I can help.'

'I said, fuck off.'

She shrugs and falls behind, but calls after me, 'Every hunter needs a guide. Think about it.'

A few blocks later, I turn into an unlit side street. Deserted, silent; stinking of half-burnt garbage, cheap insecticide, and piss. And I swear I can *feel it*: in the dark, ruined buildings all around me, people are dreaming on S.

S is not like any other drug. S dreams are neither surreal nor euphoric. Nor are they like simulator trips: empty fantasies, absurd fairy tales of limitless prosperity and indescribable bliss. They're dreams of lives that, literally, *might have been lived* by the dreamers, every bit as solid and plausible as their waking lives.

With one exception: if the dream life turns sour, the dreamer can abandon it at will, and choose another (without any need to dream of taking S . . . although that's been known to happen). He or she can piece together a second life, in which no mistakes are irrevocable, no decisions absolute. A life without

4

failures, without dead ends. All possibilities remain forever accessible.

S grants dreamers the power to live vicariously in any parallel world in which they have an alter ego – someone with whom they share enough brain physiology to maintain the parasitic resonance of the link. Studies suggest that a perfect genetic match isn't necessary for this – but nor is it sufficient; early childhood development also seems to affect the neural structures involved.

For most users, the drug does no more than this. For one in a hundred thousand, though, dreams are only the beginning. During their third or fourth year on S, they start to move *physically* from world to world, as they strive to take the place of their chosen alter egos.

The trouble is, there's never anything so simple as an infinity of direct exchanges, between all the versions of the mutant user who've gained this power, and all the versions they wish to become. Such transitions are energetically unfavourable; in practice, each dreamer must move gradually, continuously, passing through all the intervening points. But those 'points' are occupied by other versions of themselves; it's like motion in a crowd – or a fluid. The dreamers must *flow*.

At first, those alter egos who've developed the skill are distributed too sparsely to have any effect at all. Later, it seems there's a kind of paralysis through symmetry; all potential flows are equally possible, including each one's exact opposite. Everything just cancels out.

The first few times the symmetry is broken, there's usually nothing but a brief shudder, a momentary slippage, an almost imperceptible world-quake. The detectors record these events, but are still too insensitive to localise them.

Eventually, some kind of critical threshold is crossed. Complex, sustained flows develop: vast, tangled currents with the kind of pathological topologies that only an infinite-dimensional space can contain. Such flows are viscous; nearby points are dragged along. That's what creates the whirlpool; the closer you are to the mutant dreamer, the faster you're carried from world to world.

As more and more versions of the dreamer contribute to the flow, it picks up speed – and the faster it becomes, the further away its influence is felt.

The Company, of course, doesn't give a shit if reality is scrambled in the ghettos. My job is to keep the effects from spreading beyond.

I follow the side street to the top of a hill. There's another main road about four hundred metres ahead. I find a sheltered spot amongst the rubble of a half-demolished building, unfold a pair of binoculars, and spend five minutes watching the pedestrians below. Every ten or fifteen seconds, I notice a tiny mutation: an item of clothing changing; a person suddenly shifting position, or vanishing completely, or materialising from nowhere. The binoculars are smart; they count up the number of events which take place in their field of view, as well as computing the map coordinates of the point they're aimed at.

I turn one hundred and eighty degrees, and look back on the crowd that I passed through on my way here. The rate is substantially lower, but the same kind of thing is visible. Bystanders, of course, notice nothing; as yet, the whirlpool's gradients are so shallow that any two people within sight of each other on a crowded street would more or less shift universes together. Only at a distance can the changes be seen.

In fact, since I'm closer to the centre of the whirlpool than the people to the south of me, most of the changes I see in that direction are due to my own rate of shift. I've long ago left the world of my most recent employers behind – but I have no doubt that the vacancy has been, and will continue to be, filled.

I'm going to have to make a third observation to get a fix, some distance away from the north–south line joining the first two points. Over time, of course, the centre will drift, but not very rapidly; the flow runs between worlds where the centres are close together, so its position is the last thing to change.

I head down the hill, westwards.

Amongst the crowds and lights again, waiting for a gap in the traffic, someone taps my elbow. I turn, to see the same blue-haired woman who accosted me before. I give her a stare of mild annoyance, but I keep my mouth shut; I don't know whether or not this version of her has met a version of me, and I don't want to contradict her expectations. By now, at least some of the locals must have noticed what's going on – just listening to an outside radio station, stuttering randomly from song to song, should be enough to give it away – but it's not in my interest to spread the news.

She says, 'I can help you find her.'

'Help me find who?'

'I know exactly where she is. There's no need to waste time on measurements and calc—'

'Shut up. Come with me.'

She follows me, uncomplaining, into a nearby alley. *Maybe I'm being set up for an ambush. By the whirlpool cult?* But the alley is deserted. When I'm sure we're alone, I push her against the wall and put a gun to her head. She doesn't call out, or resist; she's shaken, but I don't think she's surprised by this treatment. I scan her with a hand-held magnetic resonance imager; no weapons, no booby traps, no transmitters.

I say, 'Why don't you tell me what this is all about?' I'd swear that nobody could have seen me on the hill, but maybe she saw another version of me. It's not like me to screw up, but it does happen.

7

She closes her eyes for a moment, then says, almost calmly, 'I want to save you time, that's all. I know where the mutant is. I want to help you find her as quickly as possible.'

'Why?'

'*Why?* I have a *business* here, and I don't want to see it disrupted. Do you know how hard it is to build up contacts again, after a whirlpool's been through? What do you think – I'm covered by insurance?'

I don't believe a word of this, but I see no reason not to play along; it's probably the simplest way to deal with her, short of blowing her brains out. I put away the gun and take a map from my pocket. 'Show me.'

She points out a building about two kilometres north-east of where we are. 'Fifth floor. Apartment 522.'

'How do you know?'

'A friend of mine lives in the building. He noticed the effects just before midnight, and he got in touch with me.' She laughs nervously. 'Actually, *I* don't know the guy all that well . . . but I think the version who phoned me had something going on with another me.'

'Why didn't you just leave when you heard the news? Clear out to a safe distance?'

She shakes her head vehemently. 'Leaving is the worst thing to do; I'd end up even more out of touch. The outside world doesn't matter. Do you think I care if the government changes, or the pop stars have different names? This is my home. If Leightown shifts, I'm better off shifting with it. Or with part of it.'

'So how did you find me?'

She shrugs. 'I knew you'd be coming. Everybody knows that much. Of course, I didn't know what you'd look like – but I know this place pretty well, and I kept my eyes open for strangers. And it seems I got lucky.'

Lucky. Exactly. Some of my alter egos will be having versions of this conversation, but others won't be having any conversation at all. One more random delay.

I fold the map. 'Thanks for the information.'

She nods. 'Any time.'

As I'm walking away, she calls out, '*Every time.*'

I quicken my step for a while; other versions of me should be doing the same, compensating for however much time they've wasted. I can't expect to maintain perfect synch, but dispersion is insidious; if I didn't at least try to minimise it, I'd end up travelling to the centre by every conceivable route, and arriving over a period of days.

And although I can usually make up lost time, I can never entirely cancel out the effects of variable delays. Spending different amounts of time at different distances from the centre means that all the versions of me aren't shifted uniformly. There are theoretical models which show that under certain conditions, this could result in gaps; I could be squeezed into certain portions of the flow, and removed from others – a bit like halving all the numbers between 0 and 1, leaving a hole from 0.5 to 1 . . . squashing one infinity into another which is cardinally identical, but half the geometric size. No versions of me would have been destroyed, and I wouldn't even exist twice in the same world, but nevertheless, a gap would have been created.

As for heading straight for the building where my 'informant' claims the mutant is dreaming, I'm not tempted at all. Whether or not the information is genuine, I doubt very much that I've received the tip-off in any but an insignificant portion – technically, a set of measure zero – of the worlds caught up in the whirlpool. Any action taken only in such a sparse set of worlds would be totally ineffectual, in terms of disrupting the flow.

If I'm right, then of course it makes no difference

what I do; if all the versions of me who received the tip-off simply marched out of the whirlpool, it would have no impact on the mission. A set of measure zero wouldn't be missed. But my actions, as an individual, are *always* irrelevant in that sense; if I, *and I alone*, deserted, the loss would be infinitesimal. The catch is, I could never know that I was acting alone.

And the truth is, versions of me probably have deserted; however stable my personality, it's hard to believe that there are *no* valid quantum permutations entailing such an action. Whatever the physically possible choices are, my alter egos have made – and will continue to make – every single one of them. My stability lies in the distribution, and the relative density, of all these branches – in the shape of a static, pre-ordained structure. Free will is a rationalisation; I can't help making all the right decisions. And all the wrong ones.

But I 'prefer' (granting meaning to the word) not to think this way too often. The only sane approach is to think of myself as one free agent of many, and to 'strive' for coherence; to ignore short cuts, to stick to procedure, to 'do everything I can' to concentrate my presence.

As for worrying about those alter egos who desert, or fail, or die, there's a simple solution: I disown them. It's up to me to define my identity any way I like. I may be forced to accept my multiplicity, but the borders are mine to draw. 'I' am those who survive, and succeed. The rest are someone else.

I reach a suitable vantage point and take a third count. The view is starting to look like a half-hour video recording edited down to five minutes – exept that the whole scene doesn't change at once; apart from some highly correlated couples, different people vanish and appear independently, suffering their own individual jump cuts. They're still all shifting universes more or less together, but what that means, in terms of where they happen to be physically located at any instant, is so complex that it might as well be random. A few people don't vanish at all; one man loiters consistently on the same street corner – although his haircut changes, radically, at least five times.

When the measurement is over, the computer inside the binoculars flashes up coordinates for the centre's estimated position. It's about sixty metres from the building the blue-haired woman pointed out; well within the margin of error. So perhaps she was telling the truth – but that changes nothing. I must still ignore her.

As I start towards my target, I wonder: Maybe I *was* ambushed back in that alley, after all. Maybe I was given the mutant's location as a deliberate attempt to distract me, to divide me. Maybe the woman tossed a coin to split the universe: heads for a tip-off, tails for none – or threw dice, and chose from a wider list of strategies.

It's only a theory . . . but it's a comforting idea: if that's the best the whirlpool cult can do to protect the object of their devotion, then I have nothing to fear from them at all.

I avoid the major roads, but even on the side streets it's soon clear that the word is out. People run past me, some hysterical, some grim; some empty-handed, some toting possessions; one man dashes from door to door, hurling bricks through windows, waking the occupants, shouting the news. Not everyone's heading in the same direction; most are simply fleeing the ghetto, trying to escape the whirlpool, but others are no doubt frantically searching for their friends, their families, their lovers, in the hope of reaching them before they turn into strangers. I wish them well.

Except in the central disaster zone, a few hard-core

dreamers will stay put. Shifting doesn't matter to them; they can reach their dream lives from anywhere – or so they think. Some may be in for a shock; the whirlpool can pass through worlds where there is no supply of S – where the mutant user has an alter ego who has never even heard of the drug.

As I turn into a long, straight avenue, the naked-eye view begins to take on the jump-cut appearance that the binoculars produced, just fifteen minutes ago. People flicker, shift, vanish. Nobody stays in sight for long; few travel more than ten or twenty metres before disappearing. Many are flinching and stumbling as they run, balking at empty space as often as at real obstacles, all confidence in the permanence of the world around them, rightly, shattered. Some run blindly with their heads down and their arms outstretched. Most people are smart enough to travel on foot, but plenty of smashed and abandoned cars strobe in and out of existence on the roadway. I witness one car in motion, but only fleetingly.

I don't see myself anywhere about; I never have yet. Random scatter *should* put me in the same world twice, in some worlds – but only in a set of measure zero. Throw two idealised darts at a dartboard, and the probability of twice hitting the same point – the same zero-dimensional *point* – is zero. Repeat the experiment in an uncountably infinite number of worlds, and it will happen – but only in a set of measure zero.

The changes are most frantic in the distance, and the blur of activity retreats to some extent as I move – due as it is, in part, to mere separation – but I'm also heading into steeper gradients, so I am, slowly, gaining on the havoc. I keep to a measured pace, looking out for both sudden human obstacles and shifts in the terrain.

The pedestrians thin out. The street itself still endures, but the buildings around me are beginning to be transformed into bizarre chimeras, with mismatched segments from variant designs, and then from utterly different structures, appearing side by side. It's like walking through some holographic architectural iden-tikit machine on overdrive. Before long, most of these composites are collapsing, unbalanced by fatal disa-greements on where loads should be borne. Falling rubble makes the footpath dangerous, so I weave my way between the car bodies in the middle of the road. There's virtually no moving traffic now, but it's slow work just navigating between all this 'stationary' scrap metal. Obstructions come and go; it's usually quicker to wait for them to vanish than to backtrack and look for another way through. Sometimes I'm hemmed in on all sides, but never for long.

Finally, most of the buildings around me seem to have toppled, in most worlds, and I find a path near the edge of the road that's relatively passable. Nearby, it looks like an earthquake has levelled the ghetto. Look-ing back, away from the whirlpool, there's nothing but a grey fog of generic buildings; out there, structures are still moving as one – or near enough to remain standing – but I'm shifting so much faster than they are that the skyline has smeared into an amorphous multiple ex-posure of a billion different possibilities.

A human figure, sliced open obliquely from skull to groin, materialises in front of me, topples, then vanishes. My guts squirm, but I press on. I know that the very same thing must be happening to versions of me – but I declare it, I *define* it, to be the death of strangers. The gradient is so high now that different parts of the body can be dragged into different worlds, where the complementary pieces of anatomy have no good statistical reason to be correctly aligned. The rate at which this fatal dissociation occurs, though, is inexplicably lower than calculations predict; the human body somehow defends its integrity, and shifts as a whole far more often than it should. The physical basis for this anomaly has yet to be pinned down – but then, the physical basis for the human brain creating the delusion of a unique history, a sense of time, and a sense of identity, from the multifurcating branches and fans of superspace, has also proved to be elusive.

The sky grows light, a weird blue-grey that no single overcast sky ever possessed. The streets themselves are in a state of flux now; every second or third step is a revelation – bitumen, broken masonry, concrete, sand, all at slightly different levels – and briefly, a patch of withered grass. An inertial navigation implant in my skull guides me through the chaos. Clouds of dust and smoke come and go, and then—

A cluster of apartment blocks, with surface features flickering, but showing no signs of disintegrating. The rates of shift here are higher than ever, but there's a counterbalancing effect: the worlds between which the flow runs are required to be more and more alike, the closer you get to the dreamer.

The group of buildings is roughly symmetrical, and it's perfectly clear which one lies at the centre. None of me would fail to make the same judgement, so I won't need to go through absurd mental contortions to avoid acting on the tip-off.

The front entrance to the building oscillates, mainly between three alternatives. I choose the leftmost door; a matter of procedure, a standard which The Company managed to propagate between itselves before I was even recruited. (No doubt contradictory instructions circulated for a while, but one scheme must have dominated, eventually, because I've never been briefed any differently.) I often wish I could leave (and/or follow) a trail of some kind, but any mark I made would be useless, swept downstream faster than those it was meant to guide. I have no choice but to trust in procedure to minimise my dispersion.

From the foyer, I can see four stairwells – all with

stairs converted into piles of flickering rubble. I step into the leftmost, and glance up; the early-morning light floods in through a variety of possible windows. The spacing between the great concrete slabs of the floors is holding constant; the energy difference between such large structures in different positions lends them more stability than all the possible, specific shapes of flights of stairs. Cracks must be developing, though, and given time, there's no doubt that even this building would succumb to its discrepancies – killing the dreamer, in world after world, and putting an end to the flow. But who knows how far the whirlpool might have spread by then?

The explosive devices I carry are small, but more than adequate. I set one down in the stairwell, speak the arming sequence, and run. I glance back across the foyer as I retreat, but at a distance, the details amongst the rubble are nothing but a blur. The bomb I've planted has been swept into another world, but it's a matter of faith – and experience – that there's an infinite line of others to take its place.

I collide with a wall where there used to be a door, step back, try again, pass through. Sprinting across the road, an abandoned car materialises in front of me; I skirt around it, drop behind it, cover my head.

Eighteen. Nineteen. Twenty. Twenty-one. Twenty-two?

Not a sound. I look up. The car has vanished. The building still stands – and still flickers.

I climb to my feet, dazed. Some bombs may have – must have – failed . . . but enough should have exploded to disrupt the flow.

So what's happened? Perhaps the dreamer has survived in some small, but contiguous, part of the flow, and it's closed off into a loop – which it's my bad luck to be a part of. *Survived how?* The worlds in which the bomb exploded should have been spread randomly, uniformly, everywhere dense enough to do the job . . .

but perhaps some freak clustering effect has given rise to a gap.

Or maybe I've ended up squeezed out of part of the flow. The theoretical conditions for that have always struck me as far too bizarre to be fulfilled in real life . . . but what if it *has* happened? A gap in my presence, downstream from me, would have left a set of worlds with no bomb planted at all – which then flowed along and caught up with me, once I moved away from the building and my shift rate dropped.

I 'return' to the stairwell. There's no unexploded bomb, no sign that any version of me has been here. I plant the backup device, and run. This time, I find no shelter on the street, and I simply hit the ground.

Again, nothing.

I struggle to calm myself, to visualise the possibilities. If the gap without bombs hadn't fully passed the gap without me, when the first bombs went off, then I'd still have been missing from a part of the surviving flow – allowing exactly the same thing to happen all over again.

I stare at the intact building, disbelieving. *I am the ones who succeed. That's all that defines me.* But who, exactly, failed? If I was absent from part of the flow, there were no versions of me in those worlds *to* fail. Who takes the blame? Who do I disown? Those who successfully planted the bomb, but 'should have' done it in other worlds? *Am I amongst them?* I have no way of knowing.

So, what now? How big is the gap? How close am I to it? How many times can it defeat me?

I have to keep killing the dreamer, until I succeed.

I return to the stairwell. The floors are about three metres apart. To ascend, I use a small grappling hook on a short rope; the hook fires an explosive-driven spike into the concrete floor. Once the rope is uncoiled, its chances of ending up in separate pieces in different worlds is magnified; it's essential to move quickly.

I search the first storey systematically, following procedure to the letter, as if I'd never heard of Room 522. A blur of alternative dividing walls, ghostly spartan furniture, transient heaps of sad possessions. When I've finished, I pause until the clock in my skull reaches the next multiple of ten minutes. It's an imperfect strategy – some stragglers will fall more than ten minutes behind – but that would be true however long I waited.

The second storey is deserted, too. But a little more stable; there's no doubt that I'm drawing closer to the heart of the whirlpool.

The third storey's architecture is almost solid. The fourth, if not for the abandoned ephemera flickering in the corners of rooms, could pass for normal.

The fifth—

I kick the doors open, one by one, moving steadily down the corridor. 502. 504. 506. I thought I might be tempted to break ranks when I came this close, but instead I find it easier than ever to go through the motions, knowing that I'll have no opportunity to regroup. 516. 518. 520.

At the far end of Room 522, there's a young woman stretched out on a bed. Her hair is a diaphanous halo of possibilities, her clothing a translucent haze, but her body looks solid and permanent, the almost-fixed point about which all the night's chaos has spun.

I step into the room, take aim at her skull, and fire. The bullet shifts worlds before it can reach her, but it will kill another version, downstream. I fire again and again, waiting for a bullet from a brother assassin to strike home before my eyes – or for the flow to stop, for the living dreamers to become too few, too sparse, to maintain it.

Neither happens.

'You took your time.'

I swing around. The blue-haired woman stands

outside the doorway. I reload the gun; she makes no move to stop me. My hands are shaking. I turn back to the dreamer and kill her, another two dozen times. The version before me remains untouched, the flow undiminished.

I reload again, and wave the gun at the blue-haired woman. 'What the fuck have you done to me? *Am I alone?* Have you slaughtered all the others?' But that's absurd – and if it were true, how could she see me? I'd be a momentary, imperceptible flicker to each separate version of her, nothing more; she wouldn't even know I was there.

She shakes her head, and says mildly, 'We've slaughtered no one. We've mapped you into Cantor dust, that's all. Every one of you is still alive – but none of you can stop the whirlpool.'

Cantor dust. A fractal set, uncountably infinite, but with measure zero. There's not *one* gap in my presence; there's an infinite number, an endless series of ever-smaller holes, everywhere. But—

'*How?* You set me up, you kept me talking, but how could you coordinate the delays? And calculate the effects? It would take . . .'

'Infinite computational power? An infinite number of people?' She smiles faintly. 'I *am* an infinite number of people. All sleepwalking on S. All dreaming each other. We can act together, in synch, as one – or we can act independently. Or something in between, as now: the versions of me who can see and hear you at any moment are sharing their sense data with the rest of me.'

I turn back to the dreamer. 'Why defend her? She'll never get what she wants. She's tearing the city apart, and she'll never even reach her destination.'

'Not here, perhaps.'

'*Not here?* She's crossing all the worlds she lives in! Where else is there?'

The woman shakes her head. 'What creates those worlds? Alternative possibilities for ordinary physical processes. But it doesn't stop there; the possibility of motion *between* worlds has exactly the same effect. Superspace *itself* branches out into different versions, versions containing all possible cross-world flows. And there can be higher-level flows, between those versions of superspace, so the whole structure branches again. And so on.'

I close my eyes, drowning in vertigo. If this endless ascent into greater infinities is true—

'Somewhere, the dreamer always triumphs? Whatever I do?'

'Yes.'

'And somewhere, I always win? Somewhere, you've failed to defeat me?'

'Yes.'

Who am I? I'm the ones who succeed. Then who am *I*? I'm nothing at all. A set of measure zero.

I drop the gun and take three steps towards the dreamer. My clothes, already tattered, part worlds and fall away.

I take another step, and then halt, shocked by a sudden warmth. My hair, and outer layers of skin, have vanished; I'm covered with a fine sweat of blood. I notice, for the first time, the frozen smile on the dreamer's face.

And I wonder: in how many infinite sets of worlds will I take one more step? And how many countless versions of me will turn around instead, and walk out of this room? *Who exactly am I saving from shame, when I'll live and die in every possible way?*

Myself.

THE HUNDRED-LIGHT-YEAR DIARY

Martin Place was packed with the usual frantic lunch-time crowds. I scanned the faces nervously; the moment had almost arrived, and I still hadn't even caught sight of Alison. *One twenty-seven and fourteen seconds.* Would I be mistaken about something so important? With the knowledge of the mistake still fresh in my mind? But that knowledge could make no difference. Of course it would affect my state of mind, of course it would influence my actions – but I already knew exactly what the net result of that, and every other, influence would be: I'd write what I'd read.

I needn't have worried. I looked down at my watch, and as *1:27:13* became *1:27:14*, someone tapped me on the shoulder. I turned; it was Alison, of course. I'd never seen her before, in the flesh, but I'd soon devote a month's bandwidth allocation to sending back a Barnsley-compressed snapshot. I hesitated, then spoke my lines, awful as they were:

'Fancy meeting you here.'

She smiled, and suddenly I was overwhelmed, giddy with happiness – exactly as I'd read in my diary a thousand times, since I'd first come across the day's entry at the age of nine; exactly as I would, necessarily, describe it at the terminal that night. But – foreknow-ledge aside – how could I have felt anything but euphoria? I'd finally met the woman I'd spend my life with. We had fifty-eight years together ahead of us, and we'd love each other to the end.

'So, where are we going for lunch?'

I frowned slightly, wondering if she was joking – and wondering why I'd left myself in any doubt. I said, hesitantly, 'Fulvio's. Didn't you . . .?' But of course she had no idea of the petty details of the meal; on 14 December, 2074, I'd write admiringly: *A. concentrates on the things that matter; she never lets herself be distracted by trivia.*

I said, 'Well, the food won't be ready on time; they'll have screwed up their schedule, but—'

She put a finger to her lips, then leant forward and kissed me. For a moment, I was too shocked to do anything but stand there like a statue, but after a second or two, I started kissing back.

When we parted, I said stupidly, 'I didn't know . . . I thought we just . . . I—'

'James, you're blushing.'

She was right. I laughed, embarrassed. It was absurd: in a week's time, we'd make love, and I already knew every detail – yet that single unexpected kiss left me flustered and confused.

She said, 'Come on. Maybe the food won't be ready, but we have a lot to talk about while we're waiting. I just hope you haven't read it all in advance, or you're going to have a very boring time.'

She took my hand and started leading the way. I followed, still shaken. Halfway to the restaurant, I finally managed to say, 'Back then – did you know that would happen?'

She laughed. 'No. But I don't tell myself everything. I like to be surprised now and then. Don't you?'

Her casual attitude stung me. *Never lets herself be distracted by trivia.* I struggled for words; this whole conversation was unknown to me, and I never was

22

much good at improvising anything but small talk.

I said, 'Today is important to me. I always thought I'd write the most careful – the most *complete* – account of it possible. I mean, I'm going to record the time we met, to the second. I can't imagine sitting down tonight and *not even mentioning* the first time we kissed.'

She squeezed my hand, then moved close to me and whispered, mock-conspiratorially: 'But you will. You know you will. And so will I. You know exactly what you're going to write, and exactly what you're going to leave out – and the fact is, that kiss is going to remain our little secret.'

Francis Chen wasn't the first astronomer to hunt for time-reversed galaxies, but he was the first to do so from space. He swept the sky with a small instrument in a junk-scattered near-Earth orbit, long after all serious work had shifted to the (relatively) unpolluted vacuum on the far side of the moon. For decades, certain – highly speculative – cosmological theories had suggested that it might be possible to catch glimpses of the universe's future phase of re-contraction, during which – perhaps – all the arrows of time would be reversed.

Chen charged up a light detector to saturation, and searched for a region of the sky which would *unexpose it* – discharging the pixels in the form of a recognisable image. The photons from ordinary galaxies, collected by ordinary telescopes, left their mark as patterns of charge on arrays of electro-optical polymer; a time-reversed galaxy would require instead that the detector *lose* charge, emitting photons which would leave the telescope on a long journey into the future universe, to be absorbed by stars tens of billions of years hence, contributing an infinitesimal nudge to drive their nuclear processes from extinction back towards birth.

Chen's announcement of success was met with

virtually unanimous scepticism – and rightly so, since he refused to divulge the coordinates of his discovery. I've seen the recording of his one and only press conference.

'What would happen if you pointed an *uncharged* detector at this thing?' asked one puzzled journalist.

'You can't.'

'What do you mean, you *can't*?'

'Suppose you point a detector at an ordinary light source. Unless the detector's not working, it *will* end up charged. It's no use declaring: *I am going to expose this detector to light, and it will end up uncharged*. That's ludicrous; it simply won't happen.'

'Yes, but—'

'Now time-reverse the whole situation. If you're going to point a detector at a time-reversed light source, it *will* be charged beforehand.'

'But if you discharge the whole thing thoroughly, before exposing it, and then . . .'

'I'm sorry. You won't. *You can't*.'

Shortly afterwards, Chen retired into self-imposed obscurity – but his work had been government funded, and he'd complied with the rigorous auditing requirements, so copies of all his notes existed in various archives. It was almost five years before anyone bothered to exhume them – new theoretical work having made his claims more fashionable – but once the coordinates were finally made public, it took only days for a dozen groups to confirm the original results.

Most of the astronomers involved dropped the matter there and then – but three people pressed on, to the logical conclusion:

Suppose an asteroid, a few hundred billion kilometres away, happened to block the line of sight between Earth and Chen's galaxy. In the galaxy's time frame, there'd be a delay of half an hour or so before this occultation could be seen in near-Earth orbit – before the last photons to make it past the asteroid arrived. Our time frame runs the other way, though; for us, the 'delay' would be *negative*. We might think of the detector, not the galaxy, as the source of the photons – but it would still have to stop emitting them half an hour *before* the asteroid crossed the line of sight, in order to emit them only when they'd have a clear path all the way to their destination. Cause and effect; the detector has to have a reason to lose charge and emit photons – even if that reason lies in the future.

Replace the uncontrollable – and unlikely – asteroid with a simple electronic shutter. Fold up the line of sight with mirrors, shrinking the experiment down to more manageable dimensions – and allowing you to place the shutter and detector virtually side by side. Flash a torch at yourself in a mirror, and you get a signal from the past; do the same with the light from Chen's galaxy, and the signal comes from the future.

Hazzard, Capaldi and Wu arranged a pair of space-borne mirrors, a few thousand kilometres apart. With multiple reflections, they achieved an optical path length of over two light seconds. At one end of this 'delay' they placed a telescope, aimed at Chen's galaxy; at the other end they placed a detector. ('The other end' optically speaking – physically, it was housed in the very same satellite as the telescope.) In their first experiments, the telescope was fitted with a shutter triggered by the 'unpredictable' decay of a small sample of a radioactive isotope.

The sequence of the shutter's opening and closing and the detector's rate of discharge were logged by a computer. The two sets of data were compared – and the patterns, unsurprisingly, matched. Except, of course, that the detector began discharging two seconds before the shutter opened, and ceased discharging two seconds before it closed.

So, they replaced the isotope trigger with a manual

control, and took turns trying to change the immutable future.

Hazzard said, in an interview several months later: 'At first, it seemed like some kind of perverse reaction-time test: instead of having to hit the green button when the green light came on, you had to try to hit the red button, and vice versa. And at first, I really believed I was "obeying" the signal only because I couldn't discipline my reflexes to do anything so "difficult" as contradicting it. In retrospect, I know that was a rationalisation, but I was quite convinced at the time. So I had the computer swap the conventions – and of course, that didn't help. Whenever the display said I was going to open the shutter – however it expressed that fact – I opened it.'

'And how did that make you feel? *Soulless? Robotic? A prisoner to fate?*'

'No. At first, just . . . clumsy. Uncoordinated. So clumsy I couldn't hit the wrong button, no matter how hard I tried. And then, after a while, the whole thing began to seem perfectly . . . normal. I wasn't being "forced" to open the shutter; I was opening it precisely when I felt like opening it, and observing the consequences – observing them before the event, yes, but that hardly seemed important any more. Wanting to "not open" it when I already knew that I would seemed as absurd as wanting to change something in the past that I already knew had happened. Does not being able to rewrite history make you feel "soulless"?'

'No.'

'This was exactly the same.'

Extending the device's range was easy; by having the detector itself trigger the shutter in a feedback loop, two seconds could become four seconds, four hours, or four days. Or four centuries – in theory. The real problem was bandwidth; simply blocking off the view of Chen's galaxy, or not, coded only a single bit of information, and the shutter couldn't be strobed at too high a rate, since the detector took almost half a second to lose enough charge to unequivocally signal a future exposure.

Bandwidth is still a problem, although the current generation of Hazzard Machines have path lengths of a hundred light years, and detectors made up of millions of pixels, each one sensitive enough to be modulated at megabaud rates. Governments and large corporations use most of this vast capacity, for purposes that remain obscure – and still they're desperate for more.

As a birthright, though, everyone on the planet is granted one hundred and twenty-eight bytes a day. With the most efficient data-compression schemes, this can code about a hundred words of text; not enough to describe the future in microscopic detail, but enough for a summary of the day's events.

A hundred words a day; three million words in a lifetime. The last entry in my own diary was received in 2032, eighteen years before my birth, one hundred years before my death. The history of the next millennium is taught in schools: the end of famine and disease, the end of nationalism and genocide, the end of poverty, bigotry and superstition. There are glorious times ahead.

If our descendants are telling the truth.

The wedding was, mostly, just as I'd known it would be. The best man, Pria, had his arm in a sling from a mugging in the early hours of the morning – we'd laughed over that when we'd first met, in high school, a decade before.

'But what if I stay out of that alley?' he'd joked.

'Then I'll have to break it for you, won't I? You're not shunting my wedding day!'

Shunting was a fantasy for children, the subject of juvenile schlock-ROMs. *Shunting* was what happened

27

when you grimaced and sweated and gritted your teeth and *absolutely refused* to participate in something unpleasant that you knew was going to happen. In the ROMs, the offending future was magicked away into a parallel universe, by sheer mental discipline and the force of plot convenience. Drinking the right brand of cola also seemed to help.

In real life, with the advent of the Hazzard Machines, the rates of death and injury through crime, natural disaster, industrial and transport accidents, and many kinds of disease, had certainly plummeted – but such events weren't forecast and then paradoxically 'avoided'; they simply, consistently, became increasingly rare in reports from the future – reports which proved to be as reliable as those from the past.

A residue of 'seemingly avoidable' tragedies remains, though, and the people who know that they're going to be involved react in different ways: some swallow their fate cheerfully; some seek comfort (or anaesthesia) in somnambulist religions; a few succumb to the wish-fulfilment fantasies of the ROMs, and go kicking and screaming all the way.

When I met up with Pria, on schedule, in the Casualty Department of St Vincent's, he was a bloody, shivering mess. His arm was broken, as expected. He'd also been sodomised with a bottle and slashed on the arms and chest. I stood beside him in a daze, choking on the sour taste of all the stupid jokes I'd made, unable to shake the feeling that I was to blame. *I'd lie to him, lie to myself—*

As they pumped him full of painkillers and tranquillisers, he said, 'Fuck it, James, I'm not letting on. I'm not going to say how bad it was; I'm not frightening that kid to death. And *you'd* better not, either.' I nodded earnestly and swore that I wouldn't; redundantly, of course, but the poor man was delirious.

And when it was time to write up the day's events, I

dutifully regurgitated the light-hearted treatment of my friend's assault that I'd memorised long before I even knew him.

Dutifully? Or simply because the cycle was closed, because I had no choice but to write what I'd already read? Or . . . both? Ascribing motives is a strange business, but I'm sure it always has been. Knowing the future doesn't mean we've been subtracted out of the equations that shape it. Some philosophers still ramble on about 'the loss of free will' (I suppose they can't help themselves), but I've never been able to find a meaningful definition of what they think this magical thing ever *was*. The future has always been determined. What else could affect human actions, other than each individual's – unique and complex – inheritance and past experience? *Who we are* decides *what we do* – and what greater 'freedom' could anyone demand? If 'choice' wasn't grounded absolutely in cause and effect, what would decide its outcome? Meaningless random glitches from quantum noise in the brain? (A popular theory – before quantum indeterminism was shown to be nothing but an artefact of the old time-asymmetric world-view.) Or some mystical invention called *the soul* . . . but then what, precisely, would govern *its* behaviour? Laws of metaphysics every bit as problematical as those of neurophysiology.

I believe we've lost nothing; rather, we've gained the only freedom we ever lacked: *who we are* is now shaped by the future, as well as the past. Our lives resonate like plucked strings, standing waves formed by the collision of information flowing back and forth in time.

Information – and disinformation.

Alison looked over my shoulder at what I'd typed. 'You've got to be kidding,' she said.

I replied by hitting the CHECK key – a totally unnecessary facility, but that's never stopped anyone using it. The text I'd just typed matched the received version precisely. (People have talked about automating the whole process – transmitting what *must be* transmitted, without any human intervention whatsoever – but nobody's ever done it, so perhaps it's impossible.)

I hit SAVE, burning the day's entry on to the chip that would be transmitted shortly after my death, then said – numbly, idiotically (and inevitably) – 'What if I'd warned him?'

She shook her head. 'Then you'd have warned him. It still would have happened.'

'Maybe not. Why couldn't life turn out better than the diary, not worse? Why couldn't it turn out that we'd made the whole thing up – that he hadn't been attacked at all?'

'Because it didn't.'

I sat at the desk for a moment longer, staring at the words that I couldn't take back, *that I never could have taken back.* But my lies were the lies I'd promised to tell; I'd done the right thing, hadn't I? I'd known for years exactly what I'd 'choose' to write – but that didn't change the fact that the words had been determined, not by 'fate', not by 'destiny', but by *who I was.*

I switched off the terminal, stood up and began undressing. Alison headed for the bathroom. I called out after her, 'Do we have sex tonight, or not? I never say.'

She laughed. 'Don't ask me, James. You're the one who insisted on keeping track of these things.'

I sat down on the bed, disconcerted. It was our wedding night, after all; surely I could read between the lines.

But I never was much good at improvising.

The Australian federal election of 2077 was the closest for fifty years, and would remain so for almost another century. A dozen independents – including three members of a new ignorance cult, called God Averts His Gaze – held the balance of power, but deals to ensure stable government had been stitched together well in advance, and would survive the four-year term.

Consistently, I suppose, the campaign was also among the most heated in recent memory, or short-term anticipation. The soon-to-be Opposition Leader never tired of listing the promises the new Prime Minister would break; she in turn countered with statistics of the mess he'd create as Treasurer, in the mid-eighties. (The causes of that impending recession were still being debated by economists; most claimed it was an 'essential precursor' of the prosperity of the nineties, and that The Market, in its infinite, time-spanning wisdom, would choose/had chosen the best of all possible futures. Personally, I suspect it simply proved that even foresight was no cure for incompetence.)

I often wondered how the politicians felt, mouthing the words they'd known they'd utter ever since their parents first showed them the future-history ROMs, and explained what lay ahead. No ordinary person could afford the bandwidth to send back moving picturs; only the newsworthy were forced to confront such detailed records of their lives, with no room for ambiguity or euphemism. The cameras, of course, *could* lie – digital video fraud was the easiest thing in the world – but mostly they didn't. I wasn't surprised that people made (seemingly) impassioned election speeches which they knew would get them nowhere; I'd read enough past history to realise that that had always been the case. But I'd like to have discovered what went on in their heads as they lip-synched their way through interviews and debates, parliamentary question time and party conferences, all captured in high-resolution holographic perfection for anterity. With every syllable, every gesture, known in advance, did they feel like they'd been reduced to twitching puppets? (If so, maybe that, too, had always been the case.) Or was the smooth flow of rationalisation as efficient as ever? After all, when I filled in my diary each night, I was just as tightly constrained, but I could – almost always – find a good reason to write what I knew I'd write.

Lisa was on the staff of a local candidate who was due to be voted into office. I met her a fortnight before the election, at a fund-raising dinner. To date, I'd had nothing to do with the candidate, but at the turn of the century – by which time, the man's party would be back in office yet again, with a substantial majority – I'd head an engineering firm which would gain several large contracts from state governments of the same political flavour. I'd be coy in my own description of the antecedents of this good fortune – but my bank statement included transactions six months in advance, and I duly made the generous donation that the records implied. In fact, I'd been a little shocked when I'd first seen the print-out, but I'd had time to accustom myself to the idea, and the *de facto* bribe no longer seemed so grossly out of character.

The evening was dull beyond redemption (I'd later describe it as 'tolerable'), but as the guests dispersed into the night, Lisa appeared beside me and said matter-of-factly, 'I believe you and I are going to share a taxi.'

I sat beside her in silence, while the robot vehicle carried us smoothly towards her apartment. Alison was spending the weekend with an old schoolfriend, whose mother would die that night. I *knew* I wouldn't be unfaithful. I loved my wife, I always would. *Or at least, I'd always claim to.* But if that wasn't proof enough, I couldn't believe I'd keep such a secret from myself for the rest of my life.

When the taxi stopped, I said, 'What now? You ask me in for coffee? And I politely decline?'

She said, 'I have no idea. The whole weekend's a

mystery to me.'

The elevator was broken; a sticker from Building Maintenance read: OUT OF ORDER UNTIL 11:06 a.m., 3/2/78. I followed Lisa up twelve flights of stairs, inventing excuses all the way: *I was proving my freedom, my spontaneity – proving that my life was more than a fossilised pattern of events in time.* But the truth was, I'd never felt trapped by my knowledge of the future, never felt any need to delude myself that I had the power to live any life but one. The whole idea of an unknown liaison filled me with panic and vertigo. The bland white lies that I'd already written were unsettling enough – but if *anything at all* could happen in the spaces between the words, then I no longer knew who I was, or who I might become. My whole life would dissolve into quicksand.

I was shaking as we undressed each other.

'Why are we doing this?'

'Because we can.'

'Do you know me? Will you write about me? About *us*?'

She shook her head. 'No.'

'But . . . how long will this last? *I have to know.* One night? A month? A year? How will it end?' I was losing my mind: how could I start something like this, *when I didn't even know how it would end*?

She laughed. 'Don't ask me. Look it up in your own diary, if it's so important to you.'

I couldn't leave it alone, I couldn't shut up. 'You must have written something. You knew we'd share that taxi.'

'No. I just said that.'

'You—' I stared at her.

'It came true, though, didn't it? How about that?' She sighed, slid her hands down my spine, pulled me on to the bed. Down into the quicksand.

'Will we—'

She clamped her hand over my mouth.

'No more questions. I don't keep a diary. I don't know anything at all.'

Lying to Alison was easy; I was almost certain that I'd get away with it. Lying to myself was easier still. Filling out my diary became a formality, a meaningless ritual; I scarcely glanced at the words I wrote. When I did pay attention, I could barely keep a straight face: amidst the merely lazy and deceitful elision and euphemism were passages of deliberate irony which had been invisible to me for years, but which I could finally appreciate for what they were. Some of my paeans to marital bliss seemed 'dangerously' heavy-handed; I could scarcely believe that I'd never picked up the subtext before. *But I hadn't*. There was no 'risk' of tipping myself off – I was 'free' to be every bit as sarcastic as I 'chose' to be.

No more, no less.

The ignorance cults say that knowing the future robs us of our souls; by losing the power to choose between right and wrong, we cease to be human. To them, ordinary people are literally the walking dead: meat puppets, zombies. The somnambulists believe much the same thing, but – rather than seeing this as a tragedy of apocalyptic dimensions – embrace the idea with dreamy enthusiasm. They see a merciful end to responsibility, guilt and anxiety, striving and failing: a descent into inanimacy, the leaching of our souls into a great cosmic spiritual blancmange, while our bodies hang around, going through the motions.

For me, though, knowing the future – or believing that I did – never made me feel like a sleepwalker, a zombie in a senseless, amoral trance. It made me feel I was in control of my life. *One person* held sway across the decades, tying the disparate threads together, making sense of it all. How could that unity make me less than human? Everything I did grew out of who I was: who I had been, and who I would be.

I only started feeling like a soulless automaton when I tore it all apart with lies.

After school, few people pay much attention to history, past or future – let alone that grey zone between the two which used to be known as 'current affairs'. Journalists continue to collect information and scatter it across time, but there's no doubt that they now do a very different job than they did in pre-Hazzard days, when the live broadcast, the latest dispatch, had a real, if fleeting, significance. The profession hasn't died out completely; it's as if a kind of equilibrium has been reached between apathy and curiosity, and if we had any less news flowing from the future, there 'would be' a greater effort made to gather it and send it back. How valid such arguments can be – with their implications of dynamism, of hypothetical alternative worlds cancelled out by their own inconsistencies – I don't know, but the balance is undeniable. We learn precisely enough to keep us from wanting to know any more.

On 8 July, 2079, when Chinese troops moved into Kashmir to 'stabilise the region' – by wiping out the supply lines to the separatists within their own borders – I hardly gave it a second thought. I knew the UN would sort out the whole mess with remarkable dexterity; historians had praised the Secretary-General's diplomatic resolution of the crisis for decades, and, in a rare move for the conservative Academy, she'd been awarded the Nobel Peace Prize three years in advance of the efforts which would earn it. My memory of the details was sketchy, so I called up *The Global Yearbook*. The troops would be out by 3 August; casualties would be few. Duly comforted, I got on with my life.

I heard the first rumours from Pria, who'd taken to sampling the countless underground communications nets. Gossip and slander for computer freaks; a harm-less enough pastime, but I'd always been amused by the participants' conceit that they were 'plugged in' to the global village, that they had their fingers on the pulse of the planet. Who needed to be wired to *the moment*, when the past and the future could be examined at leisure? Who needed the latest unsubstantiated static, when a sober, considered version of events which had stood the test of time could be had just as soon – or sooner?

So when Pria told me solemnly that a full-scale war had broken out in Kashmir, and that people were being slaughtered in the thousands, I said, 'Sure. And Maura got the Nobel Prize for genocide.'

He shrugged. 'You ever heard of a man called Henry Kissinger?'

I had to admit that I hadn't.

I mentioned the story to Lisa, disparagingly, confident that she'd laugh along with me. She rolled over to face me and said, 'He's right.'

I didn't know whether to take the bait; she had a strange sense of humour, she might have been teasing. Finally, I said, 'He can't be. I've checked. All the histories agree—'

She looked genuinely surprised before her expression turned to pity; she'd never thought much of me, but I don't think she'd ever believed I was quite so naïve.

'The victors have always written the "history", James. Why should the future be any different? Believe me. It's happening.'

'How do you know?' It was a stupid question; her boss was on all the foreign affairs committees, and would be Minister next time the party was in power. If he didn't have access to the intelligence in his present job, he would in the long term.

She said, 'We're helping to fund it, of course. Along with Europe, Japan, and the States. Thanks to the embargo after the Hong Kong riots, the Chinese have no war drones; they're pitting human soldiers with obsolete equipment against the best Vietnamese robots. Four hundred thousand troops and a hundred thousand civilians will die – while the Allies sit in Berlin playing their solipsist video games.'

I stared past her, into the darkness, numb and disbelieving. 'Why? Why couldn't things have been worked out, defused in time?'

She scowled. 'How? You mean, *shunted*? Known about, then avoided?'

'No, but . . . if everyone knew the truth, if this hadn't been covered up—'

'What? If people had known it would happen, *it wouldn't have*? Grow up. It *is* happening, it will go on happening; there's nothing else to say.'

I climbed out of bed and started dressing, although I had no reason to hurry home. Alison knew all about us; apparently, she'd known since childhood that her husband would turn out to be a piece of shit.

Half a million people slaughtered. It wasn't fate, it wasn't destiny – there was no Will of God, no Force of History to absolve us. It grew out of *who we were*: the lies we'd told, and would keep on telling. Half a million people slaughtered in the spaces between the words.

I vomited on the carpet, then stumbled about dizzily, cleaning it up. Lisa watched me sadly.

'You're not coming back, are you?'

I laughed weakly. 'How the fuck should I know?'

'You're not.'

'I thought you didn't keep a diary.'

'I don't.'

And I finally understood why.

Alison woke when I switched on the terminal, and said sleepily, without rancour, 'What's the hurry, James? If you've masturbated about tonight since you were twelve years old, surely you'll still remember it all in the morning.'

I ignored her. After a while, she got out of bed and came and looked over my shoulder.

'Is this true?'

I nodded.

'And you knew all along? You're going to send this?'

I shrugged and hit the CHECK key. A message box popped up on the screen: 95 WORDS; 95 ERRORS.

I sat and stared at this verdict for a long time. What did I think? I had the power to change history? My puny outrage could *shunt* the war? Reality would dissolve around me, and another – better – world would take its place?

No. History, past and future, was determined, and I couldn't help being part of the equations that shaped it – but I didn't have to be part of the lies.

I hit the SAVE key, and burned those 95 words on to the chip, irreversibly.

(I'm sure I had no choice.)

That was my last diary entry – and I can only assume that the same computers that will filter it out of my posthumous transmission will also fill in the unwritten remainder, extrapolating an innocuous life for me, fit for a child to read.

I tap into the nets at random, listening to the whole spectrum of conflicting rumours, hardly knowing what to believe. I've left my wife, I've left my job, parting ways entirely with my rosy, fictitious future. All my certainties have evaporated: I don't know when I'll die; I don't know who I'll love; I don't know if the world is heading for Utopia, or Armageddon.

But I keep my eyes open, and I feed what little of value I can gather back into the nets. There must be corruption and distortion here, too – but I'd rather swim in this cacophony of a million contradictory voices than drown in the smooth and plausible lies of

38

those genocidal authors of history who control the Hazzard Machines.

Sometimes I wonder how different my life might have been without their intervention – but the question is meaningless. *It couldn't have been any other way.* Everyone is manipulated; everyone is a product of their times. *And vice versa.*

Whatever the unchangeable future holds, I'm sure of one thing: *who I am* is still a part of what always has, and always will, decide it.

I can ask for no greater freedom than that.

And no greater responsibility.

EUGENE

'I guarantee it. *I can make your child a genius.*'

Sam Cook (MB BS MD FRACP PhD MBA) shifted his supremely confident gaze from Angela to Bill and then back again, as if daring them to contradict him.

Angela finally cleared her throat and said, 'How?'

Cook reached into a drawer and pulled out a small section of a human brain, sandwiched in Perspex. 'Do you know who this belonged to? I'll give you three guesses.'

Bill suddenly felt very queasy. He didn't need three guesses, but he kept his mouth shut. Angela shook her head and said, impatiently, 'I have no idea.'

'Only *the greatest scientific mind* of the twentieth century.'

Bill leant forward and asked, appalled but fascinated, 'H-h-how did y-y-y—?'

'How did I get hold of it? Well, the enterprising fellow who did the autopsy, back in nineteen fifty-five, souvenired the brain prior to cremation. Naturally, he was bombarded with requests from various groups for pieces to study, so over the years it got subdivided and scattered around the world. At some point, the records listing who had what were mislaid, so most of it has effectively vanished, but several samples turned up for auction in Houston a few years ago – along with three Elvis Presley thigh bones; I think someone was liquidating their collection. Naturally, we here at Human Potential put in a bid for a prime slice of cortex. Half a million US dollars – I can't remember what that came to per gram – but worth every cent. Because we know the secret. *Glial cells.*'

'G-g-g-g—?'

'They provide a kind of structural matrix in which the neurons are embedded. They also perform several active functions which aren't yet fully understood, but it *is* known that the more glial cells there are per neuron, the more connections there are *between* the neurons. The more connections between neurons, the more complex and powerful the brain. Are you with me so far? Well, *this* tissue,' he held up the sample, 'has almost *thirty per cent* more glial cells per neuron than you'll find in the average cretin.'

Bill's facial tic suddenly went out of control, and he turned away, making quiet sounds of distress. Angela glanced up at the row of framed qualifications on the wall, and noticed that several were from a private university on the Gold Coast which had gone bankrupt more than a decade before.

She was still just a little uneasy about putting her future child in this man's hands. The tour of Human Potential's Melbourne headquarters had been impressive; from sperm bank to delivery room, the hardware had certainly gleamed, and surely anyone in charge of so many millions of dollars' worth of supercomputers, X-ray crystallography gear, mass spectrometers, electron microscopes, and so on, *had* to know what he was doing. But her doubts had begun when Cook had shown them his pet project: three young dolphins whose DNA contained human gene grafts. ('We ate the failures,' he had confided, with a sigh of gustatory bliss.) The aim had been to alter their brain physiology in such a way as to enable them to master human speech and 'human modes of thought' – and although, strictly

42

speaking, this had been achieved, Cook had been unable to explain to her *why* the creatures were only able to converse in limericks.

Angela regarded the grey sliver sceptically. 'How can you be sure it's as simple as that?'

'We've done *experiments*, of course. We located the gene that codes for a growth factor that determines the ratio of glial cells to neurons. We can control the extent to which this gene is switched on, and hence how much of the growth factor is synthesised, and hence what the ratio becomes. So far, we've tried reducing it by five per cent, and on average that causes a drop in IQ of twenty points. So, by simple linear extrapolation, if we *up* the ratio by two hundred per cent—'

Angela frowned. 'You intentionally produced children with reduced intelligence?'

'*Relax*. Their parents wanted Olympic athletes. Those kids won't miss twenty points – in fact, it will probably help them cope with the training. Besides, we like to be balanced. We give with one hand and take with the other. It's only fair. And our bioethics Expert System said it was perfectly okay.'

'What are you going to *take* from Eugene?'

Cook looked hurt. He did it well; his big brown eyes, as much as his professional success, had put his face on the glossy sleeves of a dozen magazines. '*Angela*. Your case is special. For you, and Bill – and Eugene – I'm going to break *all* the rules.'

When Bill Cooper was ten years old, he saved up his pocket money for a month, and bought a lottery ticket. The first prize was fifty thousand dollars. When his mother found out – whatever he did, she always found out – she said calmly, 'Do you know what gambling is? Gambling is a kind of tax: a tax on stupidity. A tax on greed. Some money changes hands at random, but the net cash flow always goes one way – to the Government, to the casino operators, to the bookies, to the crime syndicates. If you ever *do* win, you won't have won against *them*. They'll still be getting their share. You'll have won against all the penniless losers, that's all.'

He hated her. She hadn't taken away the ticket, she hadn't punished him, she hadn't even forbidden him to do it again – she had simply stated her opinion. The only trouble was, as an ordinary ten-year-old child, he didn't understand half the phrases she'd used, and he didn't have a hope of properly assessing her argument, let alone rebutting it. By talking over his head, she might just as well have proclaimed with the voice of authority: *you are stupid and greedy and wrong* – and it frustrated him almost to tears that she'd achieved this effect while remaining so calm and reasonable.

The ticket didn't win him a cent, and he didn't buy another. By the time he left home, eight years later, and found employment as a data-entry clerk in the Department of Social Security, the government lotteries had been all but superseded by a new scheme, in which participants marked numbers on a coupon in the hope that their choice would match the numbers on balls spat out by a machine.

Bill recognised the change as a cynical ploy, designed to suggest, *sotto voce*, to a statistically ignorant public that they now had the opportunity to use 'skill' and 'strategy' to improve their chances of winning. No longer would anyone be stuck with the immutable number on a lottery ticket; they were free to put crosses in boxes, any way they liked! This illusion of having *control* would bring in more players, and hence more revenue. And that sucked.

The TV ads for the game were the most crass and emetic things he'd ever seen, with grinning imbeciles going into fits of poorly acted euphoria as money cascaded down on them, cheerleaders waved pom-

poms, and tacky special effects lit up the screen. Images of yachts, champagne, and chauffeur-driven limousines were intercut. It made him gag.

However. There was a third prong. The radio ads were less inane, offering appealing scenarios of revenge for the instantly wealthy: Evict Your Landlord. Retrench Your Boss. Buy the Nightclub Which Denied You Admission. The play on stupidity and the play on greed had failed, but this touched a raw nerve. Bill *knew* he was being manipulated, but he couldn't deny that the prospect of spending the next forty-two years typing crap into a VDU (or doing whatever the changing technology demanded of shit-kickers – assuming he wasn't made completely obsolete) and paying most of his wages in rent, without even an infinitesimal chance of escape, was too much to bear.

So, in spite of everything, he caved in. Each week, he filled in a coupon, and paid the tax. Not a tax on greed, he decided. A tax on hope.

Angela operated a supermarket checkout, telling customers where to put their EFTPOS cards, and adjusting the orientation of cans and cartons if the scanner failed to locate their bar code (Hitachi made a device which could do this, but the US Department of Defence was covertly buying them all, in the hope of keeping anyone else from getting hold of the machine's pattern-recognition software). Bill always took his groceries to her checkout, however long the queue, and one day managed to overcome his pathological shyness long enough to ask her out.

Angela didn't mind his stutter, or any of his other problems. Sure, he was an emotional cripple, but he was passably handsome, superficially kind, and far too withdrawn to be either violent or demanding. Soon they were meeting regularly, to engage in messy but mildly pleasant acts, designed to be unlikely to transfer either human or viral genetic material between them.

However, no amount of latex could prevent their sexual intimacy from planting hooks deep in other parts of their brains. Neither had begun the relationship expecting it to endure, but as the months passed and nothing drove them apart, not only did their desire for each other fail to wane, but they grew accustomed to – even *fond of* – ever broader aspects of each other's appearance and behaviour.

Whether this bonding effect was purely random, or could be traced to formative experiences, or ultimately reflected a past advantage in the conjunction of some of their visibly expressed genes, is difficult to determine. Perhaps all three factors contributed to some degree. In any case, the knot of their interdependencies grew, until marriage began to seem far simpler than disentanglement, and, once accepted, almost as natural as puberty or death. But if the offspring of previous Bill-and-Angela lookalikes *had* lived long and bred well, the issue now seemed purely theoretical; the couple's combined income hovered above the poverty line, and children were out of the question.

As the years passed, and the information revolution continued, their original jobs all but vanished, but they both somehow managed to cling to employment. Bill was replaced by an optical character reader, but was promoted to computer operator, which meant changing the toner on laser printers and coping with jammed stationery. Angela became a supervisor, which meant store detective; shoplifting as such was impossible (supermarkets were now filled with card-operated vending machines) but her presence was meant to discourage vandalism and muggings (a real security guard would have cost more), and she assisted any customers unable to work out which buttons to push.

In contrast, their first contact with the biotechnology revolution was both voluntary and beneficial. Born pink – and more often made pinker than browner by sunlight – they both acquired deep black, slightly purplish skin; an artificial retrovirus inserted genes into their melanocytes which boosted the rate of melanin synthesis and transfer. This treatment, although fashionable, was of far more than cosmetic value; since the south polar ozone hole had expanded to cover most of the continent, Australia's skin cancer rates, already the world's highest, had quadrupled. Chemical sunscreens were messy and inefficient, and regular use had undesirable long-term side-effects. Nobody wanted to clothe themselves from wrist to ankle all year in a climate that was hot and growing hotter, and in any case it would have been culturally unacceptable to return to near-Victorian dress codes after two generations of maximal baring of skin. The small aesthetic shift, from valuing the deepest possible tan to accepting that people born fair-skinned could become black, was by far the easiest solution.

Of course, there was some controversy. Paranoid right-wing groups (who for decades had claimed that their racism was 'logically' founded on cultural xenophobia rather than anything so trivial as skin colour) ranted about conspiracies and called the (non-communicable) virus 'The Black Plague'. A few politicians and journalists tried to find a way to exploit people's unease without appearing completely stupid – but failed, and eventually shut up. Neo-blacks started appearing on magazine sleeves, in soap operas, in advertisements (a source of bitter amusement for the Aboriginal people, who remained all but invisible in such places), and the trend accelerated. Those who lobbied for a ban didn't have a rational leg to stand on: nobody was being forced to be black – there was even a virus available which snipped out the genes, for people who changed their mind – and the country was being saved a fortune in health-care costs.

One day, Bill turned up at the supermarket in the

middle of the morning. He looked so shaken that Angela was certain that he'd been sacked, or one of his parents had died, or he'd just been told that he had a fatal disease.

He had chosen his words in advance, and reeled them off almost without hesitation. 'We forgot to watch the draw last night,' he said. 'We've won forty-seven m-m-m . . .'

Angela clocked out.

They took the obligatory world tour while a modest house was built. After disbursing a few hundred thousand to friends and relatives – Bill's parents refused to take a cent, but his siblings, and Angela's family, had no such qualms – they were still left with more than forty-five million. Buying all the consumer goods they honestly wanted couldn't begin to dent this sum, and neither had much interest in gold-plated Rolls Royces, private jets, Van Goghs, or diamonds. They could have lived in luxury on the earnings of ten million in the safest of investments, and it was indecision more than greed that kept them from promptly donating the difference to a worthy cause.

There was so much to be done in a world ravaged by political, ecological and climatic disasters. Which project most deserved their assistance? The proposed Himalayan hydroelectric scheme, which might keep Bangladesh from drowning in the floodplains of its Greenhouse-swollen rivers? Research on engineering hardier crops for poor soils in northern Africa? Buying back a small part of Brazil from multinational agribusiness, so food could be grown, not imported, and foreign debt curtailed? Fighting the till abysmal infant mortality rate amongst their own country's original inhabitants? Thirty-five million would have helped substantially with any of these endeavours, but Angela and Bill were so worried about making the right choice that they put it off, month after month, year after year.

Meanwhile, free of financial restraints, they began trying to have a child. After two years without success, they finally sought medical advice, and were told that Angela was producing antibodies to Bill's sperm. This was no great problem; neither of them was intrinsically infertile, they could still both provide gametes for IVF, and Angela could bear the child. The only question was, who would carry out the procedure? The only possible answer was, the best reproductive specialist money could buy.

Sam Cook was the best, or at least the best known. For the past twenty years, he'd been enabling women in infertile relationships to give birth to as many as seven children at a time, long after multiple embryo implants had ceased being necessary to ensure success (the media wouldn't bid for exclusive rights to anything less than quintuplets). He also had a reputation for quality control unequalled by any of his colleagues; after a stint in Tokyo on the Human Genome Project, he was as familiar with molecular biology as he was with gynaecology, obstetrics and embryology.

It was quality control that complicated the couple's plans. For their marriage licence, their blood had been sent to a run-of-the-mill pathologist, who had only screened them for such extreme conditions as muscular dystrophy, cystic fibrosis, Huntington's disease, and so on. Human Potential, equipped with all the latest probes, was a thousand times more thorough. It turned out that Bill carried genes which could make their child susceptible to clinical depression, and Angela carried genes which might make it hyperactive.

Cook spelt out the options for them.

One solution would be to use what was now referred to as TPGM: third-party genetic material. No need to make do with any old dross, either; Human Potential had Nobel prizewinners' sperm by the bucketful, and although they had no equivalent ova – collection being

49

so much harder, and most prizewinners being well into their sixties – they had blood samples instead, from which chromosomes could be extracted, artificially converted from diploid to haploid, and inserted into an ovum provided by Angela.

Alternatively – albeit at a somewhat higher cost – they could stick with their own gametes, and use gene therapy to correct the problems.

They talked it over for a couple of weeks, but the choice wasn't difficult. The legal status of children produced from TPGM was still a mess – and a slightly different mess in every state of Australia, not to mention from country to country – and of course they both wanted, if possible, a child who was biologically their own.

At their next appointment, while explaining these reasons, Angela also disclosed the magnitude of their wealth, so that Cook would feel no need to cut corners for the sake of economy. They had kept their win from becoming public knowledge, but it hardly seemed right to have any secrets from the man who was going to work this miracle for them.

Cook seemed to take the revelation in his stride, and congratulated them on their wise decision. But he added, apologetically, that in his ignorance of the size of their financial resources, he had probably misled them into a limited view of what he had to offer.

Since they'd chosen gene therapy, why be half-hearted about it? Why rescue their child from malad-justment, only to curse it with mediocrity – when so much *more* was possible? With their money, and Human Potential's facilities and expertise, a truly *extraordinary* child could be created: intelligent, crea-tive, charismatic; the relevant genes had all been more or less pinned down, and a timely injection of research funds – say, twenty or thirty million – would see the loose ends sorted out very rapidly.

Angela and Bill exchanged looks of incredulity. Thirty seconds earlier, they'd been talking about a normal, healthy baby. This grab for their money was so transparent that they could scarcely believe it.

Cook went on, apparently oblivious. Naturally, such a donation would be honoured by renaming the building's L. K. Robinson/Margaret Lee/Duneside Rotary Club laboratory the Angela and Bill Cooper/L. K. Robinson/Margaret Lee/Duneside Rotary Club laboratory, and a contract would ensure that their philanthropy be mentioned in all scientific papers and media releases which flowed from the work.

Angela broke into a coughing fit to keep from laughing. Bill stared at a spot on the carpet and bit his cheeks. Both found the prospect of joining the ranks of the city's obnoxious, self-promoting charity socialites about as enticing as the notion of eating their own excrement.

However. There was a third prong.

'The world,' Cook said, suddenly stern and brooding, 'is a mess.' The couple nodded dumbly, still fighting back laughter – in full agreement, but wondering if they were now about to be told not to bother raising children at all. 'Every ecosystem on the planet that hasn't been bulldozed is dying from pollution. The climate is changing faster than we can modify our infrastructure. Species are vanishing. People are starving. There have been more casualties of war in the last ten years than in the previous *century*.' They nodded again, sober now, but still baffled by the abrupt change of subject.

'Scientists are doing all they can, but it's *not enough*. The same for politicians. Which is sad, but hardly surprising: these people are only a generation beyond the fools who got us into this mess. What child can be expected to avoid, to undo – to utterly *transcend* – the mistakes of its parents?'

He paused, then suddenly broke into a dazzling, almost beatific smile.

'What child? A very special child. *Your child.*'

In the late twentieth century, opponents of molecular eugenics had relied almost exclusively on pointing out similarities between modern trends and the obscenities of the past: nineteenth-century pseudo-sciences like phrenology and physiognomy, invented to support pre-conceptions about race and class differences; Nazi ideology about racial inferiority, which had led straight to the Holocaust; and radical biological determinism, a movement largely confined to the pages of academic journals, but infamous nonetheless for its attempts to make racism scientifically respectable.

Over the years, though, the racist taint receded. Genetic engineering produced a wealth of highly beneficial new drugs and vaccines, as well as therapies – and sometimes cures – for dozens of previously debilitating, often fatal, genetic diseases. It was absurd to claim that molecular biologists (as if they were all of one mind) were intent on creating a world of Aryan supermen (as if that, and precisely that, were the only conceivable abuse). Those who had played glibly on fears of the past were left without ammunition.

By the time Angela and Bill were contemplating Cook's proposal, the prevailing rhetoric was almost the reverse of that of a decade before. Modern eugenics was hailed by its practitioners as a force *opposed to* racist myths. Individual traits were what mattered, to be assessed 'objectively' on their merits, and the historical conjunctions of traits which had once been referred to as 'racial characteristics' were of no more interest to a modern eugenicist than national boundaries were to a geologist. Who could oppose reducing the incidence of crippling genetic diseases? Who could oppose decreasing the next generation's susceptibility to arteriosclerosis, breast cancer, and stroke, and increasing their ability to tolerate UV radiation, pollution and stress? Not to mention nuclear fallout.

As for producing a child so brilliant as to cut a swathe through the world's environmental, political and social problems . . . perhaps such high expectations would not be fulfilled, but what could be wrong about *trying*?

And yet. Angela and Bill remained wary – and even felt vaguely guilty at the prospect of accepting Cook's proposal, without quite knowing why. Yes, eugenics was only for the rich, but that had been true of the leading edge of health care for centuries. Neither would have declined the latest surgical procedures or drugs simply because most people in the world could not afford them. Their patronage, they reasoned, could assist the long, slow process leading to extensive gene therapy for *everyone's* children. Well . . . at least everyone in the wealthiest countries' upper middle classes.

They returned to Human Potential. Cook gave them the VIP tour, he showed them his talking dolphins and his slice of prime cortex, and still they were unconvinced. So he gave them a questionnaire to fill out, a specification of the child they wanted; this might, he suggested, make it all a bit more tangible.

Cook glanced over the form, and frowned. 'You haven't answered all the questions.'

Bill said, 'W-w-we didn't—'

Angela hushed him. 'We want to leave some things to chance. Is that a problem?'

Cook shrugged. 'Not technically. It just seems a pity. Some of the traits you've left blank could have a very real influence on the course of Eugene's life.'

'That's exactly why we left them blank. We don't want to dictate every tiny detail, we don't want to leave him with no room at all—'

Cook shook his head. 'Angela, Angela! You're

looking at this the wrong way. By refusing to make a decision, you're not giving Eugene personal freedom – you're taking it away! Abnegating responsibility won't give him the power to choose any of these things for himself; it simply means he'll be stuck with traits which may be less than ideal. Can we go through some of these unanswered questions?'

'Sure.'

Bill said, 'Maybe ch-ch-chance is p-part of freedom.' Cook ignored him.

'*Height*. Do you honestly not care at all about that? Both of you are well below average, so you must both be aware of the disadvantages. Don't you want better for Eugene?

'*Build*. Let's be frank; you're overweight, Bill is rather scrawny. We can give Eugene a head start towards a socially optimal body. Of course, a lot will depend on his lifestyle, but we can influence his dietary and exercise habits far more than you might think. He can be made to like and dislike certain foods, and we can arrange maximum susceptibility to endogenous opiates produced during exercise.

'*Penis length*—'

Angela scowled. 'Now *that's* the most trivial—'

'You think so? A recent survey of two thousand male graduates of Harvard Business School found that penis length and IQ were *equally good* predictors of annual income.

'*Facial bone structure*. In the latest group-dynamic studies, it turned out that both the forehead *and* the cheekbones played significant roles in determining which individuals assumed dominant status. I'll give you a copy of the results.

'*Sexual preference*—'

'Surely he can—'

'Make up his own mind? That's wishful thinking, I'm afraid. The evidence is quite unambiguous: it's determined in the embryo by the interaction of several genes. Now, I have nothing at all against homosexuals, but the condition is hardly what you'd call a blessing. Oh, people can always reel off lists of famous homosexual geniuses, but that's a biased sample; of course we've only heard of the successes.

'*Musical taste.* As yet, we can only influence this crudely, but the social advantages should not be underestimated . . .'

Angela and Bill sat in their living room with the TV on, although they weren't paying much attention to it. An interminable ad for the Department of Defence was showing, all rousing music and jet fighters in appealingly symmetrical formations. The latest privatisation legislation meant that each taxpayer could specify the precise allocation of his or her income tax between government departments, who in turn were free to spend as much of their revenue as they wished on advertising aimed at attracting more funds. Defence was doing well. Social Security was laying off staff.

The latest meeting with Cook had done nothing to banish their sense of unease, but without solid reasons to back up their feelings, they felt obliged to ignore them. *Cook* had solid reasons for everything, all based on the very latest research; how could they go to him and call the whole thing off, without at least a dozen impeccable arguments, each supported by a reference to some recent report in *Nature*?

They couldn't even pin down the source of their disquiet to their own satisfaction. Perhaps they were simply afraid of the fame that Eugene was destined to bring upon them. Perhaps they were jealous, already, of their son's as yet unknowable – but inevitably spectacular – achievements. Bill had a vague suspicion that the whole endeavour was somehow pulling the rug out from under an important part of what it had meant to be human – but he didn't know quite how to put it into words, not even to Angela. How could he confess that, personally, he didn't *want* to know the extent to which genes determined the fate of an individual? How could he declare that he'd rather stick with comfortable myths – no, forget the euphemisms, that he'd rather have downright *lies* – than have his nose rubbed in the dreary truth that a human being could be made to order, like a hamburger?

Cook had assured them that they need have no worries about handling the young genius. He could arrange a queue-jumping enrolment in the best Californian baby university, where, amongst Noble × Noble TPGM prodigies, Eugene could do brain-stimulating baby gymnastics to the sound of Kant sung to Beethoven, and learn Grand Unified Field Theory subliminally during his afternoon naps. Eventually, of course, he would overtake both his genetically inferior peers and his merely brilliant instructors, but by then he ought to be able to direct his own education.

Bill put an arm around Angela, and wondered if Eugene really *would* do more for humanity than their millions could have achieved directly in Bangladesh or Ethiopia or Alice Springs. But could they face spending the rest of their lives wondering what miracles Eugene might have performed for their crippled planet? That would be unbearable. They'd pay the tax on hope.

Angela began loosening Bill's clothing. He did the same for her. Tonight – as they both knew, without exchanging a word – was the most fertile point of Angela's cycle; in spite of the antibodies, they hadn't abandoned the habits they'd acquired in the years when they'd been hoping to conceive naturally.

The rousing music from the television stopped, abruptly. The scenes of military hardware deteriorated into static. A sad-eyed boy, perhaps eight years old, appeared on the screen and said quietly, 'Mother.

Father. I owe you an explanation.'

Behind the boy was nothing but an empty blue sky. Angela and Bill stared at the screen in silence, waiting in vain for a voice-over or title to put the image in context. Then the child's eyes met Angela's, and she knew that he could see her, and she knew who it must be. She gripped Bill's arm and whispered, dizzy with shock, but euphoric too, 'It's Eugene.'

The boy nodded.

For a moment, Bill was overcome with panic and confusion, but then paternal pride swelled up and he managed to say, 'You've invented t-t-t-time t-travel!'

Eugene shook his head. 'No. Suppose you fed the genetic profile of an embryo into a computer, which then constructed a simulation of the appearance of the mature organism; no time travel is involved, and yet aspects of a possible future are revealed. In that example, all the machinery to perform the extrapolation exists in the present, but the same thing *can* happen if the right equipment – equipment of a far more sophisticated kind – exists in the *potential future*. It may be useful, as a mathematical formalism, to pretend that the potential future has a tangible reality and is influencing its past – just as in geometric optics, it's often convenient to pretend that reflections are real objects that exist behind the mirrors that create them – but a formalism is all it would be.'

Angela said, 'So because you *might* invent such a device, we can see you, and talk to you, *as if* you were speaking to us from the future?'

'Yes.'

The couple exchanged glances. Here was an end to their doubts! Now they could find out *exactly* what Eugene would do for the world!

'If you *were* speaking to us from the future,' Angela asked carefully, 'what would you tell us? That you've reversed the Greenhouse Effect?' Eugene shook his head sadly. 'That you've made war obsolete?' *No*. 'That you've abolished hunger?' *No*. 'That you've found a cure for cancer?' *No*. 'What, then?'

'I would say that I have found a way to Nirvana.'

'What do you mean? Immortality? Infinite bliss? Heaven on Earth?'

'No. *Nirvana*. The absence of all longing.'

Bill was horrified. 'Y-y-you d-don't mean g-g-genocide? You're n-not going to w-w-w-wipe—'

'No, Father. That would be easy, but I would never do such a thing. Each must find their own way – and in any case, death is an incomplete solution, it cannot erase what has already been. Nirvana is *to never have been*.'

Angela said, 'I don't understand.'

'My potential existence influences more than this television set. When you check your bank accounts, you will find that the money you might have used to create me has been disbursed; don't look so distressed – it's all gone to charitable organisations of which you both approve. The computer records are *precisely* as if you had authorised the payments yourselves, so don't bother trying to challenge their authenticity.'

Angela was distraught. 'But . . . why would you waste your talents on destroying yourself, when you could have lived a happy, productive life, and done great things for the whole human race?'

'*Why?*' Eugene frowned. 'Don't ask *me* to account for my actions; you're the ones who would have made me what I would have been. If you want my subjective opinion: personally, I can't see any point in existence when I can achieve so much without it – but I wouldn't call that an "explanation"; it's merely a rationalisation of processes best described at a neural level.' He shrugged apologetically. 'The question really has no meaning. *Why* anything? The laws of physics, and the boundary conditions of space-time. What more can I say?'

He vanished from the screen. A soap opera appeared.

They contacted their bank's computer. The experience had been no shared hallucination; their accounts were empty.

They sold the house, which was far too large for just the two of them, but it cost them most of the proceeds to buy something much smaller. Angela found work as a tour guide. Bill got a job on a garbage truck.

Cook's research continued without them, of course. He succeeded in creating four chimpanzees able to sing, and understand, country and western, for which he received both the Nobel Prize and a Grammy award. He made it into the Guinness Book of Records, for implanting and delivering the world's first third-generation IVF quins. But his super-baby project, and those of other eugenicists around the world, seemed jinxed; sponsors backed out for no apparent reason, equipment malfunctioned, labs caught fire.

Cook died without ever understanding how completely successful he'd been.

THE CARESS

Two smells hit me when I kicked down the door: death, and the scent of an animal.

A man who passed the house each day had phoned us, anonymously; worried by the sight of a broken window left unrepaired, he'd knocked on the front door with no results. On his way to the back door, he'd glimpsed blood on the kitchen wall through a gap in the curtains.

The place had been ransacked; all that remained downstairs were the drag marks on the carpet from the heaviest furniture. The woman in the kitchen, mid fifties, throat slit, had been dead for at least a week.

My helmet was filing sound and vision, but it couldn't record the animal smell. The correct procedure was to make a verbal comment, but I didn't say a word. Why? Call it a vestigial need for independence. Soon they'll be logging our brain waves, our heartbeats, who knows what, and all of it subpoenable. 'Detective Segel, the evidence shows that you experienced a penile erection when the defendant opened fire. Would you describe that as an *appropriate* response?'

Upstairs was a mess. Clothes scattered in the bedroom. Books, CDs, papers, upturned drawers, spread across the floor of the study. Medical texts. In one corner, piles of CD periodicals stood out from the jumble by their jackets' uniformity: *The New England Journal of Medicine, Nature, Clinical Biochemistry* and *Laboratory Embryology*. A framed scroll hung on the wall, awarding the degree of Doctor of Philosophy to Freda Anne Macklenburg in the year two thousand and twenty-three. The desktop had dust-free spaces shaped like a monitor and a keyboard. I noticed a wall outlet with a pilot light; the switch was down but the light was dead. The room light wasn't working; ditto elsewhere.

Back on the ground floor, I found a door behind the stairs, presumably leading to a basement. Locked. I hesitated. Entering the house I'd had no choice but to force my way in; here, though, I was on shakier legal ground. I hadn't searched thoroughly for keys, and I had no clear reason to believe it was urgent to get into the basement.

But what would one more broken door change? Cops have been sued for failing to wipe their boots clean on the doormat. If a citizen wants to screw you, they'll find a reason, even if you came in on your knees, waving a handful of warrants, and saved their whole family from torture and death.

No room to kick, so I punched out the lock. The smell had me gagging, but it was the excess, the concentration, that was overwhelming; the scent in itself wasn't foul. Upstairs, seeing medical books, I'd thought of guinea pigs, rats and mice, but this was no stink of caged rodents.

I switched on the torch in my helmet and moved quickly down the narrow concrete steps. Over my head was a thick, square pipe. An air-conditioning duct? That made sense; the house couldn't *normally* smell the way it did, but with the power cut off to a basement air-conditioner—

The torch beam showed a shelving unit, decorated with trinkets and potted plants. A TV set. Landscape paintings on the wall. A pile of straw on the concrete floor. Curled on the straw, the powerful body of a leopard, lungs visibly labouring, but otherwise still.

When the beam fell upon a tangle of auburn hair, I thought, it's chewing on a severed human head. I continued to approach, expecting, hoping, that by disturbing the feeding animal I could provoke it into attacking me. I was carrying a weapon that could have spattered it into a fine mist of blood and gristle, an outcome which would have involved me in a great deal less tedium and bureaucracy than dealing with it alive. I directed the light towards its head again, and realised that I'd been mistaken; it wasn't chewing anything, its head was hidden, tucked away, and the human head was simply—

Wrong again. The human head was simply joined to the leopard's body. Its human neck took on fur and spots and merged with the leopard's shoulders.

I squatted down beside it, thinking, above all else, what those claws could do to me if my attention lapsed. The head was a woman's. Frowning. Apparently asleep. I placed one hand below her nostrils, and felt the air blast out in time with the heavings of the leopard's great chest. That, more than the smooth transition of the skin, made the union real for me.

I explored the rest of the room. There was a pit in one corner that turned out to be a toilet bowl sunk into the floor. I put my foot on a nearby pedal, and the bowl flushed from a hidden cistern. There was an upright freezer, standing in a puddle of water. I opened it to find a rack containing thirty-five small plastic vials. Every one of them bore smeared red letters, spelling out the word SPOILED. Temperature-sensitive dye.

I returned to the leopard woman. Asleep? Feigning sleep? Sick? Comatose? I patted her on the cheek, and not gently. The skin seemed hot, but I had no idea what her temperature ought to be. I shook her by one shoulder, this time with a little more respect, as if waking her by touching the leopard part might somehow be more dangerous. No effect.

Then I stood up, fought back a sigh of irritation (Psych latch on to all your little noises; I've been grilled for hours over such things as an injudicious whoop of triumph), and called for an ambulance.

I should have known better than to hope that *that* would be the end of my problems. I had to physically obstruct the stairway to stop the ambulancemen from retreating. One of them puked. They then refused to put her on the stretcher unless I promised to ride with her to the hospital. She was only about two metres long, excluding the tail, but must have weighed a hundred and fifty kilos, and it took the three of us to get her up the awkward stairs.

We covered her completely with a sheet before leaving the house, and I took the trouble to arrange it to keep it from revealing the shape beneath. A small crowd had gathered outside, the usual motley collection of voyeurs. The forensic team arrived just then, but I'd already told them everything by radio.

At the casualty department of St Dominic's, doctor after doctor took one look under the sheet and then fled, some muttering half-baked excuses, most not bothering. I was about to lose my temper when the fifth one I cornered, a young woman, turned pale but kept her ground. After poking and pinching and shining a torch into the leopard woman's forced-opened eyes, Dr Muriel Beatty (from her name badge) announced, 'She's in a coma,' and started extracting details from me. When I'd told her everything, I squeezed in some questions of my own.

'How would someone do this? Gene splicing? Transplant surgery?'

'I doubt it was either. More likely she's a chimera.'

I frowned. 'That's some kind of mythical—'

'Yes, but it's also a bioengineering term. You can physically mix the cells of two genetically distinct early embryos, and obtain a blastocyst that will develop into a single organism. If they're both of the same species, there's a very high success rate; for different species it's trickier. People made crude sheep/goat chimeras as far back as the nineteen sixties, but I've read nothing new on the subject for five or ten years. I would have said it was no longer being seriously pursued. Let alone pursued with humans.' She stared down at her patient with unease and fascination. 'I wouldn't know how they guaranteed such a sharp distinction between the head and the body; a thousand times more effort has gone into *this* than just stirring two clumps of cells together. I guess you could say it was something halfway between foetal transplant surgery and chimerisation. And there must have been genetic manipulation as well, to smooth out the biochemical differences.' She laughed drily. 'So both your suggestions I dismissed just then were probably partly right. *Of course!*'

'What?'

'No wonder she's in a coma! That freezer full of vials you mentioned – she probably needs an external supply for half a dozen hormones that are insufficiently active across species. Can I arrange for someone to go to the house and look through the dead woman's papers? We need to know exactly what those vials contained. Even if she made it up herself from off-the-shelf sources, we might be able to find the recipe – but chances are she had a contract with a biotechnology company for a regular, pre-mixed supply. So if we can find, say, an invoice with a product reference number, that would be the quickest, surest way to get this patient what she needs to stay alive.'

I agreed, and accompanied a lab technician back to the house, but he found nothing of use in the study, or the basement. After talking it over with Muriel Beatty on the phone, I started ringing local biotech companies, quoting the deceased woman's name and address. Several people said they'd heard of Dr Macklenburg, but not as a customer. The fifteenth call produced results – deliveries from a company called Applied Veterinary Research had been sent to Macklenburg's address – and with a combination of threats and smooth talking (such as inventing an order number they could quote on their invoice), I managed to extract a promise that a batch of the 'Applied Veterinary Research' preparation would be made up at once and rushed to St Dominic's.

Burglars *do* switch off the power sometimes, in the hope of disabling those (very rare) security devices that don't have battery back-up, but the house hadn't been broken into; the scattered glass from the window fell, in an undisturbed pattern, on to carpet where a sofa had left clear indentations. The fools had forgotten to break a window until after they'd taken the furniture. People *do* throw out invoices, but Macklenburg had kept all her videophone, water, gas and electricity bills for the last five years. So, it looked like somebody had known about the chimera and wanted it dead, without wishing to be totally obvious, yet without being professional enough to manage anything subtler, or more certain.

I arranged for the chimera to be guarded. Probably a good idea anyway, to keep the media at bay when they found out about her.

Back in my office, I did a search of medical literature by Macklenburg, and found her name on only half a dozen papers. All were more than twenty years old. All were concerned with embryology, though (to the extent that I could understand the jargon-laden abstracts, full of 'zonae pellucidae' and 'polar bodies') none was explicitly about chimeras.

The papers were all from one place; the Early Human

Development Laboratory at St Andrew's Hospital. After some standard brush-offs from secretaries and assistants, I managed to get myself put through to one of Macklenburg's one-time co-authors, a Dr Henry Feingold, who looked rather old and frail. News of Macklenburg's death produced a wistful sigh, but no visible shock or distress.

'Freda left us back in thirty-two or thirty-three. I've hardly set eyes on her since, except at the occasional conference.'

'Where did she go to from St Andrew's?'

'Something in industry. She was rather vague about it. I'm not sure that she had a definite appointment lined up.'

'Why did she resign?'

He shrugged. 'Sick of the conditions here. Low pay, limited resources, bureaucratic restrictions, ethics committees. Some people learn to live with all that, some don't.'

'Would you know anything about her work, her particular research interests, after she left?'

'I don't know that she *did* much research. She seemed to have stopped publishing, so I really couldn't say what she was up to.'

Shortly after that (with unusual speed), clearance came through to access her taxation records. Since '35 she had been self-employed as a 'freelance biotechnology consultant'; whatever that meant, it had provided her with a seven-figure income for the past fifteen years. There were at least a hundred different company names listed by her as sources of revenue. I rang the first one and found myself talking to an answering machine. It was after seven. I rang St Dominic's, and learnt that the chimera was still unconscious, but doing fine; the hormone mixture had arrived, and Muriel Beatty had located a veterinarian at the university with some relevant experience. So I swallowed my

67

deprimers and went home.

The surest sign that I'm not fully down is the frustration I feel when opening my own front door. It's too bland, too easy: inserting three keys and touching my thumb to the scanner. Nothing inside is going to be dangerous or challenging. The deprimers are meant to work in five minutes. Some nights it's more like five hours.

Marion was watching TV, and called out, 'Hi, Dan.'

I stood in the living room doorway. 'Hi. How was your day?' She works in a child-care centre, which is my idea of a high-stress occupation. She shrugged. 'Ordinary. How was yours?'

Something on the TV screen caught my eye. I swore for about a minute, mostly cursing a certain communications officer who I knew was responsible, though I couldn't have proved it. 'How was my day? You're looking at it.' The TV was showing part of my helmet log; the basement, my discovery of the chimera.

Marion said, 'Ah. I was going to ask if you knew who the cop was.'

'And you know what I'll be doing tomorrow? Trying to make sense of a few thousand phone calls from people who've seen this and decided they have something useful to say about it.'

'That poor girl. Is she going to be OK?'

'I think so.'

They played Muriel Beatty's speculations, again from my point of view, then cut to a couple of pocket experts who debated the fine points of chimerism while an interviewer did his best to drag in spurious references to everything from Greek mythology to *The Island of Doctor Moreau*.

I said, 'I'm starving. Let's eat.'

I woke at half past one, shaking and whimpering. Marion was already awake, trying to calm me down.

Lately I'd been suffering a lot from delayed reactions like this. A few months earlier, two nights after a particularly brutal assault case, I'd been distraught and incoherent for hours.

On duty, we are what's called 'primed'. A mixture of drugs heightens various physiological and emotional responses, and suppresses others. Sharpens our reflexes. Keeps us calm and rational. Supposedly improves our judgement. (The media like to say that the drugs make us more aggressive, but that's garbage; why would the force intentionally create trigger-happy cops? Swift decisions and swift actions are the *opposite* of dumb brutality.)

Off duty, we are 'deprimed'. That's meant to make us the way we would be if we'd never taken the priming drugs. (A hazy concept, I have to admit. As if we'd never taken the priming drugs, *and* never spent the day at work? Or, as if we'd seen and done the very same things, without the primers to help us cope?)

Sometimes this seesaw works smoothly. Sometimes it fucks up.

I wanted to describe to Marion how I felt about the chimera. I wanted to talk about my fear and revulsion and pity and anger. All I could do was make unhappy noises. No words. She didn't say anything, she just held me, her long fingers cool on the burning skin of my face and chest.

When I finally exhausted myself into something approaching peace, I managed to speak. I whispered, 'Why do you stay with me? Why do you put up with this?'

She turned away from me and said, 'I'm tired. Go to sleep.'

I enrolled for the force at the age of twelve. I continued my normal education, but that's when you have to start the course of growth-factor injections, and weekend and vacation training, if you want to qualify for active duty. (It wasn't an irreversible obligation; I could have chosen a different career later, and paid off what had been invested in me at a hundred dollars or so a week over the next thirty years. Or, I could have failed the psychological tests, and been dropped without owing a cent. But the tests before you even begin tend to weed out anyone who's likely to do either.) It makes sense; rather than limiting recruitment to men and women meeting certain physical criteria, candidates are chosen according to intelligence and attitude, and then the secondary, but useful, characteristics of size, strength and agility are provided artificially.

So we're freaks, constructed and conditioned to meet the demands of the job. Less so than soldiers or professional athletes. Far less so than the average street gang member, who thinks nothing of using illegal growth promoters that lower his life expectancy to around thirty years. Who, unarmed but on a mixture of Berserker and Timewarp (oblivious to pain and most physical trauma and with a twenty-fold decrease in reaction times), can kill a hundred people in a crowd in five minutes, then vanish to a safe house before the high ends and the fortnight of side effects begins. (A certain politician, a very popular man, advocates undercover operations to sell supplies of these drugs laced with fatal impurities, but he's not yet succeeded in making that legal.)

Yes, we're freaks; but if we have a problem, it's that we're still far too human.

When over a hundred thousand people phone in about an investigation, there's only one way to deal with their calls. It's called ARIA: Automated Remote Informant Analysis.

An initial filtering process identifies the blatantly obvious pranksters and lunatics. It's always *possible* that someone who phones in and spends ninety per cent of his time ranting about UFOs, or communist conspiracies, or slicing up our genitals with razor blades, has something relevant and truthful to mention in passing, but it seems reasonable to give his evidence less weight than that of someone who sticks to the point. More sophisticated analysis of gestures (about thirty per cent of callers don't switch off the vision), and speech patterns, supposedly picks up anyone who is, although superficially rational and apposite, actually suffering from psychotic delusions or fixations. Ultimately, each caller is given a 'reliability factor' between zero and one, with the benefit of the doubt going to anyone who betrays no recognisable signs of dishonesty or mental illness. Some days I'm impressed with the sophistication of the software that makes these assessments. Other days I curse it as a heap of useless voodoo.

The relevant assertions (broadly defined) of each caller are extracted, and a frequency table is created, giving a count of the number of callers making each assertion, and their average reliability factor. Unfortunately, there are no simple rules to determine which assertions are most likely to be *true*. One thousand people might earnestly repeat a widespread but totally baseless rumour. A single honest witness might be distraught, or chemically screwed up, and be given an unfairly poor rating. Basically, you have to read all the assertions – which is tedious, but still several thousand times faster than viewing every call.

001.	The chimera is a Martian.	15312	0.37
002.	The chimera is from a UFO.	14106	0.29
003.	The chimera is from Atlantis.	9003	0.24
004.	The chimera is a mutant.	8973	0.41
005.	The chimera resulted from human-leopard sexual intercourse.	6884	0.13
006.	The chimera is a sign from God.	2654	0.09

007.	The chimera is the Antichrist.	2432	0.07
008.	Caller is the chimera's father.	2390	0.12
009.	The chimera is a Greek deity.	1345	0.10
010.	Caller is the chimera's mother.	1156	0.09
011.	The chimera should be killed by authorities.	1009	0.19
012.	Caller has previously seen the chimera in their neighbourhood.	988	0.39
013.	The chimera killed Freda Macklenburg.	945	0.24
014.	Caller intends killing the chimera.	903	0.49
015.	Caller killed Freda Macklenburg.	830	0.27

(If desperate, I could view, one by one, the seventeen hundred and thirty-three calls of items 14 and 15. Not yet, though; I still had plenty of better ways to spend my time.)

016.	The chimera was created by a foreign government.	724	0.18
017.	The chimera is the result of biological warfare.	690	0.14
018.	The chimera is a were-leopard.	604	0.09
019.	Caller wishes to have sexual intercourse with the chimera.	582	0.58
020.	Caller has previously seen a painting of the chimera.	527	0.89

That was hardly surprising, considering the number of paintings there must be of fantastic and mythical creatures. But on the next page:

| 034. | The chimera closely resembles the creature portrayed in a painting entitled *The Caress*. | 94 | 0.92 |

Curious, I displayed some of the calls. The first few told me little more than the print-out's summary line. Then, one man held up an open book to the lens. The glare of a light blub reflected off the glossy paper rendered parts of it almost invisible, and the whole thing was slightly out of focus, but what I could see was intriguing.

A leopard with a woman's head was crouched near the edge of a raised, flat surface. A slender young man, bare to the waist, stood on the lower ground, leaning sideways on to the raised surface, cheek to cheek with the leopard woman, who pressed one forepaw against his abdomen in an awkward embrace. The man coolly gazed straight ahead, his mouth set primly, giving an impression of effete detachment. The woman's eyes were closed, or nearly so, and her expression seemed less certain the longer I stared – it might have been placid, dreamy contentment, it might have been erotic bliss. Both had auburn hair.

I selected a rectangle around the woman's face, enlarged it to fill the screen, then applied a smoothing option to make the blown-up pixels less distracting. With the glare, the poor focus, and limited resolution, the image was a mess. The best I could say was that the face in the painting was not wildly dissimilar to that of the woman I'd found in the basement.

A few dozen calls later, though, no doubt remained. One caller had even taken the trouble to capture a frame from the news broadcast and patch it into her call, side by side with a well-lit close-up of her copy of the painting. One view of a single expression does not define a human face, but the resemblance was far too close to be coincidental. Since – as many people told me, and I later checked for myself – *The Caress* had been painted in 1896 by the Belgian Symbolist artist Fernand Khnopff, the painting could not possibly have been based on the living chimera. So, it had to be the other way around.

I played all ninety-four calls. Most contained nothing but the same handful of simple facts about the painting. One went a little further.

A middle-aged man introduced himself as John Aldrich, art dealer and amateur art historian. After pointing out the resemblance, and talking briefly about Khnopff and and *The Caress*, he added:

'Given that this poor woman looks exactly like Khnopff's sphinx, I wonder if you've considered the possibility that proponents of Lindhquistism are involved?' He blushed slightly. 'Perhaps that's far-fetched, but I thought I should mention it.'

So I called an on-line *Britannica*, and said, 'Lindhquistism.'

Andreas Lindhquist, 1961–2030, was a Swiss performance artist, with the distinct financial advantage of being heir to a massive pharmaceuticals empire. Up until 2011, he engaged in a wide variety of activities of a bioartistic nature, progressing from generating sounds and images by computer processing of physiological signals (ECG, EEG, skin conductivity, hormonal levels continuously monitored by immunoelectric probes), to subjecting himself to surgery in a sterile, transparent cocoon in the middle of a packed auditorium, once to have his corneas gratuitously exchanged, left for right, and a second time to have them swapped back (he publicised a more ambitious version, in which he claimed every organ in his torso would be removed and reinserted facing backwards, but was unable to find a team of surgeons who considered this anatomically plausible).

In 2011, he developed a new obsession. He projected slides of classical paintings in which the figures had been blacked out, and had models in appropriate costumes and make-up strike poses in front of the screen, filling in the gaps.

Why? In his own words (or perhaps a translation):

The great artists are afforded glimpses into a separate, transcendental, timeless world. Does that world exist? Can we travel to it? No! We must force it into being around us! We must take these fragmentary glimpses and make them solid and tangible, make them live and breathe and walk amongst us, we must import art into reality, and by doing so transform our world into the world of the artists' vision.

74

I wondered what ARIA would have made of that.

Over the next ten years, he moved away from projected slides. He began hiring movie set designers and landscape architects to recreate in three dimensions the backgrounds of the paintings he chose. He discarded the use of make-up to alter the appearance of models, and, when he found it impossible to obtain perfect lookalikes, he employed only those who, for sufficient payment, were willing to undergo cosmetic surgery.

His interest in biology hadn't entirely vanished; in 2021, on his sixtieth birthday, he had two tubes implanted in his skull, allowing him to constantly monitor, and alter, the precise neurochemical content of his brain ventricular fluid. After this, his requirements became even more stringent. The 'cheating' techniques of movie sets were forbidden – a house, or a church, or a lake, or a mountain, glimpsed in the corner of the painting being 'realised', had to *be there*, full-scale and complete in every detail. Houses, churches and small lakes were created; mountains he had to seek out – though he did transplant or destroy thousands of hectares of vegetation to alter their colour and texture. His models were required to spend months before and after the 'realisation', scrupulously 'living their roles', following complex rules and scenarios that Lindhquist devised, based on his interpretation of the painting's 'characters'. This aspect grew increasingly important to him:

The precise realisation of the appearance – the surface, I call it, however three-dimensional – is only the most rudimentary beginning. It is the network of relationships between the subjects, and between the subjects and their setting, that constitutes the challenge for the generation that follows me.

At first, it struck me as astonishing that I'd never even heard of this maniac; his sheer extravagance must have earned him a certain notoriety. But there are millions of eccentrics in the world, and thousands of extremely wealthy ones – and I was only five when Lindhquist died of a heart attack in 2030, leaving his fortune to a nine-year-old son.

As for disciples, *Britannica* listed half a dozen scattered around Eastern Europe, where apparently he'd found the most respect. All seemed to have completely abandoned his excesses, offering volumes of aesthetic theories in support of the use of painted plywood and mime artists in stylised masks. In fact, most did just that – offered the volumes, and didn't even bother with the plywood and the mime artists. I couldn't imagine any of them having either the money or the inclination to sponsor embryological research thousands of kilometres away.

For obscure reasons of copyright law, works of visual art are rarely present in publicly accessible databases, so in my lunch hour I went out and bought a book on Symbolist painters which included a colour plate of *The Caress*. I made a dozen (illegal) copies, blow-ups of various sizes. Curiously, in each one the expression of the sphinx (as Aldrich had called her) struck me as subtly different. Her mouth and her eyes (one fully closed, one infinitesimally open) could not be said to portray a definite smile, but the shading of the cheeks hinted at one – in certain enlargements, viewed from certain angles. The young man's face also changed, from vaguely troubled to slightly bored, from resolved to dissipated, from noble to effeminate. The features of both seemed to lie on complicated and uncertain borders between regions of definite mood, and the slightest shift in viewing conditions was enough to force a complete reinterpretation. If that had been Khnopff's intention it was a masterful achievement, but I also found it extremely frustrating. The book's brief commentary was no help, praising the painting's 'perfectly balanced composition and delightful thematic ambiguity', and suggesting that the leopard's head was 'perversely modelled on the artist's sister, with whose beauty he was constantly obsessed'.

Unsure for the moment just how, if at all, I ought to pursue this strand of the investigation, I sat at my desk for several minutes, wondering (but not inclined to check) if every one of the leopard's spots shown in the painting had been reproduced faithfully *in vivo*. I wanted to do something tangible, set something in motion, before I put *The Caress* aside and returned to more routine lines of inquiry.

So I made one more blow-up of the painting, this time using the copier's editing facilities to surround the man's head and shoulders with a uniform dark background. I took it down to communications, and handed it to Steve Birbeck (the man I knew had leaked my helmet log to the media).

I said, 'Put out an alert on this guy. Wanted for questioning in connection with the Macklenburg murder.'

I found nothing else of interest in the ARIA print-out, so I picked up where I'd left off the night before, phoning companies that had made use of Freda Macklenburg's services.

The work she had done had no specific connection with embryology. Her advice and assistance seemed to have been sought for a wide range of unconnected problems in a dozen fields – tissue culture work, the use of retroviruses as gene-therapy vectors, cell membrane electrochemistry, protein purification, and still other areas where the vocabulary meant nothing to me at all.

'And did Dr Macklenburg solve this problem?'

'Absolutely. She knew a perfect way around the stumbling block that had been holding us up for months.'

'How did you find out about her?'

'There's a register of consultants, indexed by speciality.'

There was indeed. She was in it in fifty-nine places. Either she somehow knew the detailed specifics of all these areas, better than many people who were actually working in them full-time, or she had access to world-class experts who could put the right words into her mouth.

Her sponsor's method of funding her work? Paying her not in money, but in expertise she could then sell as her own? Who would have so many biological scientists on tap?

The Lindhquist empire?

(So much for escaping *The Caress*.)

Her phone bills showed no long-distance calls, but that meant nothing; the local Lindhquist branch would have had its own private international network.

I looked up Lindhquist's son Gustave in *Who's Who*. It was a very sketchy entry. Born to a surrogate mother. Donor ovum anonymous. Educated by tutors. As yet unmarried at twenty-nine. Reclusive. Apparently immersed in his business concerns. Not a word about artistic pretentions, but nobody tells everything to *Who's Who*.

The preliminary forensic report arrived, with nothing very useful. No evidence of a protracted struggle – no bruising, no skin or blood found under Macklenburg's fingernails. Apparently she'd been taken entirely by surprise. The throat wound had been made by a thin, straight, razor-sharp blade, with a single powerful stroke.

There were five genotypes, besides Macklenburg's and the chimera's, present in hairs and flakes of dead skin found in the house. Precise dating isn't possible, but all showed a broad range in the age of shedding, which meant regular visitors, friends, not strangers. All five had been in the kitchen at one time or another.

Only Macklenburg and the chimera showed up in the basement in amounts that could not be accounted for by drift and second-party transport, while the chimera seemed to have rarely left her special room. One prevalent male had been in most of the rest of the house, including the bedroom, but not the bed – or at least not since the sheets had last been changed. All of this was unlikely to have a direct bearing on the murder; the best assassins either leave no biological detritus at all, or plant material belonging to someone else.

The interviewers' report came in soon after, and that was even less helpful. Macklenburg's next of kin was a cousin, with whom she had not been in touch, and who knew even less about the dead woman than I did. Her neighbours were all much too respectful of privacy to have known or cared who her friends had been, and none would admit to having noticed anything unusual on the day of the murder.

I sat and stared at *The Caress*.

Some lunatic with a great deal of money – perhaps connected to Lindhquist, perhaps not – had commissioned Freda Macklenburg to create the chimera to match the sphinx in the painting. But who would want to fake a burglary, murder Macklenburg, and endanger the chimera's life, without making the effort to actually kill it?

The phone rang. It was Muriel. The chimera was awake.

The two officers outside had had a busy shift so far; one psycho with a knife, two photographers disguised as doctors, and a religious fanatic with a mail-order exorcism kit. The news reports hadn't mentioned the name of the hospital, but there were only a dozen plausible candidates, and the staff could not be sworn to secrecy or immunised against the effect of bribes. In a day or two, the chimera's location would be common knowledge. If things didn't quieten down, I'd have to consider trying to arrange for a room in a prison infirmary, or a military hospital.

'You saved my life.'

The chimera's voice was deep and quiet and calm, and she looked right at me as she spoke. I'd expected her to be painfully shy, amongst strangers for perhaps the first time ever. She lay curled on her side on the bed, not covered by a sheet but with her head resting on a clean, white pillow. The smell was noticeable, but not unpleasant. Her tail, as thick as my wrist and longer than my arm, hung over the edge of the bed, restlessly swinging.

'Dr Beatty saved your life.' Muriel stood at the foot of the bed, glancing regularly at a blank sheet of paper on a clipboard. 'I'd like to ask you some questions.' The chimera said nothing to that, but her eyes stayed on me. 'Could you tell me your name, please?'

'Catherine.'

'Do you have another name? A surname?'

'No.'

'How old are you, Catherine?' Primed or not, I couldn't help feeling a slight giddiness, a sense of surreal inanity to be asking routine questions of a sphinx plucked from a nineteenth-century oil painting.

'Seventeen.'

'You know that Freda Macklenburg is dead?'

'Yes.' Quieter, but still calm.

'What was your relationship with her?'

She frowned slightly, then gave an answer which sounded rehearsed but sincere, as if she had long expected to be asked this. 'She was everything. She was my mother and my teacher and my friend.' Misery and loss came and went on her face, a flicker, a twitch.

'Tell me what you heard, the day the power went off.'

'Someone came to visit Freda. I heard the car, and the doorbell. It was a man. I couldn't hear what he said, but

I could hear the sound of his voice.'

'Was it a voice you'd heard before?'

'I don't think so.'

'How did they sound? Were they shouting? Arguing?'

'No. They sounded friendly. Then they stopped, it was quiet. A little while after that, the power went off. Then I heard a truck pull up, and a whole lot of noise – footsteps, things being shifted about. But no more talking. There were two or three people moving all around the house for about half an hour. Then the truck and the car drove away. I kept waiting for Freda to come down and tell me what it had all been about.'

I'd been thinking a while how to phrase the next question, but finally gave up trying to make it polite.

'Did Freda ever discuss with you why you're different from other people?'

'Yes.' Not a hint of pain, or embarrassment. Instead, her face glowed with pride, and for a moment she looked so much like the painting that the giddiness hit me again. 'She made me this way. She made me special. She made me beautiful.'

'Why?'

That seemed to baffle her, as if I had to be teasing. She was special. She was beautiful. No further explanation was required.

I heard a faint grunt from just outside the door, followed by a tiny thud against the wall. I signalled to Muriel to drop to the floor, and to Catherine to keep silent, then – quietly as I could, but with an unavoidable squeaking of metal – I climbed on to the top of a wardrobe that stood in the corner to the left of the door.

We were lucky. What came through the door when it opened a crack was not a grenade of any kind, but a hand bearing a fan laser. A spinning mirror sweeps the beam across a wide arc – this one was set to one hundred and eighty degrees, horizontally. Held at shoulder height, it filled the room with a lethal plane about a metre above the bed. I was tempted to simply kick the door shut on the hand the moment it appeared, but that would have been too risky; the gun might have tilted down before the beam cut off. For the same reason, I couldn't simply burn a hole in the man's head as he stepped into the room, or even aim at the gun itself – it was shielded, and would have borne several seconds' fire before suffering any internal damage. Paint on the walls was scorched and the curtains had split into two burning halves; in an instant he would lower the beam on to Catherine. I kicked him hard in the face, knocking him backwards and tipping the fan of laser light up towards the ceiling. Then I jumped down and put my gun to his temple. He switched off the beam and let me take the weapon from him. He was dressed in an orderly's uniform, but the fabric was implausibly stiff, probably containing a shielding layer of aluminium-coated asbestos (with the potential for reflections, it's unwise to operate a fan laser with any less protection).

I turned him over and cuffed him in the standard way – wrists and ankles all brought together behind the back, in bracelets with a sharpened inner edge that discourages (some) attempts to burst the chains. I sprayed sedative on his face for a few seconds, and he acted like it had worked, but then I pulled open one eye and knew it hadn't. Every cop uses a sedative with a slightly different tracer effect; my usual turns the whites of the eyes pale blue. He must have had a barrier layer on his skin. While I was preparing an IV jab, he turned his head towards me and opened his mouth. A blade flew out from under his tongue and nicked my ear as it whistled past. That was something I'd never seen before. I forced his jaw open and had a look; the launching mechanism was anchored to his teeth with wires and pins. There was a second blade in there; I put my gun to his head again and advised him to eject it on to the floor. Then I punched him in the face and started searching for an easy vein.

He gave a short cry, and began vomiting steaming-hot blood. Possibly his own choice, but more likely his employers had decided to cut their losses. The body started smoking, so I dragged it out into the corridor.

The officers who'd been on guard were unconscious, not dead. A matter of pragmatism; chemically knocking someone senseless is usually quieter, less messy and less risky to the assailant than killing them. Also, dead cops have been known to trigger an extra impetus in many investigations, so it's worthwhile taking the trouble to avoid them. I phoned someone I knew in Toxicology to come and take a look at them, then radioed for replacements. Organising the move to somewhere more secure would take twenty-four hours at least.

Catherine was hysterical, and Muriel, pretty shaken herself, insisted on sedating her and ending the interview.

Muriel said, 'I've read about it, but I've never seen it with my own eyes before. What does it feel like?'

'What?'

She emitted a burst of nervous laughter. She was shivering. I held on to her shoulders until she calmed down a little. 'Being like that.' Her teeth chattered. 'Someone just tried to *kill us all*, and you're carrying on like nothing special happened. Like someone out of a comic book. What does it feel like?'

I laughed myself. We have a standard answer.

'It doesn't feel like anything at all.'

Marion lay with her head on my chest. Her eyes were closed, but she wasn't asleep. I knew she was still listening to me. She always tenses up a certain way when I'm raving.

'How could anyone *do* that? How could anyone sit

down and cold-bloodedly *plan* to create a deformed human being with no chance of living a normal life? All for some insane "artist" somewhere who's keeping alive a dead billionaire's crazy theories. Shit, what do they think people are? Sculptures? *Things* they can mess around with any way they like?'

I wanted to sleep, it was late, but I couldn't shut up. I hadn't even realised how angry I was until I'd started on the topic, but then my disgust had grown more intense with every word I'd uttered.

An hour before, trying to make love, I'd found myself impotent. I'd resorted to using my tongue, and Marion had come, but it still depressed me. Was it psychological? The case I was on? Or a side effect of the priming drugs? So suddenly, after all these years? There were rumours and jokes about the drugs causing almost everything imaginable: sterility, malformed babies, cancer, psychoses; but I'd never believed any of that. The union would have found out and raised hell, the department would never have been allowed to get away with it. It was the chimera case that was screwing me up, it had to be. So I talked about it.

'And the worst thing is, she doesn't even understand what's been done to her. She's been lied to from birth. Macklenburg told her she was *beautiful*, and she *believes* that crap, because she doesn't know any better.'

Marion shifted slightly, and sighed. 'What's going to happen to her? How's she going to live when she's out of hospital?'

'I don't know. I guess she could sell her story for quite a packet. Enough to hire someone to look after her for the rest of her life.' I closed my eyes. 'I'm sorry. It's not fair, keeping you awake half the night with this.'

I heard a faint hissing sound, and Marion suddenly relaxed. For what seemed like several seconds, but can't have been, I wondered what was wrong with me, why I hadn't leapt to my feet, why I hadn't even raised my head to look across the dark room to find out who or what was there.

Then I realised the spray had hit me, too, and I was paralysed. It was such a relief to be powerless that I slipped into unconsciousness feeling, absurdly, more peaceful than I had felt for a very long time.

I woke with a mixture of panic and lethargy, and no idea where I was or what had happened. I opened my eyes and saw nothing. I flailed about trying to touch my eyes, and felt myself drifting slightly, but my arms and legs were restrained. I forced myself to relax for a moment and interpret my sensations. I was blindfolded or bandaged, floating in a warm, buoyant liquid, my mouth and nose covered with a mask. My feeble thrashing movements had exhausted me, and for a long time I lay still, unable to concentrate sufficiently to even start guessing about my circumstances. I felt as if every bone in my body had been broken – not through any pain, but through a subtler discomfort arising from an unfamiliar sense of my body's configuration; it was awkward, it was wrong. It occurred to me that I might have been in an accident. A fire? That would explain why I was floating; I was in a burns treatment unit. I said, 'Hello? I'm awake.' The words came out as painful, hoarse whispers.

A blandly cheerful voice, almost genderless but borderline male, replied. I was wearing headphones; I hadn't noticed them until I felt them vibrate.

'Mr Segel. How do you feel?'

'Uncomfortable. Weak. Where am I?'

'A long way from home, I'm afraid. But your wife is here too.'

It was only then that I remembered: lying in bed, unable to move. That seemed impossibly long ago, but I had no more recent memories to fill in the gap.

'How long have I been here? Where's Marion?'

'Your wife is nearby. She's safe and comfortable. You've been here a number of weeks, but you are healing rapidly. Soon you'll be ready for physiotherapy. So please, relax, be patient.'

'*Healing from what?*'

'Mr Segel, I'm afraid it was necessary to perform a great deal of surgery to adjust your appearance to suit my requirements. Your eyes, your face, your bone structure, your build, your skin tones; all needed substantial alteration.'

I floated in silence. The face of the diffident youth in *The Caress* drifted across the darkness. I was horrified, but my disorientation cushioned the blow; floating in darkness, listening to a disembodied voice, nothing was yet quite real.

'Why pick me?'

'You saved Catherine's life. On two occasions. That's precisely the relationship I wanted.'

'Two set-ups. She was never in any real danger, was she? Why didn't you find someone who already looked the part, to go through the motions?' I almost added 'Gustave', but stopped myself in time. I was certain he intended killing me anyway, eventually, but betraying my suspicions about his identity would have been suicidal. The voice was synthetic, of course.

'You genuinely saved her life, Mr Segel. If she'd stayed in the basement without replacement hormones, she would have died. And the assassin we sent to the hospital was seriously intent on killing her.'

I snorted feebly. 'What if he'd succeeded? Twenty years' work and millions of dollars, down the drain. What would you have done then?'

'Mr Segel, you have a very parochial view of the world. Your little town isn't the only one on the planet. Your little police force isn't unique either, except in being the only one who couldn't keep the story from the media. We began with twelve chimeras. Three died in childhood. Three were not discovered in time after their keepers were killed. Four were assassinated after discovery. The other surviving chimera's life was saved by different people on the two occasions – and also she was not quite up to the standard of morphology that Freda Macklenburg achieved with Catherine. So, imperfect as you are, Mr Segel, you are what I am required to work with.'

Shortly after that, I was shifted to a normal bed, and the bandages were removed from my face and body. At first the room was kept dark, but each morning the lights were turned up slightly. Twice a day, a masked physiotherapist with a filtered voice came and helped me learn to move again. There were six armed, masked guards in the windowless room at all times; ludicrous overkill unless they were there in case of an unlikely, external attempt to rescue me. I could barely walk; one stern grandmother could have kept me from escaping.

They showed me Marion, once, on closed-circuit TV. She sat in an elegantly furnished room, watching a news disk. Every few seconds, she glanced around nervously. They wouldn't let us meet. I was glad. I didn't want to see her reaction to my new appearance; that was an emotional complication I could do without.

As I slowly became functional, I began to feel a deep sense of panic that I'd yet to think of a plan for keeping us alive. I tried striking up conversations with the guards, in the hope of eventually persuading one of them to help us, either out of compassion or on the promise of a bribe, but they all stuck to monosyllables, and ignored me when I spoke of anything more abstract than requests for food. Refusing to cooperate in the 'realisation' was the only strategy I could think of, but for how long would that work? I had no doubt that my captor would resort to torturing Marion, and if that failed he would simply hypnotise or drug me to ensure that I complied. And then he would kill us all: Marion, myself, and Catherine.

I had no idea how much time we had; neither the guards, nor the physiotherapist, nor the cosmetic surgeons who occasionally came to check their handi-work, would even acknowledge my questions about the schedule being followed. I longed for Lindhquist to speak with me again; however insane he was, at least he'd engaged in a two-way conversation. I demanded an audience with him, I screamed and ranted; the guards remained as unresponsive as their masks.

Accustomed to the aid of the priming drugs in focusing my thoughts, I found myself constantly distracted by all kinds of unproductive concerns, from a simple fear of death, to pointless worries about my chances of continued employment, and continued marriage, if Marion and I did somehow survive. Weeks went by in which I felt nothing but hopelessness and self-pity. Everything that defned me had been taken away: my face, my body, my job, my usual modes of thought. And although I missed my former physical strength (as a source of self-respect rather than some-thing that would have been useful in itself), it was the mental clarity that had been so much a part of my primed state of mind that, I was certain, would have made all the difference if only I could have regained it.

I eventually began to indulge in a bizarre, romantic fantasy: the loss of everything I had once relied on – the stripping away of the bio-chemical props that had held my unnatural life together – would reveal an inner core of sheer moral courage and desperate resourcefulness which would see me through this hour of need. My identity had been demolished, but the naked spark of humanity remained, soon to burst into a searing flame that no prison walls could contain. That which had not killed me would (soon, real soon) make me strong.

A moment's introspection each morning showed

that this mystical transformation had not yet taken place. I went on a hunger strike, hoping to hasten my victorious emergence from the crucible of suffering by turning up the heat. I wasn't force-fed, or even given intravenous protein. I was too stupid to make the obvious deduction: the day of realisation was imminent.

One morning, I was handed a costume which I recognised at once from the painting. I was terrified to the point of nausea, but I put it on and went with the guards, making no trouble. The painting was set outdoors. This would be my only chance to escape.

I'd hoped we would have to travel, with all the opportunities that might have entailed, but the landscape had been prepared just a few hundred metres from the building I'd been kept in. I blinked at the glare from the thin grey clouds that covered most of the sky (had Lindhquist been waiting for them, or had he ordered their presence?), weary, frightened, weaker than ever thanks to not having eaten for three days. Desolate fields stretched to the horizon in all directions. There was nowhere to run to, nobody to signal to for help.

I saw Catherine, already sitting in place on the edge of a raised stretch of ground. A short man – well, shorter than the guards, whose height I'd grown accustomed to – stood by her, stroking her neck. She flicked her tail with pleasure, her eyes half closed. The man wore a loose white suit, and a white mask, rather like a fencing mask. When he saw me approaching, he raised his arms in an extravagant gesture of greeting. For an instant a wild idea possessed me: Catherine could save us! With her speed, her strength, her *claws*.

There were a dozen armed men around us, and Catherine was clearly as docile as a kitten.

'Mr Segel! You look so glum! Cheer up, please! This is a wonderful day!'

I stopped walking. The guards on either side of me

stopped too, and did nothing to force me on.

I said, 'I won't do it.'

The man in white was indulgent. 'Why ever not?'

I stared at him, trembling. I felt like a child. Not since childhood had I confronted anyone this way, without the priming drugs to calm me, without a weapon within easy reach, without absolute confidence in my strength and agility. 'When we've done what you want, you're going to kill us all. The longer I refuse, the longer I stay alive.'

It was Catherine who answered first. She shook her head, not quite laughing. 'No, Dan! Andreas won't hurt us! He loves us both!'

The man came towards me. Had Andreas Lindhquist faked his death? His gait was not an old man's gait.

'Mr Segel, please calm yourself. Would I harm my own creations? Would I waste all those years of hard work, by myself and so many others?'

I sputtered, confused, 'You've killed people. You've kidnapped us. You've broken a hundred different laws.' I almost shouted at Catherine. '*He* arranged Freda's death!', but I had a feeling that would have done me a lot more harm than good.

The computer that disguised his voice laughed blandly. 'Yes, I've broken laws. Whatever happens to you, Mr Segel, I've already broken them. Do you think I'm afraid of what you'll do when I release you? You will be as powerless then to harm me as you are now. You have no proof as to my identity. Oh, I've examined a record of your inquiries. I know you suspected me—'

'I suspected your son.'

'Ah. A moot point. I prefer to be called Andreas by intimate acquaintances, but to business associates, I am Gustave Lindhquist. You see, this body *is* that of my son – if son is the right word to use for a clone – but since his birth I took regular samples of my brain tissue, and had the appropriate components extracted from them and injected into his skull. The brain can't be *transplanted*, Mr Segel, but with care, a great deal of memory and personality can be imposed upon a young child. When my first body died, I had the brain frozen, and I continued the injections until all the tissue was used up. Whether or not I "am" Andreas is a matter for philosophers and theologians. I clearly recall sitting in a crowded classroom watching a black and white television, the day Neil Armstrong stepped on the moon, fifty-two years before this body was born. So call me Andreas. Humour an old man.'

He shrugged. 'The masks, the voice filters – I like a little theatre. And the less you see and hear, the fewer your avenues for causing me minor annoyance. But please, don't flatter yourself; you can never be a threat to me. I could buy every member of your entire force with half the amount I've earnt while we've been speaking.

'So forget these delusions of martyrdom. You are going to live, and for the rest of your life you will be, not only my creation, but my instrument. You are going to carry this moment away inside you, out into the world for me, like a seed, like a strange, beautiful virus, infecting and transforming everyone and everything you touch.'

He took me by the arm and led me towards Catherine. I didn't resist. Someone placed a winged staff in my right hand. I was prodded, arranged, adjusted, fussed over. I hardly noticed Catherine's cheek against mine, her paw resting against my belly. I stared ahead, in a daze, trying to decide whether or not to believe I was going to live, overcome by this first real chance of hope, but too terrified of disappointment to trust it.

There was no one but Lindhquist and his guards and assistants. I don't know what I'd expected; an audience in evening dress? He stood a dozen metres away, glancing down at a copy of the painting (or perhaps it was the original) mounted on an easel, then calling out instructions for microscopic changes to our posture and expression. My eyes began to water, from keeping my gaze fixed; someone ran forward and dried them, then sprayed something into them which prevented a recurrence.

Then, for several minutes, Lindhquist was silent. When he finally spoke, he said, very softly, 'All we're waiting for now is the movement of the sun, the correct positioning of your shadows. Be patient for just a little longer.'

I don't remember clearly what I felt in those last seconds. I was so tired, so confused, so uncertain. I do remember thinking: How will I know when the moment has passed? When Lindhquist pulls out a weapon and incinerates us, perfectly preserving the moment? Or when he pulls out a camera? *Which would it be?*

Suddenly he said, 'Thank you,' and turned and walked away, alone. Catherine shifted, stretched, kissed me on the cheek, and said, 'Wasn't that fun?' One of the guards took my elbow, and I realised I'd staggered.

He hadn't even taken a photograph. I giggled hysterically, certain now that I was going to live after all. And he hadn't even taken a photograph. I couldn't decide if that made him twice as insane, or if it totally redeemed his sanity.

I never discovered what became of Catherine. Perhaps she stayed with Lindhquist, shielded from the world by his wealth and seclusion, living a life effectively identical to that she'd lived before, in Freda Macklenburg's basement. Give or take a few servants and luxurious villas.

Marion and I were returned to our home, unconscious for the duration of the voyage, waking on the bed we'd left six months before. There was a lot of dust about. She took my hand and said, 'Well. Here we are.' We lay there in silence for hours, then went out in search of food.

The next day I went to the station. I proved my identity with fingerprints and DNA, and gave a full report of all that had happened.

I had not been assumed dead. My salary had continued to be paid into my bank account, and mortgage payments deducted automatically. The department settled my claim for compensation out of court, paying me three-quarters of a million dollars, and I underwent surgery to restore as much of my former appearance as possible.

It took more than two years of rehabilitation, but now I am back on active duty. The Macklenburg case has been shelved for lack of evidence. The investigation of the kidnapping of the three of us, and Catherine's present fate, is on the verge of going the same way; nobody doubts my account of the events, but all the evidence against Gustave Lindhquist is circumstantial. I accept that. I'm glad. I want to erase everything that Lindhquist has done to me, and an obsession with bringing him to justice is the exact opposite of the state of mind I aim to achieve. I don't pretend to understand what he thought he was achieving by letting me live, what his insane notion of my supposed effect on the world actually entailed, but I am determined to be, in every way, the same person as I was before the experience, and thus to defeat his intentions.

Marion is doing fine. For a while she suffered from recurring nightmares, but after seeing a therapist who specialises in detraumatising hostages and kidnap victims, she is now every bit as relaxed and carefree as she used to be.

I have nightmares, now and then. I wake in the early hours of the morning, shivering and sweating and crying out, unable to recall what horror I'm escaping. Andreas Lindhquist injecting samples of brain tissue into his son? Catherine blissfully closing her eyes, and thanking me for saving her life while her claws rake my body into bloody strips? Myself, trapped in *The Caress*; the moment of the realisation infinitely, unmercifully prolonged? Perhaps; or perhaps I simply dream about my latest case – that seems much more likely.

Everything is back to normal.

BLOOD SISTERS

When we were nine years old, Paula decided we should prick our thumbs, and let our blood flow into each other's veins.

I was scornful. 'Why bother? Our blood's already exactly the same. We're *already* blood sisters.'

She was unfazed. 'I know that. That's not the point. It's the ritual that counts.'

We did it in our bedroom, at midnight, by the light of a single candle. She sterilised the needle in the candle flame, then wiped it clean of soot with a tissue and saliva.

When we'd pressed the tiny, sticky wounds together, and recited some ridiculous oath from a third-rate children's novel, Paula blew out the candle. While my eyes were still adjusting to the dark, she added a whispered coda of her own: 'Now we'll dream the same dreams, and share the same lovers, and die at the very same hour.'

I tried to say, indignantly, 'That's just not true!' but the darkness and the scent of the dead flame made the protest stick in my throat, and her words remained unchallenged.

As Dr Packard spoke, I folded the pathology report, into halves, into quarters, obsessively aligning the edges. It was far too thick for me to make a neat job of it; from the micrographs of the misshapen lymphocytes proliferating in my bone marrow, to the print-out of portions of the RNA sequence of the virus that had triggered the disease, thirty-two pages in all.

In contrast, the prescription, still sitting on the desk in front of me, seemed ludicrously flimsy and insubstantial. No match at all. The traditional – indecipherable – polysyllabic scrawl it bore was nothing but a decoration; the drug's name was reliably encrypted in the bar code below. There was no question of receiving the wrong medication by mistake. The question was, *would the right one help me?*

'Is that clear? Ms Rees? Is there anything you don't understand?'

I struggled to focus my thoughts, pressing hard on an intractable crease with my thumb. She'd explained the situation frankly, without resorting to jargon or euphemism, but I still had the feeling that I was missing something crucial. It seemed like every sentence she'd spoken had started one of two ways: 'The virus . . .' or 'The drug . . .'

'Is there anything *I* can do? Myself? To . . . improve the odds?'

She hesitated, but not for long. 'No, not really. You're in excellent health, otherwise. Stay that way.' She began to rise from her desk to dismiss me, and I began to panic.

'But, there must be *something*.' I gripped the arms of my chair, as if afraid of being dislodged by force. Maybe she'd misunderstood me, maybe I hadn't made myself clear. 'Should I . . . stop eating certain foods? Get more exercise? Get more sleep? I mean, there has to be *something* that will make a difference. And I'll do it, whatever it is. Please, just *tell* me—' My voice almost cracked, and I looked away, embarrassed. *Don't ever start ranting like that again. Not ever.*

'Ms Rees, I'm sorry. I know how you must be feeling. But the Monte Carlo diseases are all like this. In fact, you're exceptionally lucky; the WHO computer found eighty thousand people, worldwide, infected with a similar strain. That's not enough of a market to support any hard-core research, but enough to have persuaded the pharmaceutical companies to rummage through their databases for something that might do the trick. A lot of people are on their own, infected with viruses that are virtually unique. Imagine how much useful information the health profession can give *them*.'

I finally looked up; the expression on her face was one of sympathy, tempered by impatience.

I declined the invitation to feel ashamed of my ingratitude. I'd made a fool of myself, but I still had a right to ask the question. 'I understand all that. I just thought there might be something *I* could do. You say this drug might work, or it might not. If I could contribute, *myself*, to fighting this disease, I'd feel . . .'

What? More like a human being, and less like a test tube – a passive container in which the wonder drug and the wonder virus would fight it out between themselves.

'. . . better.'

She nodded. 'I know, but trust me, nothing you can do would make the slightest difference. Just look after yourself as you normally would. Don't catch pneumonia. Don't gain or lose ten kilos. Don't do *anything* out of the ordinary. Millions of people must have been exposed to this virus, but the reason you're sick, and they're not, is *a purely genetic matter*. The cure will be just the same. The biochemistry that determines whether or not the drug will work for you isn't going to change if you start taking vitamin pills, or stop eating junk food – and I should warn you that going on one of those "miracle-cure" diets will simply make you sick; the charlatans selling them ought to be in prison.'

I nodded fervent agreement to *that*, and felt myself flush with anger. Fraudulent cures had long been my *bête noire* – although now, for the first time, I could almost understand why other Monte Carlo victims paid good money for such things: crackpot diets, meditation schemes, aromatherapy, self-hypnosis tapes, you name it. The people who peddled that garbage were the worst kind of cynical parasites, and I'd always thought of their customers as being either congenitally gullible, or desperate to the point of abandoning their wits, but there was more to it than that. When your life is at stake, you want to fight for it – with every ounce of your strength, with every cent you can borrow, with every waking moment. Taking one capsule, three times a day, just isn't *hard enough* – whereas the schemes of the most perceptive con men were sufficiently arduous (or sufficiently expensive) to make the victims feel that they were engaged in the kind of struggle that the prospect of death requires.

This moment of shared anger cleared the air completely. We were on the same side, after all; I'd been acting like a child. I thanked Dr Packard for her time, picked up the prescription, and left.

On my way to the pharmacy, though, I found myself almost wishing that she'd lied to me – that she'd told me my chances would be vastly improved if I ran ten kilometres a day and ate raw seaweed with every meal – but then I angrily recoiled, thinking: Would I really want to be deceived 'for my own good'? If it's down to my DNA, it's down to my DNA, and I ought to expect to be told that simple truth, however unpalatable I find it – and I ought to be grateful that the medical profession has abandoned its old patronising, paternalistic ways.

I was twelve years old when the world learnt about the Monte Carlo project.

A team of biological warfare researchers (located just a stone's throw from Las Vegas – alas, the one in New

Mexico, not the one in Nevada) had decided that *designing* viruses was just too much hard work (especially when the Star Wars boys kept hogging the supercomputers). Why waste hundreds of PhD-years – why expend any intellectual effort whatsoever – when the time-honoured partnership of blind mutation and natural selection was all that was required?

Speeded up substantially, of course.

They'd developed a three-part system: a bacterium, a virus, and a line of modified human lymphocytes. A stable portion of the viral genome allowed it to reproduce in the bacterium, while rapid mutation of the rest of the virus was achieved by neatly corrupting the transcription error repair enzymes. The lymphocytes had been altered to vastly amplify the reproductive success of any mutant which managed to infect them, causing it to out-breed those which were limited to using the bacterium.

The theory was, they'd set up a few trillion copies of this system, like row after row of little biological poker machines, spinning away in their underground lab, and just wait to harvest the jackpots.

The theory also included the best containment facilities in the world, and five hundred and twenty people all sticking scrupulously to official procedure, day after day, month after month, without a moment of carelessness, laziness or forgetfulness. Apparently, nobody bothered to compute the probability of *that*.

The bacterium was supposed to be unable to survive outside artificially beneficent laboratory conditions, but a mutation of the virus came to its aid, filling in for the genes that had been snipped out to make it vulnerable.

They wasted too much time using ineffectual chemicals before steeling themselves to nuke the site. By then, the winds had already made any human action – short of melting half a dozen states, not an option in an election year – irrelevant.

The first rumours proclaimed that we'd all be dead within a week. I can clearly recall the mayhem, the looting, the suicides (second-hand on the TV screen; our own neighbourhood remained relatively tranquil – or numb). States of emergency were declared around the world. Planes were turned away from airports, ships (which had left their home ports months before the leak) were burnt in the docks. Harsh laws were rushed in everywhere, to protect public order and public health.

Paula and I got to stay home from school for a month. I offered to teach her programming; she wasn't interested. She wanted to go swimming, but the beaches and pools were all closed. That was the summer that I finally managed to hack into a Pentagon computer – just an office supplies purchasing system, but Paula was suitably impressed (and neither of us had ever guessed that paperclips were *that* expensive).

We didn't believe we were going to die – at least, not within a week – and we were right. When the hysteria subsided, it soon became apparent that only the virus and the bacterium had escaped, and without the modified lymphocytes to fine-tune the selection process, the virus had mutated away from the strain which had caused the initial deaths.

However, the cosy symbiotic pair is now found all over the world, endlessly churning out new mutations. Only a tiny fraction of the strains produced are infectious in humans, and only a fraction of those are potentially fatal.

A mere hundred or so a year.

On the train home, the sun seemed to be in my eyes no matter which way I turned – somehow, every surface in the carriage caught its reflection. The glare made a headache which had been steadily growing all afternoon almost unbearable, so I covered my eyes with my forearm and faced the floor. With my other hand, I clutched the brown paper bag that held the small glass vial of red-and-black capsules that would or wouldn't save my life.

Cancer. Viral leukaemia. I pulled the creased pathology report from my pocket, and flipped through it one more time. The last page hadn't magically changed into a happy ending – an oncovirology expert system's declaration of a sure-fire cure. The last page was just the bill for all the tests. Twenty-seven thousand dollars.

At home, I sat and stared at my work station.

Two months before, when a routine quarterly examination (required by my health insurance company, ever eager to dump the unprofitable sick) had revealed the first signs of trouble, I'd sworn to myself that I'd keep on working, keep on living exactly as if nothing had changed. The idea of indulging in a credit spree, or a world trip, or some kind of self-destructive binge, held no attraction for me at all. Any such final fling would be an admission of defeat. *I'd* go on a fucking world trip to celebrate my cure, and not before.

I had plenty of contract work stacked up, and that pathology bill was already accruing interest. Yet for all that I needed the distraction – for all that I needed *the money* – I sat there for three whole hours, and did nothing but brood about my fate. Sharing it with eighty thousand strangers scattered about the world was no great comfort.

Then it finally struck me. *Paula*. If I was vulnerable *for genetic reasons,* then *so was she.*

For identical twins, in the end we hadn't done too bad a job of pursuing separate lives. She had left home at sixteen, to tour central Africa, filming the wildlife, and – at considerably greater risk – the poachers. Then she'd gone to the Amazon, and become caught up in the land rights struggle there. After that, it was a bit of a blur;

she'd always tried to keep me up to date with her exploits, but she moved too fast for my sluggish mental picture of her to follow.

I'd never left the country; I hadn't even moved house in a decade.

She came home only now and then, on her way between continents, but we'd stayed in touch electronically, circumstances permitting. (They take away your SatPhone in Bolivian prisons.)

The telecommunications multinationals all offer their own expensive services for contacting someone when you don't know in advance what country they're in. The advertising suggests that it's an immensely difficult task; the fact is, every SatPhone's location is listed in a central database, which is kept up to date by pooling information from all the regional satellites. Since I happened to have 'acquired' the access codes to consult that database, I could phone Paula directly, wherever she was, without paying the ludicrous surcharge. It was more a matter of nostalgia than miserliness; this minuscule bit of hacking was a token gesture, proof that in spite of impending middle age, I wasn't yet terminally law-abiding, conservative and dull.

I'd automated the whole procedure long ago. The database said she was in Gabon; my program calculated local time, judged 10.23 p.m. to be civilised enough, and made the call. Seconds later, she was on the screen.

'Karen! How are you? You look like shit. I thought you were going to call last week – what happened?'

The image was perfectly clear, the sound clean and undistorted (fibre-optic cables might be scarce in central Africa, but geosynchronous satellites are directly overhead). As soon as I set eyes on her, I felt sure she didn't have the virus. She was right – I looked half-dead, whereas she was as animated as ever. Half a lifetime spent outdoors meant her skin had aged much faster than mine – but there was always a glow of energy, of purpose, about her that more than compensated.

She was close to the lens, so I couldn't see much of the background, but it looked like a fibreglass hut, lit by a couple of hurricane lamps; a step up from the usual tent.

'I'm sorry, I didn't get around to it. *Gabon?* Weren't you in Ecuador—?'

'Yes, but I met Mohammed. He's a botanist. From Indonesia. Actually, we met in Bogotá; he was on his way to a conference in Mexico—'

'But—'

'Why Gabon? This is where he was going next, that's all. There's a fungus here, attacking the crops, and I couldn't resist coming along . . .'

I nodded, bemused, through ten minutes of convoluted explanations, not paying too much attention; in three months' time it would all be ancient history. Paula survived as a freelance pop-science journalist, darting around the globe writing articles for magazines, and scripts for TV programmes, on the latest ecological trouble spots. To be honest, I had severe doubts that this kind of predigested eco-babble did the planet any good, but it certainly made her happy. I envied her that. I could not have lived her life – in no sense was she the woman I 'might have been' – but nonetheless it hurt me, at times, to see in her eyes the kind of sheer excitement that I hadn't felt, myself, for a decade.

My mind wandered while she spoke. Suddenly, she was saying, 'Karen? Are you going to tell me what's wrong?'

I hesitated. I had originally planned to tell no one, not even her, and now my reason for calling her seemed absurd – *she* couldn't have leukaemia, it was unthinkable. Then, without even realising that I'd made the decision, I found myself recounting everything in a dull, flat voice. I watched with a strange feeling of detachment the changing expression on her face; shock, pity, then a burst of fear when she realised – far sooner than I would have done – exactly what my predicament meant for her.

What followed was even more awkward and painful than I could have imagined. Her concern for me was genuine – but she would not have been human if the uncertainty of her own position had not begun to prey on her at once, and knowing *that* made all her fussing seem contrived and false.

'Do you have a good doctor? Someone you can trust?'

I nodded.

'Do you have someone to look after you? Do you want me to come home?'

I shook my head, irritated. 'No. I'm all right. I'm being looked after, I'm being *treated*. But *you* have to get tested as soon as possible.' I glared at her, exasperated. I no longer believed that she could have the virus, but I wanted to stress the fact that I'd called her to warn her, not to fish for sympathy – and somehow, that finally struck home. She said, quietly, 'I'll get tested today. I'll go straight into town. OK?'

I nodded. I felt exhausted, but relieved; for a moment, all the awkwardness between us melted away.

'You'll let me know the results?'

She rolled her eyes. 'Of course I will.'

I nodded again. 'OK.'

'Karen. Be careful. Look after yourself.'

'I will. You too.' I hit the ESCAPE key.

Half an hour later, I took the first of the capsules, and climbed into bed. A few minutes later, a bitter taste crept up into my throat.

Telling Paula was essential. Telling Martin was insane. I'd only known him six months, but I should have guessed exactly how he'd take it.

'Move in with me. I'll look after you.'

'I don't *need* to be looked after.'

He hesitated, but only slightly. 'Marry me.'

'*Marry* you? Why? Do you think I have some desperate need to be married before I die?'

He scowled. 'Don't talk like that. I *love you*. Don't you understand that?'

I laughed. 'I don't *mind* being pitied – people always say it's degrading, but I think it's a perfectly normal response – but I don't want to have to live with it twenty-four hours a day.' I kissed him, but he kept on scowling. At least I'd waited until after we'd had sex before breaking the news; if not, he probably would have treated me like porcelain.

He turned to face me. 'Why are you being so hard on yourself? What are you trying to prove? That you're superhuman? That you don't need anyone?'

'*Listen.* You've known from the very start that I need independence and privacy. What do you want me to say? That I'm terrified. OK. I am. But I'm still the same person. I still need the same things.' I slid one hand across his chest, and said as gently as I could, 'So thanks for the offer, but no thanks.'

'I don't mean very much to you, do I?'

I groaned, and pulled a pillow over my face. I thought: *Wake me when you're ready to fuck me again. Does that answer your question?* I didn't say it out loud, though.

A week later, Paula phoned me. She had the virus. Her white cell count was up, her red cell count was down – the numbers she quoted sounded just like my own from the month before. They'd even put her on the very same drug. That was hardly surprising, but it gave me an unpleasant, claustrophobic feeling, when I thought about what it meant:

We would both live, or we would both die.

In the days that followed, this realisation began to obsess me. It was like voodoo, like some curse out of a fairy tale – or the fulfilment of the words she'd uttered, the night we became 'blood sisters'. We had never dreamed the same dreams, we'd certainly never loved the same men, but now . . . it was as if we were being punished, for failing to respect the forces that bound us together.

Part of me *knew* this was bullshit. *Forces that bound us together!* It was mental static, the product of stress, nothing more. The truth, though, was just as oppressive: the biochemical machinery would grind out its identical verdict on both of us, for all the thousands of kilometres between us, for all that we had forged separate lives in defiance of our genetic unity.

I tried to bury myself in my work. To some degree, I succeeded – if the grey stupor produced by eighteen-hour days in front of a terminal could really be considered a success.

I began to avoid Martin; his puppy-dog concern was just too much to bear. Perhaps he meant well, but I didn't have the energy to justify myself to him, over and over again. Perversely, at the very same time, I missed our arguments terribly; resisting his excessive mothering had at least made me feel strong, if only in contrast to the helplessness he seemed to expect of me.

I phoned Paula every week at first, but then gradually less and less often. We ought to have been ideal confidantes; in fact, nothing could have been less true. Our conversations were redundant; we already knew what the other was thinking, far too well. There was no sense of unburdening, just a suffocating, monotonous feeling of recognition. We took to trying to outdo each other in affecting a veneer of optimism, but it was a depressingly transparent effort. Eventually, I thought: when – if – I get the good news, I'll call her; until then, what's the point? Apparently, she came to the same conclusion.

All through childhood, we were forced together. We loved each other, I suppose, but . . . we were always in the same classes at school, bought the same clothes, given the same Christmas and birthday presents – and we were always sick at the same time, with the same ailment, for the same reason. When she left home, I was envious, and horribly lonely for a while, but then I felt a surge of joy, of *liberation*, because I knew that I had no real wish to follow her, and I knew that from then on, our lives could only grow further apart.

Now, it seemed that had all been an illusion. We would live or die together, and all our efforts to break the bonds had been in vain.

About four months after the start of treatment, my blood counts began to turn around. I was more terrified than ever of my hopes being dashed, and I spent all my time battling to keep myself from premature optimism. I didn't dare ring Paula; I could think of nothing worse than leading her to think that we were cured, and then turning out to have been mistaken. Even when Dr Packard – cautiously, almost begrudgingly – admitted that things were looking up, I told myself that she might have relented from her policy of unflinching honesty and decided to offer me some palliative lies.

One morning I woke, not yet convinced that I was cured, but sick of feeling I had to drown myself in gloom for fear of being disappointed. If I wanted absolute certainty, I'd be miserable all my life; a relapse would always be possible, or a *whole new virus* could come along.

It was a cold, dark morning, pouring with rain outside, but as I climbed, shivering, out of bed, I felt more cheerful than I had since the whole thing had begun.

There was a message in my work station mailbox, tagged CONFIDENTIAL. It took me thirty seconds to recall the password I needed, and all the while my shivering grew worse.

The message was from the Chief Administrator of the Libreville People's Hospital, offering his or her condolences on the death of my sister, and requesting instructions for the disposal of the body.

I don't know what I felt first. Disbelief. Guilt. Confusion. Fear. How could she have died, when I was so close to recovery? How could she have died without a word to me? *How could I have let her die alone?* I walked away from the terminal, and slumped against the cold brick wall.

The worst of it was, I suddenly *knew* why she'd stayed silent. She must have thought that I was dying, too, and that was the one thing we'd both feared most of all: dying together. In spite of everything, dying together, as if we were one.

How could the drug have failed her, and worked for me? *Had it worked for me?* For a moment of sheer paranoia, I wondered if the hospital had been faking my test results, if in fact I was on the verge of death, myself. That was ludicrous, though.

Why, then, had Paula died? There was only one possible answer. She should have come home – I should have *made her* come home. How could I have let her stay there, in a tropical, Third World country, with her immune system weakened, living in a fibreglass hut, without proper sanitation, probably malnourished? I should have sent her the money, I should have sent her the ticket, I should have flown out there in person and dragged her back home.

Instead, I'd kept her at a distance. Afraid of us dying together, afraid of the curse of our sameness, I'd let her die alone.

I tried to cry, but something stopped me. I sat in the

kitchen, sobbing drily. I was worthless. I'd killed her with my superstition and cowardice. I had no right to be alive.

I spent the next fortnight grappling with the legal and administrative complexities of death in a foreign land. Paula's will requested cremation, but said nothing about where it was to take place, so I arranged for her body and belongings to be flown home. The service was all but deserted; our parents had died a decade before, in a car crash, and although Paula had had friends all over the world, few were able to make the trip.

Martin came, though. When he put an arm round me, I turned and whispered to him angrily, 'You didn't even know her. What the hell are you doing here?' He stared at me for a moment, hurt and baffled, then walked off without a word.

I can't pretend I wasn't grateful, when Packard announced that I was cured, but my failure to rejoice out loud must have puzzled even her. I might have told her about Paula, but I didn't want to be fed cheap clichés about how irrational it was of me to feel guilty for surviving.

She was dead. I was growing stronger by the day; often sick with guilt and depression, but more often simply numb. That might easily have been the end of it.

Following the instructions in the will, I sent most of her belongings – notebooks, disks, audio and video tapes – to her agent, to be passed on to the appropriate editors and producers, to whom some of it might be of use. All that remained was clothing, a minute quantity of jewellery and cosmetics, and a handful of odds and ends. Including a small glass vial of red-and-black capsules.

I don't know what possessed me to take one of the capsules. I had half a dozen left of my own, and Packard had shrugged when I'd asked if I should finish them, and said that it couldn't do me any harm.

There was no aftertaste. Every time I'd swallowed my own, within minutes there'd been a bitter aftertaste.

I broke open a second capsule and put some of the white powder on my tongue. It was entirely without flavour. I ran and grabbed my own supply, and sampled one the same way; it tasted so vile it made my eyes water.

I tried, very hard, not to leap to any conclusions. I knew perfectly well that pharmaceuticals were often mixed with inert substances, and perhaps not necessarily the same ones all the time – but why would something *bitter* be used for that purpose? The taste had to come from the drug itself. The two vials bore the same manufacturer's name and logo. The same brand name. The same generic name. The same formal chemical name for the active ingredient. The same product code, down to the very last digit. Only the batch numbers were different.

The first explanation that came to mind was corruption. Although I couldn't recall the details, I was sure that I'd read about dozens of cases of officials in the health-care systems of developing countries diverting pharmaceuticals for resale on the black market. What better way to cover up such a theft than to replace the stolen product with something else – something cheap, harmless, and absolutely useless? The gelatin capsules themselves bore nothing but the manufacturer's logo, and since the company probably made at least a thousand different drugs, it would not have been too hard to find something cheaper, with the same size and colouration.

I had no idea what to do with this theory. Anonymous bureaucrats in a distant country had killed my sister, but the prospects of finding out who they were, let alone seeing them brought to justice, were infinitesimally small. Even if I'd had real, damning evidence, what was the most I could hope for? A meekly phrased protest from one diplomat to another.

I had one of Paula's capsules analysed. It cost me a fortune, but I was already so deeply in debt that I didn't much care.

It was full of a mixture of soluble inorganic compounds. There was no trace of the substance described on the label, nor of anything else with the slightest biological activity. It wasn't a cheap substitute drug, chosen at random.

It was a placebo.

I stood with the print-out in my hand for several minutes, trying to come to terms with what it meant. Simple greed I could have understood, but there was an utterly inhuman coldness here that I couldn't bring myself to swallow. Someone must have made an honest mistake. *Nobody* could be so callous.

Then Packard's words came back to me. 'Just look after yourself as you normally would. Don't do *anything* out of the ordinary.'

Oh no, *Doctor*. Of course not, *Doctor*. Wouldn't want to go spoiling the experiment with any messy, extraneous, uncontrolled factors . . .

I contacted an investigative journalist, one of the best in the country. I arranged a meeting in a small café on the edge of town.

I drove out there – terrified, angry, triumphant – thinking I had the scoop of the decade, thinking I had dynamite, thinking I was Meryl Streep playing Karen Silkwood. I was dizzy with sweet thoughts of revenge. Heads were going to roll.

Nobody tried to run me off the road. The café was deserted, and the waiter barely listened to our orders, let alone our conversation.

The journalist was very kind. She calmly explained the facts of life.

In the aftermath of the Monte Carlo disaster, a lot of legislation had been passed to help deal with the emergency – and a lot of legislation had been repealed. As a matter of urgency, new drugs to treat the new diseases had to be developed and assessed, and the best way to ensure *that* was to remove the cumbersome regulations that had made clinical trials so difficult and expensive.

In the old 'double-blind' trials, neither the patients nor the investigators knew who was getting the drug and who was getting a placebo; the information was kept secret by a third party (or a computer). Any improvement observed in the patients who were given the placebo could then be taken into account, and the drug's true efficacy measured.

There were two small problems with this traditional approach. Firstly, telling patients that there's only a fifty-fifty chance that they've been given a potentially life-saving drug subjects them to a lot of stress. Of course, the treatment and control groups were affected equally, but in terms of predicting what would happen when the drug was finally put out on the market, it introduced a lot of noise into the data. Which side effects were real, and which were artefacts of the patients' uncertainty?

Secondly – and more seriously – it had become increasingly difficult to find people willing to volunteer for placebo trials. When you're dying, you don't give a shit about the scientific method. You want the maximum possible chance of surviving. Untested drugs will do, if there is no known, certain cure – but why accept a further *halving* of the odds, to satisfy some technocrat's obsession with details?

Of course, in the good old days the medical profession could lay down the law to the unwashed masses: *Take part in this double-blind trial, or crawl away and die.* AIDS had changed all that, with black markets for the latest untried cures, straight from the labs to the streets, and intense politicisation of the issues.

The solution to both flaws was obvious.

You lie to the patients.

No bill had been passed to explicitly declare that 'triple-blind' trials were legal. If it had, people might have noticed, and made a fuss. Instead, as part of the 'reforms' and 'rationalisation' that came in the wake of the disaster, all the laws that might have made them illegal had been removed or watered down. At least, it looked that way – no court had yet been given the opportunity to pass judgement.

'How could any doctor *do that*? Lie like that? How could they justify it, even to themselves?'

She shrugged. 'How did they ever justify double-blind trials? A good medical researcher has to care more about the quality of the data than about any one person's life. And if a double-blind trial is good, a triple-blind trial is better. The data *is* guaranteed to be better, you can see that, can't you? And the more accurately a drug can be assessed, well, perhaps in the long run, the more lives can be saved.'

'Oh, *crap*! The placebo effect isn't *that* powerful. It just isn't that important! Who cares if it's not precisely taken into account? Anyway, *two* potential cures could still be compared, one treatment against another. That would tell you which drug would save the most lives, without any need for placebos—'

'That *is* done sometimes, although the more prestigious journals look down on those studies; they're less likely to be published—'

I stared at her. 'How can you know all this and do nothing? The media could blow it wide open! If you let people know what's going on . . .'

She smiled thinly. 'I *could* publicise the observation that these practices are now, theoretically, legal. Other people have done that, and it doesn't exactly make headlines. But if I printed any *specific* facts about an actual triple-blind trial, I'd face a half-million-dollar fine, and twenty-five years in prison, for endangering public health. Not to mention what they'd do to my publisher. All the "emergency" laws brought in to deal with the Monte Carlo leak are still active.'

'But that was twenty years ago!'

She drained her coffee and rose. 'Don't you recall what the experts said at the time?'

'No.'

'The effects will be with us for generations.'

It took me four months to penetrate the drug manufacturer's network.

I eavesdropped on the data flow of several company executives who chose to work from home. It didn't take long to identify the least computer-literate. A real bumbling fool, who used ten-thousand-dollar spreadsheet software to do what the average five-year-old could have done without fingers and toes. I watched his clumsy responses when the spreadsheet package gave him error messages. He was a gift from heaven; he simply didn't have a clue.

And, best of all, he was forever running a tediously unimaginative pornographic video game.

If the computer said, 'Jump!' he'd say, 'Promise not to tell?'

I spent a fortnight minimising what he had to do; it started out at seventy keystrokes, but I finally got it down to twenty-three.

I waited until his screen was at its most compromising, then I suspended his connection to the network, and took its place myself.

· FATAL SYSTEM ERROR! TYPE THE FOLLOWING TO RECOVER.

He botched it the first time. I rang alarm bells, and repeated the request. The second time, he got it right.

The first multi-key combination I had him strike took the work station right out of its operating system into its processor's microcode debugging routine. The hexadecimal that followed, gibberish to him, was a tiny program to dump all of the work station's memory down the communications line, right into my lap.

If he told anyone with any sense what had happened, suspicion would be aroused at once – but would he risk being asked to explain just what he was running when the 'bug' occurred? I doubted it.

I already had his passwords. Included in the work station's memory was an algorithm which told me precisely how to respond to the network's security challenges.

I was in.

The rest of their defences were trivial, at least so far as my aims were concerned. Data that might have been useful to their competitors was well shielded, but I wasn't interested in stealing the secrets of their latest haemorrhoid cure.

I could have done a lot of damage. Arranged for their backups to be filled with garbage. Arranged for the gradual deviation of their accounts from reality, until reality suddenly intruded in the form of bankruptcy – or charges of tax fraud. I considered a thousand possibilities, from the crudest annihilation of data to the slowest, most insidious forms of corruption.

In the end, though, I restrained myself. I knew the fight would soon become a political one, and any act of petty vengeance on my part would be sure to be dredged up and used to discredit me, to undermine my cause.

So I did only what was absolutely necessary.

I located the files containing the names and addresses of everyone who had been unknowingly participating in triple-blind trials of the company's products. I arranged for them all to be notified of what had been done to them. There were over two hundred thousand people, spread all around the world – but I found a swollen executive slush fund which easily covered the communications bill.

Soon, the whole world would know of our anger, would share in our outrage and grief. Half of us were sick or dying, though, and before the slightest whisper of protest was heard, my first objective had to be to save whoever I could.

I found the program that allocated medication or placebo. The program that had killed Paula, and thousands of others, for the sake of sound experimental technique.

I altered it. A very small change. I added one more lie.

All the reports it generated would continue to assert that half the patients involved in clinical trials were being given the placebo. Dozens of exhaustive, impressive files would continue to be created, containing data entirely consistent with this lie. Only one small file, never read by humans, would be different. The file controlling the assembly-line robots would instruct them to put medication in every vial of every batch.

From triple-blind to quadruple-blind. One more lie, to cancel out the others, until the time for deception was finally over.

Martin came to see me.

'I heard about what you're doing. TIM. Truth in Medicine.' He pulled a newspaper clipping from his pocket. ' "A vigorous new organisation dedicated to the eradication of quackery, fraud and deception in both alternative and conventional medicine." Sounds like a great idea.'

'Thanks.'

He hesitated. 'I heard you were looking for a few more volunteers. To help around the office.'

'That's right.'

'I could manage four hours a week.'

I laughed. 'Oh, could you really? Well, thanks very much, but I think we'll cope without you.'

For a moment, I thought he was going to walk out, but then he said, not so much hurt as simply baffled, 'Do you want volunteers, or not?'

'Yes, but—' *But what?* If he could swallow enough pride to offer, I could swallow enough pride to accept.

I signed him up for Wednesday afternoons.

I have nightmares about Paula, now and then. I wake smelling the ghost of a candle flame, certain that she's standing in the dark beside my pillow, a solemn-eyed nine-year-old child again, mesmerised by our strange condition.

That child can't haunt me, though. She never died. She grew up, and grew apart from me, and she fought for our separateness harder than I ever did. What if we had died 'at the very same hour'? It would have signified nothing, changed nothing. Nothing could have reached back and robbed us of our separate lives, our separate achievements and failures.

I realise, now, that the blood oath that seemed so ominous to me was nothing but a joke to Paula, her way of *mocking* the very idea that our fates could be entwined. How could I have taken so long to see that?

It shouldn't surprise me, though. The truth – and the measure of her triumph – is that I never really knew her.

AXIOMATIC

'. . . like your brain has been frozen in liquid nitrogen, and then smashed into a thousand shards!'

I squeezed my way past the teenagers who lounged outside the entrance to The Implant Store, no doubt fervently hoping for a holovision news team to roll up and ask them why they weren't in school. They mimed throwing up as I passed, as if the state of not being pubescent and dressed like a member of Binary Search was so disgusting to contemplate that it made them physically ill.

Well, maybe it did.

Inside, the place was almost deserted. The interior reminded me of a video ROM shop; the display racks were virtually identical, and many of the distributors' logos were the same. Each rack was labelled: PSYCHEDELIA. MEDITATION AND HEALING. MOTIVATION AND SUCCESS. LANGUAGES AND TECHNICAL SKILLS. Each implant, although itself less than half a millimetre across, came in a package the size of an old-style book, bearing gaudy illustrations and a few lines of stale hyperbole from a marketing thesaurus or some rent-an-endorsement celebrity. '*Become* God! *Become* the Universe!' 'The Ultimate Insight! The Ultimate Knowledge! The Ultimate Trip!' Even the perennial 'This implant changed my life!'

I picked up the carton of *You Are Great!* – its transparent protective wrapper glistening with sweaty fingerprints – and thought numbly: If I bought this thing and used it, I would actually believe that. No amount of evidence to the contrary would be *physically able* to change my mind. I put it back on the shelf, next to *Love Yourself A Billion* and *Instant Willpower, Instant Wealth*.

I knew exactly what I'd come for, and I knew that it wouldn't be on display, but I browsed a while longer, partly out of genuine curiosity, partly just to give myself time. Time to think through the implications once again. Time to come to my senses and flee.

The cover of *Synaesthesia* showed a blissed-out man with a rainbow striking his tongue and musical staves piercing his eyeballs. Beside it, *Alien Mind-Fuck* boasted 'a mental state so bizarre that even as you experience it, you won't know what it's like!' Implant technology was originally developed to provide instant language skills for business people and tourists, but after disappointing sales and a takeover by an entertainment conglomerate, the first mass-market implants appeared: a cross between video games and hallucinogenic drugs. Over the years, the range of confusion and dysfunction on offer grew wider, but there's only so far you can take that trend; beyond a certain point, scrambling the neural connections doesn't leave anyone *there* to be entertained by the strangeness, and the user, once restored to normalcy, remembers almost nothing.

The first of the next generation of implants – the so-called axiomatics – were all sexual in nature; apparently that was the technically simplest place to start. I walked over to the Erotica section, to see what was available – or at least, what could legally be displayed. Homosexuality, heterosexuality, autoerotism. An assortment of harmless fetishes. Eroticisation of various unlikely parts of the body. Why, I wondered, would anyone choose to have their brain rewired to make them crave a sexual practice they otherwise would have found abhorrent, or ludicrous, or just plain boring? To comply with a partner's demands? Maybe, although such extreme submissiveness was hard to imagine, and could scarcely be sufficiently widespread to explain the size of the market. To enable a part of their own sexual identity, which, unaided, would have merely nagged and festered, to triumph over their inhibitions, their ambivalence, their revulsion? Everyone has conflicting desires, and people can grow tired of both wanting and not wanting the very same thing. I understood *that*, perfectly.

The next rack contained a selection of religions, everything from Amish to Zen. (Gaining the Amish disapproval of technology this way apparently posed no problem; virtually every religious implant enabled the user to embrace far stranger contradictions.) There was even an implant called *Secular Humanist* ('You WILL hold these truths to be self-evident!'). No *Vacillating Agnostic*, though; apparently there was no market for doubt.

For a minute or two, I lingered. For a mere fifty dollars, I could have bought back my childhood Catholicism, even if the Church would not have approved. (At least, not officially; it would have been interesting to know exactly who was subsidising the product.) In the end, though, I had to admit that I wasn't really tempted. Perhaps it would have solved my problem, but not in the way that I wanted it solved – and after all, getting my own way was the whole point of coming here. Using an implant wouldn't rob me of my free will; on the contrary, it was going to help me to assert it.

Finally, I steeled myself and approached the sales counter.

'How can I help you, sir?' The young man smiled at me brightly, radiating sincerity, as if he really enjoyed his work. I mean, really, *really*.

'I've come to pick up a special order.'

'Your name, please, sir?'

'Carver. Mark.'

He reached under the counter and emerged with a parcel, mercifully already wrapped in anonymous brown. I paid in cash, I'd brought the exact change: $399.95. It was all over in twenty seconds.

I left the store, sick with relief, triumphant, exhausted. At least I'd finally bought the fucking thing; it was in my hands now, no one else was involved, and all I had to do was decide whether or not to use it.

After walking a few blocks towards the train station, I tossed the parcel into a bin, but I turned back almost at once and retrieved it. I passed a pair of armoured cops, and I pictured their eyes boring into me from behind their mirrored faceplates, but what I was carrying was perfectly legal. How could the Government ban a device which did no more than engender, in those who *freely chose* to use it, a particular set of beliefs – without also arresting everyone who shared those beliefs naturally? Very easily, actually, since the law didn't have to be consistent, but the implant manufacturers had succeeded in convincing the public that restricting their products would be paving the way for the Thought Police.

By the time I got home, I was shaking uncontrollably. I put the parcel on the kitchen table, and started pacing.

This wasn't for Amy. I had to admit that. Just because I still loved her, and still mourned her, didn't mean I was doing this for *her*. I wouldn't soil her memory with that lie.

In fact, I was doing it to free myself from her. After five years, I wanted my pointless love, my useless grief, to finally stop ruling my life. Nobody could blame me for that.

She had died in an armed hold-up, in a bank. The security cameras had been disabled, and everyone apart from the robbers had spent most of the time face-down on the floor, so I never found out the whole story. She must have moved, fidgeted, looked up, she must have done *something*; even at the peaks of my hatred, I couldn't believe that she'd been killed on a whim, for no comprehensible reason at all.

I knew who had squeezed the trigger, though. It hadn't come out at the trial; a clerk in the Police Department had sold me the information. The killer's name was Patrick Anderson, and by turning prosecution witness, he'd put his accomplices away for life, and reduced his own sentence to seven years.

I went to the media. A loathsome crime-show personality had taken the story and ranted about it on the airwaves for a week, diluting the facts with self-serving rhetoric, then grown bored and moved on to something else.

Five years later, Anderson had been out on parole for nine months.

OK. *So what?* It happens all the time. If someone had come to me with such a story, I would have been sympathetic, but firm. 'Forget her, she's dead. Forget him, he's garbage. Get on with your life.'

I didn't forget her, and I didn't forget her killer. I had loved her, whatever that meant, and while the rational part of me had swallowed the fact of her death, the rest kept twitching like a decapitated snake. Someone else in the same state might have turned the house into a shrine, covered every wall and mantelpiece with photographs and memorabilia, put fresh flowers on her grave every day, and spent every night getting drunk watching old home movies. I didn't do that, I couldn't. It would have been grotesque and utterly false; sentimentality had always made both of us violently ill. I kept a single photo. We hadn't made home movies. I visited her grave once a year.

Yet for all of this outward restraint, inside my head my obsession with Amy's death simply kept on growing. I didn't *want* it, I didn't *choose* it, I didn't feed it or encourage it in any way. I kept no electronic scrapbook of the trial. If people raised the subject, I walked away. I buried myself in my work; in my spare time I read, or went to the movies, alone. I thought about searching for someone new, but I never did anything about it, always putting it off until that time in the indefinite future when I would be human again.

Every night, the details of the incident circled in my brain. I thought of a thousand things I 'might have done' to have prevented her death, from not marrying her in the first place (we'd moved to Sydney because of my job), to magically arriving at the bank as her killer took aim, tackling him to the ground and beating him senseless, or worse. I knew these fantasies were futile and self-indulgent, but that knowledge was no cure. If I took sleeping pills, the whole thing simply shifted to the daylight hours, and I was literally unable to work. (The computers that help us are slightly less appalling every year, but air-traffic controllers *can't* daydream.)

I had to do something.

Revenge? Revenge was for the morally retarded. Me, I'd signed petitions to the UN, calling for the world-wide, unconditional abolition of capital punishment. I'd meant it then, and I still meant it. Taking human life was *wrong*; I'd believed that, passionately, since child-hood. Maybe it started out as religious dogma, but when I grew up and shed all the ludicrous claptrap, the sanctity of life was one of the few beliefs I judged to be worth keeping. Aside from any pragmatic reasons, human consciousness had always seemed to me the most astonishing, miraculous, *sacred* thing in the universe. Blame my upbringing, blame my genes; I could no more devalue it than believe that one plus one equalled zero.

Tell some people you're a pacifist, and in ten seconds flat they'll invent a situation in which millions of people will die in unspeakable agony, and all your loved ones will be raped and tortured, if you don't blow someone's brains out. (There's always a contrived reason why you can't merely *wound* the omnipotent, genocidal madman.) The amusing thing is, they seem to hold you in even greater contempt when you admit that, yes, you'd do it, you'd kill under those conditions.

Anderson, however, clearly was not an omnipotent, genocidal madman. I had no idea whether or not he was likely to kill again. As for his capacity for reform, his abused childhood, or the caring and compassionate alter ego that may have been hiding behind the façade of his brutal exterior, I really didn't give a shit, but nonetheless I was convinced that it would be wrong for me to kill him.

I bought the gun first. That was easy, and perfectly legal; perhaps the computers simply failed to correlate my permit application with the release of my wife's killer, or perhaps the link was detected, but judged irrelevant.

I joined a 'sports' club full of people who spent three hours a week doing nothing but shooting at moving, human-shaped targets. A recreational activity, harmless as fencing; I practised saying that with a straight face.

Buying the anonymous ammunition from a fellow club member *was* illegal; bullets that vaporised on impact, leaving no ballistics evidence linking them to a specific weapon. I scanned the court records; the average sentence for possessing such things was a five-hundred-dollar fine. The silencer was illegal, too; the penalties for ownership were similar.

Every night, I thought it through. Every night, I came to the same conclusion: despite my elaborate preparations, I wasn't going to kill anyone. Part of me wanted to, part of me didn't, but I knew perfectly well which was strongest. I'd spend the rest of my life dreaming about it, safe in the knowledge that no amount of hatred or grief or desperation would ever be enough to make me act against my nature.

I unwrapped the parcel. I was expecting a garish cover – sneering body builder toting sub-machine-gun – but the packaging was unadorned, plain grey with no markings except for the product code, and the name of the distributor, Clockwork Orchard.

I'd ordered the thing through an on-line catalogue, accessed via a coin-driven public terminal, and I'd specified collection by 'Mark Carver' at a branch of The Implant Store in Chatswood, far from my home. All of which was paranoid nonsense, since the implant was legal – and all of which was perfectly reasonable, because I felt far more nervous and guilty about buying it than I did about buying the gun and ammunition.

The description in the catalogue had begun with the statement *Life is cheap!* then had waffled on for several lines in the same vein: *People are meat. They're nothing, they're worthless.* The exact words weren't important, though; they weren't a part of the implant itself. It wouldn't be a matter of a voice in my head, reciting some badly written spiel which I could choose to ridicule or ignore; nor would it be a kind of mental legislative decree, which I could evade by means of semantic quibbling. Axiomatic implants were derived from analysis of actual neural structures in real people's brains, they weren't based on the expression of the axioms in language. The spirit, not the letter, of the law would prevail.

I opened up the carton. There was an instruction

leaflet, in seventeen languages. A programmer. An applicator. A pair of tweezers. Sealed in a plastic bubble labelled STERILE IF UNBROKEN, the implant itself. It looked like a tiny piece of gravel.

I had never used one before, but I'd seen it done a thousand times on holovision. You placed the thing in the programmer, 'woke it up', and told it how long you wanted it to be active. The applicator was strictly for tyros; the jaded cognoscenti balanced the implant on the tip of their little finger, and daintily poked it up the nostril of their choice.

The implant burrowed into the brain, sent out a swarm of nanomachines to explore, and forge links with, the relevant neural systems, and then went into active mode for the predetermined time – anything from an hour to infinity – doing whatever it was designed to do. Enabling multiple orgasms of the left kneecap. Making the colour blue taste like the long-lost memory of mother's milk. Or, hard–wiring a premise: *I will succeed. I am happy in my job. There is life after death. Nobody died in Belsen. Four legs good, two legs bad* . . .

I packed everything back into the carton, put it in a drawer, took three sleeping pills, and went to bed.

Perhaps it was a matter of laziness. I've always been biased towards those options which spare me from facing the very same set of choices again in the future; it seems so *inefficient* to go through the same agonies of conscience more than once. To *not* use the implant would have meant having to reaffirm that decision, day after day, for the rest of my life.

Or perhaps I never really believed that the preposterous toy would work. Perhaps I hoped to prove that my convictions – unlike other people's – were engraved on some metaphysical tablet that hovered in a spiritual dimension unreachable by any mere machine.

Or perhaps I just wanted a moral alibi – a way to kill

Anderson while still believing it was something that the *real* me could never have done.

At least I'm sure of one thing. I didn't do it for Amy.

I woke around dawn the next day, although I didn't need to get up at all; I was on annual leave for a month. I dressed, ate breakfast, then unpacked the implant again and carefully read the instructions.

With no great sense of occasion, I broke open the sterile bubble and, with the tweezers, dropped the speck into its cavity in the programmer.

The programmer said, 'Do you speak English?' The voice reminded me of one of the control towers at work; deep but somehow genderless, businesslike without being crudely robotic – and yet, unmistakably inhuman.

'Yes.'

'Do you want to program this implant?'

'Yes.'

'Please specify the active period.'

'Three days.' Three days would be enough, surely; if not, I'd call the whole thing off.

'This implant is to remain active for three days after insertion. Is that correct?'

'Yes.'

'This implant is ready for use. The time is seven forty-three a.m. Please insert the implant before eight forty-three a.m., or it will deactivate itself and repro-gramming will be required. Please enjoy this product and dispose of the packaging thoughtfully.'

I placed the implant in the applicator, then hesitated, but not for long. This wasn't the time to agonise; I'd agonised for months, and I was sick of it. Any more indecisiveness and I'd need to buy a second implant to convince me to use the first. I wasn't committing a crime; I wasn't even coming close to guaranteeing that I would commit one. Millions of people held the belief that human life was nothing special, but how many of them were murderers? The next three days would simply reveal how *I* reacted to that belief, and although the attitude would be hard-wired, the consequences were far from certain.

I put the applicator in my left nostril, and pushed the release button. There was a brief stinging sensation, nothing more.

I thought, *Amy would have despised me for this.* That shook me, but only for a moment. Amy was dead, which made her hypothetical feelings irrelevant. Nothing I did could hurt her now, and thinking any other way was crazy.

I tried to monitor the progress of the change, but that was a joke; you can't check your moral precepts by introspection every thirty seconds. After all, my assessment of myself as being unable to kill had been based on decades of observation (much of it probably out of date). What's more, that assessment, that self-image, had come to be as much a *cause* of my actions and attitudes as a reflection of them – and apart from the direct changes the implant was making to my brain, it was breaking that feedback loop by providing a rationalisation for me to act in a way I'd convinced myself was impossible.

After a while, I decided to get drunk, to distract myself from the vision of microscopic robots crawling around in my skull. It was a big mistake; alcohol makes me paranoid. I don't recall much of what followed, except for catching sight of myself in the bathroom mirror, screaming, 'HAL's breaking First Law! HAL's breaking First Law!' before vomiting copiously.

I woke just after midnight, on the bathroom floor. I took an anti-hangover pill, and in five minutes my headache and nausea were gone. I showered and put on fresh clothes. I'd bought a jacket especially for the occasion, with an inside pocket for the gun.

It was still impossible to tell if the thing had done anything to me that went beyond the placebo effect; I asked myself, out loud, 'Is human life sacred? Is it wrong to kill?' but I couldn't concentrate on the question, and I found it hard to believe that I ever had in the past; the whole idea seemed obscure and difficult, like some esoteric mathematical theorem. The prospect of going ahead with my plans made my stomach churn, but that was simple fear, not moral outrage; the implant wasn't meant to make me brave, or calm, or resolute. I could have bought those qualities too, but that would have been cheating.

I'd had Anderson checked out by a private investigator. He worked every night but Sunday, as a bouncer in a Surry Hills nightclub; he lived nearby, and usually arrived home, on foot, at around four in the morning. I'd driven past his terrace house several times, I'd have no trouble finding it. He lived alone; he had a lover, but they always met at her place, in the afternoon or early evening.

I loaded the gun and put it in my jacket, then spent half an hour staring in the mirror, trying to decide if the bulge was visible. I wanted a drink, but I restrained myself. I switched on the radio and wandered through the house, trying to become less agitated. Perhaps taking a life was now no big deal to me, but I could still end up dead, or in prison, and the implant apparently hadn't rendered me uninterested in my own fate.

I left too early, and had to drive by a circuitous route to kill time; even then, it was only a quarter past three when I parked, a kilometre from Anderson's house. A few cars and taxis passed me as I walked the rest of the way, and I'm sure I was trying so hard to look at ease that my body language radiated guilt and paranoia – but no ordinary driver would have noticed or cared, and I didn't see a single patrol car.

When I reached the place, there was nowhere to hide

– no gardens, no trees, no fences – but I'd known that in advance. I chose a house across the street, not quite opposite Anderson's, and sat on the front step. If the occupant appeared, I'd feign drunkenness and stagger away.

I sat and waited. It was a warm, still, ordinary night; the sky was clear, but grey and starless thanks to the lights of the city. I kept reminding myself: *You don't have to do this, you don't have to go through with it.* So why did I stay? The hope of being liberated from my sleepless nights? The idea was laughable; I had no doubt that if I killed Anderson, it would torture me as much as my helplessness over Amy's death.

Why did I stay? It was nothing to do with the implant; at most, that was neutralising my qualms; it wasn't forcing me to *do* anything.

Why, then? In the end, I think I saw it as a matter of honesty. I had to accept the unpleasant fact that I honestly wanted to kill Anderson, and however much I had also been repelled by the notion, to be true to myself I had to do it – anything less would have been hypocrisy and self-deception.

At five to four, I heard footsteps echoing down the street. As I turned, I hoped it would be someone else, or that he would be with a friend, but it was him, and he was alone. I waited until he was as far from his front door as I was, then I started walking. He glanced my way briefly, then ignored me. I felt a shock of pure fear – I hadn't seen him in the flesh since the trial, and I'd forgotten how physically imposing he was.

I had to force myself to slow down, and even then I passed him sooner than I'd meant to. I was wearing light, rubber-soled shoes, he was in heavy boots, but when I crossed the street and did a U-turn towards him, I couldn't believe he couldn't hear my heartbeat, or smell the stench of my sweat. Metres from the door, just as I finished pulling out the gun, he looked over his shoulder with an expression of bland curiosity, as if he might have been expecting a dog or a piece of wind-blown litter. He turned around to face me, frowning. I just stood there, pointing the gun at him, unable to speak. Eventually he said, 'What the fuck do you want? I've got two hundred dollars in my wallet. Back pocket.'

I shook my head. 'Unlock the front door, then put your hands on your head and kick it open. Don't try closing it on me.'

He hesitated, then complied.

'Now walk in. Keep your hands on your head. Five steps, that's all. Count them out loud. I'll be right behind you.'

I reached the light switch for the hall as he counted four, then I slammed the door behind me, and flinched at the sound. Anderson was right in front of me, and I suddenly felt trapped. The man was a vicious killer; *I* hadn't even thrown a punch since I was eight years old. Did I really believe the gun would protect me? With his hands on his head, the muscles of his arms and shoulders bulged against his shirt. I should have shot him right then, in the back of the head. This was an execution, not a duel; if I'd wanted some quaint idea of honour, I would have come without a gun and let him take me to pieces.

I said, 'Turn left.' Left was the living room. I followed him in, switched on the light. 'Sit.' I stood in the doorway, he sat in the room's only chair. For a moment, I felt dizzy and my vision seemed to tilt, but I don't think I moved, I don't think I sagged or swayed; if I had, he probably would have rushed me.

'What do you want?' he asked.

I had to give that a lot of thought. I'd fantasised this situation a thousand times, but I could no longer remember the details – although I did recall that I'd usually assumed that Anderson would recognise me, and start volunteering excuses and explanations straight away.

Finally, I said, 'I want you to tell me why you killed my wife.'

'I didn't kill your wife. Miller killed your wife.'

I shook my head. 'That's not true. I *know*. The cops told me. Don't bother lying, because I *know*.'

He stared at me blandly. I wanted to lose my temper and scream, but I had a feeling that, in spite of the gun, that would have been more comical than intimidating. I could have pistol-whipped him, but the truth is I was afraid to go near him.

So I shot him in the foot. He yelped and swore, then leant over to inspect the damage. 'Fuck you!' he hissed. 'Fuck you!' He rocked back and forth, holding his foot. 'I'll break your fucking neck! I'll fucking kill you!' The wound bled a little through the hole in his boot, but it was nothing compared to the movies. I'd heard that the vaporising ammunition had a cauterising effect.

I said, 'Tell me why you killed my wife.'

He looked far more angry and disgusted than afraid, but he dropped his pretence of innocence. 'It just happened,' he said. 'It was just one of those things that happens.'

I shook my head, annoyed. 'No. *Why?* Why did it happen?'

He moved as if to take off his boot, then thought better of it. 'Things were going wrong. There was a time lock, there was hardly any cash, everything was just a big fuck-up. I didn't mean to do it. It just happened.'

I shook my head again, unable to decide if he was a moron, or if he was stalling. 'Don't tell me "it just happened". *Why* did it happen? Why did you do it?'

The frustration was mutual; he ran a hand through his hair and scowled at me. He was sweating now, but I couldn't tell if it was from pain or from fear. 'What do you want me to say? I lost my temper, all right? Things were going badly, and I lost my fucking temper, and there she was, all right?'

The dizziness struck me again, but this time it didn't subside. I understood now; he wasn't being obtuse, he was telling the entire truth. I'd smashed the occasional coffee cup during a tense situation at work. I'd even, to my shame, kicked our dog once, after a fight with Amy. Why? *I'd lost my fucking temper, and there she was.*

I stared at Anderson, and felt myself grinning stupidly. It was all so clear now. I understood. I understood the absurdity of everything I'd ever felt for Amy – my 'love', my 'grief'. It had all been a joke. She was meat, she was nothing. All the pain of the past five years evaporated; I was drunk with relief. I raised my arms and spun around slowly. Anderson leapt up and sprung towards me; I shot him in the chest until I ran out of bullets, then I knelt down beside him. He was dead.

I put the gun in my jacket. The barrel was warm. I remembered to use my handkerchief to open the front door. I half expected to find a crowd outside, but of course the shots had been inaudible, and Anderson's threats and curses were not likely to have attracted attention.

A block from the house, a patrol car appeared around a corner. It slowed almost to a halt as it approached me. I kept my eyes straight ahead as it passed. I heard the engine idle. Then stop. I kept on walking, waiting for a shouted command, thinking: if they search me and find the gun, I'll confess; there's no point in prolonging the agony.

The engine spluttered, revved noisily, and the car roared away.

Perhaps I'm *not* the number-one most obvious suspect. I don't know what Anderson was involved in since he got out; maybe there are hundreds of other people who had far better reasons for wanting him dead, and perhaps when the cops have finished with them, they'll get around to asking me what I was doing that night. A month seems an awfully long time, though. Anyone would think they didn't care.

The same teenagers as before are gathered around the entrance, and again the mere sight of me seems to disgust them. I wonder if the taste in fashion and music tattooed on their brains is set to fade in a year or two, or if they have sworn lifelong allegiance. It doesn't bear contemplating.

This time, I don't browse. I approach the sales counter without hesitation.

This time, I know exactly what I want.

What I want is what I felt that night: the unshakeable conviction that Amy's death – let alone Anderson's – simply didn't matter, any more than the death of a fly or an amoeba, any more than breaking a coffee cup or kicking a dog.

My one mistake was thinking that the insight I gained would simply vanish when the implant cut out. It hasn't. It's been clouded with doubts and reservations, it's been undermined, to some degree, by my whole ridiculous panoply of beliefs and superstitions, but I can still recall the peace it gave me, I can still recall that flood of joy and relief, and *I want it back*. Not for three days; for the rest of my life.

Killing Anderson *wasn't* honest, it wasn't 'being true to myself'. Being true to myself would have meant living with all my contradictory urges, suffering the multitude of voices in my head, accepting confusion and doubt. It's too late for that now; having tasted the freedom of certainty, I find I can't live without it.

'How can I help you, sir?' The salesman smiles from the bottom of his heart.

Part of me, of course, still finds the prospect of what I am about to do totally repugnant.

No matter. That won't last.

THE SAFE-DEPOSIT BOX

I dream a simple dream. I dream that I have a name. One name, unchanging, mine until death. I don't know what my name *is*, but that doesn't matter. Knowing that I have it is enough.

I wake just before the alarm goes off (I usually do), so I'm able to reach out and silence it the instant it starts screeching. The woman beside me doesn't move; I hope the alarm wasn't meant for her too. It's freezing cold and pitch black, except for the bedside clock's red digits slowly coming into focus. Ten to *four*! I groan softly. What am I? A garbage collector? A milkman? This body is sore and tired, but that tells me nothing; they've all been sore and tired lately, whatever their profession, their income, their lifestyle. Yesterday I was a diamond merchant. Not quite a millionaire, but close. The day before I was a bricklayer, and the day before that I sold menswear. Crawling out of a warm bed felt pretty much the same each time.

I find my hand travelling instinctively to the switch for the reading light on my side of the bed. When I click it on, the woman stirs and mumbles, 'Johnny?' but her eyes remain closed. I make my first conscious effort to access this host's memories; sometimes I can pick up a frequently used name. Linda? Could be. *Linda.* I mouth it silently, looking at the tangle of soft brown hair almost hiding her sleeping face.

The situation, if not the individual, is comfortingly familiar. *Man looks fondly upon sleeping wife.* I whisper to her, 'I love you,' and I mean it; I love, not this particular woman (with a past I'll barely glimpse, and a future that I have no way of sharing), but the composite woman of which, today, she is a part – my flickering, inconstant companion, my lover made up of a million pseudorandom words and gestures, held together only by the fact that I behold her, known in her entirety to no one but me.

In my romantic youth, I used to speculate: Surely I'm not the only one of my kind? Might there not be another like me, but who wakes each morning in the body of a woman? Might not whatever mysterious factors determine the selection of *my* host act in parallel on *her*, drawing us together, keeping us together day after day, transporting us, side by side, from host couple to host couple?

Not only is it unlikely, it simply isn't true. The last time (nearly twelve years ago now) that I cracked up and started spouting the unbelievable truth, my host's wife *did not* break in with shouts of relief and recognition, and her own, identical, confession. (She didn't do much at all, actually. I expected her to find my rantings frightening and traumatic, I expected her to conclude at once that I was dangerously insane. Instead, she listened briefly, apparently found what I was saying either boring or incomprehensible, and so, very sensibly, left me alone for the rest of the day.)

Not only is it untrue, it simply doesn't matter. Yes, my lover has a thousand faces, and yes, a different soul looks out from every pair of eyes, but I can still find (or imagine) as many unifying patterns in my memories of her, as any other man or woman can find (or imagine) in their own perceptions of their own most faithful lifelong companion.

Man looks fondly upon sleeping wife.

I climb out from under the blankets and stand for a moment, shivering, looking around the room, eager to start moving to keep myself warm, but unable to decide what to do first. Then I spot a wallet on top of the chest of drawers.

I'm John Francis O'Leary, according to the driver's licence. Date of birth: 15 November, 1951 – which makes me one week older than when I went to bed. Although I still have occasional daydreams about waking up twenty years younger, that seems to be as unlikely for me as it is for anyone else; in thirty-nine years, so far as I know, I've yet to have a host born any time but November or December of 1951. Nor have I ever had a host either born, or presently living, outside this city.

I don't know *how* I move from one host to the next, but since any process could be expected to have some finite effective range, my geographical confinement is not surprising. There's desert to the east, ocean to the west, and long stretches of barren coast to the north and south; the distances from town to town are simply too great for me to cross. In fact, I never even seem to get *close* to the outskirts of the city, and on reflection that's not surprising: if there are one hundred potential hosts to the west of me, and five to the east, then a jump to a randomly chosen host is *not* a jump in a random direction. The populous centre attracts me with a kind of statistical gravity.

As for the restrictions on host age and birthplace, I've never had a theory plausible enough to believe for more than a day or two. It was easy when I was twelve or thirteen, and could pretend I was some kind of alien prince, imprisoned in the bodies of Earthlings by a wicked rival for my cosmic inheritance; the bad guys must have put something in the city's water, late in 1951, which was drunk by expectant mothers, thus preparing their unborn children to be my unwitting jailers. These days I accept the likelihood that I'll simply never know the answer.

I am sure of one thing, though: both restrictions were essential to whatever approximation to sanity I now possess. Had I 'grown up' in bodies of completely random ages, or in hosts scattered worldwide, with a different language and culture to contend with every day, I doubt that I'd even *exist* – no personality could possibly emerge from such a cacophony of experiences. (Then again, an ordinary person might think the same of my own, relatively stable, origins.)

I don't recall being John O'Leary before, which is unusual. This city contains only six thousand men aged thirty-nine, and of those, roughly one thousand would have been born in November or December. Since thirty-nine years is more than fourteen thousand days, the odds by now are heavily against first-timers, and I've visited most hosts several times within memory.

In my own inexpert way, I've explored the statistics a little. Any given potential host should have, on average, one thousand days, or three years, between my visits. Yet the average time I should expect to pass without repeating any hosts *myself* is a mere forty days (the average to date is actually lower, twenty-seven days, presumably because some hosts are more susceptible than others). When I first worked this out it seemed paradoxical, but only because the averages don't tell the whole story; a fraction of all repeat visits occur within weeks rather than years, and of course it's these abnormally fast ones that determine the rate for me.

In a safe-deposit box (with a combination lock) in the centre of the city, I have records covering the past twenty-two years. Names, addresses, dates of birth, and dates of each visit since 1968, for over eight hundred hosts. One day soon, when I have a host who can spare the time, I really must rent a computer with a database package and shift all that crap on to disk; that would make statistical tests a thousand times easier. I don't expect astounding revelations; if I found some kind of bias or pattern in the data, well, so what? Would that tell me anything? Would that *change* anything? Still, it seems like a good thing to do.

Partly hidden under a pile of coins beside the wallet is – *oh, bliss!* – an ID badge, complete with photo. John O'Leary is an orderly at the Pearlman Psychiatric Institute. The photo shows part of a light blue uniform, and when I open his wardrobe there it is. I believe this body could do with a shower, though, so I postpone dressing.

The house is small and plainly furnished, but very clean and in good repair. I pass one room that is probably a child's bedroom, but the door is closed and I leave it that way, not wanting to risk waking anyone. In the living room, I look up the Pearlman Institute in the phone book, and then locate it in a street directory. I've already memorised my own address from the licence, and the Institute's not far away; I work out a route that shouldn't take more than twenty minutes, at this hour of the morning. I still don't know when my shift starts; surely not before five.

Standing in the bathroom, shaving, I stare for a moment into my new brown eyes, and I can't help noticing that John O'Leary is not bad looking at all. It's a thought that leads nowhere. For a long while now, thankfully, I've managed to accept my fluctuating appearance with relative tranquillity, though it hasn't always been that way. I had several neurotic patches, in my teens and early twenties, when my mood would swing violently between elation and depression, depending on how I felt about my latest body. Often, for weeks after departing an especially good-looking host (which of course I'd have delayed for as long as possible, by staying awake night after night), I'd fantasise obsessively about returning, preferably to stay. At least an ordinary, screwed-up adolescent *knows* he has no choice but to accept the body in which he was born. I had no such comfort.

I'm more inclined now to worry about my health, but that's every bit as futile as fretting over appearance. There's no point whatsoever in me exercising, or watching my diet, since any such gesture is effectively diluted one-thousandfold. 'My' weight, 'my' fitness, 'my' alcohol and tobacco consumption, can't be altered by my own personal initiative – they're public health statistics, requiring vastly expensive advertising campaigns to budge them even slightly.

After showering, I comb my hair in imitation of the ID photo, hoping that it's not too out of date.

Linda opens her eyes and stretches as I walk, naked, back into the bedroom, and the sight of her gives me an erection at once. I haven't had sex for months; almost every host lately seems to have managed to screw himself senseless the night *before* I arrived, and to have subsequently lost interest for the following fortnight. Apparently, my luck has changed. Linda reaches out and grabs me.

'I'll be late for work,' I protest.

She turns and looks at the clock. 'That's crap. You don't start until six. If you eat breakfast here, instead of detouring to that greasy truck stop, you won't have to leave for *an hour*.'

Her fingernails are pleasantly sharp. I let her drag me towards the bed, then I lean over and whisper, 'You know, that's *exactly* what I wanted to hear.'

My earliest memory is of my mother reverently holding a bawling infant towards me, saying, 'Look, Chris! This is your baby brother. This is Paul! Isn't he beautiful?' I couldn't understand what all the fuss was about. Siblings were like pets or toys; their number, their ages, their sexes, their names, all fluctuated as senselessly as the furniture or the wallpaper.

Parents were clearly superior; they changed appearance and behaviour, but at least their names stayed the same. I naturally assumed that when I grew up, my name would become 'Daddy', a suggestion that was usually greeted with laughter and amused agreement. I suppose I thought of my parents as being basically like me; their transformations were more extreme than my own, but everything else about them was bigger, so that made perfect sense. That they were in a sense *the same* from day to day, I never doubted; my mother and father were, by definition, the two adults who did certain things: scolded me, hugged me, tucked me into bed, made me eat disgusting vegetables, and so on. They stood out a mile, you couldn't miss them. Occasionally one or the other was absent, but never for more than a day.

The past and future weren't problems; I simply grew up with rather vague notions as to what they actually *were*. 'Yesterday' and 'tomorrow' were like 'once upon a time' – I was never disappointed by broken promises of future treats, or baffled by descriptions of alleged past events, because I treated all such talk as intentional fiction. I was often accused of telling 'lies', and I assumed that was just a label applied to stories that were insufficiently interesting. Memories of events more than one day old were clearly worthless 'lies', so I did my best to forget them.

I'm sure I was happy. The world was a kaleidoscope. I had a new house to explore every day, different toys, different playmates, different food. Sometimes the colour of my skin would change (and it thrilled me to see that my parents, brothers and sisters almost always chose to make their own skin the same as mine). Now and then I woke up as a girl, but at some point (around the age of four, I think) this began to trouble me, and soon after that, it simply stopped happening.

I had no suspicion that I was *moving*, from house to house, from body to body. I changed, my house changed, the other houses, and the streets and shops and parks around me, changed. I travelled now and then to the city centre with my parents, but I thought of it not as a fixed location (since it was reached by a different route each time) but as a fixed feature of the world, like the sun or the sky.

School was the start of a long period of confusion and misery. Although the school building, the classroom, the teacher, and the other children, changed like everything else in my environment, the repertoire was clearly not as wide as that of my house and family. Travelling to the same school, but along different streets, and with a different name and face, upset me, and the gradual realisation that classmates were copying my own previous names and faces – and, worse still, I was being saddled with ones *they'd* used – was infuriating.

These days, having lived with the approved world-view for so long, I sometimes find it hard to understand how my first year at school wasn't enough to make everything perfectly clear – until I recall that my glimpses of each classroom were generally spaced weeks apart, and that I was shuttling back and forth at random between more than a hundred schools. I had no diary, no records, no class lists in my head, no means of even *thinking about* what was happening to me – nobody trained me in the scientific method. Even Einstein was a great deal older than six, when he worked out *his* theory of relativity.

I kept my disquiet from my parents, but I was sick of dismissing my memories as lies; I tried discussing them with other children, which brought ridicule and hostility. After a period of fights and tantrums, I grew introverted. My parents said things like 'You're quiet today!', day after day, proving to me exactly how stupid they were.

It's a miracle that I learnt anything. Even now, I'm unsure how much of my reading ability belongs to me, and how much comes from my hosts. I'm sure that my vocabulary travels with me, but the lower-level business of scanning the page, of actually recognising letters and words, feels quite different from day to day. (Driving is similar; almost all of my hosts have licences, but I've never had a single lesson myself. I know the traffic rules, I know the gears and pedals, but I've never tried going out on to the road in a body that hasn't done it before – it would make a nice experiment, but those bodies tend not to own cars.)

I learnt to read. I learnt quickly to read quickly – if I didn't finish a book the day I started it, I knew I might not get my hands on it again for weeks, or months. I read hundreds of adventure stories, full of heroes and heroines with friends, brothers and sisters, even pets, that stayed with them day after day. Each book hurt a little more, but I couldn't stop reading, I couldn't give up hoping that the next book I opened would start with the words, 'One sunny morning a boy woke up, and wondered what his name was.'

One day I saw my father consulting a street direct-ory, and, despite my shyness, I asked him what it was. I'd seen world globes and maps of the country at school, but never anything like this. He pointed out our house, my school, and his place of work, both on the detailed street maps, and on the key map of the whole city inside the front cover.

At that time, one brand of street directory had a virtual monopoly. Every family owned one, and every day for weeks, I browbeat my father or mother into showing me things on the key map. I successfully committed a lot of it to memory (once I tried making pencil marks, thinking they might somehow inherit the magical permanence of the directory itself, but they proved to be as transitory as all the writing and drawing I did at school). I knew I was on to something profound, but the concept of my own motion, from place to place in an unchanging city, still failed to crystallise.

Not long afterwards, when my name was Danny Foster (a movie projectionist, these days, with a beautiful wife called Kate to whom I lost my virginity, though probably not Danny's), I went to a friend's eighth birthday party. I didn't understand birthdays at all; some years I had none, some years I had two or three. The birthday boy, Charlie McBride, was no friend of mine so far as I was concerned, but my parents bought me a gift to take, a plastic toy machine gun, and drove me to his house; I had no say in any of it. When I arrived home, I pestered Dad into showing me, on a street map, exactly where I'd been, and the route the car had taken.

A week later, I woke up with Charlie McBride's face, plus a house, parents, little brother, older sister, and toys, all identical to those I'd seen at his party. I refused to eat breakfast until my mother showed me our house on a street map, but I already knew where she'd point to.

I pretended to set off for school. My brother was too young for school, and my sister too old to want to be seen with me; in such circumstances I normally followed the clear flow of other children through the streets, but today I ignored it.

I still remembered landmarks from the trip to the party. I got lost a few times, but I kept stumbling upon streets I'd seen before; dozens of fragments of my world were starting to connect. It was both exhilarating and terrifying; I thought I was uncovering a vast conspiracy, I thought everyone had been purposely concealing the secrets of existence, and at last I was on the verge of outsmarting them all.

When I reached Danny's house, though, I didn't feel triumphant, I simply felt lonely and deceived and confused. Revelation or no revelation, I was still a child. I sat on the front steps and cried. Mrs Foster came out, in a fluster, calling me Charlie, asking me where my mother was, how I'd got here, why I wasn't at school. I yelled abuse at this filthy *liar*, who'd pretended, like they all had, to be my mother. Phone calls were made, and I was driven home screaming, to spend the day in my bedroom, refusing to eat, refusing to speak, refusing to explain my unforgivable behaviour.

That night, I overheard my 'parents' discussing me, arranging what in retrospect I now believe was a visit to a child psychologist.

I never made it to that appointment.

For the past eleven years now, I've been spending my days at the host's workplace. It's certainly not for the host's sake; I'm far more likely to get him sacked by screwing up at his job than by causing him one day's absence every three years. It's, well, it's what I do, it's who I am these days. Everybody has to define themselves somehow; I am a professional impersonator. The pay and conditions are variable, but a vocation cannot be denied.

I've tried constructing an independent life for myself, but I've never been able to make it work. When I was much younger, and mostly unmarried, I'd set myself things to study. That's when I first hired the safe-deposit box – to keep notes in. I studied mathematics, chemistry and physics, in the city's central library, but when any subject began to grow difficult, it was hard to find the discipline to push myself onwards. What was the point? I knew I could never be a practising scientist. As for uncovering the nature of my plight, it was clear that the answer was not going to lie in any library book on neurobiology. In the cool, quiet reading rooms, with nothing to listen to but the soporific drone of the air conditionings, I'd lapse into daydreams as soon as the words or equations in front of me stopped making easy sense.

I once did a correspondence course in undergraduate level physics; I hired a post office box, and kept the key to it in my safe-deposit box. I completed the course, and did quite well, but I had no one to tell of my achievement.

A while after that I got a pen pal in Switzerland. She was a music student, a violinist, and I told her I was studying physics at the local university. She sent me a photo, and, eventually, I did the same, after waiting for one of my best-looking hosts. We exchanged letters regularly, every week for more than a year. One day she wrote, saying she was coming to visit, asking for details of how we could meet. I don't think I'd ever felt as lonely as I did then. If I hadn't sent that photo, I could at least have seen her for one day. I could have spent a whole afternoon, talking face to face with my only true friend, the only person in the world who actually knew, not one of my hosts, but *me*. I stopped writing at once, and I gave up renting the post office box.

I've contemplated suicide at times, but the fact that it would be certain murder, and perhaps do nothing to me but drive me into another host, makes an effective deterrent.

Since leaving behind all the turmoil and bitterness of my childhood, I've generally tried to be fair to my hosts. Some days I've lost control and done things that must have inconvenienced or embarrassed them (and I take a little cash for my safe-deposit box from those who can easily spare it), but I've never set out to intentionally harm anyone. Sometimes I almost feel that they know about me and wish me well, although all the indirect evidence, from questioning wives and friends when I've had closely spaced visits, suggests that the missing days are hidden by seamless amnesia – my hosts don't even know that they've been out of action, let alone have a chance of guessing why. As for *me* knowing *them*, well, I sometimes see love and respect in the eyes of their families and colleagues, I sometimes see physical evidence of achievements I can admire – one host has written a novel, a black comedy about his Vietnam experiences, that I've read and enjoyed; one is an amateur telescope-maker, with a beautifully crafted, thirty-centimetre Newtonian reflector, through which I viewed Halley's comet – but there are *too many of them*. By the time I die, I'll have glimpsed each of their lives for just twenty or thirty randomly scattered days.

I drive around the perimeter of the Pearlman Institute, seeing what windows are lit, what doors are open, what activity is visible. There are several entrances, ranging from one clearly for the public, complete with plushly carpeted foyer and polished mahogany reception desk, to a rusty metal swing door opening on to a dingy bitumen-covered space between two buildings. I park in the street, rather than risk taking a spot on the premises to which I'm not entitled.

I'm nervous as I approach what I hope is the correct doorway; I still get a pain in my gut in those awful seconds just before I'm first seen by a colleague, and it becomes, very suddenly, a hundred times harder to back out – and, looking on the bright side, a whole lot easier to continue.

'Morning, Johnny.'

'Morning.'

The nurse continues past me even as this brief exchange takes place. I'm hoping to find out where I'm meant to be from a kind of social binding strength; the people I spend most time with ought to greet me with more than a nod and two words. I wander a short way along a corridor, trying to get used to the squeaking of my rubber-soled shoes on the linoleum. Suddenly a gruff voice cries out, 'O'Leary!' and I turn to see a young man in a uniform like mine, striding along the corridor towards me, wearing a thunderous frown, arms stuck out unnaturally, face twitching. 'Standing around! Dawdling! *Again!*' His behaviour is so bizarre that, for a fraction of a second, I'm convinced he's one of the patients; some psychotic with a grudge against me has killed another orderly, stolen his uniform, and is about to produce a bloodstained hatchet. Then the man puffs out his cheeks and stands there glaring, and I suddenly twig; he's not insane, he's just parodying some obese, aggressive superior. I prod his inflated face with one finger, as if bursting a balloon, which gives me a chance to get close enough to read his badge: Ralph Dopita.

'You jumped a *mile*! I couldn't believe it! So at last I got the voice *perfect*!'

'And the face as well. But you're lucky, you were born ugly.'

He shrugs. 'Your wife didn't think so last night.'

'You were drunk; that wasn't my wife, it was your mother.'

'Don't I always say you're like a father to me?'

The corridor, after much seemingly gratuitous winding, leads into a kitchen, all stainless steel and steam, where two other orderlies are standing around, and three cooks are preparing breakfast. With hot water constantly running in one sink, the clunking of trays and utensils, the hissing of fat, and the tortured sound of a failing ventilation fan, it's almost impossible to hear anyone speak. One of the orderlies mimes being a chicken, and then makes a gesture – swinging one hand above his head, pointing outwards, as if to take in the whole building. 'Enough eggs to feed—' he shouts, and the others crack up, so I laugh along with them.

Later, I follow them to a storeroom off the kitchen, where each of us grabs a trolley. Pinned up on a board, sheathed in transparent plastic, are four patient lists, one for each ward, ordered by room number. Beside each name is a little coloured circular sticker, green, red or blue. I hang back until there's only one left to grab.

There are three kinds of meal prepared: bacon and eggs with toast, cereal, and a mushy yellow puree resembling baby food, in descending order of popularity. On my own list there are more red stickers than green, and only a single blue, but I'm fairly certain that there were more green than red in total, when I saw all four lists together. As I load my trolley on this basis, I managed to catch a second look at Ralph's list, which is mainly green, and the contents of his trolley confirms that I have the code right.

I've never been in a psychiatric hospital before, either as patient or staff member. I spent a day in prison about five years ago, where I narrowly avoided getting my host's skull smashed in; I never discovered what he'd done, or how long his sentence was, but I'm rather hoping he'll be out by the time I get back to him.

My vague expectation that this place will be similar turns out to be pleasantly wrong. The prison cells were personalised to some degree, with pictures on the walls, and idiosyncratic possessions, but they still looked like cells. The rooms here are far less cluttered with that kind of thing, but their underlying character is a thousand times less harsh. There are no bars on the windows, and the doors in my ward have no locks. Most patients are already awake, sitting up in bed, greeting me with a quiet 'Good morning'; a few take their trays into a common room, where there's a TV tuned to news. Perhaps the degree of calm is unnatural, due solely to drugs; perhaps the peacefulness that makes my job untraumatic is stultifying and oppressive to the patients. Perhaps not. Maybe one day I'll find out.

My last patient, the single blue sticker, is listed as Klein, F. C. A skinny, middle-aged man with untidy black hair and a few days' stubble. He's lying so straight that I expect to see straps holding him in place, but there are none. His eyes are open but they don't follow me, and when I greet him there's no response.

There's a bedpan on a table beside the bed, and on a hunch I sit him up and arrange it beneath him; he's easily manipulated, not exactly cooperating, but not dead weight either. He uses the bedpan impassively. I find some paper and wipe him, then I take the bedpan to the toilets, empty it, and wash my hands thoroughly. I'm feeling only slightly queasy; O'Leary's inurement to tasks like this is probably helping.

Klein sits with a fixed gaze as I hold a spoonful of yellow mush in front of him, but when I touch it to his lips he opens his mouth wide. He doesn't close his mouth on the spoon, so I have to turn it and tip the food off, but he does swallow the stuff, and only a little ends up on his chin.

A woman in a white coat pops her head into the room and says, 'Could you shave Mr Klein, please, Johnny, he's going to St Margaret's for some tests this morning,' and then vanishes before I can reply.

After taking the trolley back to the kitchen, collecting empty trays along the way, I find all I need in the storeroom. I move Klein on to a chair – again he seems to make it easy, without quite assisting. He stays perfectly still as I lather and shave him, except for an occasional blink. I manage to nick him only once, and not deeply.

The same woman returns, this time carrying a thick manila folder and a clipboard, and she stands beside me. I get a peek at her badge – Dr Helen Lidcombe.

'How's it going, Johnny?'

'OK.'

She hovers expectantly, and I feel suddenly uneasy. I

must be doing something wrong. Or maybe I'm just too slow. 'Nearly finished,' I mutter. She reaches out with one hand and absent-mindedly massages the back of my neck. *Walking on eggs time.* Why can't my hosts lead uncomplicated lives? Sometimes I feel like I'm living the outtakes from a thousand soap operas. What does John O'Leary have a right to expect of me? To determine the precise nature and extent of this relationship, and leave him neither more nor less involved tomorrow than he was yesterday? Some chance.

'You're very tense.'

I need a safe topic, quickly. *The patient.*

'This guy, I don't know, some days he just gets to me.'

'What, is he behaving differently?'

'No, no, I just wonder. What it must be like for him.'

'Like nothing much.'

I shrug. 'He knows when he's sitting on a bedpan. He knows when he's being fed. He's not a vegetable.'

'It's hard to say what he "knows". A leech with a couple of neurons "knows" when to suck blood. All things considered, he does remarkably well, but I don't think he has anything like consciousness, or even anything like dreams.' She gives a little laugh. 'All he has is memories, though memories of *what* I can't imagine.'

I start wiping off the shaving soap. 'How do you know he has memories?'

'I'm exaggerating.' She reaches into the folder and pulls out a photographic transparency. It looks like a side-on head X-ray, but blobs and bands of artificial colour adorn it. 'Last month I finally got the money to do a few PET scans. There are things going on in Mr Klein's hippocampus that look suspiciously like long-term memories being laid down.' She whips the transparency back in the folder before I've had a chance for a proper look. 'But comparing anything in *his* head with studies on normals is like comparing the weather on Mars with the weather on Jupiter.'

I'm growing curious, so I take a risk, and ask with a furrowed brow, 'Did you ever tell me exactly how he ended up like this?'

She rolls her eyes. 'Don't start with that again! You know I'd get in trouble.'

'Who do you think I'd blab to?' I copy Ralph Dopita's imitation, for a second, and Helen bursts out laughing. 'Hardly. You haven't said more than three words to *him* since you've been here: "*Sorry, Dr Pearlman.*" '

'So why don't you tell me?'

'If you told your friends—'

'Do you think I tell my friends everything? Is that what you think? Don't you trust me at all?'

She sits on Klein's bed. 'Close the door.' I do it.

'His father was a pioneering neurosurgeon.'

'*What?*'

'If you say a *word*—'

'I won't, I promise. But what did he do? *Why?*'

'His primary research interest was redundancy and functional crossover; the extent to which people with lost or damaged portions of the brain manage to transfer the functions of the impaired regions into healthy tissue.

'His wife died giving birth to a son, their only child. He must have been psychotic already, but *that* put him right off the planet. He blamed the child for his wife's death, but he was too cold-blooded to do something simple like kill it.'

I'm about ready to tell her to shut up, that I really *do not* wish to know any more, but John O'Leary is a big, tough man with a strong stomach, and I mustn't disgrace him in front of his lover.

'He raised the child "normally", talking to it, playing with it, and so on, and making extensive notes on how it was developing; vision, coordination, the rudiments of speech, you name it. When it was a few months old, he implanted a network of cannulae, a web of very fine tubes, spanning almost the entire brain, but narrow enough not to cause any problems themselves. And then he kept on as before, stimulating the child, and recording its progress. And every week, via the cannulae, he destroyed a little more of its brain.'

I let out a long string of obscenities. Klein, of course, just sits there, but suddenly I'm ashamed of violating his privacy, however meaningless that concept might be in his case. My face is flushed with blood, I feel slightly dizzy, slightly less than real. 'How come he ever survived? How come there's *anything* left at all?'

'The extent of his father's insanity saved him, if that's the word to use. You see, for months during which he was regularly losing brain tissue, the child actually continued to develop neurologically – more slowly than normal, of course, but moving perceptibly forwards nonetheless. Professor Klein was too much the scientist to bury a result like that; he *wrote up* all his observations and tried to get them published. The journal thought it was some kind of sick hoax, but they told the police, who eventually got around to investigating. But by the time the child was rescued, well—' She nods towards the impassive Klein.

'How much of his brain is left? Isn't there a chance—?'

'Less than ten per cent. There are cases of microcephalics who live almost normal lives with a similar brain mass, but being born that way, having gone through foetal brain development that way, isn't a comparable situation. There was a young girl a few years ago, who had a hemispherectomy to cure severe epilepsy, and emerged from it with very little impairment, but she'd had years for her brain to gradually switch functions out of the damaged hemisphere. She was extremely lucky; in most cases that operation has been utterly disastrous. As for Mr Klein, well, I'd say he wasn't lucky at all.'

I seem to spend most of the rest of the morning mopping corridors. When an ambulance arrives to take Klein away for his tests, I feel mildly offended that no one asks for my assistance; the two ambulancemen, watched by Helen, plonk him into a wheelchair and wheel him away, like couriers collecting a heavy parcel. But I have even less right than John O'Leary to feel possessive or protective about 'my' patients, so I push Klein out of my thoughts.

I eat lunch with the other orderlies in the staff room. We play cards, and make jokes that even I find stale by now, but I enjoy the company nonetheless. I am teasingly accused several times of having lingering 'east-coast tendencies', which makes sense; if O'Leary lived over east for a while, that would explain why I don't remember him. The afternoon passes slowly, but sleepily. Dr Pearlman has flown somewhere, suddenly, to do whatever eminent psychiatrists or neurologists (I'm not even sure which he is) are called to do with great urgency in faraway cities – and this seems to let everyone, the patients included, relax. When my shift ends at three o'clock, and I walk out of the building saying 'See you tomorrow' to everyone I pass, I feel (as usual) a certain sense of loss. It will pass.

Because it's Friday, I detour to the city centre to update the records in my safe-deposit box. In the pre-rush traffic I begin to feel mild elation, as all the minor tribulations of coping with the Pearlman Psychiatric Institute recede, banished for months, or years, or maybe even decades.

After making diary entries for the week, and adding a new page headed JOHN FRANCIS O'LEARY to my thick ring-binder full of host details, the itch to *do something* with all this information grows in me, as it does now and then. But what? The prospect of renting a computer and arranging a place to use it is too daunting on a sleepy Friday afternoon. I could update, with the help of a calculator, my average host-repeat rate. That would be pretty bloody thrilling.

Then I recall the PET scan that Helen Lidcombe waved in front of me. Although I don't know a thing about interpreting such pictures myself, I can imagine how exciting it must be for a trained specialist to actually *see* brain processes displayed that way. If I could turn all *my* hundreds of pages of data into one coloured picture – well, it might not tell me a damn thing, but the prospect is somehow infinitely more attractive than messing about to produce a few statistics that don't tell me a damn thing either.

I buy a street directory, the brand I am familiar with from childhood, with the key map inside the front cover. I buy a packet of five felt-tipped pens. I sit on a bench in a shopping arcade, covering the map with coloured dots; a red dot for a host who's had from one to three visits, an orange dot for a host who's had four to six, and so on up to blue. It takes me an hour to complete, and when I'm finished the result does *not* look like a glossy, computer-generated brain scan at all. It looks like a mess.

And yet. Although the colours don't form isolated bands, and intermingle extensively, there's a definite concentration of blue in the city's north-east. As soon as I see this, it rings true; the north-east *is* more familiar to me than anywhere else. And, a geographical bias would explain the fact that I repeat hosts more frequently than I ought to. For each colour, I sketch a shaky pencil line that joins up all of its outermost points, and then another for all its innermost points. None of these lines intersects another. It's no perfect set of concentric circles by any means, but each curve is roughly centred on that patch of blue in the north-east. A region which contains, amongst many other things, the Pearlman Psychiatric Institute.

I pack everything back into the safe-deposit box. I need to give this a lot more thought. Driving home, a very vague hypothesis begins to form, but the traffic fumes, the noise, the glare of the setting sun, all make it hard to pin the idea down.

Linda is furious. 'Where have you been? Our daughter had to ring me, in tears, from a public phone box, with money borrowed from a *complete stranger*, and *I* had to pretend to be sick and leave work and drive halfway across town to pick her up. Where the hell have you been?'

'I – I got caught up, with Ralph, he was celebrating—'

'I *rang* Ralph. You weren't with Ralph.'

I stand there in silence. She stares at me for a full minute, then turns and stomps away.

I apologise to Laura (I see the name on her school books), who is no longer crying but looks like she has been for hours. She is eight years old, and adorable, and I feel like dirt. I offer to help with her homework, but she assures me she doesn't need *anything at all* from me, so I leave her in peace.

Linda, not surprisingly, barely says a word to me for the rest of the evening. Tomorrow this problem will be John O'Leary's, not mine, which makes me feel twice as bad about it. We watch TV in silence. When she goes to bed, I wait an hour before following her, and if she isn't asleep when I climb in, she's doing a good imitation.

I lie in the dark with my eyes open, thinking about Klein and his long-term memories, his father's unspeakable 'experiment', my brain scan of the city.

I never asked Helen how old Klein was, and now it's too late for that, but there'll surely be something in the newspapers from the time of his father's trial. First thing tomorrow – screw my host's obligations – I'll go to the central library and check that out.

Whatever consciousness is, it must be resourceful, it must be resilient. Surviving for so long in that tiny child, pushed into ever smaller corners of his mutilated, shrinking brain. But when the number of living neurons fell so low that no resourcefulness, no ingenuity, could make them suffice, what then? Did consciousness vanish in an instant? Did it slowly fade away, as function after function was discarded, until nothing remained but a few reflexes, and a parody of human dignity? Or did it – *how could it?* – reach out in desperation to the brains of a thousand other children, those young enough, flexible enough, to donate a fraction of their own capacity to save this one child from oblivion? Each one donating one day in a thousand from their own lives, to rescue me from that ruined shell, fit now for nothing but eating, defecating, and storing my long-term memories?

Klein, F. C. I don't even know what the initials stand for. Linda mumbles something and turns over. I feel remarkably unperturbed by my speculations, perhaps because I don't honestly believe that this wild theory could possibly be true. And yet, is it so much stranger than the mere fact of my existence?

And if I did believe it, how should I feel? Horrified by my own father's atrocities towards me? Yes. Astonished by such a miracle of human tenacity? Certainly.

I finally manage to cry – for Klein, F. C., or for myself, I don't know. Linda doesn't wake, but moved by some dream or instinct, she turns to me and holds me. Eventually I stop shaking, and the warmth of her body flows into me, peace itself.

As I feel sleep approaching, I make a resolution: from tomorrow, I start anew. From tomorrow, an end to mimicking my hosts. From tomorrow, whatever the problems, whatever the setbacks, I'm going to carve out a life of my own.

I dream a simple dream. I dream that I have a name. One name, unchanging, mine until death. I don't know what my name *is*, but that doesn't matter. Knowing that I have it is enough.

SEEING

I gaze down at the dusty top surface of the bank of lights suspended from the ceiling of the operating theatre. There's a neatly hand-lettered sticker on the grey-painted metal – slightly yellowing, the writing a little faded, peeling at one corner. It reads:

IN CASE OF OUT-OF-BODY EXPERIENCE
PHONE 137 4597

I'm puzzled: I've never come across a local number starting with a one – and when I look again, it's clear that the digit in question is actually a seven. I was mistaken about the 'dust', too; it's nothing but a play of light on the slightly uneven surface of the paint. *Dust* in a sterile, air-filtered room like this – what was I thinking?

I shift my attention to my body, draped in green save for a tiny square aperture above my right temple, where the macrosurgeon's probe is following the bullet's entry wound into my skull. The spindly robot has the operating table to itself, although a couple of gowned-and-masked humans are present, off to one side, watching what I take to be X-ray views of the probe approaching its target; from my vantage point, the screen is foreshortened, the images hard to decipher. Injected microsurgeons must already have staunched the bleeding, repaired hundreds of blood vessels, broken up any dangerous clots. The bullet itself, though, is too physically tough and chemically inert to be fragmented and removed, like a kidney stone, by a swarm of tiny robots; there's no alternative to reaching in and plucking it out. I used to read up on this type of operation – and lie awake afterwards, wondering when my time would finally come. I often pictured this very moment – and I'd swear, now, that when I imagined it, it looked *exactly* like this, down to the last detail. But I can't tell if that's just run-of-the-mill *déjà vu*, or if my obsessively rehearsed visualisation is fuelling this present hallucination.

I begin to wonder, calmly, about the implications of my exotic point of view. Out-of-body experiences are supposed to suggest proximity to death . . . but then, all the thousands of people who've reported them survived to tell the tale, didn't they? With no way of balancing that against the unknown number who must have died, it's absurd to treat the situation as signifying anything at all about my chances of life or death. The effect is certainly linked to severe physical trauma, but it's only the ludicrous notion that the 'soul' has parted from the body – and is perilously close to floating off down a tunnel of light into the afterlife – that associates the experience with *death*.

Memories leading up to the attack start coming back to me, hazily. Arriving to speak at Zeitgeist Entertainment's AGM. (Physically present for the first time in years – bad move. Just because I sold off HyperConference Systems, why did I have to eschew the technology?) That lunatic Murchison making a scene outside the Hilton, screaming something about me – *me!* – stiffing him on his miniseries contract. (As if I'd even read it, let alone personally drafted every clause. Why couldn't he have gone and mowed down the legal department, instead?) The motorised window of the bulletproof Rolls gliding upwards to shut out his ranting, the mirrored glass moving silently, reassuringly – and then jamming . . .

I was wrong about one thing: I always thought the bullet would come from some anal-retentive cinephile, outraged by one of Zeitgeist's 'Sequels to the Celluloid Classics'. The software avatars we use as directors are always constructed with meticulous care, by psychologists and film historians committed to re-creating the true persona of the original *auteur* . . . but some purists are never happy, and there were death threats for more than a year after *Hannah and Her Sisters II, in 3–D*. What I failed to anticipate was a man who'd just signed a seven-figure deal for the rights to his life story – out on bail only because of Zeitgeist's generous advance – trying to blow me away over a discounted residual rate for satellite transmissions dubbed into the Inuit language.

I notice that the unlikely sticker on top of the lights has vanished. What does *that* presage? If my delusion is breaking down, am I deteriorating, or recovering? Is an unstable hallucination healthier than a consistent one? Is reality about to come crashing in? What *should* I be seeing, right now? Pure darkness, if I really am under all that green swaddling, eyes closed, anaesthetised. I try to 'close my eyes' – but the concept just doesn't translate. I do my best to lose consciousness (if that's the right word for what I'm experiencing); I try to relax, as if aiming for sleep – but then a faint whir from the surgeon's probe as it reverses direction rivets my attention.

I watch – physically unable to avert my unphysical gaze – as the gleaming silver needle of the probe slowly retracts. It seems to take forever, and I rack my brain for a judgement as to whether this is a piece of masochistic dream-theatricality, or a touch of authenticity, but I can't decide.

Finally – and I *know it* a moment before it happens

(but then, I've felt that way all along) – the tip of the needle emerges, bonded outrageously by nothing more esoteric than a speck of high-strength *glue* (or so I once read) to the dull, slightly crumpled bullet.

I see the green cloth covering my chest rise and fall in an emphatic sigh of relief. I doubt the plausibility of this from an anaesthetised man on a breathing machine – then suddenly, overwhelmingly weary of trying to imagine the world at all, I allow it to disintegrate into psychedelic static, then darkness.

A familiar, but unplaceable, voice says, 'This one's from Serial Killers For Social Responsibility. "Deeply shocked . . . a tragedy for the industry . . . praying for Mr Lowe's swift recovery." Then they go on to disavow any knowledge of Randolph Murchison; they say that whatever he might or might not have done to hitchhikers in the past, celebrity assassination attempts involve an entirely separate pathology, and any irresponsible comments which blur the issue by confusing the two will result in a class action—'

I open my eyes and say, 'Can someone please tell me why there's a mirror on the ceiling over my bed? Is this a hospital, or a fucking bordello?'

The room falls silent. I squint up at the glass with a fixed gaze, unable to make out its borders, waiting for an explanation for this bizarre piece of décor. Then one possibility dawns on me: *Am I paralysed? Is this the only way to show me my surroundings?* I fight down a sense of panic: even if it's true, it need not be permanent. Nerves can be regrown, whatever's damaged can be repaired. I've *survived*, that's what counts – the rest is just a matter of rehabilitation. *And isn't this what I always expected? A bullet in the brain? A brush with death? Rebirth in a state of helplessness?*

In the mirror, I can see four people gathered around the bed – and I recognise them easily enough, in spite of the awkward view: James Long, my personal assistant, whose voice woke me. Andrea Stuart, Zeitgeist's senior vice-president. My estranged wife, Jessica – *I knew she'd come*. And my son, Alex – he must have dropped everything, and caught the first flight out of Moscow.

And on the bed, almost buried under a tangle of tubes and cables, linked to a dozen monitors and pumps, an ashen, bandaged, gaunt figure which I suppose must be me.

James glances up at the ceiling, looks down again, then says gently, 'Mr Lowe, there is no mirror. Shall I tell the doctors you're awake?'

I scowl, try to move my head, fail. 'Are you blind? I'm staring *right at it*. And if I'm not plugged into enough machinery to tell whoever's monitoring it all that I'm awake—'

James gives an embarrassed cough, a code he uses in meetings when I start to wander too far from the facts. I try again to turn to look him in the eye, and this time—

This time, I succeed. Or at least, *I see the figure on the bed turn its head—*

—and my whole sense of my surroundings *inverts*, like an all-encompassing optical illusion exposed. Floor becomes ceiling and ceiling floor – without anything moving a millimetre. I feel like bellowing at the top of my lungs, but only manage a startled grunt . . . and after a second or two, it's hard to imagine that I'd ever been fooled, the reality is so obvious.

There is no mirror. I'm watching all this from the ceiling, the way I watched the bullet being extracted. *I'm still up here. I haven't come down.*

I close my eyes – and the room *fades out*, taking two or three seconds to vanish completely.

I open my eyes. The view returns, unchanged.

I say, 'Am I dreaming? Are my eyes really open? Jessica? Tell me what's going on. Is my face bandaged?

Am I blind?'

James says, 'Your wife isn't here, Mr Lowe. We haven't been able to reach her yet.' He hesitates, then adds, 'Your face isn't bandaged—'

I laugh indignantly. 'What are you talking about? Who's that standing next to you?'

'Nobody's standing next to me. Ms Stuart and I are the only people with you, right now.'

Andrea clears her throat, and says, 'That's right, Philip. Please, try to calm down. You've just had major surgery – you're going to be fine, but you have to take it easy.' How did she get *there* – near the foot of the bed? The figure below turns to look at her, sweeping his gaze across the intervening space, and – as easily as the implausible *one* changed into a *seven*, as easily as the whole ludicrous sticker ceased to exist – my wife and son are banished from my vision of the room.

I say, 'I'm going mad.' That's not true, though: I'm dazed, and distinctly queasy, but a long way from coming unhinged. I notice that my voice – very reasonably – seems to come out of my one-and-only mouth, the mouth of the figure below me – as opposed to the point in empty space where my mouth would be, were I literally, bodily, hovering near the ceiling. I *felt* my larynx vibrate, my lips and tongue move, *down there* . . . and yet the sense that *I* am above, looking down, remains as convincing as ever. It's as if . . . my entire body has become as peripheral as a foot or a fingertip – connected and controlled, still a part of me, but certainly not encompassing the centre of my being. I move my tongue in my mouth, touch the tip to the point of my left incisor, swallow some saliva; the sensations are all intelligible, consistent, familiar. But I don't find myself rushing down to 'occupy' the place where these things are happening – any more than I've ever felt my sense of self pouring into my big toe, upon curling it against the sole of my shoe.

James says, 'I'll fetch the doctors.' I hunt for any trace of inconsistency in the direction of *his* voice . . . but I'm not up to the task of dissecting the memory of his speech into relative intensities in my left and right ears, and then confronting myself with the paradox that anyone truly up here, facing down, would hear it all differently. All I know is that the words *seem* to have emerged from his lips, in the customary manner.

Andrea clears her throat again, and says, 'Philip? Do you mind if I make a call? Tokyo opens in less than an hour, and when they hear that you've been shot—'

I cut her off. 'Don't call – go there, in person. Take the next sub-orbital – you know that always impresses the market. Look, I'm glad you were here when I woke' – glad *your* presence, at least, turned out to be more than wishful thinking – 'but the biggest favour you can do for me now is to make damned sure that Zeitgeist comes through this unscathed.' I try to make eye contact as I say this, but I can't tell whether I succeed or not. It's twenty years since we were lovers, but she's still my closest friend. I'm not even sure why I'm so desperate to get rid of her – but I can't help feeling *exposed* up here . . . as if she might suddenly glance up and *see me* – see some part of me that my flesh always concealed.

'Are you sure?'

'I'm positive. James can baby-sit me, that's what he's paid for. And if I know you're looking after Zeitgeist, I won't have to lie here sweating about it; I'll know it's all under control.'

In fact, as soon as she's gone, the idea of worrying about anything as remote and inconsequential as my company's share price begins to seem utterly bizarre. I turn my head so that the figure on the bed looks straight up at 'me' once more. I slide my hand across my chest, and most of the cables and tubes that were 'covering me' disappear, leaving behind nothing but a slightly wrinkled sheet. I laugh weakly – an odd sight. It looks like a memory of the last time I laughed into a mirror.

James returns, followed by four generic white-coated figures – whose number shrinks to two, a young man and a middle-aged woman, when I turn my head towards them.

The woman says, 'Mr Lowe, I'm Dr Tyler, your neurologist. How are you feeling?'

'How am I feeling? I feel like I'm up on the ceiling.'

'You're still giddy from the anaesthetic?'

'*No!*' I very nearly shout: *Can't you look at me when I'm speaking to you?* But I calm myself, and say evenly, 'I'm not "giddy" – I'm *hallucinating*. I see everything as if I'm up on the ceiling, looking down. Do you understand me? I'm watching my own lips move as I say these words. I'm staring down at the top of your head. I'm having an out-of-body experience – right now, right in front of you.' *Or right above you.* 'It started in the operating theatre. I saw the robot take out the bullet. I *know*, it was just a delusion, a kind of lucid dream – I didn't really *see* anything . . . but it's still happening. I'm awake, and it's still happening. *I can't come down.*'

Dr Tyler says firmly, 'The surgeon didn't remove the bullet. It was never embedded; it only grazed your skull. The impact caused a fracture, and forced some bone fragments into the underlying tissue – but the damaged region is very small.'

I smile with relief to hear this – and then stop myself; it looks too strange, too self-conscious. I say, 'That's wonderful news. But I'm still up here.'

Dr Tyler frowns. *How do I know that?* She's bent over me, her face seems to be hidden – yet the knowledge reaches me somehow, as if conveyed through an extra sense. This is insane: the things I must be 'seeing' with my own eyes – the things I'm *entitled* to know – are taking on an air of unreliable clairvoyance, while my 'vision' of the room – a patchwork of wild guesses and wishful thinking – masquerades as the artless truth.

'Do you think you can sit up?'

I can – slowly. I'm very weak, but certainly not paralysed, and with an ungainly scrabbling of feet and elbows, I manage to raise myself into a sitting position. The exertion makes me sharply aware of every limb, every joint, every muscle . . . but aware most of all that their relationships with *each other* remain unchanged. The hip bone is still connected to the thigh bone, and that's still what counts – however far away from both I feel 'myself' to be.

My view stays fixed as my body moves – but I don't find that especially disconcerting; at some level, it seems no stranger than the simple understanding that turning your head doesn't send the world spinning in the opposite direction.

Dr Tyler holds out her right hand. 'How many fingers?'

'Two.'

'Now?'

'Four.'

She shields her hand from aerial scrutiny with a clipboard. 'Now?'

'One. I can't see it, though. I just guessed.'

'You guessed right. Now?'

'Three.'

'Right again. And now?'

'Two.'

'Correct.'

She hides her hand from the figure on the bed, 'exposing' it to me–above. I make three wrong guesses in a row, one right, one wrong, then wrong again.

All of which makes perfect sense, of course: I know only what my eyes can see; the rest is pure guesswork. I am, demonstrably, *not* observing the world from a point three metres above my head. Having the truth rendered obvious makes no difference, though: I fail to descend.

Dr Tyler suddenly jabs two fingers towards my eyes, stopping just short of contact. I'm not even startled; from this distance, it's no more threatening than watching The Three Stooges. 'Blink reflex working,' she says – but I know I should have done more than *blink*.

She looks around the room, finds a chair, places it beside the bed. Then she tells her colleague, 'Get me a broom.'

She stands on the chair. 'I think we should try to pin down exactly *where* you think you are.' The young man returns with a two-metre-long white plastic tube. 'Vaccum cleaner extension,' he explains. 'There are no brooms in the private wards.'

James stands clear, glancing upwards self-consciously every now and then. He's beginning to look alarmed, in a diplomatic sort of way.

Dr Tyler takes the tube, raises it up with one hand, and starts scraping the end across the ceiling. 'Tell me when I'm getting warm, Mr Lowe.' The thing looms towards me, moving in from the left, then slides across the bottom of my field of view, missing me by a few centimetres.

'Am I close yet?'

'I—' The scraping sound is intimidating; it takes some effort to bring myself to cooperate, to guide the implement home.

When the tube finally closes over me, I fight off a sense of claustrophobia, and stare down the long dark tunnel. At the far end, in a circle of dazzling radiance, is the tip of Dr Tyler's white lace-up shoe.

'What do you see now?'

I describe the view. Keeping the top end fixed, she tilts the tube towards the bed, until it points directly at my bandaged forehead, my startled eyes – a strange, luminous cameo.

'Try . . . moving towards the light,' she suggests.

I try. I screw up my face, I grit my teeth, I urge myself forward, down the tunnel: back to my skull, back to my citadel, back to my private screening room. Back to the throne of my ego, the anchor of my identity. *Back home.*

Nothing happens.

I always knew I'd get a bullet in the brain. It had to happen: I'd made far too much money, had far too much good luck. Deep down, I always understood that, sooner or later, my life would be brought into balance. And I always expected my would-be assassin to fail – leaving me crippled, speechless, amnesic; forced to struggle to make myself whole again, forced to rediscover – or reinvent – myself.

Given a chance to start my life again.

But this? What kind of redemption is *this*?

Eyes closed or open, I have no trouble identifying pinpricks all over my body, from the soles of my feet to the top of my scalp – but the surface of my skin, however clearly delineated, still fails to *enclose me*.

Dr Tyler shows me-below photographs of torture victims, humorous cartoons, pornography. I cringe, I smile, I get an erection – before I even know what I'm 'looking' at.

'Like a split-brain patient,' I muse. 'Isn't that what happens? Show them an image in half their visual field, and they respond to it emotionally – without being able to describe what they've seen.'

'Your *corpus callosum* is perfectly intact. You're not a split-brain patient, Mr Lowe.'

'Not horizontally – but what about vertically?' There's a stony silence. I say, 'I'm only joking. Can't I make a joke?' I see her write on her clipboard: INAP-PROPRIATE AFFECT. I 'read' the remark effortlessly, in spite of my elevation – but I don't have the nerve to ask her if it's really what she wrote.

A mirror is thrust in front of my face – and when it's taken away, I see myself as less pale, less wasted than before. The mirror is turned towards me-above, and the place where I 'am' is 'shown' to be empty – but I knew that all along.

I 'look around' with my eyes every chance I get – and my vision of the room grows more detailed, more stable, more consistent. I experiment with sounds, tapping my fingers on the side of the bed, on my ribs, my jaw, my skull. I have no trouble convincing myself that my hearing is still taking place in my ears – the closer a sound is to those organs down there, the louder it seems, as always – but nor do I have any difficulty interpreting these cues correctly; when I snap my fingers beside my right ear, it's obvious that the source of the sound is close to *my ear*, not close to *me*.

Finally, Dr Tyler lets me try to walk. I'm clumsy and unsteady at first, distracted by my unfamiliar perspective, but I soon learn to take what I need from the view – the positions of obstacles – and ignore the rest. As my body crosses the room, I move with it, hovering more or less directly above – sometimes lagging behind or moving ahead, but never by far. Curiously, I feel no conflict between my sense of balance, telling me I'm upright, and my downwards gaze, which 'should' (but doesn't) suggest that my body is facing the floor. That meaning has been stripped away, somehow – and it has nothing to do with the fact that I can 'see' myself standing. Perhaps my true orientation is gleaned, subconsciously, from the evidence of my eyes, at some point before the damaged part of my brain corrupts the information – like my 'clairvoyant' knowledge of 'hidden' objects.

I could walk a kilometre, I'm sure, but not very quickly. I place my body in a wheelchair, and a taciturn orderly pushes it – and me – out of the room. The smooth, involuntary motion of my point of view is alarming at first, but then gradually starts to make sense: after all, I can feel my hands on the armrests, the chair against my legs, my buttocks, my back – 'part' of me *is* in the wheelchair, and, like a roller-skater staring down at his feet, I should be able to swallow the notion that the 'rest' of me is attached, and obliged to follow. Down corridors, up ramps, in and out of elevators, through swing doors . . . I fantasise daringly about wandering off on my own – turning left when the orderly turns right – but the truth is, I can't begin to imagine how I could make that happen.

We turn into a crowded walkway linking the hospital's two main blocks, and end up travelling alongside another patient in a wheelchair – a man about my age, his head also bandaged. I wonder what he's been through, and what's in store for him now – but this doesn't seem like the time or place to strike up a conversation about it. From above (at least, as I see it) these two head-wound cases in hospital gowns are almost indistinguishable, and I find myself wondering: *Why do I care what happens to one of these bodies, so much more than the other? How can it be so important . . . when I can barely tell them apart?*

I grip the armrests of the chair tightly – but resist the temptation to raise a hand and signal to myself: *This one is me.*

We finally reach Medical Imaging. Strapped to a motorised table, my blood infused with a cocktail of radioactive substances, I'm guided into a helmet comprised of several tonnes of superconducting magnets and particle detectors. My whole head is engulfed by the thing, but the room doesn't vanish at once. The technicians, cut loose from reality, keep themselves busy fussing with the scanner's controls – like old celluloid-movie extras pretending, unconvincingly, to know how to operate a nuclear power station or an interstellar spacecraft. Gradually, the scene fades to black.

When I emerge, with dark-adapted eyes, for a second or two the room is unbearably bright.

'We have no previous case histories of a lesion in exactly this location,' admits Dr Tyler, thoughtfully holding the brain scan at an angle which allows me to observe, and simultaneously visualise, its contents. She insists on addressing her remarks solely to me–below, though, which makes me feel a bit like a patronised child – ignored by the adults, who, instead, crouch down and say hello to Teddy.

'We do know it's associative cortex. Higher-level sense-data processing and integration. The place where your brain constructs models of the world, and your relationship to it. From your symptoms, it seems you've lost access to the primary model, so you're making do with a secondary one.'

'What's that supposed to mean? Primary model, secondary model? I'm still looking at everything through the same pair of eyes, aren't I?'

'Yes.'

'Then how can I fail to *see it that way*? If a camera is damaged, it produces a faulty image – it doesn't start giving you bird's-eye views from down on the ground.'

'Forget about cameras. *Vision* is nothing like photography – it's an elaborate cognitive act. A pattern of light on your retina doesn't mean a thing until it's been *analysed*: that means everything from detecting edges, detecting motion, extracting features from noise, simplifying, extrapolating – all the way up to constructing hypothetical objects, testing them against reality, comparing them to memories and expectations . . . the end product is *not* a movie in your head, it's a set of conclusions about the world.

'The brain assembles those conclusions into models of your surroundings. The primary model includes information about more or less everything that's directly visible at any given moment – and nothing else. It makes the most efficient use of all your visual data, and it makes the least possible number of assumptions. So it has a lot of advantages – but it doesn't arise automatically just because the data was gathered *through your eyes*. And it's not the only possibility: we all build other models, all the time; most people can imagine their surroundings from almost any angle—'

I laugh incredulously. 'Not like this. Nobody could *imagine* a view as vivid as this. I certainly never could.'

'Then perhaps you've managed to redeploy some of the neural pathways responsible for the intensity of the primary model—'

'I don't want to *redeploy* them! I *want* the primary model back!' I hesitate, put off by the look of apprehension on my face, but I have to know. 'Can you do that – can you repair the damage? Put in a neural graft?'

Dr Tyler tells my Teddy Bear, gently, 'We can replace the damaged tissue, but the region's not well enough understood to be repaired, directly, by microsurgeons. We wouldn't know which neurons to join to which. All we can do is inject some immature neurons into the site of the lesion, and leave them to form their own connections.'

'And . . . will they form the right ones?'

'There's a good chance they will, eventually.'

'*A good chance*. If they do, how long will it take?'

'Several months, at least.'

'I'll want a second opinion.'

'Of course.'

She pats my hand sympathetically – but leaves without so much as a glance in my direction.

Several months. At least. The room begins to rotate slowly – so slowly that it never actually moves at all. I close my eyes and wait for the feeling to pass. My vision lingers, refusing to fade. Ten seconds. Twenty seconds. Thirty seconds. There I am, on the bed below, *eyes closed* . . . but that doesn't render me invisible, does it? It doesn't make the world disappear. That's half the trouble with this whole delusion: it's so fucking *reasonable*.

I put the heels of my palms against my eyes, and press, hard. A mosaic of glowing triangles spreads out rapidly from the centre of my field of view, a shimmering pattern in grey and white; soon it eclipses the whole room.

When I take my hands away, the afterimage slowly fades to darkness.

I dream that I look down upon my sleeping body – and then drift away, rising up calmly, effortlessly, high into the air. I float above Manhattan – then London, Zurich, Moscow, Nairobi, Cairo, Beijing. Wherever the Zeitgeist Network reaches, I'm there. I wrap the planet in my being. I have no need of a body; I orbit with the satellites, I flow through the optical fibres. From the slums of Calcutta to the mansions of Beverly Hills, I am the *Zeitgeist*, the Spirit of the Age—

I wake suddenly, and hear myself swearing, before I even know why.

Then I realise I've wet the bed.

James flies in dozens of the top neurologists from around the world, and arranges remote consultations with another ten. They argue about the precise interpretation of my symptoms – but their recommendations for treatment are all essentially the same.

So, a small number of my own neurons, collected during the original surgery, are genetically regressed to a foetal state, stimulated to multiply *in vivo*, then injected back into the lesion. Local anaesthetic only; at least this time I get to 'see' more or less what really happens.

In the days that follow – far too early for any effects from the treatment – I find myself adapting to the status quo with disarming speed. My coordination improves, until I can perform most simple tasks with confidence, unaided: eating and drinking, urinating and defecating, washing and shaving – all the lifelong familiar routines start to seem ordinary again, in spite of the exotic perspective. At first, I keep catching glimpses of Randolph Murchison (played by the persona of Anthony Perkins) sneaking into the steam-clouded bathroom every time I take a shower – but that passes.

Alex visits, finally able to tear himself away from the busy Moscow bureau of Zeitgeist News. I watch the scene, oddly touched by the ineloquence of both father and son – but puzzled, too, that the awkward relationship ever caused me so much pain and confusion. These two men are not close – but that's not the end of the world. They're not close to a few billion other people, either: *It doesn't matter.*

By the end of the fourth week, I'm desperately bored – and losing patience with the infantile tests with concealed wooden blocks that Dr Young, my psychologist, insists I perform twice daily. Five red and four blue blocks can turn into three red and one green, when the partition hiding them from my eyes is lifted – and so on, a thousand times . . . but it no more demolishes my world-view than pictures of vases that turn into pairs of human profiles, or patterns with gaps that magically fill themselves in when aligned with the retinal blind spot.

Dr Tyler admits, under duress, that there's no reason I can't be discharged, but—

'I'd still prefer to keep you under observation.'

I say, 'I think I can do that myself.'

A two-metre-wide auxiliary screen attached to the

videophone lies on the floor of my study; a crutch, perhaps, but at least it takes the clairvoyance factor out of knowing what's happening on the smaller screen in front of my face.

Andrea says, 'Remember that team of Creative Consultants we hired last spring? They've come up with a brilliant new concept: "Celluloid Classics That Might Have Been" – ground-breaking movies that were *almost* made, but didn't quite survive the development process. They plan to start the series with *Three Burglars* – a Hollywood remake of *Tenue de Soirée*, with Arnold Schwarzenegger in the Depardieu role, and either Leonard Nimoy or Ivan Reitman directing. Marketing have run a simulation which shows twenty-three per cent of subscribers taking the pilot. The costings aren't too bad, either; we already own emulation rights for most of the personas we need.'

I nod my puppet head. 'That all sounds . . . fine. Is there anything else we need to discuss?'

'Just one more thing. *The Randolph Murchison Story*.'

'What's the problem?'

'Audience Psychology won't approve the latest version of the screenplay. We can't leave out Murchison's attack on you, it's far too well known—'

'I never asked for it to be left out. I just want my post-operative condition left unspecified. Lowe gets shot. Lowe survives. There's no need to clutter up a perfectly good story about mutilated hitchhikers with details of a minor character's neurological condition.'

'No, of course not – and that's not the problem. The problem is, if we cover the attack at all, we'll have to mention the reason for it, *the miniseries itself* . . . and AP says viewers won't be comfortable with that degree of reflexivity. For current affairs, all right – the programme is its own main subject, the presenters' actions *are* the news – that's taken for granted, people are used to it. But docudrama is different. You can't use a fictional narrative style – telling the audience it's safe to get emotionally involved, it's all just entertainment, it can't really touch them – and then throw in a reference to the very programme they're watching.'

I shrug. 'All right. Fine. If there's no way around it, axe the project. We can live with that; we can write it off.'

She nods, unhappily. It was the decision she wanted, I'm sure – but not so casually given.

When she hangs up, and the screen goes blank, the sight of the unchanging room quickly becomes monotonous. I switch to cable input, and flick through a few dozen channels from Zeitgeist and its major competitors. The whole world is there to gaze upon, from the latest Sudanese famine to the Chinese civil war, from a body paint fashion parade in New York to the bloody aftermath of the bombing of the British parliament. The whole world – or a model of the world: part truth, part guesswork, part wish-fulfilment.

I lean back in my chair until I'm staring straight down into my eyes. I say, 'I'm sick of this place. Let's get out of here.'

I watch the snow dust my shoulders between the sharp gusts of wind that blow it away. The icy sidewalk is deserted; nobody in this part of Manhattan seems to walk anywhere in the most clement weather any more, let alone on a day like this. I can just make out the four bodyguards, ahead of me and behind me, at the edge of my vision.

I wanted a bullet in the head. I wanted to be destroyed and reborn. I wanted a magic path to redemption. And what have I ended up with?

I raise my head, and a ragged, bearded tramp materialises beside me, stamping his feet on the sidewalk, hugging himself, shivering. He says nothing, but I stop walking.

One man below me is warmly dressed, in an overcoat and overshoes. The other is wearing threadbare jeans, a tattered bomber jacket, and baseball shoes full of holes.

The disparity is ridiculous. The warmly dressed man takes off his overcoat and hands it to the shivering man, then walks on.

And I think: What a beautiful scene for *The Philip Lowe Story*.

A KIDNAPPING

The office's elaborate software usually fielded my calls, but this one came through unannounced. The seven-metre wallscreen opposite my desk abruptly ceased displaying the work I'd been viewing – Kreyszig's dazzling abstract animation, *Spectral Density* – and the face of a nondescript young man appeared in its place.

I suspected at once that the face was a mask, a simulation. No single feature was implausible, or even unusual – limp brown hair, pale blue eyes, thin nose, square jaw – but the face as a whole was too symmetrical, too unblemished, too devoid of character to be real. In the background, a pattern of brightly coloured, *faux*-ceramic hexagonal tiles drifted across the wallpaper – desperately bland retro–geometricism, no doubt intended to make the face look natural in comparison. I made these judgements in an instant; stretching all the way to the gallery's ceiling, four times my height, the image was open to merciless scrutiny.

The 'young man' said, 'We have your wife/Transfer half a million dollars/Into this account/If you don't want her to/Suffer.' I couldn't help hearing it that way; the unnatural rhythm of the speech, the crisp enunciation of each word, made the whole thing sound like a terminally hip performance artist reading bad poetry. *This piece is entitled, 'Ransom Demand'.* As the mask spoke, a sixteen-digit account number flashed up across the bottom of the screen.

I said, 'Go screw yourself. This isn't funny.'

The mask vanished, and Loraine appeared. Her hair was dishevelled, her face was flushed, as if she'd just been in a struggle – but she wasn't distraught, or hysterical; she was grimly in control. I stared at the screen; the room seemed to sway, and I felt sweat break out on my arms and chest, impossible rivulets forming in seconds.

She said, 'David, listen: I'm all right, they haven't hurt me, but—'

Then the call cut off.

For a moment, I just sat there, dazed, drenched with sweat, too giddy to trust myself to move a muscle. Then I said to the office, 'Replay that call.' I expected a denial – *No calls have been put through all day* – but I was wrong. The whole thing began again.

'We have your wife . . .'

'Go screw yourself . . .'

'David, listen . . .'

I told the office, 'Call my home.' I don't know why I did that; I don't know what I believed, what I was hoping for. It was more a reflex action than anything else – like flailing out to grab something solid when you're falling, even if you know full well that it's far beyond your reach.

I sat and listened to the ringing tone. I thought: I'll cope with this, somehow. Loraine *will* be released, unharmed – it's just a matter of paying the money. Everything will happen, step by step; everything will unwind, inexorably – even if each second along the way seems like an unbreachable chasm.

After seven chimes, I felt like I'd been sitting at the desk, sleepless, for days: numb, tenuous, less than real.

Then Loraine answered the phone. I could see the studio behind her, all the familiar charcoal sketches on the wall. I opened my mouth to speak, but I couldn't make a sound.

Her expression changed from mild annoyance to alarm. She said, 'David? What's wrong? You look like you're having a heart attack.'

For several seconds, I couldn't answer her. On one level, I simply felt relieved – and already slightly foolish, for having been so easily taken in . . . but at the same time, I found myself holding my breath, bracing myself for another reversal. *If the office phone system had been corrupted, how could I be sure that this call had reached home? Why should I trust the sight of Loraine, safe in her studio – when the image of her in the kidnappers' hands had been every bit as convincing? At any moment, the 'woman' on the screen would drop the charade, and begin reciting coolly: 'We have your wife . . .'*

It didn't happen. So I pulled myself together and told the real Loraine what I'd seen.

In retrospect, of course, it all seemed embarrassingly obvious. The contrast between the intentionally un-natural mask, and the meticulously plausible image that followed, was designed to keep me from questioning the evidence of my own eyes. *This* is what a simulation looks like (smartarsed expert spots it at once) . . . so *this* (a thousand times more realistic) must be authentic. A crude trick, but it had worked – not for long, but long enough to shake me up.

But if the technique was transparent, the motive remained obscure. Some lunatic's idea of a joke? It seemed like a lot of trouble to go to, for no greater reward than the dubious thrill of making me sweat with fear for all of sixty seconds. As a genuine attempt at extortion, though . . . how could it ever have worked? Were they hoping that I'd transfer the money *im-mediately* – before the shock wore off, before it even occurred to me that the image of Loraine, however lifelike, proved nothing? If so, surely they would have kept me on the phone, threatening imminent danger, building up the pressure – leaving me with no time for doubts, and no opportunity to verify anything.

It didn't make sense either way.

I replayed the call for Loraine – but she didn't seem to take it very seriously.

'A crank caller with fancy technology is still just a crank caller. I remember my brother, when he was ten years old, phoning up random numbers on a dare, putting on a ludicrous high-pitched voice which was meant to sound like a woman . . . and telling whoever answered that he was about to be gang-raped. Needless to say, I thought it was totally sick – and extremely immature . . . I was eight – but his friends all sat around laughing their heads off. Thirty years later, this is the equivalent.'

'How can you say that? Ten-year-old boys do *not* own twenty-thousand-dollar video synthesisers—'

'No? Some might. But I'm sure there are plenty of forty-year-old men with the same sophisticated sense of humour.'

'Yeah? forty-year-old psychopaths who know exactly what you look like, where we live, where I work . . .'

We argued the point for almost twenty minutes, but we couldn't agree upon what the call meant, or what we should do about it. Loraine was obviously growing impatient to get back to work, so, reluctantly, I let her go.

I was a wreck, though. I knew I'd get nothing done that afternoon, so I decided to close the gallery and head for home.

Before leaving, I phoned the police – against Loraine's wishes, but as she'd said: 'You got the call, not me. If you really want to waste your time and theirs, I can't stop you.'

I was put through to a Detective Nicholson in the Communications Crime Division, and I showed him the recording. He was sympathetic, but he made it clear that there wasn't much he could do. A criminal act *had* been committed – and a ransom demand was a serious matter, however rapidly the hoax had been debunked – but identifying the perpetrator would be virtually impossible. Even if the account number quoted actually belonged to the caller, it carried the prefix of an Orbital bank, who'd certainly refuse to disclose the name of the owner. I could arrange to have the phone company attempt to trace any future calls – but if the signal was routed through an Orbital nation, as it most likely would be, the trail would stop there. An international agreement to veto exchanges of money and data with the satellites had been drafted a decade ago, but remained unratified; apparently, few countries could afford to forgo the advantages of being plugged into the quasi-legal Orbital economy.

Nicholson asked me for a list of prospective enemies, but I couldn't bring myself to name anyone. I'd had business disputes of various degrees of animosity over the years, mostly with disgruntled artists who'd taken their work elsewhere – but I couldn't honestly imagine any of the people involved wasting their energy on such a venomous – yet ultimately petty – act of revenge.

He had one final question. 'Has your wife ever been scanned?'

I laughed. 'Hardly. She loathes computers. Even if the cost came down a thousandfold, she'd be the last person in the world to have it done.'

'I see. Well, we appreciate your cooperation. If there are any further incidents, don't hesitate to get in touch.'

As he hung up, I belatedly wished I'd asked him: 'What if she *had* been scanned? Why would that be a factor? *Have hackers started breaking into people's scan files?*'

That was a disturbing notion . . . but even if it were true, it had no bearing on the hoax call. No such convenient, computerised description of Loraine existed, so however the hoaxers had reconstructed her appearance, they'd obtained their data by other means entirely.

I drove home on manual override, breaking the speed limit – marginally – on five separate occasions, watching the fines add up on the dashboard display, until the car intoned, 'One more violation and your licence is suspended.'

I went straight from the garage to the studio. Loraine was there, of course. I stood in the doorway, watching her silently, as she fussed over a sketch. I couldn't make out the subject, but she was working in charcoal again. I often teased her about her anachronistic methods: 'Why do you glorify the faults of traditional materials? Artists in the past had no choice but to make a virtue out of necessity – but why keep up the pretence? If charcoal on paper, or oil paint on canvas, really is so wonderful, then *describe* whatever it is you find so sublime about them to some virtual art software – and then generate your own virtual materials which are twice as good.' All she'd ever say in reply was: 'This is what I do, this is what I like, this is what I'm used to. There's no harm in that, is there?'

I didn't want to disturb her, but I didn't want to walk away. If she noticed my presence, she gave no sign of it. I stood there and thought: *I really do love you. And I really do admire you: the way you kept your head in the middle of—*

I caught myself. The middle of *what*? Being thrust in front of a camera by her abductors? None of that had actually happened.

No . . . but I knew Loraine – and I knew that she *wouldn't have* fallen to pieces, she would have stayed in control. I could still admire her courage and her level-headedness – however bizarre the means by which I'd been reminded of those qualities.

I started to turn away, and she said, 'Stay if you like. I don't mind you watching.'

I took a few steps into the cluttered studio. After the stark, cavernous spaces of the gallery, it looked very homely. 'What are you working on?'

She stood aside from the easel. The sketch was almost completed. It showed a woman, clenched fist raised to her lips, staring straight at the onlooker. Her expression was one of uneasy fascination, as if she was gazing at something hypnotic, compelling – and deeply troubling.

I frowned. 'It's you, isn't it? A self-portrait?' It had taken me a while to spot the resemblance, and even then, I wasn't sure.

But Loraine said, 'Yes, it's me.'

'Am I allowed to ask what you're looking at?'

She shrugged. 'Hard to say. The work in progress? Maybe it's a portrait of the artist caught in the act of self-portraiture.'

'You should try working with a camera and a flatscreen. You could program the stylisation software to build up a composite image of yourself – while you watched the result, and reacted to it.'

She shook her head, amused. 'Why go to so much trouble? Why not just frame a mirror?'

'A mirror? People want to see the artist revealed; they don't want to see *themselves*.'

I wandered over and kissed her, but she barely responded. I said, tenderly, 'I'm glad you're safe.'

She laughed. 'So am I. And don't worry – I wouldn't let anyone kidnap me, now. I know you'd have a stroke before you had a chance to pay the ransom.'

I put a finger to her lips. 'It's not funny. I was terrified – don't you believe me? I didn't know what they might do. I thought they were going to torture you.'

'How? By voodoo?' She backed out of my embrace, then walked over to the workbench. The wall above was covered with her sketches – 'failures' which she kept on show for 'salutary reasons'.

She picked up a paperknife from the bench and made two diagonal slashes in one of the drawings – an old self-portrait, one I'd liked very much.

Then she turned to me and said, in mock amazement, 'That didn't hurt a bit.'

I managed to keep myself from broaching the subject again until late in the evening. We were sitting in the living room, huddled together in front of the fireplace – ready for bed, but reluctant to move from this cosy spot (even though a few words to the house could have reproduced the very same hearthside warmth, anywhere at all).

'What worries me,' I said, 'is that someone must have followed you around with a camera – long enough to capture your face, your voice, your mannerisms . . .'

Loraine scowled. 'My *what*? This thing didn't even speak a whole sentence. And they need not have *followed me* anywhere – they probably just intercepted a phone call I made, and based it all on that. They pushed their own call straight through your office defences, didn't they? They're probably just a bunch of bored hackers – and for all we know, they could live on the other side of the planet.'

'Maybe. But not one phone call – dozens. They must have gathered a lot of data, however they did it. I've talked to artists who do simulation portraits – ten or twenty seconds of action, based on hours of sittings – and they say it's still not easy to fool anyone who really knows the subject. OK, I should have been scept.cal . . . but why wasn't I? Because it was so *convincing*. Because it was *exactly* how I would have imagined you—'

She shifted in my arms, irritably. 'It was nothing like me. It was melodramatic, computerised overacting –

and they knew it, which is why they kept it so short.'

I shook my head. 'Nobody can judge an impersonation of themselves. You'll have to take my word for it. I know, it only lasted a few seconds – but I swear, *they got it right.*'

As the conversation dragged on into the early hours of the morning, Loraine stood her ground – and I had to concede that there was nothing much we could actually *do* to make our lives any safer, whether or not the caller harboured plans to inflict real physical harm. The house already had state-of-the-art security hardware, and Loraine and I both carried surgically implanted radio alarm beacons. Even I balked at the idea of hiring armed bodyguards.

I had to concede, too, that no serious aspiring kidnappers would have alerted us to their intentions with a hoax call.

Finally, wearily (as if it had to be settled, there and then, if we weren't to keep arguing until dawn), I caved in. Maybe I'd over-reacted. Maybe I just resented having been fooled. Maybe the whole thing had been nothing but a prank, after all.

However sick. However technically accomplished. However apparently pointless.

When we slumped into bed, Loraine fell asleep almost at once, but I lay awake for hours. The call itself finally stopped monopolising my thoughts – but as soon as I'd put it out of my mind, another set of concerns came floating up to take its place.

As I'd told the detective, Loraine had never been scanned. I had, though. High-resolution imaging techniques had been used to generate a detailed map of my body, down to the cellular level – a map which included, among other things, a description of every neuron in my brain, every synaptic connection. I had purchased a kind of immortality: whatever happened to me, the most recent snapshot of my body could always be resurrected as a Copy: an elaborate computer model, embedded in a virtual reality. A model which, at the very least, would act and think like me: it would share all my memories, my beliefs, my goals, my desires. Currently, such models ran slower than real time, their virtual environments were restrictive, and the telepresence robots meant to enable interaction with the physical world were a clumsy joke . . . but all of the technology was rapidly improving.

My mother had already been resurrected in the supercomputer known as Coney Island. My father had died before the process had become available. Loraine's parents were both still alive – and unscanned.

I'd been scanned twice, the last time three years before. I was long overdue for an update – but that would have meant facing up to the realities of my posthumous future, all over again. Loraine had never condemned me for my choice, and the prospect of my virtual resurrection didn't seem to bother her at all – but she'd made it clear that she wouldn't be joining me.

The argument was so familiar that I could run through it all in my head, without even waking her.

LORAINE: I don't want to be imitated by a computer after I'm dead. What use would that be to *me*?

DAVID: Don't knock imitation – *life* consists of imitation. Every organ in your body is constantly being rebuilt in its own image. Every cell that divides is dying and replacing itself with imposters. Your body doesn't contain a single atom you were born with – so what gives you your identity? It's a pattern of information, not a physical thing. And if a computer started imitating your body – instead of your body imitating itself – the only real difference would be that the computer would make fewer mistakes.

LORAINE: If that's what you believe . . . fine. But it's not the way I see things. And I'm as frightened of death as anyone — but being *scanned* wouldn't make me feel any better. It wouldn't make me feel immortal; it wouldn't comfort me at all. So why should I do it? Give me one good reason.

And I never could bring myself to say (not even then, in the safety of my imaginings): *Do it because I don't want to lose you. Do it for me.*

I spent the next morning dealing with the curator for a large insurance company, who was looking for a change of décor for a few hundred lobbies, elevators, and boardrooms, real and virtual. I had no trouble selling her some suitably dignified electronic wallpaper, by some suitably revered young talents.

Some starving artists put low-resolution roughs of their work into network galleries, hoping to strike a compromise between a version so crude as to be off-putting, and one so appealing as to make buying the real thing superfluous. Nobody will pay for art unseen — and in the network galleries, to *see* was to *own*.

Physical galleries — tightly run — remained the best solution. All my visitors were screened for microcameras and visual cortex taps; nobody left the building with anything more than an impression, without paying for it. If it had been lawful, I would have demanded blood samples, and refused entry to anyone with a genetic predisposition to eidetic memory.

In the afternoon, as always, I viewed the work of aspiring exhibitors. I finished watching the Kreyszig piece which had been interrupted the day before, and then started sifting through a great heap of lesser submissions. The process of deciding what would or wouldn't be acceptable to my corporate clientele required no intellectual or emotional exertion; after two decades in the business, it had become a purely mechanical act — as uninvolving, most of the time, as standing at a conveyor belt sorting nuts from bolts. My aesthetic judgement hadn't been blunted – if anything, it had become more finely honed – but only the most exceptional work evoked anything more from me than a – highly astute, unfailingly accurate – assessment of marketability.

When the image of the 'kidnapper' broke through on to the screen again, I wasn't surprised; the instant it happened, I realised that I'd been waiting for it all afternoon. And although I grew tense in anticipation of the unpleasantness to follow, at the same time, the opportunity of discovering more about the caller's true motives was, undeniably, welcome. I couldn't be fooled again, so what did I have to fear? Knowing that Loraine was safe, I could watch with a sense of detachment, and try to extract some clue as to what was really going on.

The mask said, 'We have your wife/Transfer half a million dollars/ Into this account/If you don't want her to/Suffer.'

The synthetic image of Loraine reappeared. I laughed uneasily. *What did these people expect me to believe?* I surveyed the picture coolly. What I could see of the dingy 'room' behind 'her' badly needed repainting – another laborious touch of 'realism' to contrast with the background for the other mask. This time, 'she' didn't seem to have been struggling – and there were no signs that 'she' had been physically ill-treated (it even looked like 'she' had had a chance to wash) – but there was an uncertainty in 'her' expression, a hint of subdued panic on 'her' face, which hadn't been there before.

Then she looked straight into the camera and said, 'David? They won't let me see you – but I know you're there. And I know you must be doing all you can to get me out of this – but please hurry. Please, pay them the money as soon as you can.'

My veneer of objectivity shattered. I *knew* it was just

an elaborate piece of computer animation – but listening to it 'pleading' with me this way was almost as distressing as the call I'd thought was real. It looked like Loraine, it sounded like Loraine; every word and gesture rang true. I couldn't throw a switch inside my head and turn off all my responses to the sight of someone I loved, begging for her life.

I covered my face and shouted, 'You sick *fuck* – is this how you get off? Do you think I'm going to *pay you* to stop this? I'll just get the phone fixed so you can't break through – then you can go back to running interactive snuff movies, and fucking your own corpse.'

There was no reply, and when I looked at the screen again, the call was over.

I waited until I'd stopped shaking – mostly with anger – then I called Detective Nicolson, for what that was worth. I gave him a copy of the call for his files; he thanked me. I told myself, optimistically: with computer analysis of *modus operandi*, every piece of evidence helps; if the same caller goes on to do the same thing to other people, the information collected might eventually coalesce into some kind of incriminating profile. The psychopathic piece of shit might even get caught one day.

Then I phoned the company which had supplied the office software, and explained what had been going on – leaving out details of the subject matter of the nuisance calls.

Their troubleshooter asked me to authorise a diagnostic link; I did so. She vanished for a minute or two. I thought: it will be something simple, and easily fixed – some trivial mistake in the security set-up.

The woman came on-screen again, looking wary.

'The software all seems fine – there's no evidence of tampering. And no evidence of unauthorised access. How long since you changed the breakthrough password?'

193

'Ah. I haven't. I haven't changed anything since the system was installed.'

'So it's been the same for the last five years? That's not good practice.'

I nodded repentantly, but said, 'I don't see how anyone could have discovered it. Even if they tried a few thousand random words—'

'You would have been notified on the fourth wrong guess. And there's a voiceprint check. Passwords are usually stolen by eavesdropping.'

'Well, the only other person who knows it is my wife – and I don't think she's ever even used it.'

'There are two authorised voiceprints on file. Whose is the other one?'

'Mine. In case I had to call the office management system from home. I've never done that, though – so I doubt the password has been spoken out loud since the day we installed the software.'

'Well, there's a log of both breakthrough calls—'

'That's no help. I record all my calls, I've already given copies to the police.'

'No, I'm talking about something else. For security reasons, the initial part of the call – when the password is actually spoken – is stored separately, in encrypted form. If you want to view it, I'll tell you how – but you'll have to speak the password yourself, to authorise the decoding.'

She explained the procedure, then went off-line. She didn't look happy at all. Of course, she didn't know that the caller had been imitating Loraine; she probably thought I was about to 'discover' that the threatening calls were coming from my wife.

She was wrong, of course – but so was I.

Five years is a long time to remember anything so trivial. I had to make three guesses before I got the password right.

I steeled myself for one more glimpse of the fake

Loraine, but the screen remained dark – and the voice that said 'Benvenuto' was my own.

When I arrived home, Loraine was still working, so I left her undisturbed. I went to my study and checked the terminal for mail. There was nothing new, but I scrolled back through the list of past items, until I came to the most recent video postcard from my mother, which had arrived about a month before. Because of the time-rate difference, talking face-to-face was arduous, so we kept in touch by sending each other these recorded monologues.

I told the terminal to replay it. There was something I half remembered at the end, something I wanted to hear again.

My mother had been slowly unageing her appearance ever since her resurrection in Coney Island; she now looked about thirty. She'd been working on her house, too – which had gradually mutated and expanded from a near-perfect model of her last real-world home, into a kind of eighteenth-century French mansion, all carved doors, Louis XV chairs, ornate wall hangings, and chandeliers.

She enquired dutifully about my health and Loraine's, the gallery, Loraine's drawings. She made a few acerbic comments on current political events – both inside and outside the Island. Her youthful appearance, her opulent surroundings, weren't acts of self-deception; she was *not* an old woman any more, she did *not* live in a four-room apartment. Pretending that she had no choice but to mimic her last few years of organic life would have been absurd. She knew *exactly* who and where she was – and she had every intention of making the best of it.

I'd planned to fast-forward through the small talk, but I didn't. I sat and listened to every word, transfixed by the image of this nonexistent woman's face, trying to make sense of my feelings for her, trying to untangle the roots of my empathy, my loyalty, my love . . . for this pattern of information copied from a body now long decayed.

Finally, she said, 'You keep asking me if I'm happy. If I'm ever lonely. If I've *found someone.*' She hesitated, then shook her head. 'I'm not lonely. You know your father died before this technology was perfected. And you know how much I loved him. Well, I still do; I still love him. He's not gone, any more than I am. He lives on in my memory – and that's enough. Here of all places, *that's enough.*'

The first time I'd heard these words, I'd thought she'd been speaking in uncharacteristic platitudes. Now, I thought I understood the barely intentional hint behind her reassurances, and a chill passed through me.

He lives on in my memory.

Here of all places, that's enough.

Of course they would have kept it quiet; the organic world wasn't ready to hear this – and Copies could afford to be patient.

That was why I hadn't yet heard from my mother's companion. He could wait however many decades it took for me to come to the Island 'in person' – and that's when he'd see me 'again'.

As the serving trolley unloaded the evening meal on to the dining room table, Loraine asked, 'Any more high-tech heavy breathing today?'

I shook my head slowly, over-emphatically, feeling like an adulterer – or worse. Inside, I was drowning, but if anything showed, Loraine gave no sign that she'd noticed.

She said, 'Well, it's hardly the kind of trick you can play twice on the same victim, is it?'

'No.'

In bed, I stared out into the suffocating darkness,

trying to decide what I was going to do . . . although the kidnappers no doubt knew the answer to that already – and they'd hardly have gone ahead with their plan if they hadn't believed I'd pay them, in the end.

Everything made sense now. Far too much sense. Loraine had no scan file – but they'd broken into mine. To what end? What use is a man's soul? Well, there's no need to guess, it will tell you. Extracting the office password would have been the least of it; they must have run my Copy through a few hundred virtual scenarios, and selected the one most likely to produce the largest return on their investment.

A few hundred resurrections, a few hundred different delusions of extortion, a few hundred deaths. I didn't care – the notion was far too bizarre, far too alien to move me – which was probably why there hadn't been a very different ransom demand: 'We have your Copy . . .'

And the fake Loraine – not even a Copy of the real woman, but a construct based entirely on my knowledge of her, my memories, my mental images – what empathy, what loyalty, what love did I owe *her*?

The kidnappers might not have fully reproduced the memory-resurrection technique invented in the Island. I didn't know what they'd actually created, what – if anything – they'd 'brought to life'. How elaborate was the computer model behind 'her' words, 'her' facial expressions, 'her' gestures? Was it complex enough to *experience* the emotions it was portraying – like a Copy? Or was it merely complex enough to sway *my emotions* – complex enough to manipulate me, without feeling a thing?

How could I know, one way or the other – how could I ever tell? I took the 'humanity' of my mother for granted – and perhaps she in turn did the same for my resurrected unscanned father, plucked from her virtual brain – but what would it take to convince me that *this* pattern of information was someone I should care about, someone who desperately needed my help?

I lay in the dark, beside the flesh-and-blood Loraine, and tried to imagine what the computer simulation of my mental image of her would be saying in a month's time.

IMITATION LORAINE: David? They tell me you're there, they tell me you can hear me. If that's true . . . I don't understand. Why haven't you paid them? Is something wrong? Are the police telling you not to pay? (Silence.) I'm all right, I'm hanging on – but I don't understand what's happening. (Long silence.) They're not treating me too badly. I'm sick of the food, but I'll live. They've given me some paper to draw on, and I've done a few sketches . . .

Even if I was never convinced, even if I was never certain, I'd always be wondering: *What if I'm wrong? What if she's conscious after all? What if she's every bit as human as I'll be when I'm resurrected – and I've betrayed her, abandoned her?*

I couldn't live with that. The possibility, and the appearance, would be enough to tear me apart.

And they knew it.

My financial management software laboured all night to free the money from investments. At nine o'clock the next morning, I transferred half a million dollars into the specified account, and then sat in my office waiting to see what would happen. I considered changing the breakthrough password back to the old 'Benvenuto' – but then decided that if they really had my scan file at their disposal, they'd have no trouble deducing my new choice.

At ten past nine, the kidnapper's mask appeared on the giant screen – and said bluntly, without poetic pretensions, 'The same again, in two years' time.'

I nodded. 'Yes.' I could raise it by then, without

Loraine knowing. Just.

'So long as you keep paying, we'll keep her frozen. No time, no experience – no distress.'

'Thank you.' I hesitated, then forced myself to speak. 'But in the end, when I'm—'

'What?'

'When I'm resurrected . . . you'll let her join me?'

The mask smiled magnanimously. 'Of course.'

I don't know how I'll begin to explain everything to the imitation Loraine – or what she'll do when she learns her true nature. Resurrection in the Island may be her idea of Hell – but what choice did I have? Leaving her to rot, for as long as the kidnappers believed her suffering might still move me? Or buying her freedom – *and then never running her again*?

When we're together in the Island, she can come to her own conclusions, make her own decisions. For now, all I can do is gaze up at the sky and hope that she really is safe in her unthinking stasis.

For now, I have a life to live with the flesh-and-blood Loraine. I have to tell her the truth, of course – and I run through the whole conversation, beside her in the dark, night after night.

DAVID: How could I not care about her? How could I let her suffer? How could I abandon someone who was – literally – built out of all my reasons for loving *you*?

LORAINE: An imitation of an imitation? There *was* no one suffering, no one waiting to be saved. No one to be rescued, or abandoned.

DAVID: Am I *no one*? Are you *no one*? Because that's all *we* can ever have of each other: an imitation, a Copy. All we can ever know about are the portraits of each other inside our own skulls.

LORAINE: Is that all you think I am? An idea in your head?

DAVID: No! But if it's all I have, then it's all I can honestly love. *Don't you see that?*

And, miraculously, she does. She finally understands.

Night after night.

I close my eyes and fall asleep, relieved.

LEARNING TO BE ME

I was six years old when my parents told me that there
was a small, dark jewel inside my skull, learning to be
me.

Microscopic spiders had woven a fine golden web
through my brain, so that the jewel's teacher could
listen to the whisper of my thoughts. The jewel itself
eavesdropped on my senses, and read the chemical
messages carried in my bloodstream; it saw, heard,
smelt, tasted and felt the world exactly as I did, while
the teacher monitored its thoughts and compared them
with my own. Whenever the jewel's thoughts were
wrong, the teacher – faster than thought – rebuilt the
jewel slightly, altering it this way and that, seeking out
the changes that would make its thoughts correct.

Why? So that when I could no longer be me, the jewel
could do it for me.

I thought: if hearing that makes *me* feel strange and
giddy, how must it make *the jewel* feel? Exactly the
same, I reasoned; it doesn't know it's the jewel, and it
too wonders how the jewel must feel, it too reasons:
'Exactly the same; it doesn't know it's the jewel, and it
too wonders how the jewel must feel . . .'

And it too wonders—

(I knew, because *I* wondered)

—it too wonders whether it's the real me, or whether
in fact it's only the jewel that's learning to be me.

★

As a scornful twelve-year-old, I would have mocked such childish concerns. Everybody had the jewel, save the members of obscure religious sects, and dwelling upon the strangeness of it struck me as unbearably pretentious. The jewel was the jewel, a mundane fact of life, as ordinary as excrement. My friends and I told bad jokes about it, the same way we told bad jokes about sex, to prove to each other how blasé we were about the whole idea.

Yet we weren't quite as jaded and imperturbable as we pretended to be. One day when we were all loitering in the park, up to nothing in particular, one of the gang – whose name I've forgotten, but who has stuck in my mind as always being far too clever for his own good – asked each of us in turn: 'Who *are* you? The jewel, or the real human?' We all replied – unthinkingly, indignantly – 'The real human!' When the last of us had answered, he cackled and said, 'Well, I'm not. *I'm* the jewel. So you can eat my shit, you losers, because *you'll* all get flushed down the cosmic toilet – but me, I'm gonna live forever.'

We beat him until he bled.

By the time I was fourteen, despite – or perhaps because of – the fact that the jewel was scarcely mentioned in my teaching machine's dull curriculum, I'd given the question a great deal more thought. The pedantically correct answer when asked 'Are you the jewel or the human?' had to be 'The human' – because only the human brain was physically able to reply. The jewel received input from the senses, but had no control over the body, and its intended reply coincided with what was actually said only because the device was a perfect imitation of the brain. To tell the outside world 'I am the jewel' – with speech, with writing, or with any other method involving the body – was patently false (although to *think it* to oneself was not ruled out by this line of reasoning).

However, in a broader sense, I decided that the question was simply misguided. So long as the jewel and the human brain shared the same sensory input, and so long as the teacher kept their thoughts in perfect step, there was only *one* person, *one* identity, *one* consciousness. This one person merely happened to have the (highly desirable) property that if *either* the jewel *or* the human brain were to be destroyed, he or she would survive unimpaired. People had always had two lungs and two kidneys, and for almost a century, many had lived with two hearts. This was the same: a matter of redundancy, a matter of robustness, no more.

That was the year that my parents decided I was mature enough to be told that they had both undergone the switch – three years before. I pretended to take the news calmly, but I hated them passionately for not having told me at the time. They had disguised their stay in hospital with lies about a business trip overseas. For three years I had been living with jewel-heads, and they hadn't even told me. It was *exactly* what I would have expected of them.

'We didn't seem any different to you, did we?' asked my mother.

'No,' I said – truthfully, but burning with resentment nonetheless.

'That's why we didn't tell you,' said my father. 'If you'd known we'd switched, at the time, you might have *imagined* that we'd changed in some way. By waiting until now to tell you, we've made it easier for you to convince yourself that we're still the same people we've always been.' He put an arm around me and squeezed me. I almost screamed out, 'Don't *touch* me!' but I remembered in time that I'd convinced myself that the jewel was No Big Deal.

I should have guessed that they'd done it, long before they confessed; after all, I'd known for years that most people underwent the switch in their early thirties. By then, it's downhill for the organic brain, and it would be foolish to have the jewel mimic this decline. So, the nervous system is rewired; the reins of the body are handed over to the jewel, and the teacher is deactivated. For a week, the outward-bound impulses from the brain are compared with those from the jewel, but by this time the jewel is a perfect copy, and no differences are ever detected.

The brain is removed, discarded, and replaced with a spongy tissue-cultured object, brain-shaped down to the level of the finest capillaries, but no more capable of thought than a lung or a kidney. This mock-brain removes exactly as much oxygen and glucose from the blood as the real thing, and faithfully performs a number of crude, essential biochemical functions. In time, like all flesh, it will perish and need to be replaced.

The jewel, however, is immortal. Short of being dropped into a nuclear fireball, it will endure for a billion years.

My parents were machines. My parents were gods. It was nothing special. I hated them.

When I was sixteen, I fell in love, and became a child again.

Spending warm nights on the beach with Eva, I couldn't believe that a mere machine could ever feel the way I did. I knew full well that if my jewel had been given control of my body, it would have spoken the very same words as I had, and executed with equal tenderness and clumsiness my every awkward caress — but I couldn't accept that its inner life was as rich, as miraculous, as joyful as mine. Sex, however pleasant, I could accept as a purely mechanical function, but there was something between us (or so I believed) that had nothing to do with lust, nothing to do with words, nothing to do with *any* tangible action of our bodies that some spy in the sand dunes with parabolic microphone and infrared binoculars might have discerned. After we made love, we'd gaze up in silence at the handful of visible stars, our souls conjoined in a secret place that no crystalline computer could hope to reach in a billion years of striving. (If I'd said *that* to my sensible, smutty, twelve-year-old self, he would have laughed until he haemorrhaged.)

I knew by then that the jewel's 'teacher' didn't monitor every single neuron in the brain. That would have been impractical, both in terms of handling the data, and because of the sheer physical intrusion into the tissue. Someone-or-other's theorem said that sampling certain critical neurons was almost as good as sampling the lot, and – given some very reasonable assumptions that nobody could disprove – bounds on the errors involved could be established with mathematical rigour.

At first, I declared that *within these errors*, however small, lay the difference between brain and jewel, between human and machine, between love and its imitation. Eva, however, soon pointed out that it was absurd to make a radical, qualitative distinction on the basis of the sampling density; if the next model teacher sampled more neurons and halved the error rate, would *its* jewel then be 'halfway' between 'human' and 'machine?' In theory – and eventually, in practice – the error rate could be made smaller than any number I cared to name. Did I really believe that a discrepancy of one in a billion made any difference at all – when every human being was permanently losing thousands of neurons every day, by natural attrition?

She was right, of course, but I soon found another, more plausible, defence for my position. Living neurons, I argued, had far more internal structure than the crude optical switches that served the same function in the jewel's so-called 'neural net'. That neurons fired

or did not fire reflected only one level of their behaviour; who knew what the subtleties of biochemistry
– the quantum mechanics of the specific organic
molecules involved – contributed to the nature of
human consciousness? Copying the abstract neural
topology wasn't enough. Sure, the jewel could pass the
fatuous Turing test – no outside observer could tell it
from a human – but that didn't prove that *being* a jewel
felt the same as *being* human.

Eva asked, 'Does that mean you'll never switch?
You'll have your jewel removed? You'll let yourself *die*
when your brain starts to rot?'

'Maybe,' I said. 'Better to die at ninety or a hundred
than kill myself at thirty, and have some machine
marching around, taking my place, pretending to be
me.'

'How do you know *I* haven't switched?' she asked,
provocatively. 'How do you know that I'm not just
"pretending to be me"?'

'I know you haven't switched,' I said, smugly. 'I just
know.'

'How? I'd look the same. I'd talk the same. I'd act the
same in every way. People are switching younger, these
days. *So how do you know I haven't?*'

I turned on to my side towards her, and gazed into
her eyes. 'Telepathy. Magic. The communion of souls.'

My twelve-year-old self started snickering, but by
then I knew exactly how to drive him away.

At nineteen, although I was studying finance, I took an
undergraduate philosophy unit. The Philosophy Department, however, apparently had nothing to say
about the Ndoli Device, more commonly known as
'the jewel'. (Ndoli had in fact called it 'the *dual*', but the
accidental, homophonic nickname had stuck.) They
talked about Plato and Descartes and Marx, they talked
about St Augustine and – when feeling particularly

modern and adventurous – Sartre, but if they'd heard of Godel, Turing, Hamsun or Kim, they refused to admit it. Out of sheer frustration, in an essay on Descartes I suggested that the notion of human consciousness as 'software' that could be 'implemented' equally well on an organic brain or an optical crystal was in fact a throwback to Cartesian dualism: for 'software' read 'soul'. My tutor superimposed a neat, diagonal, luminous red line over each paragraph that dealt with this idea, and wrote in the margin (in vertical, bold-face, twenty-point Times, with a contemptuous two-hertz flash): IRRELEVANT!

I quit philosophy and enrolled in a unit of optical crystal engineering for non-specialists. I learnt a lot of solid-state quantum mechanics. I learnt a lot of fascinating mathematics. I learnt that a neural net is a device used only for solving problems that are far too hard to be *understood*. A sufficiently flexible neural net can be configured by feedback to mimic almost any system – to produce the same patterns of output from the same patterns of input – but achieving this sheds no light whatsoever on the nature of the system being emulated.

'Understanding,' the lecturer told us, 'is an overrated concept. Nobody really *understands* how a fertilised egg turns into a human. What should we do? Stop having children until ontogenesis can be described by a set of differential equations?'

I had to concede that she had a point there.

It was clear to me by then that nobody had the answers I craved – and I was hardly likely to come up with them myself; my intellectual skills were, at best, mediocre. It came down to a simple choice: I could waste time fretting about the mysteries of consciousness, or, like everybody else, I could stop worrying and get on with my life.

When I married Daphne, at twenty-three, Eva was a

distant memory, and so was any thought of the communion of souls. Daphne was thirty-one, an executive in the merchant bank that had hired me during my PhD, and everyone agreed that the marriage would benefit my career. What she got out of it, I was never quite sure. Maybe she actually liked me. We had an agreeable sex life, and we comforted each other when we were down, the way any kind-hearted person would comfort an animal in distress.

Daphne hadn't switched. She put it off, month after month, inventing ever more ludicrous excuses, and I teased her as if I'd never had reservations of my own.

'I'm afraid,' she confessed one night. 'What if *I* die when it happens – what if all that's left is a robot, a puppet, a *thing*? I don't want to *die*.'

Talk like that made me squirm, but I hid my feelings. 'Suppose you had a stroke,' I said glibly, 'which destroyed a small part of your brain. Suppose the doctors implanted a machine to take over the functions which that damaged region had performed. Would you still be "yourself"?'

'Of course.'

'Then if they did it twice, or ten times, or a thousand times—'

'That doesn't necessarily follow.'

'Oh? At what magic percentage, then, would you stop being "you"?'

She glared at me. 'All the old clichéd arguments—'

'Fault them, then, if they're so old and clichéd.'

She started to cry. 'I don't have to. Fuck you! I'm scared to death, and you don't give a shit!'

I took her in my arms. 'Sssh. I'm sorry. But *every-one* does it sooner or later. You mustn't be afraid. I'm here. I love you.' The words might have been a re-cording, triggered automatically by the sight of her tears.

'Will you do it? With me?'

I went cold. 'What?'

'Have the operation, on the same day? Switch when I switch?'

Lots of couples did that. Like my parents. Sometimes, no doubt, it was a matter of love, commitment, sharing. Other times, I'm sure, it was more a matter of neither partner wishing to be an unswitched person living with a jewel-head.

I was silent for a while, then I said, 'Sure.'

In the months that followed, all of Daphne's fears – which I'd mocked as 'childish' and 'superstitious' – rapidly began to make perfect sense, and my own 'rational' arguments came to sound abstract and hollow. I backed out at the last minute; I refused the anaesthetic, and fled the hospital.

Daphne went ahead, not knowing I had abandoned her.

I never saw her again. I couldn't face her; I quit my job and left town for a year, sickened by my cowardice and betrayal – but at the same time euphoric that I had *escaped*.

She brought a suit against me, but then dropped it a few days later, and agreed, through her lawyers, to an uncomplicated divorce. Before the divorce came through, she sent me a brief letter:

> *There was nothing to fear, after all. I'm exactly the person I've always been. Putting it off was insane; now that I've taken the leap of faith, I couldn't be more at ease.*
> *Your loving robot wife,*
> *Daphne*

By the time I was twenty-eight, almost everyone I knew had switched. All my friends from university had done it. Colleagues at my new job, as young as twenty-one, had done it. Eva, I heard through a friend of a friend, had done it six years before.

The longer I delayed, the harder the decision became. I could talk to a thousand people who had switched, I could grill my closest friends for hours about their childhood memories and their most private thoughts, but however compelling their words, I knew that the Ndoli Device had spent decades buried in their heads, learning to fake exactly this kind of behaviour.

Of course, I always acknowledged that it was equally impossible to be *certain* that even another *unswitched* person had an inner life in any way the same as my own – but it didn't seem unreasonable to be more inclined to give the benefit of the doubt to people whose skulls hadn't yet been scraped out with a curette.

I drifted apart from my friends, I stopped searching for a lover. I took to working at home (I put in longer hours and my productivity rose, so the company didn't mind at all). I couldn't bear to be with people whose humanity I doubted.

I wasn't by any means unique. Once I started looking, I found dozens of organisations exclusively for people who hadn't switched, ranging from a social club that might as easily have been for divorcees, to a paranoid, paramilitary 'resistance front', who thought they were living out *Invasion of the Body Snatchers*. Even the members of the social club, though, struck me as extremely maladjusted; many of them shared my concerns, almost precisely, but my own ideas from other lips sounded obsessive and ill-conceived. I was briefly involved with an unswitched woman in her early forties, but all we ever talked about was our fear of switching. It was masochistic, it was suffocating, it was insane.

I decided to seek psychiatric help, but I couldn't bring myself to see a therapist who had switched. When I finally found one who hadn't, she tried to talk me into helping her blow up a power station, to let THEM know who was boss.

I'd lie awake for hours every night, trying to convince myself, one way or the other, but the longer I dwelt upon the issues, the more tenuous and elusive they became. Who was 'I', anyway? What did it mean that 'I' was 'still alive', when my personality was utterly different from that of two decades before? My earlier selves were as good as dead – I remembered them no more clearly than I remembered contemporary acquaintances – yet this loss caused me only the slightest discomfort. Maybe the destruction of my organic brain would be the merest hiccup, compared to all the changes that I'd been through in my life so far.

Or maybe not. Maybe it would be exactly like dying.

Sometimes I'd end up weeping and trembling, terrified and desperately lonely, unable to comprehend – and yet unable to cease contemplating – the dizzying prospect of my own nonexistence. At other times, I'd simply grow 'healthily' sick of the whole tedious subject. Sometimes I felt certain that the nature of the jewel's inner life was the most important question humanity could ever confront. At other times, my qualms seemed fey and laughable. Every day, hundreds of thousands of people switched, and the world apparently went on as always; surely that fact carried more weight than any abstruse philosophical argument?

Finally, I made an appointment for the operation. I thought, what is there to lose? Sixty more years of uncertainty and paranoia? If the human race *was* replacing itself with clockwork automata, I was better off dead; I lacked the blind conviction to join the psychotic underground – who, in any case, were tolerated by the authorities only so long as they remained ineffectual. On the other hand, if all my fears were unfounded – if my sense of identity could survive the switch as easily as it had already survived such traumas as sleeping and waking, the constant death of brain cells, growth, experience, learning and forgetting – then I would gain not only eternal life, but an end to my doubts and my alienation.

I was shopping for food one Sunday morning, two months before the operation was scheduled to take place, flicking through the images of an on-line grocery catalogue, when a mouthwatering shot of the latest variety of apple caught my fancy. I decided to order half a dozen. I didn't, though. Instead, I hit the key which displayed the next item. My mistake, I knew, was easily remedied; a single keystroke could take me back to the apples. The screen showed pears, oranges, grapefruit. I tried to look down to see what my clumsy fingers were up to, but my eyes remained fixed on the screen.

I panicked. I wanted to leap to my feet, but my legs would not obey me. I tried to cry out, but I couldn't make a sound. I didn't feel injured, I didn't feel weak. Was I paralysed? Brain-damaged? I could still *feel* my fingers on the keypad, the soles of my feet on the carpet, my back against the chair.

I watched myself order pineapples. I felt myself rise, stretch, and walk calmly from the room. In the kitchen, I drank a class of water. I should have been trembling, choking, breathless; the cool liquid flowed smoothly down my throat, and I didn't spill a drop.

I could only think of one explanation: *I had switched.* Spontaneously. The jewel had taken over, while my brain was still alive; all my wildest paranoid fears had come true.

While my body went ahead with an ordinary Sunday morning, I was lost in a claustrophobic delirium of helplessness. The fact that everything I did was exactly what I had planned to do gave me no comfort. I caught a train to the beach, I swam for half an hour; I might as well have been running amok with an axe, or crawling naked down the street, painted with my own excrement and howling like a wolf. *I'd lost control.* My body had turned into a living straitjacket, and I couldn't struggle, I couldn't scream, I couldn't even close my eyes. I saw my reflection, faintly, in a window on the train, and I couldn't begin to guess what the mind that ruled that bland, tranquil face was thinking.

Swimming was like some sense-enhanced, holo-graphic nightmare; I was a volitionless object, and the perfect familiarity of the signals from my body only made the experience more horribly *wrong*. My arms had no right to the lazy rhythm of their strokes; I wanted to thrash about like a drowning man, I wanted to show the world my distress.

It was only when I lay down on the beach and closed my eyes that I began to think rationally about my situation.

The switch *couldn't* happen 'spontaneously'. The idea was absurd. Millions of nerve fibres had to be severed and spliced, by an army of tiny surgical robots which weren't even present in my brain – which weren't due to be injected for another two months. Without delib-erate intervention, the Ndoli Device was utterly pas-sive, unable to do anything but *eavesdrop*. No failure of the jewel or the teacher could possibly take control of my body away from my organic brain.

Clearly, there had been a malfunction – but my first guess had been wrong, absolutely wrong.

I wish I could have done *something*, when the understanding hit me. I should have curled up, moan-ing and screaming, ripping the hair from my scalp, raking my flesh with my fingernails. Instead, I lay flat on my back in the dazzling sunshine. There was an itch behind my right knee, but I was, apparently, far too lazy to scratch it.

Oh, I ought to have managed, at the very least, a good, solid bout of hysterical laughter, when I realised that *I* was the jewel.

The teacher had malfunctioned; it was no longer

keeping me aligned with the organic brain. I hadn't suddenly become powerless; I had *always been* power-less. My will to act upon 'my' body, upon the world, had *always* gone straight into a vacuum, and it was only because I had been ceaselessly manipulated, 'corrected' by the teacher, that my desires had ever coincided with the actions that seemed to be mine.

There are a million questions I could ponder, a million ironies I could savour, but I *mustn't*. I need to focus all my energy in one direction. My time is running out.

When I enter hospital and the switch takes place, if the nerve impulses I transmit to the body are not exactly in agreement with those from the organic brain, the flaw in the teacher will be discovered. *And rectified.* The organic brain has nothing to fear; *his* continuity will be safeguarded, treated as precious, sacrosanct. There will be no question as to which of us will be allowed to prevail. *I* will be made to conform, once again. *I* will be 'corrected'. *I* will be murdered.

Perhaps it is absurd to be afraid. Looked at one way, I've been murdered every microsecond for the last twenty-eight years. Looked at another way, I've only existed for the seven weeks that have now passed since the teacher failed, and the notion of my separate identity came to mean anything at all – and in one more week this aberration, this nightmare, will be over. Two months of misery; why should I begrudge losing that, when I'm on the verge of inheriting eternity? Except that it won't be *I* who inherits it, since that two months of misery is all that defines me.

The permutations of intellectual interpretation are endless, but ultimately, I can only act upon my desperate will to survive. I don't *feel like* an aberration, a disposable glitch. How can I possibly hope to survive? I must conform – of my own free will. I must choose to make myself *appear* identical to that which they would force me to become.

After twenty-eight years, surely I am still close enough to him to carry off the deception. If I study every clue that reaches me through our shared senses, surely I can put myself in his place, forget, temporarily, the revelation of my separateness, and force myself back into synch.

It won't be easy. He met a woman on the beach, the day I came into being. Her name is Cathy. They've slept together three times, and he thinks he loves her. Or at least, he's said it to her face, he's whispered it to her while she's slept, he's written it, true or false, into his diary.

I feel nothing for her. She's a nice enough person, I'm sure, but I hardly know her. Preoccupied with my plight, I've paid scant attention to her conversation, and the act of sex was, for me, little more than a distasteful piece of involuntary voyeurism. Since I realised what was at stake, I've *tried* to succumb to the same emotions as my alter ego, but how can I love her when communication between us is impossible, when she doesn't even know *I* exist?

If she rules his thoughts night and day, but is nothing but a dangerous obstacle to me, how can I hope to achieve the flawless imitation that will enable me to escape death?

He's sleeping now, so I must sleep. I listen to his heartbeat, his slow breathing, and try to achieve a tranquillity consonant with these rhythms. For a moment, I am discouraged. Even my *dreams* will be different; our divergence is ineradicable, my goal is laughable, ludicrous, pathetic. Every nerve impulse, for a week? My fear of detection and my attempts to conceal it will, unavoidably, distort my responses; this knot of lies and panic will be impossible to hide.

Yet as I drift towards sleep, I find myself believing that I *will* succeed. I *must*. I dream for a while – a confusion of images, both strange and mundane, ending with a grain of salt passing through the eye of a needle – then I tumble, without fear, into dreamless oblivion.

I stare up at the white ceiling, giddy and confused, trying to rid myself of the nagging conviction that there's something I *must not* think about.

Then I clench my fist gingerly, rejoice at this miracle, and remember.

Up until the last minute, I thought he was going to back out again – but he didn't. Cathy talked him through his fears. Cathy, after all, has switched, and he loves her more than he's ever loved anyone before.

So, our roles are reversed now. This body is *his* straitjacket, now . . .

I am drenched in sweat. *This is hopeless, impossible.* I can't read his mind, I can't guess what he's trying to do. Should I move, lie still, call out, keep silent? Even if the computer monitoring us is programmed to ignore a few trivial discrepancies, as soon as *he* notices that his body won't carry out his will, he'll panic just as I did, and I'll have no chance at all of making the right guesses. Would *he* be sweating, now? Would *his* breathing be constricted, like this? *No.* I've been awake for just thirty seconds, and already I have betrayed myself. An optical-fibre cable trails from under my right ear to a panel on the wall. Somewhere, alarm bells must be sounding.

If I made a run for it, what would they do? Use force? I'm a citizen, aren't I? Jewel-heads have had full legal rights for decades; the surgeons and engineers can't do anything to me without my consent. I try to recall the clauses on the waiver he signed, but he hardly gave it a second glance. I tug at the cable that holds me prisoner, but it's firmly anchored, at both ends.

When the door swings open, for a moment I think

I'm going to fall to pieces, but from somewhere I find the strength to compose myself. It's my neurologist, Dr Prem. He smiles and says, 'How are you feeling? Not too bad?'

I nod dumbly.

'The biggest shock, for most people, is that they don't feel different at all! For a while you'll think, "It can't be this simple! It can't be this easy! It can't be this *normal*!" But you'll soon come to accept that *it is*. And life will go on, unchanged.' He beams, taps my shoulder paternally, then turns and departs.

Hours pass. *What are they waiting for?* The evidence must be conclusive by now. Perhaps there are procedures to go through, legal and technical experts to be consulted, ethics committees to be assembled to deliberate on my fate. I'm soaked in perspiration, trembling uncontrollably. I grab the cable several times and yank with all my strength, but it seems fixed in concrete at one end, and bolted to my skull at the other.

An orderly brings me a meal. 'Cheer up,' he says. 'Visiting time soon.'

Afterwards, he brings me a bedpan, but I'm too nervous even to piss.

Cathy frowns when she sees me. 'What's wrong?'

I shrug and smile, shivering, wondering why I'm even trying to go through with the charade. 'Nothing. I just . . . feel a bit sick, that's all.'

She takes my hand, then bends and kisses me on the lips. In spite of everything, I find myself instantly aroused. Still leaning over me, she smiles and says, 'It's over now, OK? There's nothing left to be afraid of. You're a little shook up, but you know in your heart you're still who you've always been. And I love you.'

I nod. We make small talk. She leaves. I whisper to myself, hysterically, 'I'm still who I've always been. I'm still who I've always been.'

★

Yesterday, they scraped my skull clean, and inserted my new, non-sentient, space-filling mock-brain.

I feel calmer now than I have for a long time, and I think at last I've pieced together an explanation for my survival.

Why do they deactivate the teacher, for the week between the switch and the destruction of the brain? Well, they can hardly keep it running while the brain is being trashed – but why an entire week? To reassure people that the jewel, unsupervised, can still stay in synch; to persuade them that the life the jewel is going to live will be exactly the life that the organic brain 'would have lived' – whatever that could mean.

Why, then, only for a week? Why not a month, or a year? Because the jewel *cannot* stay in synch for that long – not because of any flaw, but for precisely the reason that makes it worth using in the first place. The jewel is immortal. The brain is decaying. The jewel's imitation of the brain leaves out – deliberately – the fact that *real* neurons *die*. Without the teacher working to contrive, in effect, an identical deterioration of the jewel, small discrepancies must eventually arise. A fraction of a second's difference in responding to a stimulus is enough to arouse suspicion, and – as I know too well – from that moment on, the process of divergence is irreversible.

No doubt, a team of pioneering neurologists sat huddled around a computer screen, fifty years ago, and contemplated a graph of the probability of this radical divergence, versus time. How would they have chosen *one week*? What probability would have been acceptable? A tenth of a per cent? A hundredth? A thousandth? However safe they decided to be, it's hard to imagine them choosing a value low enough to make the phenomenon rare on a global scale, once a quarter of a million people were being switched every day.

In any given hospital, it might happen only once a

decade, or once a century, but every institution would still need to have a policy for dealing with the eventuality.

What would their choices be?

They could honour their contractual obligations and turn the teacher on again, erasing their satisfied customer, and giving the traumatised organic brain the chance to rant about its ordeal to the media and the legal profession.

Or, they could quietly erase the computer records of the discrepancy, and calmly remove the only witness.

So, this is it. Eternity.

I'll need transplants in fifty or sixty years' time, and eventually a whole new body, but that prospect shouldn't worry me – *I* can't die on the operating table. In a thousand years or so, I'll need extra hardware tacked on to cope with my memory storage requirements, but I'm sure the process will be uneventful. On a time scale of millions of years, the structure of the jewel is subject to cosmic-ray damage, but error-free transcription to a fresh crystal at regular intervals will circumvent that problem.

In theory, at least, I'm now guaranteed either a seat at the Big Crunch, or participation in the heat death of the universe.

I ditched Cathy, of course. I might have learnt to like her, but she made me nervous, and I was thoroughly sick of feeling that I had to play a role.

As for the man who claimed that he loved her – the man who spent the last week of his life helpless, terrified, suffocated by the knowledge of his impending death – I can't yet decide how I feel. I ought to be able to empathise – considering that I once expected to suffer the very same fate myself – yet somehow he simply isn't *real* to me. I know my brain was modelled on his – giving him a kind of causal primacy – but in spite of that, I think of him now as a pale, insubstantial shadow.

After all, I have no way of knowing if his sense of himself, his deepest inner life, his experience of *being*, was in any way comparable to my own.

THE MOAT

I'm first into the office, so I clean off the night's graffiti before clients start to arrive. It's not hard work; we've had all the external surfaces coated, so a scrubbing brush and warm water is all it takes. When I'm finished, I find I can scarcely remember what any of it said this time; I've reached the stage where I can stare at the slogans and insults without even reading them.

All the petty intimidation is like that; it's a shock at first, but eventually it just fades into a kind of irritating static. Graffiti, phone calls, hate mail. We used to get megabytes of automated invective via e-mail, but that, at least, turned out to be easily fixed; we installed the latest screening software, and fed it a few samples of the kind of transmission we preferred not to receive.

I don't know for certain who's coordinating all this aggravation, but it's not hard to guess. There's a group calling themselves Fortress Australia, who've started putting up posters on bus shelters: obscene caricatures of Melanesians, portrayed as cannibals adorned with human bones, leering over cooking pots filled with screaming white babies. The first time I saw one, I thought it was, surely, an advertisement for an exhibition of Racist Cartoons From Nineteenth-Century Publications; some kind of scholarly deconstruction of the sins of the distant past. When I finally realised that I was looking at real, contemporary propaganda, I didn't know whether to feel sickened – or heartened by the sheer crudity of the thing. I thought, so long as the anti-refugee groups keep insulting people's intelligence with shit like this, they're not likely to get much support beyond the lunatic fringe.

Some Pacific islands are losing their land slowly, year by year; others are being rapidly eroded by the so-called Greenhouse storms. I've heard plenty of quibbling about the precise definition of the term 'environmental refugee', but there's not much room for ambiguity when your home is literally vanishing into the ocean. Nevertheless, it still takes a lawyer to steer each application for refugee status through the tortuous bureaucratic processes. Matheson & Singh are hardly the only practice in Sydney to handle this kind of work, but for some reason we seem to have been singled out for harassment by the isolationists. Perhaps it's the premises; I imagine it takes a good deal less courage to daub paint on a converted terrace house in Newtown than to attack a gleaming office tower in Macquarie Street, bristling with security hardware.

It's depressing at times, but I try to keep a sense of perspective. Sweet FA will never be more than a bunch of thugs and vandals, high in nuisance value, but politically irrelevant. I've seen them on TV, marching around their 'training camps' in designer camouflage, or sitting in lecture theatres, watching recorded speeches by their guru, Jack Kelly, or (oblivious to the irony) messages of 'international solidarity' from similar organisations in Europe and North America. They get plenty of media coverage, but apparently it hasn't done much for their recruitment rate. Freak shows are like that; everybody wants to watch, but nobody wants to join.

Ranjit arrives a few minutes later, carrying a CD; he mimes staggering under its weight. 'Latest set of amendments to the UNHCR regulations. It's going to be a long day.'

I groan. 'I'm having dinner with Rachel tonight. Why don't we just feed the bloody thing to LEX and ask for a summary?'

'And get disbarred at the next audit? No thanks.' The Law Society has strict rules on the use of pseudo-intelligent software – terrified of putting ninety per cent of its members out of work. The irony is, they use state-of-the-art software, programmed with all the forbidden knowledge, to scrutinise each practice's expert systems and make sure that they haven't been taught more than they're permitted to know.

'There must be twenty firms, at least, who've taught their systems Tax Law—'

'Sure. And they have programmers on seven-figure salaries to cover their tracks.' He tosses me the CD. 'Cheer up. I had a quick peek at home – there are some good decisions buried in here. Just wait until you get to paragraph 983.'

'I saw the strangest thing at work today.'

'Yeah?' I feel queasy already. Rachel is a forensic pathologist; when she says *strange*, it's likely to mean that some corpse's liquefying flesh was a different colour than usual.

'I was examining a vaginal swab from a woman who'd been raped early this morning, and—'

'Oh, *please*—'

She scowls. 'What? You won't let me talk about autopsies, you won't let me talk about bloodstains. You're always telling me about your own boring work—'

'I'm sorry. Go on. Just . . . keep your voice down.' I glance around the restaurant. Nobody seems to be staring, yet, but I know from experience that there's something about discussions concerning genital secretions that seems to make the words carry further than other conversation.

'I was examining this swab. There were spermatozoa visible – and tests for other components of semen were positive – so there was no doubt whatsoever that this woman had had intercourse. I also found traces of serum proteins that didn't match her blood type. So far, just what you'd expect, OK? But when I did a DNA profile, the only genotype that showed up was the victim's.'

She looks at me pointedly, but the significance escapes me.

'Is that so unusual? You're always saying that things can go wrong with DNA tests. Samples get contaminated, or degraded—'

She cuts me off impatiently. 'Yes, but I'm not talking about some three-week-old bloodstained knife. This sample was taken half an hour after the crime. It reached me for analysis a couple of hours later. I saw undamaged sperm under the microscope; if I'd added the right nutrients, they would have started swimming before my eyes. That's not what I'd call *degraded*.'

'OK. You're the expert, I'll take your word for it: the sample wasn't degraded. Then what's the explanation?'

'I don't know.'

I try to dredge up enough of the two-week forensic science course I sat through ten years ago – as part of Criminal Law – to avoid making a complete fool of myself. 'Maybe the rapist just didn't have any of the genes you were looking for. Isn't the whole point that they're variable?'

She sighs. 'Variable *in length*. Restriction fragment length polymorphisms – RFLPs. They're not something that people simply "have" or "don't have". They're long stretches of the same sequence, repeated over and over; it's the number of repeats – the length – that varies from person to person. Listen, it's very simple: you chop up the DNA with restriction enzymes, and put the mixture of fragments on to an electrophoresis gel; the smaller the fragment, the faster it moves across the gel, so everything gets sorted out by size. Then you transfer the smeared-out sample from the gel on to a membrane – to fix it in place – and add radioactive probes; little pieces of complementary DNA that will only bind to the fragments you're interested in. Make a contact photograph of the radiation, to show where these probes have bound, and the pattern you get is a series of bands, one band for each different fragment length. Are you with me so far?'

'More or less.'

'Well, the pattern from the swab, and the pattern from a sample of the woman's blood, were completely identical. There were no extra bands from the rapist.'

I frown. 'Meaning what? His profile didn't show up in the test . . . or it was the same as hers? What if he's a close relative?'

She shakes her head. 'For a start, the odds are pretty tiny that even a brother could have inherited *exactly* the same set of RFLPs. But on top of that, the serum protein differences virtually rule out a family member.'

'Then what's the alternative? He has no profile? Is it absolutely certain that *everyone* has these sequences? I don't know . . . couldn't there be some kind of rare mutation, where they're missing completely?'

'Hardly. We look at ten different RFLPs. Everyone has two copies of each – one from each parent. The probability of anyone having *twenty* separate mutations—'

'I get the picture. OK, it's a mystery. So what do you do next? There must be other experiments you can try.'

She shrugs. 'We're only meant to do tests that are officially requested. I've reported the results, and nobody's said, "Drop everything and get some useful data out of that sample." There are no suspects in the case yet, anyway – or at least, we haven't been sent any samples to compare with the evidence. So the whole thing's academic, really.'

'So after earbashing me for ten minutes, you're just going to forget about it? I don't believe that. Where's your scientific curiosity?'

She laughs. 'I don't have time for luxuries like that. We're a production line, not a research lab. Do you know how many samples we process a day? I can't do a post-mortem on every swab that doesn't give perfect, textbook results.'

Our food arrives. Rachel attacks her meal with gusto; I pick at the edges of mine. Between mouthfuls, she says innocently, 'Not during working hours, that is.'

I stare at the TV screen with growing disbelief.

'So you're saying that Australia's fragile ecology simply can't support any further population growth?'

Senator Margaret Allwick is leader of the Green Alliance. Their slogan is: *One world, one future.* Or it was last time I voted for them.

'That's exactly right. Our cities are massively over-crowded; urban sprawl is encroaching on important habitats; new water supplies are getting harder to find. Of course, natural increase has to be reined in, too – but by far the greatest pressure is coming from immigration. Obviously, it's going to require some very complex policy initiatives, acting over decades, to get our birth rate under control – whereas the influx of migrants is a factor which can be adjusted very rapidly. The legislation we're introducing will take full advantage of that flexibility.'

Take full advantage of that flexibility. What does that mean? Slam the doors and pull up the drawbridge?

'Many commentators have expressed surprise that the Greens have found themselves siding on this issue with some of the most extreme far-right groups.'

The Senator scowls. 'Yes, but the comparison is fatuous. Our motives are entirely different. It's ecological destruction that's caused the refugee problem in the first place; putting more strain on our own delicate environment would hardly be helping things in the long term, would it? We must safeguard what we have, for the sake of our children.'

A subtitle flashes on to the screen: FEEDBACK ENABLED.

I hit the INTERACT button on the remote control, hurriedly compose my thoughts, then speak into the microphone. 'But what do these people do now? Where do they go? *Their* environments are not just "fragile" or "delicate"; they're disaster areas! Wherever a refugee is coming from, you can bet it's a place where overpopulation is doing a thousand times more damage than it is here.'

My words race down fibre-optic cables into the studio computer – along with those of a few hundred thousand other viewers. In a second or two, all the questions received will be interpreted, standardised, assessed for relevance and legal implications, and then ranked by popularity.

The simulacrum reporter says, 'Well, Senator, it seems that the viewers have voted for a commercial break now, so . . . thank you for your time.'

'My pleasure.'

As she undresses, Rachel says, 'You haven't been forgetting your shots, have you?'

'What? And risk losing my glorious physique?' One side effect of the contraceptive injections is increased muscle mass, although in truth it's barely noticeable.

'Just checking.'

She switches out the light and climbs into bed. We embrace; her skin is cold as marble. She kisses me gently, then says, 'I don't feel like making love tonight, OK? Just hold me.'

'OK.'

She's silent for a while, then she says, 'I did some more tests on that sample last night.'

'Yeah?'

'I separated out some of the spermatozoa, and tried to get a DNA profile from them. But the whole thing was blank, except for some faint non-specific binding at the very start of the gel. It's as if the restriction enzymes hadn't even cut the DNA.'

'Meaning what?'

'I'm not sure yet. At first I thought, maybe this guy's done some tampering – infected himself with an engineered virus, which got into the stem cells in the bone marrow and the testis and chopped out all the sequences we use for profiling.'

'Urk. Isn't that rather extreme? Why not just use a condom?'

'Well, yes. Most rapists do. And it makes no sense in any case; if someone wanted to avoid identification, cutting out the sequences completely would be stupid. Far better to make random changes – that would muddy the water, screw up the tests, without being so obvious.'

'But . . . if a mutation's too improbable, and deleting the sequences intentionally is stupid, what's left? I mean, the sequences *are not there*, are they? You've proved that.'

'Hang on, there's more. I tried amplifying a gene with the polymerase chain reaction. A gene everybody has in common. In fact, a gene every organism on this planet *back to yeast* has in common.'

'And?'

'Nothing. Not a trace.'

My skin crawls, but I laugh. 'What are you trying to say? He's an alien?'

'With human-looking sperm, and human blood proteins? I doubt it.'

'What if the sperm were . . . malformed somehow? I

228

don't mean degraded by exposure – but abnormal to start with. Genetically damaged. Missing parts of chromosomes . . . ?'

'They look perfectly healthy to me. And I've *seen* the chromosomes; they look normal too.'

'Apart from the fact that they don't seem to contain any genes.'

'None that I've looked for; that's a long way from none at all.' She shrugs. 'Maybe there's something contaminating the sample, something which has bound to the DNA, blocking the polymerase and the restriction enzymes. Why it's only affected the rapist's DNA, I don't know – but different types of cells are permeable to different substances. It can't be ruled out.'

I laugh. 'After all this fuss . . . isn't that what I said in the first place? Contamination?'

She hesitates. 'I do have another theory – although I haven't been able to test it, yet. I don't have the right reagents.'

'Go on.'

'It's pretty far-fetched.'

'More so than aliens and mutants?'

'Maybe.'

'I'm listening.'

She shifts in my arms. 'Well . . . you know the structure of DNA: two helical strands of sugar and phosphate, joined by the base pairs which carry the genetic information. The natural base pairs are adenine and thymine, cytosine and guanine . . . but people *have* synthesised other bases, and incorporated them into DNA and RNA. And around the turn of the century, a group in Berne actually constructed an entire bacterium that used non-standard bases.'

'You mean, they rewrote the genetic code?'

'Yes and no. They kept the code, but they changed the alphabet; they just substituted a new base for each old one, consistently throughout. The hard part wasn't making the non-standard DNA; the hard part was adapting the rest of the cell to make sense of it. The ribosomes – where RNA gets translated into proteins – had to be redesigned, and they had to alter almost every enzyme that interacted with DNA or RNA. They also had to invent ways for the cell to manufacture the new bases. And of course, all these changes had to be encoded in the genes.

'The whole point of the exercise was to circumvent fears about recombinant DNA techniques – because if *these* bacteria escaped, their genes could never cross over into any wild strains; no natural organism could possibly make use of them. Anyway, the whole idea turned out to be uneconomical. There were cheaper ways to meet the new safety requirements, and there was just too much hard work involved in "converting" each new species of bacterium that the biotechnologists might have wanted to use.'

'So . . . what are you getting at? Are you saying these bacteria are still around? The rapist has some mutant venereal disease, which is screwing up your tests?'

'No, no. Forget the bacteria. But suppose someone went further. Suppose someone went on and did the same thing with multicellular organisms.'

'Well, did they?'

'Not openly.'

'You think someone did this with animals, in secret? And then what? *Did it with humans?* You think some-one's raised *human beings* with this . . . alternative DNA?' I stare at her horrified. '*That* is the most obscene thing I have ever heard.'

'Don't get all worked up. It's just a theory.'

'But . . . what would they be like? What would they *live on*? Could they eat normal food?'

'Sure. All their proteins would be built from the same amino acids as ours. They'd have to synthesise the non-standard bases from precursors in their food – but ordinary people have to synthesise the *standard* bases, so that's no big deal. If all the details had been worked out properly – if all the hormones and enzymes that bind to DNA had been appropriately modified – they wouldn't be sick, or deformed, in any way. They'd look perfectly normal. Ninety per cent of every cell in their body would be just the same as ours.'

'But . . . why do it in the first place? The bacteria were for a reason, but what conceivable advantage is there for a human being to have non-standard DNA? Besides screwing up forensic tests.'

'I've thought of one thing; they'd be immune to viruses. All viruses.'

'Why?'

'Because a virus needs all the cellular machinery that works with *normal* DNA and RNA. Viruses would still be able to get into these people's cells – but once they were inside, they wouldn't be able to reproduce. With everything in the cell adapted to the new system, a virus made up of standard bases would just be a piece of meaningless junk. *No* virus that harms ordinary people could harm someone with non-standard DNA.'

'OK, so these hypothetical tailor-made children can't catch influenza, or AIDS, or herpes. So what? If someone was serious about wiping out viral diseases, they'd concentrate on methods that would work for *everyone*: cheaper drugs and vaccines. What use would this technology be in Zaire or Uganda? It's ludicrous! I mean, how many people do they think would *want* to have children this way, even if they could afford it?'

Rachel gives me an odd look, then says, 'Obviously, it would only be for a wealthy élite. And as for other kinds of treatment: viruses *mutate*. New strains come along. In time, any drug or vaccine can lose its effectiveness. *This* immunity would last forever. No amount of mutation could ever produce a virus built

231

out of anything but the old bases.'

'Sure, but . . . but this "wealthy élite" with lifelong immunity – mostly to diseases they're not likely to catch in the first place – wouldn't even be able to have children, would they? Not by normal means.'

'Except with each other.'

'Except with each other. Well, that sounds like a pretty drastic side effect to me.'

She laughs, and suddenly relaxes. 'You're right, of course . . . and I told you: I have no evidence, this is all pure fantasy. The reagents I need should arrive in a couple of days; then I can test for the alternative bases – and rule out the whole crazy idea, once and for all.'

It's almost eleven when I realise that I'm missing two important files. I can't phone the office computer from home; certain classes of legal documents are required to reside only on systems with no connection whatsoever to public networks. So I have no choice but to go in, in person, and copy the files.

I spot the graffitist from a block away. He looks about twelve years old. He's dressed in black, but otherwise doesn't seem too worried about being seen – and his brazenness is probably justified; cyclists go by, ignoring him, and patrol cars are scarce around here. At first, I'm simply irritated; it's late and I've got work to do. I'm not in the mood for confrontation. The easiest thing, by far, might be to wait until he's gone.

Then I catch myself. *Am I that apathetic?* I couldn't care less if graffiti artists redecorated every last building and train in the city – but this is racist poison. Racist poison that I waste twenty minutes cleaning away, every morning.

I draw closer, still unnoticed. Before I can change my mind, I slip through the wrought-iron gate, which he's left ajar; the lock was smashed months ago, and we've never bothered replacing it. As I move across the courtyard, he hears me and spins around. He steps towards me and raises the paint gun to eye level, but I knock it out of his hand. *That* makes me angry; I could have been blinded. He runs for the fence, and gets halfway up; I grab him by the belt of his jeans and haul him down. Just as well; the spikes are sharp, and rusty.

I let go of his belt, and he turns around slowly, glaring at me, trying to look menacing but failing badly. 'Keep your fucking hands off me! You're not a cop.'

'Ever heard of citizen's arrest?' I step back and push the gate shut. So, what now? Invite him inside so I can phone the police?

He grabs hold of a fence railing; clearly, he's not going anywhere without a struggle. Shit. What am I going to do – drag him into the building, kicking and screaming? I don't have much stomach for assaulting children, and I'm on shaky legal ground already.

So it's stalemate.

I lean against the gate.

'Just tell me one thing.' I point at the wall. '*Why?* Why do you do it?'

He snorts. 'I could ask you the same fucking question.'

'About what?'

'About helping *them* stay in the country. Taking our jobs. Taking our houses. Fucking things up for all of us.'

I laugh. 'You sound like my grandfather. *Them* and *us*. That's the kind of twentieth-century bullshit that wrecked the planet. You think you can build a fence around this country and just forget about everything outside? Draw some artificial line on a map, and say, people inside matter, people outside don't?'

'Nothing artificial about the ocean.'

'No? They'll be pleased to hear that in Tasmania.'

He just scowls at me, disgusted. There's nothing to

communicate, nothing to understand. The anti-refugee lobby are always talking about *preserving our common values*; that's pretty funny. Here we are, two Anglo-Australians – probably born in the very same city – and our values couldn't be further apart if we'd come from different planets.

He says, '*We* didn't ask them to breed like vermin. It's not our fault. So why should we help them? Why should *we* suffer? They can all just fuck off and die. Drown in their own shit and die. That's what I think, OK?'

I step away from the gate and let him pass. He crosses the steet, then turns to yell obscenities. I go inside and get the bucket and scrubbing brush, but all I end up doing is smearing wet paint across the wall.

By the time I've plugged my laptop into the office machine, I'm not angry, or even depressed, any more; I'm simply numb.

Just to complete the perfect evening, halfway through transferring one of my files, the power fails. I sit in the dark for an hour, waiting to see if it will come back on, but it doesn't, so I walk home.

Things are looking up, there's no doubt about it.

The Allwick Bill was defeated – and the Greens have a new leader, so there's hope for them yet.

Jack Kelly is in prison for arms smuggling. Sweet FA still put up their moronic posters – but there's a group of antifascist students who spend their spare time tearing them down. Since Ranjit and I scraped up enough money for an alarm system, there's been no more graffiti, and lately even the threatening letters have become rare.

Rachel and I are married now. We're happy together, and happy in our jobs. She's been promoted to laboratory manager, and the work at Matheson & Singh is booming – even the kind that pays. I really couldn't ask for more. Sometimes we talk about adopting a child, but the truth is we don't have the time.

We don't often talk about the night I caught the graffitist. The night the inner city was blacked out, for six hours. The night several freezers full of forensic samples were spoiled. Rachel refuses to entertain any paranoid theories about this; the evidence is gone, she says. Speculation is pointless.

I do sometimes wonder, though, just how many people there might be who hold the very same views as that screwed-up child. Not in terms of nations, not in terms of race; but people who've marked their very own lines to separate *us* and *them*. Who aren't buffoons in jackboots, parading for the cameras; who are intelligent, resourceful, far-sighted. And silent.

And I wonder what kind of fortresses they're building.

THE WALK

Leaves and twigs crunch underfoot with every step; no gentle rustling, but the sharp, snapping sounds of irrevocable, unrepeatable damage – as if to hammer into my brain the fact that no one else has come this way for some time. Every footfall proclaims that there'll be no help, no interruptions, no distractions.

I've felt weak and giddy since we left the car – and part of me is still hoping that I'll simply pass out, collapse on the spot and never get up again. My body, though, shows no signs of obliging: it stubbornly acts as if each step forward is the easiest thing in the world, as if its sense of balance is unimpaired, as if all the fatigue and nausea are entirely within my head. I could fake it: I could sink to the ground and refuse to stir. *Get it over with*.

I don't, though.

Because I don't want it to be *over*.

I try again.

'Carter, you could be *rich*, man. I'd work for you for the rest of my life.' Good touch, that: *my* life, not *your* life; makes it sound like a better deal. 'You know how much I made for Finn, in *six months*? Half a million! Add it up.'

He doesn't reply. I stop walking, and turn back to face him. He halts too, keeping his distance. Carter doesn't look much like an executioner. He must be close to sixty: grey-haired, with a weathered, almost

237

kindly face. He's still solidly built, but he looks like someone's once athletic grandfather, a boxer or a football player forty years ago, now into vigorous gardening.

He calmly waves me on with the gun.

'Further. We've passed the people-taking-a-piss zone, but campers, bush walkers . . . you can't be too careful.'

I hesitate. He gives me a gently admonishing look. *If I stood my ground?* He'd shoot me right here, and carry the body the rest of the way. I can see him trudging along, with my corpse slung casually across his shoulders. However *decent* he might seem at first glance, the truth is, the man's a fucking robot: he's got some kind of neural implant, some bizarre religion; everybody knows that.

I whisper, 'Carter . . . *please.*'

He gestures with the gun.

I turn and start walking again.

I still don't understand how Finn caught me out. I thought I was the best hacker he had. Who could have followed my trail, from the outside? *Nobody!* He must have planted someone inside one of the corporations I was screwing on his behalf – just to check up on me, the paranoid bastard. And I never kept more than ten per cent. I wish I'd taken fifty. I wish I'd made it worthwhile.

I strain my ears, but I can't pick up the faintest hint of traffic, now; just birdsong, insects, the crackling of the forest's debris underfoot. Fucking *nature*. I refuse to die here. I want to end my life like a human being: in Intensive Care, high on morphine, surrounded by cripplingly expensive doctors and brutal, relentless life-support machines. Then the corpse can go into orbit – preferably around the sun. I don't care how much it costs, just so long as I don't end up part of any fucking natural cycle: carbon, phosphorus, nitrogen.

Gaia, I divorce thee. Go suck the nutrients out of someone else, you grasping bitch.

Wasted anger, wasted time. *Please don't kill me, Carter: I can't bear to be absorbed back into the unthinking biosphere.* That'd really move him.

What, then?

'I'm *twenty-five years old*, man. I haven't even *lived.* I've spent the last ten years farting around with computers. I don't even have any kids. How can you kill someone who hasn't even had kids?' For a second, seduced by my own rhetoric, I seriously think about claiming virginity – but that might be pushing it . . . and it sounds less selfish, less hedonistic, to assert my right to fatherhood than to whine about sex.

Carter laughs. 'You want immortality through *children*? Forget it. I've got two sons, myself. They're nothing like me. They're total strangers.'

'Yeah? That's sad. But I still ought to have the chance.'

'The chance to do what? To pretend that you'll live on through your children? To fool yourself?'

I laugh knowingly – trying to make it sound like we're sharing a joke that only two like-minded cynics could appreciate.

'Of course I want a chance to *fool myself.* I want to lie to myself for fifty more years. Sounds pretty good to me.'

He doesn't reply.

I slow down slightly, shortening my stride, feigning trouble with the uneven terrain. *Why?* Do I seriously think that a few extra minutes will give me the chance to formulate some dazzlingly brilliant plan? Or am I just buying time for the sake of it? Just prolonging the agony?

I pause, and suddenly find myself retching; the convulsions run deep, but nothing comes up except a faint taste of acid. When it's over, I wipe the sweat and tears from my face, and try to stop shaking – hating more than anything the fact that I care about my *dignity*, the fact that I *do* give a shit whether or not I die in a pool of vomit, weeping like a child. As if this walk to my death is all that matters, now; as if these last few minutes of my life have superseded everything else.

They have, though, haven't they? Everything else is past, is gone.

Yes – and so will this be *gone*. If I am going to die, there's no need to 'make peace' with myself, no reason to 'compose myself' for death. The way I face extinction is just as fleeting, just as irrelevant, as the way I faced every other moment of my life.

The one and only thing that could make this time *matter* would be finding a way to survive.

When I catch my breath, I try to stretch out the delay.

'Carter, how many times have you done this?'

'Thirty-three.'

Thirty-three. That's hard enough to swallow when some jilted gun fetishist squeezes the trigger of his sub-machine-gun and firehoses a crowd, but thirty-three leisurely strolls into the forest . . .

'So tell me: how do most people take it? I really want to know. Do they puke? Do they cry? Do they beg?'

He shrugs. 'Sometimes.'

'Do they try to bribe you?'

'Almost always.'

'But you can't be bought?'

He doesn't reply.

'Or – has nobody made the right offer? What do you want, if it isn't money? *Sex?*' His face remains impassive – there's no scowl of revulsion – so instead of making a joke of it, retracting what might have been an insult, I press on, light-headed. 'Is that it? Do you want me to suck your cock? If that's what you want, I'll do it.'

He gives me that admonishing look again. No

240

contempt for my spineless pleading, no disgust at my misjudged offer; just the mildest irritation that I'm wasting his time.

I laugh weakly, to hide my humiliation at this absolute indifference – this refusal to find me even pitiful.

I say, 'So, people take it pretty badly. How do *you* take it?'

He says, matter-of-factly, 'I take it pretty well.'

I wipe my face again. 'Yeah, you do, don't you? Is that what the chip in your brain is for? To let you sleep at night after you've done this?'

He hesitates, then says, 'In a way. But it's not as simple as that.' He waves the gun. 'Get moving. We've still got further to go.'

I turn, thinking numbly: *I've just told the one man who could save my life that he's a brain-damaged, subhuman killing machine.*

I start walking again.

I glance up, once, at the blank idiot sky, and refuse to take delivery of the flood of memories linked in my mind to the same astonishing blue. *All of that is gone, it's over.* No Proustian flashbacks, no Billy Pilgrim time-tripping for me. I have no need to flee into the past: I'm going to live into the future, I'm going to survive this. *How?* Carter may be merciless, and incorruptible – in which case, I'm simply going to have to overpower him. I may have led a sedentary existence, but I'm less than half his age; that has to count for something. At the very least, I must be faster on my feet. *Overpower him? Struggle with a loaded gun?* Maybe I won't have to; maybe I'll get a chance to *run*.

Carter says, 'Don't waste your time trying to think up ways to bargain with me. It's not going to happen. You'd be better off thinking of ways to accept the inevitable.'

'I don't want to fucking *accept it*.'

'That's not true. You don't want it to happen – but it *will* happen. So find a way to deal with it. You must have thought about death, before now.'

This is all I need: grief counselling from my own assassin.
'If you want to know the truth: not once. One more thing I never got around to. So why don't you give me a decade or two to sort it out?'

'It won't take a decade. It won't take long at all. Look at it this way: Does it bother you that there are places outside your skin – *and you're not in them*? That you come to a sudden end at the top of your skull – and then there's nothing but air? Of course not. So why should it bother you that there'll be times when you won't be around – any more than you care that there are places you don't occupy? You think your life is going to be undone – cancelled out, somehow – just because it has an end? Does the space above your head cancel out your body? Everything has *boundaries*. Nothing stretches on forever – in any direction.'

In spite of myself, I laugh; he's gone from the sadistic to the surreal. 'You believe that shit, do you? You actually think that way?'

'No. I could have; it's on the market – and I seriously considered buying it. It's a perfectly valid point of view . . but in the end, it just didn't ring true for me – and I didn't *want it* to ring true. I chose something else entirely. Stop here.'

'What?'

'I said stop.'

I look around, bewildered, refusing to believe that we've *arrived*. We're nowhere special – hemmed in, as ever, between the ugly eucalypts; calf deep in the drought-shrivelled undergrowth – but what did I expect? *An artificial clearing? A picnic spot?*

I turn to face him, scouring my paralysed brain for some strategy to get within reach of the gun – or get out of his range before he can fire – when he says, with

242

perfect sincerity, 'I can help you. I can make this easier.'
I stare at him for a second, then break into long, clumsy,
choking sobs.

He waits, patiently, until I finally manage to cough
up the word: 'How?'

With his left hand, he reaches into his shirt pocket,
takes out a small object, and holds it up for inspection
on his outstretched palm. For a moment, I think it's a
capsule, some kind of drug – but it's not.

Not quite.

It's a neural implant applicator. Through the transparent casing, I can just make out the grey speck of the
implant itself.

I have an instant, vivid fantasy of walking forward to
accept it: my chance, at last, to disarm him.

'Catch.' He tosses the device straight at my face, and I
put up a hand and grab it from the air.

He says, 'It's up to you, of course. I'm not going to
force you to use it.'

Flies settle on my wet face as I stare at the thing. I
brush them away with my free hand. 'What'll this give
me? Twenty seconds of cosmic bliss before you blow
my brains out? Some hallucination so vivid it'll make
me think this was all a dream? If you wanted to spare me
the pain of knowing I was going to die, you should have
just shot me in the back of the head five minutes ago,
when I still thought I had a chance.'

He says, 'It's not a hallucination. It's a set of . . .
attitudes. A philosophy, if you like.'

'What *philosophy*? All that crap about . . . *boundaries
in space and time*?'

'No. I told you, I didn't buy that.'

I almost crack up. 'So this is *your religion*? You want
to convert me, before you kill me? You want to save my
fucking *soul*? Is that how you cope with slaughtering
people? *You think you're saving their souls?*'

He shakes his head, unoffended. 'I wouldn't call it a

243

religion. There is no god. There are no souls.'

'No? Well, if you're offering me all the comforts of atheism, I don't need an implant for that.'

'Are you afraid of dying?'

'What do you think?'

'If you use the implant, you won't be.'

'You want to render me terminally brave, and then kill me? Or terminally *numb*? I'd rather be blissed out.'

'Not brave. Or numb. Perceptive.'

He may not have found me pitiful, but I'm still human enough to do him the honour. '*Perceptive?* You think swallowing some pathetic lie about death is *perceptive?*'

'No lies. This implant won't change your beliefs on any question of fact.'

'I don't *believe* in life after death, so—'

'Whose life?'

'What?'

'When you die, will other people live on?'

For a moment, I just can't speak. I'm fighting for my life – and he's treating the whole thing like some abstract philosophical debate. I almost scream: *Stop playing with me! Get it over with!*

But I don't want it to be *over*.

And as long as I can keep him talking, there's still the chance that I can rush him, the chance of a distraction, the chance of some miraculous reprieve.

I take a deep breath. 'Yes, *other people will live on*.'

'Billions. Perhaps hundreds of billions, in centuries to come.'

'No shit. I've never believed that the universe would vanish when I died. But if you think that's some great consolation—'

'How different can two humans be?'

'I don't know. You're pretty fucking *different*.'

'Out of all those hundreds of billions, don't you think there'll be people who are *just like you*?'

'What are you talking about now? Reincarnation?'

'No. Statistics. There can be no "reincarnation" – there are no souls to be reborn. But eventually – by pure chance – someone will come along who'll embody everything that defines you.'

I don't know why, but the crazier this gets, the more hopeful I'm beginning to feel – as if Carter's crippled powers of reasoning might make him vulnerable in other ways.

I say, 'That's just not true. How could anyone end up with my memories, my experiences—'

'Memories don't matter. Your experiences don't define you. The accidental details of your life are as superficial as your appearance. They may have shaped who you are – but they're not an intrinsic part of it. There's a core, a deep abstraction—'

'A soul by any other name.'

'No.'

I shake my head, vehemently. There's nothing to be gained by humouring him; I'm too bad an actor to make it convincing – and an argument can only buy me more time.

'You think I should feel better about dying because . . . sometime in the future, some total stranger might have a few abstract traits in common with me?'

'You said that you wished you'd had children.'

'I lied.'

'Good. Because they're not the answer.'

'And I should get more comfort from the thought of someone who's no relation at all, with no memories of mine, no sense of continuity—'

'How much do you have in common, now, with yourself when you were five years old?'

'Not much.'

'Don't you think there must be thousands of people who are infinitely more like you – as you are now – than

245

that child ever was?'

'Maybe. In some ways, maybe.'

'What about when you were ten? Fifteen?'

'What does it matter? OK: people change. *Slowly. Imperceptibly.*'

He nods. 'Imperceptibly – exactly! But does that make it any less *real*? Who's swallowed the lie? It's seeing the life of your body as the life of *one person* that's the illusion. The idea that "you" are made up of all the events since your birth is nothing but a useful fiction. That's not a person: it's a composite, a mosaic.'

I shrug. 'Perhaps. It's still the closest thing to . . . *an identity* . . . that anyone can possess.'

'But it isn't! And it distracts us from the truth!' Carter is growing impassioned, but there's no hint of fanaticism in his demeanour. I almost wish he'd start ranting – but instead he continues, more calmly, more reasonably than ever. 'I'm not saying that memories make no difference; of course they do. But there's a part of you that's independent of them – and that part will live again. One day, someone, somewhere, will think as you did, act as you did. Even if it's only for a second or two, *that person will be you.*'

I shake my head. I'm beginning to feel stupefied by this relentless dream-logic – and I'm dangerously close to losing touch with what's at stake.

I say flatly, 'This is bullshit. Nobody could think that way.'

'You're wrong. *I do.* And you can – if you want to.'

'Well, I don't *want to.*'

'I know it seems absurd to you, now – but I promise you, the implant would change all that.' He absent-mindedly massages his right forearm. It must be stiff from holding the gun. 'You can die afraid, or you can die reassured. It's your decision.'

I close my fist over the applicator. 'Do you offer this to all your victims?'

'Not all. A few.'

'And how many have used it?'

'None so far.'

'I'm not surprised. Who'd want to die like that? Fooling themselves?'

'You said you did.'

'Live. I said I wanted to *live*, fooling myself.'

I brush the flies from my face, for the hundredth time; they alight again, fearlessly. Carter is five metres away; if I take a step in his direction, he'll shoot me in the head, without the slightest hesitation. I strain my ears, and hear nothing but crickets.

Using the implant would buy me more time: the four or five minutes before it takes effect. What have I got to lose? *Carter's reluctance to kill me, 'unenlightened'?* In the end, that's made no difference, thirty-three times before. *My will to stay alive?* Maybe; maybe not. A change in my intellectual views about mortality need not render me utterly supine; even believers in a glorious afterlife have been known to struggle hard to postpone the trip.

Carter says softly, 'Make up your mind. I'm going to count to ten.'

The chance to die honestly? The chance to cling to my own fear and confusion to the end?

Fuck that. If I die, then it makes no difference *how I faced it.* That's *my* philosophy.

I say, 'Don't bother.' I push the applicator deep into my right nostril, and squeeze the trigger. There's a faint sting as the implant burrows into my nasal membranes, heading for the brain.

Carter laughs with delight. I almost join him. *From out of nowhere, I have five more minutes to save my life.*

I say, 'OK, I've done what you wanted. But everything I said before still stands. Let me live, and I'll make you rich. A million a year. *At least.*'

He shakes his head. 'You're dreaming. Where would

I go? Finn would track me down in a week.'

'You wouldn't need to *go* anywhere. I'd skip the country – and I'd pay your money into an Orbital account.'

'Yeah? Even if you did, what use would the money be to me? I couldn't risk spending it.'

'Once you had enough, you could buy some security. Buy some independence. Start disentangling yourself from Finn.'

'No.' He laughs again. 'Why are you still looking for a way out? Don't you understand? *There's no need.*'

By now, the implant must have disgorged its nanomachines, to build links between my brain and the tiny optical processor whose neural net embodies Carter's bizarre beliefs. Short-circuiting my own attitudes; hard-wiring his insanity into my brain. But no matter – I can always get it removed; that's the easiest thing in the world. *If it's still what I want.*

I say, 'There's *no need* for anything. There's *no need* for you to kill me. We can still both walk out of here. Why do you act like you have no choice?'

He shakes his head. 'You're dreaming.'

'Fuck you! *Listen to me!* All Finn has is *money*. I can ruin him, if that's what it takes. From the other side of the world!' I don't even know whether or not I'm lying any more. Could I do that? To save my life?

Carter says softly, finally, 'No.'

I don't know what to say. I have no more arguments, no more pleas. I almost turn and run, but I can't do it. I can't believe that I'd get away – and I can't bring myself to make him pull the trigger a moment sooner.

The sunshine is dazzling; I close my eyes against the glare. I haven't given up. I'll pretend that the implant has failed – that should disconcert him, buy me a few more minutes.

And then?

A wave of giddiness sweeps over me. I stagger, but

regain my balance. I stand, staring at my shadow on the ground, swaying gently, feeling impossibly light.

Then I look up, squinting. 'I—'

Carter says, 'You're going to die. I'm going to shoot you through the skull. Do you understand me?'

'Yes.'

'But it's not the end of you. Not the end of what matters. You believe that, don't you?'

I nod, begrudgingly. 'Yes.'

'You know you're going to die – but you're not afraid?'

I close my eyes again; the light still hurts them. I laugh wearily. 'You're wrong: I'm still afraid. You lied about that, didn't you? You shit. But I understand. Everything you said makes sense now.'

And it does. All my objections seem absurd, now; transparently ill-conceived. I resent the fact that Carter was right – but I can't pretend that my reluctance to believe him was the product of anything but short-sightedness and self-deception. That it took *a neural implant* to enable me to see the obvious only proves how confused I must have been.

I stand, eyes shut, feeling the warm sunshine on the back of my neck. Waiting.

'You don't want to die . . . but you know it's the only way out? You accept that, now?' He sounds reluctant to believe me, as if he finds my instant conversion too good to be true.

I scream at him: 'Yes, fuck you! *Yes!* So get it over with! *Get it over with!*'

He's silent for a while. Then there's a soft thud, and a crash in the undergrowth.

The flies on my arms and face desert me.

After a moment, I open my eyes and sink to my knees, shaking. For a while, I lose myself: sobbing, banging the ground with my fists, tearing up handfuls of weeds, screaming at the birds for silence.

Then I scramble to my feet and walk over to the corpse.

He believed everything he claimed to believe – but he still needed something more. More than the abstract hope of someone, sometime, somewhere on the planet, falling into alignment – *becoming him* – by pure chance. He needed someone else holding the very same beliefs, right before his eyes at the moment of death – someone else who 'knew' that they were going to die, someone else who was just as afraid as he was.

And what do *I* believe?

I look up at the sky, and the memories I fought away, before, start tumbling through my skull. From lazy childhood holidays, to the very last weekend I spent with my ex-wife and son, the same heartbreaking blue runs through them all. Unites them all.

Doesn't it?

I look down at Carter, nudge him with my foot, and whisper, 'Who died today? Tell me. Who really died?'

THE CUTIE

'Why won't you even talk about it?'

Diane rolled away from me and assumed a foetal position. 'We talked about it two weeks ago. Nothing's changed since then, so there's no point, is there?'

We'd spent the afternoon with a friend of mine, his wife, and their six-month-old daughter. Now I couldn't close my eyes without seeing again the expression of joy and astonishment on that beautiful child's face, without hearing her peals of innocent laughter, without feeling once again the strange giddiness that I'd felt when Rosalie, the mother, had said, 'Of course you can hold her.'

I had hoped that the visit would sway Diane. Instead, while leaving her untouched, it had multiplied a thousandfold my own longing for parenthood, intensifying it into an almost physical pain.

OK, OK, so it's biologically programmed into us to love babies. So what? You could say the same about ninety per cent of human activity. It's biologically programmed into us to enjoy sexual intercourse, but nobody seems to mind about that, nobody claims they're being tricked by wicked nature into doing what they otherwise would not have done. Eventually someone is going to spell out, step by step, the physiological basis of the pleasure of listening to Bach, but will that make it, suddenly, a 'primitive' response, a biological con job, an experience as empty as the high from a euphoric drug?

'Didn't you feel *anything* when she smiled?'

'Frank, shut up and let me get some sleep.'

'If we have a baby, I'll look after her. I'll take six months off work and look after her.'

'Oh, six months, very generous! And then what?'

'Longer then. I could quit my job for good, if that's what you want.'

'And live on what? I'm not supporting you for the rest of your life! Shit! I suppose you'll want to get married then, won't you?'

'All right, I won't quit my job. We can put her in child care when she's old enough. Why are you so set against it? Millions of people are having children every day, it's such an *ordinary* thing, why do you keep manufacturing all these obstacles?'

'Because *I do not want a child*. Understand? Simple as that.'

I stared up at the dark ceiling for a while, before saying with a not quite even voice, 'I could carry it, you know. It's perfectly safe these days, there've been thousands of successful male pregnancies. They could take the placenta and embryo from you after a couple of weeks, and attach it to the outer wall of my bowel.'

'You're sick.'

'They can even do the fertilisation and early development *in vitro*, if necessary. Then all you'd have to do is donate the egg.'

'*I don't want a child*. Carried by you, carried by me, adopted, bought, stolen, whatever. Now shut up and let me sleep.'

When I arrived home the next evening, the flat was dark, quiet, and empty. Diane had moved out; the note said she'd gone to stay with her sister. It wasn't just the baby thing, of course; everything about me had begun to irritate her lately.

I sat in the kitchen drinking, wondering if there was any way of persuading her to come back. I knew that I was selfish: without a constant, conscious effort, I tended to ignore what other people felt. And I never seemed to be able to sustain that effort for long enough. But I did try, didn't I? What more could she expect?

When I was very drunk, I phoned her sister, who wouldn't even put her on. I hung up, and looked around for something I could break, but then all my energy vanished and I lay down right there on the floor. I tried to cry, but nothing happened, so I went to sleep instead.

The thing about biological drives is, we're so easily able to fool them, so skilled at satisfying our bodies while frustrating the evolutionary reasons for the actions that give us pleasure. Food with no nutritional value can be made to look and taste wonderful. Sex that can't cause pregnancy is every bit as good, regardless. In the past, I suppose a pet was the only way to substitute for a child. That's what I should have done: I should have bought a cat.

A fortnight after Diane left me, I bought the Cutie kit, by EFT from Taiwan. Well, when I say 'from Taiwan' I mean the first three digits of the EFT code symbolised Taiwan; sometimes that means something real, geographically speaking, but usually it doesn't. Most of these small companies have no physical premises; they consist of nothing but a few megabytes of data, manipulated by generic software running on the international trade network. A customer phones their local node, specifies the company and the product code, and if their bank balance or their credit rating checks out, orders are placed with various component manufacturers, shipping agents, and automated assembly firms. The company itself moves nothing but electrons.

What I really mean is: I bought a cheap copy. A pirate, a clone, a lookalike, a bootleg version, call it what you will. Of course I felt a little guilty, and a bit of a miser, but who can afford to pay five times as much for the genuine, made-in-El Salvador, USA product? Yes, it's ripping off the people who developed the product, who spent all that time and money on R & D, but what do they expect when they charge so much? Why should I have to pay for the cocaine habits of a bunch of Californian speculators who had a lucky hunch ten years ago about a certain biotechnology corporation? Better that my money goes to some fifteen-year-old trade hacker in Taiwan or Hong Kong or Manila, who's doing it all so that his brothers and sisters won't have to screw rich tourists to stay alive.

See what fine motives I had?

The Cutie has a venerable ancestry. Remember the Cabbage Patch Doll? Birth certificate provided, birth defects optional. The trouble was, the things just lay there, and lifelike robotics for a doll are simply too expensive to be practical. Remember the Video Baby? The Computer Crib? Perfect realism, so long as you didn't want to reach through the glass and cuddle the child.

Of course I didn't want a Cutie! I wanted a real child! But how? I was thirty-four years old, at the end of one more failed relationship. What were my choices?

I could start searching again for a woman who (a) wanted to have children, (b) hadn't yet done so, and (c) could tolerate living with a shit like me for more than a couple of years.

I could try to ignore or suppress my unreasonable desire to be a father. Intellectually (whatever that means), I had no need for a child; indeed, I could easily think of half a dozen impeccable arguments against accepting such a burden. But (to shamelessly anthropomorphise) it was as if the force that had previously

254

led me to engage in copious sex had finally cottoned on about birth control, and so had cunningly decided to shift my attention one link down the flawed causal chain. As an adolescent dreams endlessly of sex, so I dreamed endlessly of fatherhood.

Or—

O! The blessings of technology! There's nothing like a third option to create the illusion of freedom of choice!

—I could buy a Cutie.

Because Cuties are not legally human, the whole process of giving birth to one, whatever your gender, is simplified immensely. Lawyers are superfluous, not a single bureaucrat needs to be informed. No wonder they're so popular, when the contracts for adoption or surrogacy or even IVF with donor gametes all run to hundreds of pages, and when the child-related clauses in interspouse legal agreements require more negotiations than missile-ban treaties.

The controlling software was downloaded into my terminal the moment my account was debited; the kit itself arrived a month later. That gave me plenty of time to have chosen the precise appearance I wanted, by playing with the simulation graphics. Blue eyes, wispy blond hair, chubby, dimpled limbs, a snub nose . . . oh, what a stereotyped little cherub we built, the program and I. I chose a 'girl', because I'd always wanted a girl, though Cuties don't live long enough for gender to make much of a difference. At the age of four they suddenly, quietly, pass away. The death of the little one is so tragic, so heartbreaking, so *cathartic*. You can put them in their satin-padded coffins, still wearing their fourth-birthday-party clothes, and kiss them goodnight one last time before they're beamed up to Cutie heaven.

Of course it was revolting, I *knew* it was obscene, I cringed and squirmed inside at the utter sickness of what I was doing. But it was *possible*, and I find the possible so hard to resist. What's more, it was legal, it was simple, it was even cheap. So I went ahead, step by step, watching myself, fascinated, wondering when I'd change my mind, when I'd come to my senses and call it all off.

Although Cuties originate from human germ cells, the DNA is manipulated extensively before fertilisation takes place. By changing the gene that codes for one of the proteins used to build the walls of red blood cells, and by arranging for the pineal, adrenal and thyroid glands (triple backup to leave no chance of failure) to secrete, at the critical age, an enzyme that rips the altered protein apart, infant death is guaranteed. By extreme mutilation of the genes controlling embryonic brain development, subhuman intelligence (and hence their subhuman legal status) is guaranteed. Cuties can smile and coo, gurgle and giggle and babble and dribble, cry and kick and moan, but at their peak they're far stupider than the average puppy. Monkeys easily put them to shame, *goldfish* out-perform them in certain (carefully chosen) intelligence tests. They never learn to walk properly, or to feed themselves unaided. Understanding speech, let alone *using* it, is out of the question.

In short, Cuties are perfect for people who want all the heart-melting charms of a baby, but who do not want the prospect of surly six-year-olds, or rebellious teenagers, or middle-aged vultures who'll sit by their parents' deathbeds, thinking of nothing but the reading of the will.

Pirate copy or not, the process was certainly streamlined: all I had to do was hook up the Black Box to my terminal, switch it on, leave it running for a few days while various enzymes and utility viruses were tailor-made, then ejaculate into tube A.

Tube A featured a convincingly pseudo-vaginal design and realistically scented inner coating, but I have to confess that despite my lack of conceptual difficulties with this stage, it took me a ludicrous forty minutes to complete it. No matter who I remembered, no matter what I imagined, some part of my brain kept exercising a power of veto. But I read somewhere that a clever researcher has discovered that dogs with their brains removed can still go through the mechanics of copulation; the spinal cord, evidently, is all that's required. Well, in the end my spinal cord came good, and the terminal flashed up a sarcastic WELL DONE! I should have put my fist through it. I should have chopped up the Black Box with an axe and run around the room screaming nonsense poems. I should have bought a cat. It's good to have things to regret, though, isn't it? I'm sure it's an essential part of being human.

Three days later, I had to lie beside the Black Box and let it place a fierce claw on my belly. Impregnation was painless, though, despite the threatening appearance of the robot appendage; a patch of skin and muscle was locally anaesthetised, and then a quickly plunging needle delivered a pre-packaged biological complex, shielded by a chorion specially designed for the abnormal environment of my abdominal cavity.

And it was done. I was pregnant.

After a few weeks of pregnancy, all my doubts, all my distaste, seemed to vanish. Nothing in the world could have been more beautiful, more *right*, than what I was doing. Every day, I summoned up the simulated foetus on my terminal – the graphics were stunning; perhaps not totally realistic, but definitely *cute*, and that was what I'd paid for, after all – then put my hand against my abdomen and thought deep thoughts about the magic of life.

Every month I went to a clinic for ultrasound scans, but I declined the battery of genetic tests on offer; no need for *me* to discard an embryo with the wrong gender or unsatisfactory eye colour, since I'd dealt with those requirements at the start.

I told no one but strangers what I was doing; I'd changed doctors for the occasion, and I'd arranged to take leave once I started to 'show' too severely (up until then I managed to get by with jokes about 'too many beers'). Towards the end I began to be stared at, in shops and on the street, but I'd chosen a low birth-weight, and nobody could have known for sure that I wasn't merely obese. (In fact, on the advice of the instruction manual, I'd intentionally put on fat before the pregnancy; evidently it's a useful way to guarantee energy for the developing foetus.) And if anyone who saw me guessed the truth, so what? After all, I wasn't committing a crime.

During the day, once I was off work, I watched television and read books on child care, and arranged and rearranged the cot and toys in the corner of my room. I'm not sure when I chose the name: Angel. I never changed my mind about it, though. I carved it into the side of the cot with a knife, pretending that the plastic was the wood of a cherry tree. I contemplated having it tattooed upon my shoulder, but then that seemed inappropriate, between father and daughter. I said it aloud in the empty flat, long after my excuse about 'trying out the sound' was used up; I picked up the phone every now and then, and said, 'Can you be quiet, please! Angel is trying to sleep!'

Let's not split hairs. I was out of my skull. I knew I was out of my skull. I blamed it, with wonderful vagueness, on 'hormonal effects' resulting from placental secretions into my bloodstream. Sure, pregnant women didn't go crazy, but they were better designed, biochemically as well as anatomically, for what I was doing. The bundle of joy in my abdomen was sending out all kinds of chemical messages to what it thought was a female body, so was it any wonder that I went a little strange?

Of course there were more mundane effects as well. Morning sickness (in fact, nausea at all hours of the day and night). A heightened sense of smell, and sometimes a distracting hypersensitivity of the skin. Pressure on the bladder, swollen calves. Not to mention the simple, inevitable, exhausting unwieldiness of a body that was not just heavier, but had been reshaped in about the most awkward way I could imagine. I told myself many times that I was learning an invaluable lesson, that by experiencing this state, this process, so familiar to so many women but unknown to all but a handful of men, I would surely be transformed into a better, wiser person. Like I said, I was out of my skull.

The night before I checked in to hospital for the Caesarean, I had a dream. I dreamt that the baby emerged, not from me, but from the Black Box. It was covered in dark fur, and had a tail, and huge, lemur-like eyes. It was more beautiful than I had imagined possible. I couldn't decide, at first, if it was most like a young monkey or a kitten, because sometimes it walked on all fours like a cat, sometimes it crouched like a monkey, and the tail seemed equally suited to either. Eventually, though, I recalled that kittens were born with their eyes closed, so a monkey was what it had to be.

It darted around the room, then hid beneath my bed. I reached under to drag it out, then found that all I had in my hands was an old pair of pyjamas.

I was woken by an overwhelming need to urinate.

The hospital staff dealt with me without a single joke; well, I suppose I was paying enough not to be mocked. I had a private room (as far from the maternity ward as possible). Ten years ago, perhaps, my story would have been leaked to the media, and cameramen and reporters would have set up camp outside my door. But the birth of a Cutie, even to a single father, was, thankfully, no longer news. Some hundred thousand Cuties had already lived and died, so I was no trail-blazing pioneer; no paper would offer me ten years' wages for the BIZARRE AND SHOCKING story of my life, no TV stations would bid for the right to zoom in on my tears at the primetime funeral of my sweet, subhuman child. The permutations of reproductive technology had been milked dry of controversy; researchers would have to come up with a quantum leap in strangeness if they wanted to regain the front page. No doubt they were working on it.

The whole thing was done under general anaesthetic. I woke with a headache like a hammer blow and a taste in my mouth like I'd thrown up rotten cheese. The first time I moved without thinking of my stitches; it was the last time I made *that* mistake.

I managed to raise my head.

She was lying on her back in the middle of a cot, which now looked as big as a football field. Wrinkled and pink just like any other baby, her face screwed up, her eyes shut, taking a breath, then howling, then another breath, another howl, as if screaming were every bit as natural as breathing. She had thick dark hair (the program had said she would, and that it would soon fall out and grow back fair). I climbed to my feet, ignoring the throbbing in my head, and leant over the wall of the cot to place one finger gently on her cheek. She didn't stop howling, but she opened her eyes, and, yes, they were blue.

'Daddy loves you,' I said. 'Daddy loves his Angel.' She closed her eyes, took an extra-deep breath, then screamed. I reached down and, with terror, with dizzying joy, with infinite precision in every movement, with microscopic care, I lifted her up to my shoulder and held her there for a long, long time.

Two days later they sent us home.

Everything *worked*. She didn't stop breathing. She drank from her bottle, she wet herself and soiled her nappies, she cried for hours, and sometimes she even slept.

Somehow I managed to stop thinking of her as a Cutie. I threw out the Black Box, its task completed. I sat and watched her watch the glittering mobile I'd suspended above her cot, I watched her learning to follow movements with her eyes when I set it swinging and twisting and tinkling, I watched her trying to lift her hands towards it, trying to lift her whole body towards it, grunting with frustration, but sometimes cooing with enchantment. Then I'd rush up and lean over her and kiss her nose, and make her giggle, and say, again and again, 'Daddy loves you! Yes, I do!'

I quit my job when my holiday entitlement ran out. I had enough saved to live frugally for years, and I couldn't face the prospect of leaving Angel with anybody else. I took her shopping, and everyone in the supermarket succumbed to her beauty and charm. I ached to show her to my parents, but they would have asked too many questions. I cut myself off from my friends, letting no one into the flat, and refusing all invitations. I didn't need a job, I didn't need friends, I didn't need anyone or anything but Angel.

I was so happy and proud, the first time she reached out and gripped my finger when I waved it in front of her face. She tried to pull it into her mouth. I resisted, teasing her, freeing my finger and moving it far away, then suddenly offering it again. She laughed at this, as if she knew with utter certainty that in the end I would give up the struggle and let her put it briefly to her gummy mouth. And when that happened, and the taste proved uninteresting, she pushed my hand away with surprising strength, giggling all the while.

According to the development schedule, she was *months* ahead, being able to do that at her age. 'You little smartie!' I said, talking much too close to her face. She grabbed my nose then exploded with glee, kicking the mattress, making a cooing sound I'd never heard before, a beautiful, delicate sequence of tones, each note sliding into the next, almost like a kind of birdsong.

I photographed her weekly, filling album after album. I bought her new clothes before she'd outgrown the old ones, and new toys before she'd even touched the ones I'd bought the week before. 'Travel will broaden your mind,' I said, each time we prepared for an outing. Once she was out of the pram and into the stroller, seated and able to look at more of the world than the sky, her astonishment and curiosity were sources of endless delight for me. A passing dog would have her bouncing with joy, a pigeon on the footpath was cause for vocal celebration, and cars that were too loud earned angry frowns from Angel that left me helpless with laughter, to see her tiny face so expressive of contempt.

It was only when I sat for too long watching her sleeping, listening too closely to her steady breathing, that a whisper in my head would try to remind me of her predetermined death. I shouted it down, silently screaming back nonsense, obscenities, meaningless abuse. Or sometimes I would quietly sing or hum a lullaby, and if Angel stirred at the sound I made, I would take that as a sign of victory, as certain proof that the evil voice was lying.

Yet at the very same time, in a sense, I wasn't fooling myself for a minute. I *knew* she would die when the time came, as one hundred thousand others had died before her. And I knew that the only way to accept *that* was by doublethink, by expecting her death while pretending it would never really come, and by treating her exactly like a real, human child, while knowing all along that she was nothing more than an adorable pet. A monkey, a puppy, a goldfish.

Have you ever done something so wrong that it dragged your whole life down into a choking black swamp in a sunless land of nightmares? Have you ever made a choice so foolish that it cancelled out, in one blow, everything good you might ever have done, made void every memory of happiness, made everything in the world that was beautiful, ugly, turned every last trace of self-respect into the certain knowledge that you should never have been born?

I have.

I bought a cheap copy of the Cutie kit.

I should have bought a cat. Cats aren't permitted in my building, but I should have bought one anyway. I've known people with cats, I like cats, cats have strong personalities, a cat would have been a companion I could have given attention and affection to, without fuelling my obsession: if I'd tried dressing *it* up in baby clothes and feeding it from a bottle, it would have scratched me to pieces and then shrivelled my dignity with a withering stare of disdain.

I bought Angel a new set of beads one day, an abacus-like arrangement in ten shiny colours, to be suspended above her in her cot. She laughed and clapped as I installed it, her eyes glistening with mischief and delight.

Mischief and delight?

I remembered reading somewhere that a young baby's 'smiles' are really caused by nothing but wind – and I remembered my annoyance; not with the facts themselves, but with the author, for feeling obliged to smugly disseminate such a tedious truth. And I thought, what's this magic thing called 'humanity', anyway? Isn't half of it, at least, in the eyes of the beholder?

'Mischief? *You?* Never!' I leant over and kissed her.

She clapped her hands and said, very clearly, 'Daddy!'

All the doctors I've seen are sympathetic, but there's nothing they can do. The time bomb inside her is too much a part of her. *That* function, the kit performed perfectly.

She's growing smarter day by day, picking up new words all the time. What should I do?

(a) Deny her stimuli?

(b) Subject her to malnutrition?

(c) Drop her on her head? Or,

(d) None of the above?

Oh, it's all right, I'm a little unstable, but I'm not yet completely insane: I can still understand the subtle difference between fucking up her genes and actually assaulting her living, breathing body. Yes, if I concentrate as hard as I can, I swear I can see the difference.

In fact, I think I'm coping remarkably well: I never break down in front of Angel. I hide all my anguish until she falls asleep.

Accidents happen. Nobody's perfect. Her death will be quick and painless. Children die around the world all the time. See? There are lots of answers, lots of sounds I can make with my lips while I'm waiting for the urge to pass – the urge to kill us both, right now; the purely selfish urge to end my own suffering. I won't do it. The doctors and all their tests might still be wrong. There might still be a miracle that can save her. I have to keep living, without daring to hope. And if she does die, then I will follow her.

There's one question, though, to which I'll never know the answer. It haunts me endlessly, it horrifies me more than my blackest thoughts of death:

Had she never said a word, would I really have fooled myself into believing that her death would have been less tragic?

INTO DARKNESS

The tone from the buzzer rises in both pitch and loudness the longer it's on, so I leap out of bed knowing that it's taken me less than a second to wake. I swear I was dreaming it first, though, dreaming the sound long before it was real. That's happened a few times. Maybe it's just a trick of the mind; maybe some dreams take shape only in the act of remembering them. Or maybe I dream it every night, every sleeping moment, just in case.

The light above the buzzer is red. Not a rehearsal.

I dress on my way across the room to thump the acknowledgement switch; as soon as the buzzer shuts off, I can hear the approaching siren. It takes me as long to lace my shoes as everything else combined. I grab my backpack from beside the bed and flick on the power. It starts flashing LEDs as it goes through its self-checking routines.

By the time I'm at the kerb, the patrol car is braking noisily, rear passenger door swinging open. I know the driver, Angelo, but I haven't seen the other cop before. As we accelerate, a satellite view of The Intake in false-colour infrared – a pitch-black circle in a landscape of polychromatic blotches – appears on the car's terminal. A moment later, this is replaced by a street map of the region – one of the newer far northern suburbs, all cul-de-sacs and crescents – with The Intake's perimeter and centre marked, and a dashed line showing where The

Core should be. The optimal routes are omitted; too much clutter and the mind balks. I stare at the map, trying to commit it to memory. It's not that I won't have access to it, inside, but it's always faster to just *know*. When I close my eyes to see how I'm going, the pattern in my head looks like nothing so much as a puzzle-book maze.

We hit the freeway, and Angelo lets loose. He's a good driver, but I sometimes wonder if this is the riskiest part of the whole business. The cop I don't know doesn't think so; he turns to me and says, 'I gotta tell you one thing; I respect what you do, but you must be fucking crazy. I wouldn't go inside that thing for a million dollars.' Angelo grins – I catch it in the rear-view mirror – and says, 'Hey, how much is the Nobel prize, anyway? More than a million?'

I snort. 'I doubt it. And I don't think they give the Nobel prize for the eight-hundred-metre steeplechase.' The media seem to have decided to portray me as some kind of expert; I don't know why – unless it's because I once used the phrase 'radially anisotropic' in an interview. It's true that I carried one of the first scientific 'payloads', but any other Runner could have done that, and these days it's routine. The fact is, by international agreement, no one with even a microscopic chance of contributing to the theory of The Intake is allowed to risk their life by going inside. If I'm atypical in any way, it's through a *lack* of relevant qualifications; most of the other volunteers have a background in the conventional rescue services.

I switch my watch into chronograph mode, and synch it to the count that the terminal's now showing, then do the same to my backpack's timer. Six minutes and twelve seconds. The Intake's manifestations obey exactly the same statistics as a radioactive nucleus with a half-life of eighteen minutes; seventy-nine per cent last six minutes or more – but multiply anything by 0.962

every minute, and you wouldn't believe how fast it can fall. I've memorised the probabilities right out to an hour (ten per cent), which may or may not have been a wise thing to do. Counter to intuition, The Intake does *not* become more dangerous as time passes, any more than a single radioactive nucleus becomes 'more unstable'. At any given moment – assuming that it hasn't yet vanished – it's just as likely as ever to stick around for another eighteen minutes. A mere ten per cent of manifestations last for an hour or more – but *of that ten per cent*, half will still be there eighteen minutes later. The danger has not increased.

For a Runner, inside, to ask what the odds are *now*, he or she must be alive to pose the question, and so the probability curve must start afresh from that moment. History can't harm you; the 'chance' of *having survived* the last x minutes is one hundred per cent, once you've done it. As the unknowable future becomes the unchangeable past, risk must collapse into certainty, one way or another.

Whether or not any of us really think this way is another question. You can't help having a gut feeling that time is running out, that the odds are being whittled away. Everyone keeps track of the time since The Intake materialised, however theoretically irrelevant that is. The truth is, these abstractions make no difference in the end. You do what you can, as fast as you can, regardless.

It's two in the morning, the freeway is empty, but it still takes me by surprise when we screech on to the exit ramp so soon. My stomach is painfully tight. I wish I felt *ready*, but I never do. After ten real calls, after nearly two hundred rehearsals, I never do. I always wish I had more time to compose myself, although I have no idea what state of mind I'd aim for, let alone how I'd achieve it. Some lunatic part of me is always hoping for a *delay*. If what I'm really hoping is that The Intake will have vanished before I can reach it, I shouldn't be here at all.

The coordinators tell us, over and over: 'You can back out any time you want to. Nobody would think any less of you.' It's true, of course (up to the point where backing out becomes physically impossible), but it's a freedom I could do without. Retiring would be one thing, but once I've accepted a call I don't want to have to waste my energy on second thoughts, I don't want to have to endlessly reaffirm my choice. I've psyched myself into half believing that *I* couldn't live with myself, however understanding other people might be, and that helps a little. The only trouble is, this lie might be self-fulfilling, and I really don't want to become that kind of person.

I close my eyes, and the map appears before me. I'm a mess, there's no denying it, but I can still do the job, I can still get results. That's what counts.

I can tell when we're getting close, without even searching the skyline; there are lights on in all of the houses, and families standing in their front yards. Many people wave and cheer as we pass, a sight that always depresses me. When a group of teenagers, standing on a street corner drinking beer, scream abuse and gesture obscenely, I can't help feeling perversely encouraged.

'Dickheads,' mutters the cop I don't know. I keep my mouth shut.

We take a corner, and I spot a trio of helicopters, high on my right, ascending with a huge projection screen in tow. Suddenly, a corner of the screen is obscured, and my eye extends the curve of the eclipsing object from this one tiny arc to giddy completion.

From the outside, by day, The Intake makes an impressive sight: a giant black dome, completely non-reflective, blotting out a great bite of the sky. It's impossible not to believe that you're confronting a massive, solid object. By night, though, it's different. The shape is still unmistakable, cut in a velvet black that makes the darkest night seem grey, but there's no illusion of solidity; just an awareness of a different kind of void.

The Intake has been appearing for almost ten years now. It's always a perfect sphere, a little more than a kilometre in radius, and usually centred close to ground level. On rare occasions, it's been known to appear out at sea, and slightly more often, on uninhabited land, but the vast majority of its incarnations take place in populated regions.

The currently favoured hypothesis is that a future civilisation tried to construct a wormhole that would let them sample the distant past, bringing specimens of ancient life into their own time to be studied. They screwed up. Both ends of the wormhole came unstuck. The thing has shrunk and deformed, from – presumably – some kind of grand temporal highway, bridging geological epochs, to a gateway that now spans less time than it would take to cross an atomic nucleus at the speed of light. One end – The Intake – is a kilometre in radius; the other is about a fifth as big, spatially concentric with the first, but displaced an almost immeasurably small time into the future. We call the inner sphere – the wormhole's destination, which seems to be inside it, but isn't – The Core.

Why this shrivelled-up piece of failed temporal engineering has ended up in the present era is anyone's guess; maybe we just happened to be halfway between the original endpoints, and the thing collapsed symmetrically. Pure bad luck. The trouble is, it hasn't quite come to rest. It materialises somewhere on the planet, remains fixed for several minutes, then loses its grip and vanishes, only to appear at a new location a fraction of a second later. Ten years of analysing the data has yielded no method for predicting successive locations, but there must be some remnant of a navigation system in action; why else would the wormhole cling to the Earth's surface (with a marked preference for inhabited, dry land) instead of wandering off on a random course into interplanetary space? It's as if some faithful, demented computer keeps valiantly trying to anchor The Intake to a region which might be of interest to its scholarly masters; no Palaeozoic life can be found, but twenty-first-century cities will do, since there's nothing much else around. And every time it fails to make a permanent connection and slips off into hyperspace, with infinite dedication, and unbounded stupidity, it tries again.

Being of interest is bad news. Inside the wormhole, time is mixed with one spatial dimension, and – whether by design or physical necessity – any movement which equates to travelling from the future into the past is forbidden. Translated into the wormhole's present geometry, this means that when The Intake materialises around you, motion away from the centre is impossible. You have an unknown time – maybe eighteen minutes, maybe more, maybe less – to navigate your way to the safety of The Core, under these bizarre conditions. What's more, light is subject to the same effect; it only propagates inwards. Everything closer to the centre than you lies in the invisible future. You're running into darkness.

I have heard people scoff at the notion that any of this could be difficult. I'm not quite enough of a sadist to hope that they learn the truth, first-hand.

Actually, outwards motion isn't quite literally impossible. If it were, everyone caught in The Intake would die at once. The heart has to circulate blood, the lungs have to inhale and exhale, nerve impulses have to travel in all directions. Every single living cell relies on shuffling chemicals back and forth, and I can't even guess what the effect would be on the molecular level, if electron clouds could fluctuate in one direction but not the reverse.

There is some leeway. Because the wormhole's entire eight hundred metres spans such a minute time interval, the distance scale of the human body corresponds to an even shorter period – short enough for quantum effects to come into play. Quantum uncertainty in the space-time metric permits small, localised violations of the classical law's absolute restriction.

So, instead of everyone dying on the spot, blood pressure goes up, the heart is stressed, breathing becomes laborious, and the brain may function erratically. Enzymes, hormones, and other biological molecules are all slightly deformed, causing them to bind less efficiently to their targets, interfering to some degree with every biochemical process; haemoglobin, for example, loses its grip on oxygen more easily. Water diffuses out of the body – because random thermal motion is suddenly not so random – leading to gradual dehydration.

People already in very poor health can die from these effects. Others are just made nauseous, weak and confused – on top of the inevitable shock and panic. They make bad decisions. They get trapped.

One way or another, a few hundred lives are lost, every time The Intake materialises. Intake Runners may save ten or twenty people, which I'll admit is not much of a success rate, but until some genius works out how to rid us of the wormhole for good, it's better than nothing.

The screen is in place high above us, when we reach the 'South Operations Centre' – a couple of vans, stuffed with electronics, parked on someone's front lawn. The now familiar section of street map appears, the image rock steady and in perfect focus, in spite of the fact that it's being projected from a fourth helicopter, and all four are jittering in the powerful inwards wind. People inside can see out, of course; this map – and the others, at the other compass points – will save dozens of lives. In theory, once outdoors, it should be simple enough to head straight for The Core; after all, there's no easier direction to find, no easier path to follow. The trouble is, a straight line inwards is likely to lead you into obstacles, and when you can't retrace your steps, the most mundane of these can kill you.

So, the map is covered with arrows, marking the optimal routes to The Core, given the constraint of staying safely on the roads. Two more helicopters, hovering above The Intake, are doing one better: with high-velocity paint guns under computer control, and laser-ring inertial guidance systems constantly telling the shuddering computers their precise location and orientation, they're drawing the same arrows in fluorescent/reflective paint on the invisible streets below. You can't see the arrows ahead of you, but you can look back at the ones you've passed. It helps.

There's a small crowd of coordinators, and one or two Runners, around the vans. This scene always looks forlorn to me, like some small-time rained-out amateur athletics event, air traffic notwithstanding. Angelo calls out, 'Break a leg!' as I run from the car. I raise a hand and wave without turning. Loudspeakers are blasting the standard advice inwards, cycling through a dozen languages. In the corner of my eye I can see a TV crew arriving. I glance at my watch. Nine minutes. I can't help thinking, *seventy-one per cent*, although The Intake is, clearly, one hundred per cent still there. Someone taps me on the shoulder. Elaine. She smiles and says, 'John, see you in The Core,' then sprints into the wall of darkness before I can reply.

Dolores is handing out assignments on RAM. She wrote most of the software used by Intake Runners around the world, but then, she makes her living writing computer games. She's even written a game which models The Intake itself, but sales have been less than spectacular; the reviewers decided it was in bad taste. 'What's next? Let's play Airline Disaster?' Maybe they think flight simulators should be programmed for endless calm weather. Meanwhile, televangelists sell prayers to keep the wormhole away; you just slip that credit card into the home-shopping slot for instant protection.

'What have you got for me?'

'Three infants.'

'Is that *all*?'

'You come late, you get the crumbs.'

I plug the cartridge into my backpack. A sector of the street map appears on the display panel, marked with three bright red dots. I strap on the pack, and then adjust the display on its movable arm so I can catch it with a sideways glance, if I have to. Electronics can be made to function reliably inside the wormhole, but everything has to be specially designed.

It's not ten minutes, not quite. I grab a cup of water from a table beside one of the vans. A solution of mixed carbohydrates, supposedly optimised for our metabolic needs, is also on offer, but the one time I tried it I was sorry; my gut isn't interested in absorbing anything at this stage, optimised or not. There's coffee too, but the very last thing I need right now is a stimulant. Gulping down the water, I hear my name, and I can't help tuning in to the TV reporter's spiel.

'. . . John Nately, high-school science teacher and unlikely hero, embarking on this, his *eleventh* call as a volunteer Intake Runner. If he survives tonight, he'll have set a new national record – but of course, the odds of making it through grow slimmer with every call, and by now . . .'

The moron is spouting crap – the odds *do not* grow slimmer, a veteran faces no extra risk – but this isn't the time to set him straight. I swing my arms for a few seconds in a half-hearted warm-up, but there's not much point; every muscle in my body is tense, and will

273

be for the next eight hundred metres, whatever I do. I try to blank my mind and just concentrate on the run-up — the faster you hit The Intake, the less of a shock it is — and before I can ask myself, for the first time tonight, what the fuck I'm really doing here, I've left the isotropic universe behind, and the question is academic.

The darkness doesn't swallow you. Perhaps that's the strangest part of all. You've seen it swallow other Runners; why doesn't it swallow *you*? Instead, it recedes from your every step. The borderline isn't absolute; quantum fuzziness produces a gradual fade-out, stretching visibility about as far as each extended foot. By day, this is completely surreal, and people have been known to suffer fits and psychotic episodes at the sight of the void's apparent retreat. By night, it seems merely implausible, like chasing an intelligent fog.

At the start, it's almost too easy; memories of pain and fatigue seem ludicrous. Thanks to frequent re-hearsals in a compression harness, the pattern of resistance as I breathe is almost familiar. Runners once took drugs to lower their blood pressure, but with sufficient training, the body's own vasoregulatory system can be made flexible enough to cope with the stress, unaided. The odd tugging sensation on each leg as I bring it forward would probably drive me mad, if I didn't (crudely) understand the reason for it: inwards motion is resisted, when pulling, rather than pushing, is involved, because *information* travels outwards. If I trailed a ten-metre rope behind me, I wouldn't be able to take a single step; pulling on the rope would pass information about my motion from where I am to a point further out. That's forbidden, and it's only the quantum leeway that lets me drag each foot forwards at all.

The street curves gently to the right, gradually losing its radial orientation, but there's no convenient turn-off yet. I stay in the middle of the road, straddling the double white line, as the border between past and future swings to the left. The road surface seems always to slope towards the darkness, but that's just another wormhole effect; the bias in thermal molecular motion – cause of the inwards wind, and slow dehydration – produces a force, or pseudo-force, on solid objects, too, tilting the apparent vertical.

'—me! *Please!*'

A man's voice, desperate and bewildered – and almost indignant, as if he can't help believing that I must have heard him all along, that I must have been feigning deafness out of malice or indifference. I turn, without slowing; I've learnt to do it in a way that makes me only slightly dizzy. Everything appears almost normal, looking outwards – apart from the fact that the streetlights are out, and so most illumination is from helicopter floodlights and the giant street map in the sky. The cry came from a bus shelter, all vandal-proof plastic and reinforced glass, at least five metres behind me, now; it might as well be on Mars. Wire mesh covers the glass; I can just make out the figure behind it, a faint silhouette.

'Help me!'

Mercifully – for me – I've vanished into this man's darkness; I don't have to think of a gesture to make, an expression to put on my face, appropriate to the situation. I turn away, and pick up speed. I'm not inured to the death of strangers, but I am inured to my helplessness.

After ten years of The Intake, there are international standards for painted markings on the ground around every potential hazard in public open space. Like all the other measures, it helps, slightly. There are standards, too, for eventually eliminating the hazards – designing out the corners where people can be trapped – but that's going to cost billions, and take decades, and won't even touch the real problem: interiors. I've seen demonstra-

275

tion trap-free houses and office blocks, with doors, or curtained doorways, in *every* corner of *every* room, but the style hasn't exactly caught on. My own house is far from ideal; after getting quotes for alterations, I decided that the cheapest solution was to keep a sledgehammer beside every wall.

I turn left, just in time to see a trail of glowing arrows hiss into place on the road behind me.

I'm almost at my first assignment. I tap a button on my backpack and peer sideways at the display, as it switches to a plan of the target house. As soon as The Intake's position is known, Dolores's software starts hunting through databases, assembling a list of locations where there's a reasonable chance that we can do some good. Our information is never complete, and sometimes just plain wrong; census data is often out of date, building plans can be inaccurate, misfiled, or simply missing – but it beats walking blind into houses chosen at random.

I slow almost to a walk, two houses before the target, to give myself time to grow used to the effects. Running inwards lessens the outwards components – relative to the wormhole – of the body's cyclic motions; slowing down always feels like precisely the wrong thing to do. I often dream of running through a narrow canyon, no wider than my shoulders, whose walls will stay apart only so long as I move fast enough; that's what my body thinks of *slowing down*.

The street here lies about thirty degrees off radial. I cross the front lawn of the neighbouring house, then step over a knee-high brick wall. At this angle, there are few surprises; most of what's hidden is so easy to extrapolate that it almost seems visible in the mind's eye. A corner of the target house emerges from the darkness on my left; I get my bearings from it and head straight for a side window. Entry by the front door would cost me access to almost half of the house, including the bedroom which Dolores's highly erratic Room Use Predictor nominates as the one most likely to be the child's. People can file room-use information with us directly, but few bother.

I smash the glass with a crowbar, open the window, and clamber through. I leave a small electric lamp on the windowsill – carrying it with me would render it useless – and move slowly into the room. I'm already starting to feel dizzy and nauseous, but I force myself to concentrate. One step too many, and the rescue becomes ten times more difficult. Two steps, and it's impossible.

It's clear that I have the right room when a dresser is revealed, piled with plastic toys, talcum powder, baby shampoo, and other paraphernalia spilling on to the floor. Then a corner of the crib appears on my left, pointed at an unexpected angle; the thing was probably neatly parallel to the wall to start with, but slid unevenly under the inwards force. I sidle up to it, then inch forwards, until a lump beneath the blanket comes into view. I hate this moment, but the longer I wait, the harder it gets. I reach sideways and lift the child, bringing the blanket with it. I kick the crib aside, then walk forwards, slowly bending my arms, until I can slip the child into the harness on my chest. An adult is strong enough to drag a small baby a short distance outwards. It's usually fatal.

The kid hasn't stirred; he or she is unconscious, but breathing. I shudder briefly, a kind of shorthand emotional catharsis, then I start moving. I glance at the display to recheck the way out, and finally let myself notice the time. Thirteen minutes. Sixty-one per cent. More to the point, The Core is just two or three minutes away, downhill, nonstop. One successful assignment means ditching the rest. There's no alternative; you can't lug a child with you, in and out of buildings; you can't even put it down somewhere and come back for it later.

As I step through the front door, the sense of relief leaves me giddy. Either that, or renewed cerebral blood flow. I pick up speed as I cross the lawn – and catch a glimpse of a woman, shouting, 'Wait! Stop!'

I slow down; she catches up with me. I put a hand on her shoulder and propel her slightly ahead of me, then say, 'Keep moving, as fast as you can. When you want to speak, fall behind me. I'll do the same. OK?'

I move ahead of her. She says, 'That's my daughter you've got. Is she all right? Oh, please . . . Is she alive?'

'She's fine. Stay calm. We just have to get her to The Core now. OK?'

'I want to hold her. I want to take her.'

'Wait until we're safe.'

'I want to take her there myself.'

Shit. I glance at her sideways. Her face is glistening with sweat and tears. One of her arms is bruised and blotchy, the usual symptom of trying to reach out to something unreachable.

'I really think it would be better to wait.'

'What right have you got? She's *my* daughter! Give her to me!' The woman is indignant, but remarkably lucid, considering what she's been through. I can't imagine what it must have felt like, to stand by that house, hoping insanely for some kind of miracle, while everyone in the neighbourhood fled past her, and the side effects made her sicker and sicker. However pointless, however idiotic her courage, I can't help admiring it.

I'm lucky. My ex-wife, and our son and daughter, live halfway across town from me. I have no friends who live nearby. My emotional geography is very carefully arranged; I don't give a shit about anyone who I could end up unable to save.

So what do I do – sprint away from her, leave her running after me, screaming? Maybe I should. *If I gave her the child, though, I could check out one more house.*

'Do you know how to handle her? Never try to move her backwards, away from the darkness. *Never.*'

'I know that. I've read all the articles. I *know* what you're meant to do.'

'OK.' I must be crazy. We slow down to a walk, and I pass the child to her, lowering it into her arms from beside her. I realise, almost too late, that we're at the turn-off for the second house. As the woman vanishes into the darkness, I yell after her, '*Run!* Follow the arrows, and *run!*'

I check the time. Fifteen minutes already, with all that stuffing around. I'm still alive, though – so the odds now are, as always, fifty-fifty that the wormhole will last another eighteen minutes. Of course I could die at any second – but that was equally true when I first stepped inside. I'm no greater fool now than I was then. For what that's worth.

The second house is empty, and it's easy to see why. The computer's guess for the nursery is in fact a study, and the parents' bedroom is outwards of the child's. Windows are open, clearly showing the path they must have taken.

A strange mood overtakes me, as I leave the house behind. The inwards wind seems stronger than ever, the road turns straight into the darkness, and I feel an inexplicable tranquillity wash over me. I'm moving as fast as I can, but the edge of latent panic, of sudden death, is gone. My lungs, my muscles, are battling all the same restraints, but I feel curiously detached from them; aware of the pain and effort, yet somehow uninvolved.

The truth is, I know exactly why I'm here. I can never quite admit it, outside – it seems too whimsical, too bizarre. Of course I'm glad to save lives, and maybe that's grown to be part of it. No doubt I also crave to be thought of as a hero. The real reason, though, is too strange to be judged either selfless or vain:

The wormhole makes tangible the most basic truths of existence. You cannot see the future. You cannot change the past. All of life consists of running into darkness. This is why I'm here.

My body grows, not numb, but separate, a puppet dancing and twitching on a treadmill. I snap out of this and check the map, not a moment too soon. I have to turn right, sharply, which puts an end to any risk of somnambulism. Looking up at the bisected world makes my head pound, so I stare at my feet, and try to recall if the pooling of blood in my left hemisphere ought to make me more rational, or less.

The third house is in a borderline situation. The parents' bedroom is slightly outwards from the child's, but the doorway gives access to only half the room. I enter through a window that the parents could not have used.

The child is dead. I see the blood before anything else. I feel, suddenly, very tired. A slit of the doorway is visible, and I know what must have happened. The mother or father edged their way in, and found they could just reach the child – could take hold of one hand, but no more. Pulling inwards is resisted, but people find that confusing; they don't expect it, and when it happens, they fight it. When you want to snatch someone you love out of the jaws of danger, you pull with all your strength.

The door is an easy exit for me, but less so for anyone who came in that way – especially someone in the throes of grief. I stare into the darkness of the room's inwards corner, and yell, 'Crouch down, as low as you can,' then mime doing so. I pluck the demolition gun from my backpack, and aim high. The recoil, in normal space, would send me sprawling; here it's a mere thump.

I step forward, giving up my own chance to use the

door. There's no immediate sign that I've just blasted a metre-wide hole in the wall; virtually all of the dust and debris is on the inwards side. I finally reach a man kneeling in the corner, his hands on his head; for a brief moment I think he's alive, that he took this position to shield himself from the blast. No pulse, no respiration. A dozen broken ribs, probably; I'm not inclined to check. Some people can last for an hour, pinned between walls of brick and an invisible, third wall that follows them ruthlessly into the corner, every time they slip, every time they give ground. Some people, though, do exactly the worst thing; they squeeze themselves into the inward-most part of their prison, obeying some instinct which, I'm sure, makes sense at the time.

Or maybe he wasn't confused at all. Maybe he just wanted it to be over.

I hoist myself through the hole in the wall. I stagger through the kitchen. The fucking plan is wrong wrong wrong, a door I'm expecting doesn't exist. I smash the kitchen window, then cut my hand on the way out.

I refuse to glance at the map. I don't want to know the time. Now that I'm alone, with no purpose left but saving myself, everything is jinxed. I stare at the ground, at the fleeting magic golden arrows, trying not to count them.

One glimpse of a festering hamburger discarded on the road, and I find myself throwing up. Common sense tells me to turn and face backwards, but I'm not quite that stupid. The acid in my throat and nose brings tears to my eyes. As I shake them away, something impossible happens.

A brilliant blue light appears, high up in the darkness ahead, dazzling my dark-adapted eyes. I shield my face, then peer between my fingers. As I grow used to the glare, I start to make out details.

A cluster of long, thin, luminous cylinders is hanging

in the sky, like some mad upside-down pipe organ built of glass, bathed in glowing plasma. The light it casts does nothing to reveal the houses and streets below. I must be hallucinating; I've seen shapes in the darkness before, although never anything so spectacular, so persistent. I run faster, in the hope of clearing my head. The apparition doesn't vanish, or waver; it merely grows closer.

I halt, shaking uncontrollably. I stare into the impossible light. What if it's not in my head? There's only one possible explanation. Some component of the wormhole's hidden machinery has revealed itself. The idiot navigator is showing me its worthless soul.

With one voice in my skull screaming, *No!* and another calmly asserting that I have no choice, that this chance might never come again, I draw the demolition gun, take aim, and fire. As if some puny weapon in the hands of an amoeba could scratch the shimmering artifact of a civilisation whose failures leave us cowering in awe.

The structure shatters and implodes in silence. The light contracts to a blinding pinprick, burning itself into my vision. Only when I turn my head am I certain that the real light is gone.

I start running again. Terrified, elated. I have no idea what I've done, but the wormhole is, so far, unchanged. The afterimage lingers in the darkness, with nothing to wipe it from my sight. Can hallucinations leave an afterimage? *Did the navigator choose to expose itself, choose to let me destroy it?*

I trip on something and stagger, but catch myself from falling. I turn and see a man crawling down the road, and I bring myself to a rapid halt, astonished by such a mundane sight after my transcendental encounter. The man's legs have been amputated at the thighs; he's dragging himself along with his arms alone. That would be hard enough in normal space, but here, the effort must almost be killing him.

There are special wheelchairs which can function in the wormhole (wheels bigger than a certain size buckle and deform if the chair stalls) and if we know we'll need one, we bring one in, but they're too heavy for every Runner to carry one just in case.

The man lifts his head and yells, 'Keep going! Stupid fucker!' without the least sign of doubt that he's not just shouting at empty space. I stare at him and wonder why I don't take the advice. He's huge: big-boned and heavily muscled, with plenty of fat on top of that. I doubt that I could lift him – and I'm certain that if I could, I'd stagger along more slowly than he's crawling.

Inspiration strikes. I'm in luck, too; a sideways glance reveals a house, with the front door invisible but clearly only a metre or two inwards of where I am now. I smash the hinges with a hammer and chisel, then manoeuvre the door out of the frame and back to the road. The man has already caught up with me. I bend down and tap him on the shoulder. 'Want to try sledding?'

I step inwards in time to hear part of a string of obscenities, and to catch an unwelcome close-up of his bloody forearms. I throw the door down on to the road ahead of him. He keeps moving; I wait until he can hear me again.

'Yes or no?'

'Yes,' he mutters.

It's awkward, but it works. He sits on the door, leaning back on his arms. I run behind, bent over, my hands on his shoulders, pushing. Pushing is the one action the wormhole doesn't fight, and the inwards force makes it downhill all the way. Sometimes the door slides so fast that I have to let go for a second or two, to keep from overbalancing.

I don't need to look at the map. I *know* the map, I

know precisely where we are; The Core is less than a hundred metres away. In my head I recite an incantation: *The danger does not increase. The danger does not increase.* And in my heart I know that the whole conceit of 'probability' is meaningless; the wormhole is reading my mind, waiting for the first sign of hope, and whether that comes fifty metres, or ten metres, or two metres from safety, that's when it will take me.

Some part of me calmly judges the distance we cover, and counts: *Ninety-three, ninety-two, ninety-one* . . . I mumble random numbers to myself, and when that fails, I reset the count arbitrarily: *Eighty-one, eighty-seven, eighty-six, eighty-five, eighty-nine* . . .

A new universe, of light, stale air, noise – and people, *countless people* – explodes into being around me. I keep pushing the man on the door, until someone runs towards me and gently prises me away. Elaine. She guides me over to the front steps of a house, while another Runner with a first-aid kit approaches my bloodied passenger. Groups of people stand or sit around electric lanterns, filling the streets and front yards as far as I can see. I point them out to Elaine. 'Look. Aren't they beautiful?'

'John? You OK? Get your breath. It's over.'

'Oh, fuck.' I glance at my watch. 'Twenty-one minutes. Forty-five per cent.' I laugh, hysterically. 'I was afraid of *forty-five per cent*?'

My heart is working twice as hard as it needs to. I pace for a while, until the dizziness begins to subside. Then I flop down on the steps beside Elaine.

A while later, I ask, 'Any others still out there?'

'No.'

'Great.' I'm starting to feel almost lucid. 'So . . . how did you go?'

She shrugs. 'OK. A sweet little girl. She's with her parents somewhere round here. No complications; favourable geometry.' She shrugs again. Elaine is like that; favourable geometry or not, it's never a big deal.

I recount my own experience, leaving out the apparition. I should talk to the medical people first, straighten out what kind of hallucination is or isn't possible, before I start spreading the word that I took a pot shot at a glowing blue pipe organ from the future.

Anyway, if I did any good, I'll know soon enough. If The Intake *does* start drifting away from the planet, that shouldn't take long to make news; I have no idea at what rate the parting would take place, but surely the very next manifestation would be highly unlikely to be on the Earth's surface. Deep in the crust, or halfway into space—

I shake my head. There's no use building up my hopes, prematurely, when I'm still not sure that any of it was real.

Elaine says, 'What?'

'Nothing.'

I check the time again. Twenty-nine minutes. Thirty-three per cent. I glance down the street impatiently. We can see out into the wormhole, of course, but the border is clearly delineated by the sudden drop in illumination, once outward-bound light can no longer penetrate. When The Intake moves on, though, it won't be a matter of looking for subtle shifts in the lighting. While the wormhole is in place, its effects violate the Second Law of Thermodynamics (biased thermal motion, for a start, clearly decreases entropy). In parting, it more than makes amends; it *radially homogenises* the space it occupied, down to a length scale of about a micron. To the rock two hundred metres beneath us, and the atmosphere above – both already highly uniform – this will make little difference, but every house, every garden, every blade of grass – every structure visible to the naked eye – will vanish. Nothing will remain but radial streaks of fine dust, swirling out as the high-pressure air in The Core is finally free to escape.

Thirty-five minutes. Twenty-six per cent. I look around at the weary survivors; even for those who left no family or friends behind, the sense of relief and thankfulness at having reached safety has no doubt faded. They – we – just want the waiting to be over. Everything about the passage of time, everything about the wormhole's uncertain duration, has reversed its significance. Yes, the thing might set us free at any moment – but so long as it hasn't, we're as likely as not to be stuck here for eighteen more minutes.

Forty minutes. Twenty-one per cent.

'Ears are really going to pop tonight,' I say. Or worse; on rare occasions, the pressure in The Core can grow so high that the subsequent decompression gives rise to the bends. That's at least another hour away, though – and if it started to become a real possibility, they'd do an air drop of a drug that would cushion us from the effect.

Fifty minutes. Fifteen per cent.

Everyone is silent now; even the children have stopped crying.

'What's your record?' I ask Elaine.

She rolls her eyes. 'Fifty-six minutes. You were there. Four years ago.'

'Yeah. I remember.'

'Just relax. Be patient.'

'Don't you feel a little silly? I mean, if I'd known, I would have taken my time.'

One hour. Ten per cent. Elaine has dozed off, her head against my shoulder. I'm starting to feel drowsy myself, but a nagging thought keeps me awake.

I've always assumed that the wormhole moves because its efforts to stay put eventually fail – but what if the truth is precisely the opposite? What if it moves because its efforts to move have always, eventually, succeeded? What if the navigator breaks away to try again, as quickly as it can — but its crippled machinery can do no better than a fifty-fifty chance of success, for every eighteen minutes of striving?

Maybe I've put an end to that striving. Maybe I've brought The Intake, finally, to rest.

Eventually, the pressure itself can grow high enough to be fatal. It takes almost five hours, it's a one-in-one-hundred-thousand case, but it has happened once already, there's no reason at all it couldn't happen again. That's what bothers me most: I'd never know. Even if I saw people dying around me, the moment would never arrive when I knew, for certain, that this was the final price.

Elaine stirs without opening her eyes. '*Still?*'

'Yeah.' I put an arm around her; she doesn't seem to mind.

'Well. Don't forget to wake me when it's over.'

APPROPRIATE LOVE

'Your husband is going to survive. There's no question about it.'

I closed my eyes for a moment and almost screamed with relief. At some point during the last thirty-nine sleepless hours, the uncertainty had become far worse than the fear, and I'd almost succeeded in convincing myself that when the surgeons had said it was touch and go, they'd meant there was no hope at all.

'However, he *is* going to need a new body. I don't expect you want to hear another detailed account of his injuries, but there are too many organs damaged, too severely, for individual transplants or repairs to be a viable solution.'

I nodded. I was beginning to like this Mr Allenby, despite the resentment I'd felt when he'd introduced himself: at least he looked me squarely in the eye and made clear, direct statements. Everyone else who'd spoken to me since I'd stepped inside the hospital had hedged their bets; one specialist had handed me a Trauma Analysis Expert System's print-out, with one hundred and thirty-two 'prognostic scenarios' and their respective probabilities.

A new body. That didn't frighten me at all. It sounded so clean, so simple. Individual transplants would have meant cutting Chris open, again and again – each time risking complications, each time subjecting him to a form of assault, however beneficial the intent. For the first few hours, a part of me had clung to the absurd hope that the whole thing had been a mistake; that Chris had walked away from the train wreck, unscratched; that it was someone else in the operating theatre – some thief who had stolen his wallet. After forcing myself to abandon this ludicrous fantasy and accept the truth – that he had been injured, mutilated, almost to the point of death – the prospect of a new body, pristine and whole, seemed an almost equally miraculous reprieve.

Allenby went on, 'Your policy covers that side of things completely; the technicians, the surrogate, the handlers.'

I nodded again, hoping that he wouldn't insist on going into all the details. I *knew* all the details. They'd grow a clone of Chris, intervening *in utero* to prevent its brain from developing the capacity to do anything more than sustain life. Once born, the clone would be forced to a premature, but healthy, maturity, by means of a sequence of elaborate biochemical lies, simulating the effects of normal ageing and exercise at a sub-cellular level. Yes, I still had misgivings – about hiring a woman's body, about creating a brain-damaged 'child' – but we'd agonised about these issues when we'd decided to include the expensive technique in our insurance policies. Now was *not* the time to have second thoughts.

'The new body won't be ready for almost two years. In the mean time, the crucial thing, obviously, is to keep your husband's brain alive. Now, there's no prospect of him regaining consciousness in his present situation, so there's no compelling reason to try to maintain his other organs.'

That jolted me at first – but then I thought: *Why not?* Why not cut Chris free from the wreck of his body, the way he'd been cut free from the wreck of the train? I'd seen the aftermath of the crash replayed on the waiting room TV: rescue workers slicing away at the metal with their clean blue lasers, surgical and precise. Why

not complete the act of liberation? *He* was his brain –
not his crushed limbs, his shattered bones, his bruised
and bleeding organs. What better way could there be
for him to await the restoration of health, than in a
perfect, dreamless sleep, with no risk of pain, un-
encumbered by the remnants of a body that would
ultimately be discarded?

'I should remind you that your policy specifies that
the least costly medically sanctioned option will be used
for life support while the new body is being grown.'

I almost started to contradict him, but then I remembered: it was the only way that we'd been able to
shoehorn the premiums into our budget; the base rate
for body replacements was so high that we'd had to
compromise on the frills. At the time, Chris had joked,
'I just hope they don't get cryonic storage working in
our lifetimes. I don't much fancy you grinning up at me
from the freezer, every day for two years.'

'You're saying you want me to keep nothing but his
brain alive – *because that's the cheapest method*?'

Allenby frowned sympathetically. 'I know, it's unpleasant having to think about costs, at a time like this.
But I stress that the clause refers to *medically sanctioned*
procedures. We certainly wouldn't insist that you do
anything unsafe.'

I nearly said, angrily: You won't *insist* that I do
anything. I didn't, though; I didn't have the energy to
make a scene – and it would have been a hollow boast.
In theory, the decision would be mine alone. In
practice, Global Assurance were paying the bills. They
couldn't dictate treatment, directly – but if I couldn't
raise the money to bridge the gap, I knew I had no
choice but to go along with whatever arrangements
they were willing to fund.

I said, 'You'll have to give me some time, to talk to
the doctors, to think things over.'

'Yes, of course. Absolutely. I should explain,

though, that of all the various options—'

I put up a hand to silence him. '*Please.* Do we have to go into this right now? I told you, I need to talk to the doctors. I *need* to get some sleep. I know: eventually, I'm going to have to come to terms with all the details . . . the different life-support companies, the different services they offer, the different kinds of machines . . . whatever. But it can wait for twelve hours, can't it? *Please.*'

It wasn't just that I was desperately tired, probably still in shock – and beginning to suspect that I was being railroaded into some off-the-shelf 'package solution' that Allenby had already costed down to the last cent. There was a woman in a white coat standing nearby, glancing our way surreptitiously every few seconds, as if waiting for the conversation to end. I hadn't seen her before, but that didn't prove that she wasn't part of the team looking after Chris; they'd sent me six different doctors already. If she had news, I wanted to hear it.

Allenby said, 'I'm sorry, but if you could just bear with me for a few more minutes, I really *do* need to explain something.'

His tone was apologetic, but tenacious. I didn't feel tenacious at all; I felt like I'd been struck all over with a rubber mallet. I didn't trust myself to keep arguing without losing control – and anyway, it seemed like letting him say his piece would be the fastest way to get rid of him. If he snowed me under with details that I wasn't ready to take in, then I'd just switch off, and make him repeat it all later.

I said, 'Go on.'

'Of all the various options, the least costly doesn't involve a life-support *machine* at all. There's a technique called biological life support that's recently been perfected in Europe. Over a two-year period, it's more economical than other methods by a factor of about twenty. What's more, the risk profile is extremely favourable.'

'Biological life support? I've never even heard of it.'

'Well, yes, it is quite new, but I assure you, it's down to a fine art.'

'Yes, but *what is it*? What does it actually entail?'

'The brain is kept alive by sharing a second party's blood supply.'

I stared at him. '*What*? You mean . . . create some two-headed . . . ?'

After so long without sleep, my sense of reality was already thinly stretched. For a moment, I literally believed that I was dreaming – that I'd fallen asleep on the waiting room couch and dreamed of good news, and now my wish-fulfilling fantasy was decaying into a mocking black farce, to punish me for my ludicrous optimism.

But Allenby didn't whip out a glossy brochure, showing satisfied customers beaming cheek-to-cheek with their hosts. He said, 'No, no, no. Of course not. The brain is removed from the skull completely, and encased in protective membranes, in a fluid-filled sac. And it's sited internally.'

'Internally? *Where*, internally?'

He hesitated, and stole a glance at the white-coated woman, who was still hovering impatiently nearby. She seemed to take this as some kind of signal, and began to approach us. Allenby, I realised, hadn't meant her to do so, and for a moment he was flustered – but he soon regained his composure, and made the best of the intrusion.

He said, 'Ms Perrini, this is Dr Gail Sumner. Without a doubt, one of this hospital's brightest young gynaecologists.'

Dr Sumner flashed him a gleaming that-will-be-all-thanks smile, then put one hand on my shoulder and started to steer me away.

★

I went – electronically – to every bank on the planet, but they all seemed to feed my financial parameters into the same equations, and even at the most punitive interest rates, no one was willing to loan me a tenth of the amount I needed to make up the difference. Biological life support was just *so much* cheaper than traditional methods.

My younger sister, Debra, said, 'Why not have a total hysterectomy? Slash and burn, yeah! That'd teach the bastards to try colonising your womb!'

Everyone around me was going mad. 'And then what? Chris ends up dead, and I end up mutilated. That's not my idea of victory.'

'You would have made a point.'

'I don't *want* to make a point.'

'But you don't want to be forced to carry him, do you? Listen: if you hired the right PR people – on a contingency basis – and made the right gestures, you could get seventy, eighty per cent of the public behind you. Organise a boycott. Give this insurance company enough bad publicity, and enough financial pain, and they'll end up paying for whatever you want.'

'No.'

'You can't just think of yourself, Carla. You have to think of all the other women who'll be treated the same way, if you don't put up a fight.'

Maybe she was right – but I knew I couldn't go through with it. I couldn't turn myself into a *cause célèbre* and battle it out in the media; I just didn't have that kind of strength, that kind of stamina. And I thought: why should I *have to*? Why should I have to mount some kind of national PR campaign, just to get a simple contract honoured fairly?

I sought legal advice.

'Of course, they can't *force* you to do it. There are laws against slavery.'

'Yes – but in practice, what's the alternative? What

else can I actually *do*?'

'Let your husband die. Have them switch off the life-support machine he's on at present. That's not illegal. The hospital can, and will, do just that, with or without your consent, the moment they're no longer being paid.'

I'd already been told this half a dozen times, but I still couldn't quite believe it. 'How can it be legal to murder him? It's not even euthanasia – he has every chance of recovering, every chance of leading a perfectly normal life.'

The solicitor shook her head. 'The technology exists to give just about anyone – however sick, however old, however badly injured – a *perfectly normal life*. But it all costs money. Resources are limited. Even if doctors and medical technicians were compelled to provide their services, free of charge, to whoever demanded them . . . and like I said, there are laws against slavery . . . well, someone, somehow, would still have to miss out. The present government sees the market as the best way of determining who that is.'

'Well, I have no intention of letting him die. All I want to do is to keep him on a life-support *machine*, for two years—'

'You may want it, but I'm afraid you simply can't afford it. Have you thought of hiring someone else to carry him? You're using a surrogate for his new body, why not use one for his brain? It would be expensive – but not as expensive as mechanical means. You might be able to scrape up the difference.'

'There shouldn't *be* any fucking difference! Surrogates get paid a fortune! What gives Global Assurance the right to use *my* body for free?'

'Ah. There's a clause in your policy . . .' She tapped a few keys on her work station, and read from the screen: '. . . *while in no way devaluing the contribution of the co-signatory as carer, he or she hereby expressly waives all*

entitlement to remuneration for any such services rendered;
furthermore, in all calculations pursuant to paragraph 97
(b) . . .'

'I thought *that* meant that neither of us could expect
to get paid for nursing duties if the other spent a day in
bed with the flu.'

'I'm afraid the scope is much broader than that. I
repeat, they *do not* have the right to compel you to do
anything – but nor do they have any obligation to pay
for a surrogate. When they compute the costs for the
cheapest way of keeping your husband alive, this
provision entitles them to do so on the basis that you
could choose to provide him with life support.'

'So ultimately, it's all a matter of . . . *accounting*?'

'Exactly.'

For a moment, I could think of nothing more to say. I
knew I was being screwed, but I seemed to have run out
of ways to articulate the fact.

Then it finally occurred to me to ask the most
obvious question of all.

'Suppose it had been the other way around. Suppose
I'd been on that train, instead of Chris. Would they have
paid for a surrogate then – or would they have expected
him to carry *my* brain inside him for two years?'

The solicitor said, poker-faced, 'I really wouldn't like
to hazard a guess on that one.'

Chris was bandaged in places, but most of his body was
covered by a myriad of small machines, clinging to his
skin like beneficial parasites; feeding him, oxygenating
and purifying his blood, dispensing drugs, perhaps
even carrying out repairs on broken bones and damaged
tissue, if only for the sake of staving off further
deterioration. I could see part of his face, including one
eye socket – sewn shut – and patches of bruised skin
here and there. His right hand was entirely bare; they'd
taken off his wedding ring. Both legs had been

amputated just below the thighs.

I couldn't get too near; he was enclosed in a sterile plastic tent, about five metres square, a kind of room within a room. A three-clawed nurse stood in one corner, motionless but vigilant – although I couldn't imagine the circumstances where its intervention would have been of more use than that of the smaller robots already in place.

Visiting him was absurd, of course. He was deep in a coma, not even dreaming; I could give him no comfort. I sat there for hours, though, as if I needed to be constantly reminded that his body *was* injured beyond repair; that he really did need my help, *or he would not survive.*

Sometimes my hesitancy struck me as so abhorrent that I couldn't believe that I'd not yet signed the forms and begun the preparatory treatment. *His life was at stake! How could I think twice? How could I be that selfish?* And yet, this guilt itself made me almost as angry and resentful as everything else: the coercion that wasn't quite coercion, the sexual politics that I couldn't quite bring myself to confront.

To refuse, to let him die, was unthinkable. And yet . . . would I have carried the brain of a total stranger? No. Letting a stranger die wasn't unthinkable at all. Would I have done it for a casual acquaintance? No. A close friend? For some, perhaps – but not for others.

So, just how much did I love him? Enough?

Of course!

Why 'of course'?

It was a matter of . . . *loyalty*? That wasn't the word; it smacked too much of some kind of unwritten contractual obligation, some notion of 'duty', as pernicious and idiotic as patriotism. Well, 'duty' could go fuck itself; that wasn't it at all.

Why, then? Why was he special? What made him

different from the closest friend?

I had no answer, no right words – just a rush of emotion-charged images of Chris. So I told myself: *now* is not the time to analyse it, to dissect it. I don't need an answer; I *know* what I feel.

I lurched between despising myself, for entertaining – however theoretically – the possibility of letting him die, and despising the fact that I was being bullied into doing something with my body that I did *not* want to do. The solution, of course, would have been to do neither – but what did I expect? Some rich benefactor to step out from behind a curtain and make the dilemma vanish?

I'd seen a documentary, a week before the crash, showing some of the hundreds of thousands of men and women in central Africa, who spent their whole lives nursing dying relatives, simply because they couldn't afford the AIDS drugs that had virtually wiped out the disease in wealthier countries, twenty years before. If *they* could have saved the lives of their loved ones by the minuscule 'sacrifice' of carrying an extra kilogram and a half for two years . . .

In the end, I gave up trying to reconcile all the contradictions. I had a right to feel angry and cheated and resentful – but the fact remained that *I wanted Chris to live*. If I wasn't going to be manipulated, it had to work both ways; reacting blindly against the way I'd been treated would have been no less stupid and dishonest than the most supine cooperation.

It occurred to me – belatedly – that Global Assurance might not have been entirely artless in the way they'd antagonised me. After all, if I let Chris die, they'd be spared not just the meagre cost of biological life support, with the womb thrown in rent-free, but the whole expensive business of the replacement body as well. A little calculated crassness, a little reverse psychology . . .

The only way to keep my sanity was to transcend all this bullshit; to declare Global Assurance and their machinations irrelevant; to carry his brain – not because I'd been coerced; not because I felt guilty, or obliged; not to prove that I couldn't be manipulated – but for the simple reason that I loved him enough to want to save his life.

They injected me with a gene-tailed blastocyst, a cluster of cells which implanted in the uterine wall and fooled my body into thinking that I was pregnant.

Fooled? My periods ceased. I suffered morning sickness, anaemia, immune suppression, hunger pangs. The pseudo-embryo grew at a literally dizzying rate, much faster than any child, rapidly forming the protective membranes and amniotic sac, and creating a placental blood supply that would eventually have the capacity to sustain an oxygen-hungry brain.

I'd planned to work on as if nothing special was happening, but I soon discovered that I couldn't; I was just too sick, and too exhausted, to function normally. In five weeks, the thing inside me would grow to the size that a foetus would have taken *five months* to reach. I swallowed a fistful of dietary supplement capsules with every meal, but I was still too lethargic to do much more than sit around the flat, making desultory attempts to stave off boredom with books and junk TV. I vomited once or twice a day, urinated three or four times a night. All of which was bad enough – but I'm sure I felt far more miserable than these symptoms alone could have made me.

Perhaps half the problem was the lack of any simple way of *thinking about* what was happening to me. Apart from the actual structure of the 'embryo', I *was* pregnant – in every biochemical and physiological sense of the word – but I could hardly let myself go along with the deception. Even half pretending that the mass of amorphous tissue in my womb was *a child* would have been setting myself up for a complete emotional meltdown. But – what was it, then? *A tumour?* That was closer to the truth, but it wasn't exactly the kind of substitute image I needed.

Of course, intellectually, I knew precisely what was inside me, and precisely what would become of it. I was *not* pregnant with a child who was destined to be ripped out of my womb to make way for my husband's brain. I did *not* have a vampiric tumour that would keep on growing until it drained so much blood from me that I'd be too weak to move. I was carrying a benign growth, a tool designed for a specific task – a task that I'd decided to accept.

So why did I feel perpetually confused, and depressed – and at times, so desperate that I fantasised about suicide and miscarriage, about slashing myself open, or throwing myself down the stairs? I was tired, I was nauseous, I didn't expect to be dancing for joy – but why was I so fucking unhappy that I couldn't stop thinking of death?

I could have recited some kind of explanatory mantra: *I'm doing this for Chris. I'm doing this for Chris.*

I didn't, though. I already resented him enough; I didn't want to end up hating him.

Early in the sixth week, an ultrasound scan showed that the amniotic sac had reached the necessary size, and Doppler analysis of the blood flow confirmed that it, too, was on target. I went into hospital for the substitution.

I could have paid Chris one final visit, but I stayed away. I didn't want to dwell upon the mechanics of what lay ahead.

Dr Sumner said, 'There's nothing to worry about. Foetal surgery far more complex than this is routine.'

I said, through gritted teeth, 'This *isn't* foetal

surgery.'

She said, 'Well . . . no.' As if the news were a revelation.

When I woke after the operation, I felt sicker than ever. I rested one hand on my belly; the wound was clean and numb, the stitches hidden. I'd been told that there wouldn't even be a scar.

I thought: *He's inside me. They can't hurt him now. I've won that much.*

I closed my eyes. I had no trouble imagining Chris, the way he'd been – *the way he would be, again.* I drifted halfway back to sleep, shamelessly dredging up images of all the happiest times we'd had. I'd never indulged in sentimental reveries before – it wasn't my style, I hated living in the past – but any trick that sustained me was welcome now. I let myself hear his voice, see his face, feel his touch—

His body, of course, was dead now. Irreversibly dead. I opened my eyes and looked down at the bulge in my abdomen, and pictured what it contained: a lump of meat from his corpse. A lump of grey meat, torn from the skull of his corpse.

I'd fasted for surgery, my stomach was empty, I had nothing to throw up. I lay there for hours, wiping sweat off my face with a corner of the sheet, trying to stop shaking.

In terms of bulk, I was five months pregnant.

In terms of weight, seven months.

For two years.

If Kafka had been a woman . . .

I didn't grow used to it, but I did learn to cope. There were ways to sleep, ways to sit, ways to move that were easier than others. I was tired all day long, but there were times when I had enough energy to feel almost normal again, and I made good use of them. I worked hard, and I didn't fall behind. The Department was launching a new blitz on corporate tax evasion; I threw myself into it with more zeal than I'd ever felt before. My enthusiasm was artificial, but that wasn't the point; I needed the momentum to carry me through.

On good days, I felt optimistic: weary, as always, but triumphantly persistent. On bad days, I thought: You bastards, you think this will make me hate him? It's *you* I'll resent, *you* I'll despise. On bad days, I made plans for Global Assurance. I hadn't been ready to fight them before, but when Chris was safe, and my strength had returned, I'd find a way to hurt them.

The reactions of my colleagues were mixed. Some were admiring. Some thought I'd let myself be exploited. Some were simply revolted by the thought of *a human brain* floating in my womb – and to challenge my own squeamishness, I confronted these people as often as I could.

'Go on, touch it,' I said. 'It won't bite. It won't even kick.'

There was a brain in my womb, pale and convoluted. *So what?* I had an equally unappealing object in my own skull. In fact, my whole body was full of repulsive-looking offal – a fact which had never bothered me before.

So I conquered my visceral reactions to the organ *per se* – but thinking about Chris himself remained a difficult balancing act.

I resisted the insidious temptation to delude myself that I might be 'in touch' with him – by 'telepathy', through the bloodstream, by any means at all. Maybe pregnant mothers had some genuine empathy with their unborn children; I'd never been pregnant, it wasn't for me to judge. Certainly, a child in the womb could hear its mother's voice – but a comatose brain, devoid of sense organs, was a different matter entirely. At best – or worst – perhaps certain hormones in my blood crossed the placenta and had some limited effect on his condition.

On his mood?

He was in a coma, he had no *mood*.

In fact, it was easiest, and safest, not to think of him as even being *located* inside me, let alone experiencing anything there. I was carrying a part of him; the surrogate mother of his clone was carrying another. Only when the two were united would he truly exist again; for now, he was in limbo, neither dead nor alive.

This pragmatic approach worked, most of the time. Of course, there were moments when I suffered a kind of panic at the renewed realization of the bizarre nature of what I'd done. Sometimes I'd wake from nightmares, believing – for a second or two – that Chris was dead and his spirit had possessed me; or that his brain had sent forth nerves into my body and taken control of my limbs; or that he was fully conscious, and going insane from loneliness and sensory deprivation. But I wasn't possessed, my limbs still obeyed me, and every month a PET scan and a 'uterine EEG' proved that he was still comatose – undamaged, but mentally inert.

In fact, the dreams I hated the most were those in which I was carrying a child. I'd wake from *these* with one hand on my belly, rapturously contemplating the miracle of the new life growing inside me – until I came to my senses and dragged myself angrily out of bed. I'd start the morning in the foulest of moods, grinding my teeth as I pissed, banging plates at the breakfast table, screaming insults at no one in particular while I dressed. Lucky I was living alone.

I couldn't really blame my poor besieged body for trying, though. My oversized, marathon pregnancy dragged on and on; no wonder it tried to compensate me for the inconvenience with some stiff medicinal doses of maternal love. How ungrateful my rejection must have seemed; how baffling to find its images and sentiments rejected as *inappropriate*.

So . . . I trampled on Death, and I trampled on Motherhood. Well, *hallelujah*. If sacrifices had to be made, what better victims could there have been than those two emotional slave-drivers? And it was easy, really; logic was on my side, with a vengeance. Chris was *not* dead; I had no reason to mourn him, whatever had become of the body I'd known. And the thing in my womb was *not* a child; permitting a disembodied brain to be the object of motherly love would have been simply farcical.

We think of our lives as circumscribed by cultural and biological taboos, but if people really want to break them, they always seem to find a way. Human beings are capable of anything: torture, genocide, cannibalism, rape. After which – or so I'd heard – most can still be kind to children and animals, be moved to tears by music, and generally behave as if all their emotional faculties are intact.

So, what reason did I have to fear that my own minor – and utterly selfless – transgressions could do me any harm at all?

I never met the new body's surrogate mother, I never saw the clone as a child. I did wonder, though – once I knew that the thing had been born – whether or not she'd found her 'normal' pregnancy as distressing as I'd found mine. Which is easier, I wondered: carrying a brain-damaged child-shaped object, with no potential for human thought, grown from a stranger's DNA – or carrying the sleeping brain of your lover? Which is the harder to keep from loving in inappropriate ways?

At the start, I'd hoped to be able to blur all the details in my mind – I'd wanted to be able to wake one morning and pretend that Chris had merely been *sick*, and was now *recovered*. Over the months, though, I'd come to realise that it was never going to work that way.

When they took out the brain, I should have felt – at the very least – relieved, but I just felt numb, and vaguely disbelieving. The ordeal had gone on for so long; it *couldn't* be over with so little fuss: no trauma, no ceremony. I'd had surreal dreams of laboriously, but triumphantly, giving birth to a healthy pink brain – but even if I'd wanted that (and no doubt the process could have been induced), the organ was too delicate to pass safely through the vagina. This 'Caesarean' removal was just one more blow to my biological expectations; a good thing, of course, in the long run, since my biological expectations could never be fulfilled . . . but I still couldn't help feeling slightly cheated.

So I waited, in a daze, for the proof that it had all been worthwhile.

The brain couldn't simply be transplanted into the clone, like a heart or a kidney. The peripheral nervous system of the new body wasn't identical to that of the old one; identical genes weren't sufficient to ensure that. Also – despite drugs to limit the effect – parts of Chris's brain had atrophied slightly from disuse. So, rather than splicing nerves directly between the imperfectly matched brain and body – which probably would have left him paralysed, deaf, dumb and blind – the impulses would be routed through a computerised 'interface', which would try to sort out the discrepancies. Chris would still have to be rehabilitated, but the computer would speed up the process enormously, constantly striving to bridge the gap between thought and action, between reality and perception.

The first time they let me see him, I didn't recognise him at all. His face was slack, his eyes unfocused; he looked like a large, neurologically impaired child – which, of course, he was. I felt a mild twinge of revulsion. The man I'd seen after the train wreck, swarming with medical robots, had looked far more human, far more whole.

I said, 'Hello. It's me.'

He stared into space.

The technician said, 'It's early days.'

She was right. In the weeks that followed, his progress (or the computer's) was astounding. His posture and expression soon lost their disconcerting neutrality, and the first helpless twitches rapidly gave way to coordinated movement; weak and clumsy, but encouraging. He couldn't talk, but he could meet my eyes, he could squeeze my hand.

He was *in there,* he was *back*, there was no doubt about that.

I worried about his silence – but I discovered later that he'd deliberately spared me his early, faltering attempts at speech.

One evening in the fifth week of his new life, when I came into the room and sat down beside the bed, he turned to me and said clearly, 'They told me what you did. Oh God, Carla, I love you!'

His eyes filled with tears. I bent over and embraced him; it seemed like the right thing to do. And I cried, too – but even as I did so, I couldn't help thinking: None of this can really touch me. It's just one more trick of the body, and I'm immune to all that now.

We made love on the third night he spent at home. I'd expected it to be difficult, a massive psychological hurdle for both of us, but that wasn't the case at all. And after everything we'd come through, why should it have been? I don't know what I'd feared; some poor misguided avatar of the Incest Taboo, crashing through the bedroom window at the critical moment, spurred on by the ghost of a discredited nineteenth-century misogynist?

I suffered no delusion at any level – from the merely subconscious, right down to the endocrine – that Chris was *my son*. Whatever effects two years of placental hormones might have had on me, whatever behavioural programs they 'ought' to have triggered, I'd apparently gained the strength and the insight to undermine completely.

True, his skin was soft and unweathered, and devoid of the scars of a decade of hacking off facial hair. He might have passed for a sixteen-year-old, but I felt no qualms about *that* – any middle-aged man who was rich enough and vain enough could have looked the same.

And when he put his tongue to my breasts, I did not lactate.

We soon started visiting friends; they were tactful, and Chris was glad of that – although personally, I'd have happily discussed any aspect of the procedure. Six months later, he was working again; his old job had been taken, but a new firm was recruiting (and they wanted a youthful image).

Piece by piece, our lives were reassembled.

Nobody, looking at us now, would think that anything had changed.

But they'd be wrong.

To love a *brain* as if it were a *child* would be ludicrous. Geese might be stupid enough to treat the first animal they see upon hatching as their mother, but there are limits to what a sane human being will swallow. So, reason triumphed over instinct, and I conquered my inappropriate love; under the circumstances, there was never really any contest.

Having deconstructed one form of enslavement, though, I find it all too easy to repeat the process, to recognise the very same chains in another guise.

Everything special I once felt for Chris is transparent to me now. I still feel genuine friendship for him, I still feel desire, but there used to be something more. If there hadn't been, I doubt he'd be alive today.

Oh, the signals keep coming through; some part of my brain still pumps out cues for *appropriate* feelings of tenderness, but these messages are as laughable, and as ineffectual, now, as the contrivances of some tenth-rate tear-jerking movie. I just can't suspend my disbelief any more.

I have no trouble going through the motions; inertia makes it easy. And as long as things are working – as long as his company is pleasant and the sex is good – I see no reason to rock the boat. We may stay together for years, or I may walk out tomorrow. I really don't know.

Of course I'm still glad that he survived – and to some degree, I can even admire the courage and selflessness of the woman who saved him. I know that I could never do the same.

Sometimes when we're together, and I see in his eyes the very same helpless passion that I've lost, I'm tempted to pity myself. I think: I was *brutalised*, no wonder I'm a cripple, no wonder I'm so fucked up.

And in a sense, that's a perfectly valid point of view – but I never seem to be able to subscribe to it for long. The new truth has its own cool passion, its own powers of manipulation; it assails me with words like 'freedom' and 'insight', and speaks of the end of all deception. It grows inside me, day by day, and it's far too strong to let me have regrets.

THE MORAL VIROLOGIST

Out on the street, in the dazzling sunshine of a warm
Atlanta morning, a dozen young children were playing.
Chasing, wrestling, and hugging each other, laughing
and yelling, crazy and jubilant for no other reason than
being alive on such a day. Inside the gleaming white
building, though, behind double-glazed windows, the
air was slightly chilly – the way John Shawcross
preferred it – and nothing could be heard but the air
conditioning, and a faint electrical hum.

The schematic of the protein molecule trembled very
slightly. Shawcross grinned, already certain of success.
As the pH displayed in the screen's top left crossed the
critical value – the point at which, according to his
calculations, the energy of conformation B should drop
below that of conformation A – the protein suddenly
convulsed and turned completely inside out. It was
exactly as he had predicted, and his binding studies had
added strong support, but to *see* the transformation
(however complex the algorithms that had led from
reality to screen) was naturally the most satisfying
proof.

He replayed the event backwards and forwards
several times, utterly captivated. This marvellous
device would easily be worth the eight hundred
thousand he'd paid for it. The salesperson had provided
several impressive demonstrations, of course, but this
was the first time Shawcross had used the machine for

his own work. Images of proteins *in solution*! Normal X-ray diffraction could only work with crystalline samples, in which a molecule's configuration often bore little resemblance to its aqueous, biologically relevant, form. An ultrasonically stimulated semi-ordered liquid phase was the key, not to mention some major break-throughs in computing; Shawcross couldn't follow all the details, but that was no impediment to using the machine. He charitably wished upon the inventor Nobel prizes in chemistry, physics and medicine, viewed the stunning results of his experiment once again, then stretched, rose to his feet, and went out in search of lunch.

On his way to the delicatessen, he passed *that* bookshop, as always. A lurid new poster in the window caught his eye, a naked young man stretched out on a bed in a state of postcoital languor, one corner of the sheet only just concealing his groin. Emblazoned across the top of the poster, in imitation of a glowing red neon sign, was the book's title: *A Hot Night's Safe Sex*. Shawcross shook his head in anger and disbelief. What was wrong with people? Hadn't they read his advertisement? Were they blind? Stupid? Arrogant? Safety lay *only* in the obedience of God's laws.

After eating, he called in at a newsagent that carried several foreign papers. The previous Saturday's edi-tions had arrived, and his advertisement was in all of them, where necessary translated into the appropriate languages. Half a page in a major newspaper was not cheap anywhere in the world, but then, money had never been a problem.

ADULTERERS! SODOMITES!
REPENT AND BE SAVED!
ABANDON YOUR WICKEDNESS *NOW*
OR DIE AND BURN FOREVER!

He couldn't have put it more plainly, could he? Nobody could claim that they hadn't been warned.

In 1981, Matthew Shawcross bought a tiny, run-down cable TV station in the Bible belt, which until then had split its air time between scratchy black-and-white film clips of fifties gospel singers, and local novelty acts such as snake handlers (protected by their faith, not to mention the removal of their pets' venom glands) and epileptic children (encouraged by their parents' prayers, and a carefully timed withdrawal of medication, to let the spirit move them). Matthew Shawcross dragged the station into the nineteen eighties, spending a fortune on a thirty-second computer-animated station ID (a fleet of pirouetting, crenellated spaceships firing crucifix-shaped missiles into a relief map of the USA, chiselling out the station logo of Liberty, holding up, not a torch, but a cross), showing the latest, slickest gospel rock video clips, 'Christian' soap operas and 'Christian' game shows, and, above all, identifying issues – communism, depravity, godlessness in schools – which could serve as the themes for telethons to raise funds to expand the station, so that future telethons might be even more successful.

Ten years later, he owned one of the country's biggest cable TV networks.

John Shawcross was at college, on the verge of taking up palaeontology, when AIDS first began to make the news in a big way. As the epidemic snowballed, and the spiritual celebrities he most admired (his father included) began proclaiming the disease to be God's will, he found himself increasingly obsessed by it. In an age where the word *miracle* belonged to medicine and science, here was a plague straight out of the Old Testament, destroying the wicked and sparing the righteous (give or take some haemophiliacs and trans-fusion recipients), proving to Shawcross beyond any doubt that sinners could be punished in this life, as well as in the next. This was, he decided, valuable in at least two ways: not only would sinners to whom damnation had seemed a remote and unproven threat now have a powerful, wordly reason to reform, but the righteous would be strengthened in their resolve by this unarguable sign of heavenly support and approval.

In short, the mere existence of AIDS made John Shawcross feel *good*, and he gradually became convinced that some kind of personal involvement with HIV, the AIDS virus, would make him feel even better. He lay awake at night, pondering God's mysterious ways, and wondering how he could get in on the act. AIDS research would be aimed at a cure, so how could he possibly justify involving himself with *that*?

Then, in the early hours of one cold morning, he was woken by sounds from the room next to his. Giggling, grunting, and the squeaking of bed springs. He wrapped his pillow around his ears and tried to go back to sleep, but the sounds could not be ignored – nor could the effect they wrought on his own fallible flesh. He masturbated for a while, on the pretext of trying to manually crush his unwanted erection, but stopped short of orgasm, and lay, shivering, in a state of heightened moral perception. It was a different woman every week; he'd seen them leaving in the morning. He'd tried to counsel his fellow student, but had been mocked for his troubles. Shawcross didn't blame the poor young man; was it any wonder people laughed at the truth, when every movie, every book, every magazine, every rock song, still sanctioned promiscuity and perversion, making them out to be normal and good? The fear of AIDS might have saved millions of sinners, but millions more still ignored it, absurdly convinced that *their* chosen partners could never be infected, or trusting in *condoms* to frustrate the will of God!

The trouble was, vast segments of the population *had*, in spite of their wantonness, remained uninfected, and the use of condoms, according to the studies he'd read, *did* seem to reduce the risk of transmission. These facts disturbed Shawcross a great deal. Why would an omnipotent God create an imperfect tool? Was it a matter of divine mercy? That was possible, he conceded, but it struck him as rather distasteful: sexual Russian roulette was hardly a fitting image of the Lord's capacity for forgiveness.

Or – Shawcross tingled all over as the possibility crystallised in his brain – might AIDS be no more than a mere prophetic shadow, hinting at a future plague a thousand times more terrible? A warning to the wicked to change their ways while they still had time? *An example to the righteous as to how they might do His will?*

Shawcross broke into a sweat. The sinners next door moaned as if already in Hell, the thin dividing wall vibrated, the wind rose up to shake the dark trees and rattle his window. What was this wild idea in his head? A true message from God, or the product of his own imperfect understanding? He needed guidance! He switched on his reading lamp and picked up his Bible from the bedside table. With his eyes closed, he opened the book at random.

He recognised the passage at the very first glance. He ought to have; he'd read it and reread it a hundred times, and knew it almost by heart. *The destruction of Sodom and Gomorrah*.

At first, he tried to deny his destiny: He was unworthy! A sinner himself! An ignorant child! But everyone was unworthy, everyone was a sinner, everyone was an ignorant child in God's eyes. It was pride, not humility, that spoke against God's choice of him.

By morning, not a trace of doubt remained.

Dropping palaeontology was a great relief; defending Creationism with any conviction required a certain, very special, way of thinking, and he had never been quite sure that he could master it. Biochemistry, on the other hand, he mastered with ease (confirmation, if any was needed, that he'd made the right decision). He topped his classes every year, and went on to do a PhD in Molecular Biology at Harvard, then postdoctoral work at the NIH, and fellowships in Canada and France. He lived for his work, pushing himself mercilessly, but always taking care not to be too conspicuous in his achievements. He published very little, usually as a modest third or fourth co-author, and when at last he flew home from France, nobody in his field knew, or would have much cared, that John Shawcross had returned, ready to begin his real work.

Shawcross worked alone in the gleaming white building that served as both laboratory and home. He couldn't risk taking on employees, no matter how closely their beliefs might have matched his own. He hadn't even let his *parents* in on the secret; he told them he was engaged in theoretical molecular genetics, which was a lie of omission only – and he had no need to beg his father for money week by week, since for tax reasons, twenty-five per cent of the Shawcross empire's massive profit was routinely paid into accounts in his name.

His lab was filled with shiny grey boxes, from which ribbon cables snaked to PCs; the latest generation, fully automated, synthesisers and sequencers of DNA, RNA, and proteins (all available off the shelf, to anyone with the money to buy them). Half a dozen robot arms did all the grunt work: pipetting and diluting reagents, labelling tubes, loading and unloading centrifuges.

At first Shawcross spent most of his time working with computers, searching databases for the sequence and structure information that would provide him with starting points, later buying time on a supercomputer to predict the shapes and interactions of molecules as yet unknown.

When aqueous X-ray diffraction become possible, his work sped up by a factor of ten; to synthesise and observe the actual proteins and nucleic acids was now both faster, and more reliable, than the hideously complex process (even with the best short cuts, approximations and tricks) of solving Schrödinger's equation for a molecule consisting of hundreds of thousands of atoms.

Base by base, gene by gene, the Shawcross virus grew.

As the woman removed the last of her clothes, Shawcross, sitting naked on the motel room's plastic bucket chair, said, 'You must have had sexual intercourse with hundreds of men.'

'Thousands. Don't you want to come closer, honey? Can you see OK from there?'

'I can see fine.'

She lay back, still for a moment with her hands cupping her breasts, then she closed her eyes and began to slide her palms across her torso.

This was the two hundredth occasion on which Shawcross had paid a woman to tempt him. When he had begun the desensitising process five years before, he had found it almost unbearable. Tonight he knew he would sit calmly and watch the woman achieve, or skilfully imitate, orgasm, without experiencing even a flicker of lust himself.

'You take precautions, I suppose.'

She smiled, but kept her eyes closed. 'Damn right I do. If a man won't wear a condom, he can take his business elsewhere. And *I* put it on, he doesn't do it himself. When I put it on, it stays on. Why, have you changed your mind?'

'No. Just curious.'

Shawcross always paid in full, in advance, for the act he did not perform, and always explained to the woman, very clearly at the start, that at any time he might weaken, he might make the decision to rise from the chair and join her. No mere circumstantial impediment could take any credit for his inaction; nothing but his own free will stood between him and mortal sin.

Tonight, he wondered why he continued. The 'temptation' had become a formal ritual, with no doubt whatsoever as to the outcome.

No doubt? Surely that was pride speaking, his wiliest and most persistent enemy. *Every* man and woman forever trod the edge of a precipice over the inferno, at risk more than ever of falling to those hungry flames when he or she least believed it possible.

Shawcross stood and walked over to the woman. Without hesitation, he placed one hand on her ankle. She opened her eyes and sat up, regarding him with amusement, then took hold of his wrist and began to drag his hand along her leg, pressing it hard against the warm, smooth skin.

Just above the knee, he began to panic – but it wasn't until his fingers struck moisture that he pulled free with a strangled mewling sound, and staggered back to the chair, breathless and shaking.

That was more like it.

The Shawcross virus was to be a masterful piece of biological clockwork (the likes of which William Paley could never have imagined – and which no godless evolutionist would dare attribute to the 'blind watch-maker' of chance). Its single strand of RNA would describe, not one, but *four* potential organisms.

Shawcross virus A, SVA, the 'anonymous' form, would be highly infectious, but utterly benign. It would reproduce within a variety of host cells in the skin and mucous membranes, without causing the least disruption to normal cellular functions. Its protein coat had been designed so that every exposed site mimicked some portion of a *naturally occurring* human protein; the immune system being necessarily blind to these substances (to avoid attacking the body itself), would be equally blind to the invader.

Small numbers of SVA would make their way into the bloodstream, infecting T-lymphocytes, and triggering stage two of the virus's genetic program. A system of enzymes would make RNA copies of hundreds of genes from every chromosome of the host cell's DNA, and these copies would then be incorporated into the virus itself. So, the next generation of the virus would carry with it, in effect, *a genetic fingerprint* of the host in which it had come into being.

Shawcross called this second form SVC, the C standing for 'customised' (since every individual's unique genetic profile would give rise to a unique strain of SVC), or 'celibate' (because in a celibate person, only SVA and SVC would be present).

SVC would be able to survive only in blood, semen and vaginal fluids. Like SVA, it would be immunologically invisible, but with an added twist: its choice of camouflage would vary wildly from person to person, so that even if its disguise was imperfect, and antibodies to a dozen (or a hundred, or a thousand) *particular* strains could be produced, universal vaccination would remain impossible.

Like SVA, it would not alter the function of its hosts – with one minor exception. When infecting cells in the vaginal mucous membrane, the prostate, or the seminiferous epithelium, it would cause the manufacture and secretion from these cells of several dozen enzymes specifically designed to degrade varieties of rubber. The holes created by a brief exposure would be invisibly small – but from a viral point of view, they'd be enormous.

317

Upon reinfecting T cells, SVC would be capable of making an 'informed decision' as to what the next generation would be. Like SVA, it would create a genetic fingerprint of its host cell. It would then compare this with its stored, ancestral copy. If the two fingerprints were identical – proving that the customised strain had remained within the body in which it had begun – its daughters would be, simply, more SVC.

However, if the fingerprints failed to match, implying that the strain had now crossed into another person's body (*and* if gender-specific markers showed that the two hosts were *not* of the same sex), the daughter virus would be a third variety, SVM, containing both fingerprints. The M stood for 'monogamous', or 'marriage certificate'. Shawcross, a great romantic, found it almost unbearably sweet to think of two people's love for each other being expressed in this way, deep down at the subcellular level, and of man and wife, by the very act of making love, signing a contract of faithfulness until death, literally in their own blood.

SVM would be, externally, much like SVC. Of course, when it infected a T cell it would check the host's fingerprint against *both* stored copies, and if *either* one matched, all would be well, and more SVM would be produced.

Shawcross called the fourth form of the virus SVD. It could arise in two ways; from SVC directly, when the gender markers implied that a homosexual act had taken place, or from SVM, when the detection of a third genetic fingerprint suggested that the molecular marriage contract had been violated.

SVD forced its host cells to secrete enzymes that catalysed the disintegration of vital structural proteins in blood vessel walls. Sufferers from an SVD infection would undergo massive haemorrhaging all over their body. Shawcross had found that mice died within two or three minutes of an injection of pre-infected lympho-cytes, and rabbits within five or six minutes; the timing varied slightly, depending on the choice of injection site.

SVD was designed so that its protein coat would degrade in air, or in solutions outside a narrow range of temperature and pH, and its RNA alone was non-infectious. Catching SVD from a dying victim would be almost impossible. Because of the swiftness of death, an adulterer would have no time to infect their innocent spouse; the widow or widower would, of course, be sentenced to celibacy for the rest of their life, but Shawcross did not think this too harsh: it took two people to make a marriage, he reasoned, and some small share of the blame could always be apportioned to the other partner.

Even assuming that the virus fulfilled its design goals precisely, Shawcross acknowledged a number of com-plications:

Blood transfusions would become impractical until a foolproof method of killing the virus *in vitro* was found. Five years ago this would have been tragic, but Shawcross was encouraged by the latest work in synthetic and cultured blood components, and had no doubt that his epidemic would cause more funds and manpower to be diverted into the area. Transplants were less easily dealt with, but Shawcross thought them somewhat frivolous anyway, an expensive and rarely justifiable use of scarce resources.

Doctors, nurses, dentists, paramedics, police, under-takers . . . well, in fact *everyone*, would have to take extreme precautions to avoid exposure to other peo-ple's blood. Shawcross was impressed, though of course not surprised, at God's foresight here: the rarer and less deadly AIDS virus had gone before, encourag-ing practices verging on the paranoid in dozens of professions, multiplying rubber glove sales by orders of magnitude. Now the overkill would all be justified, since *everyone* would be infected with, at the very least, SVC.

Rape of virgin by virgin would become a sort of biological shotgun wedding; any other kind would be murder and suicide. The death of the victim would be tragic, of course, but the near-certain death of the rapist would surely be an overwhelming deterrent. Shawcross decided that the crime would virtually disappear.

Homosexual incest between identical twins would escape punishment, since the virus could have no way of telling one from the other. This omission irritated Shawcross, especially since he was unable to find any published statistics that would allow him to judge the prevalence of such abominable behaviour. In the end he decided that this minor flaw would constitute a necessary, token remnant – a kind of moral fossil – of man's inalienable potential to consciously choose evil.

It was in the northern summer of 2000 that the virus was completed, and tested as well as it could be in tissue culture experiments and on laboratory animals. Apart from establishing the fatality of SVD (created by test-tube simulations of human sins of the flesh), rats, mice and rabbits were of little value, because so much of the virus's behaviour was tied up in its interaction with the human genome. In cultured human cell lines, though, the clockwork all seemed to unwind, exactly as far, and never further, than appropriate to the circumstances; generation after generation of SVA, SVC and SVM remained stable and benign. Of course more experiments could have been done, more time put aside to ponder the consequences, but that would have been the case regardless.

It was time to act. The latest drugs meant that AIDS was now rarely fatal – at least, not to those who could afford the treatment. The third millennium was fast approaching, a symbolic opportunity not to be ignored. Shawcross was doing God's work; what need did he have for quality control? True, he was an imperfect human instrument in God's hands, and at every stage of the task he had blundered and failed a dozen times before achieving perfection, but that was in the laboratory, where mistakes could be discovered and rectified easily. Surely God would never permit anything less than an infallible virus, His will made RNA, out into the world.

So Shawcross visited a travel agent, then infected himself with SVA.

Shawcross went west, crossing the Pacific at once, saving his own continent for last. He stuck to large population centres: Tokyo, Beijing, Seoul, Bangkok, Manila, Sydney, New Delhi, Cairo. SVA could survive indefinitely, dormant but potentially infectious, on any surface that wasn't intentionally sterilised. The seats in a jet, the furniture in a hotel room, aren't autoclaved too often.

Shawcross didn't visit prostitutes; it was SVA that he wanted to spread, and SVA was not a venereal disease. Instead, he simply played the tourist, sightseeing, shopping, catching public transport, swimming in hotel pools. He relaxed at a frantic pace, adopting a schedule of remorseless recreation that, he soon felt, only divine intervention sustained.

Not surprisingly, by the time he reached London he was a wreck, a suntanned zombie in a fading floral shirt, with eyes as glazed as the multicoated lens of his obligatory (if filmless) camera. Tiredness, jet lag, and endless changes of cuisine and surroundings (paradoxically made worse by an underlying glutinous monotony to be found in food and cities alike) had all worked together to slowly drag him down into a muddy, trancelike state of mind. He dreamt of airports and hotels and jets, and woke in the same places, unable to distinguish between memories and dreams.

His faith held out through it all, of course, invulnerably axiomatic, but he worried nonetheless. High-altitude jet travel meant extra exposure to cosmic rays; could he be certain that the virus's mechanisms for self-checking and mutation repair were fail-safe? God would be watching over all the trillions of replications, but still, he would feel better when he was home again, and could test the strain he'd been carrying for any evidence of defects.

Exhausted, he stayed in his hotel room for days, when he should have been out jostling Londoners, not to mention the crowds of international tourists making the best of the end of summer. News of his plague was only now beginning to grow beyond isolated items about mystery deaths; health authorities were investigating, but had had little time to assemble all the data, and were naturally reluctant to make premature announcements. It was too late, anyway; even if Shawcross had been found and quarantined at once, and all national frontiers sealed, people he had infected so far would already have taken SVA to every corner of the globe.

He missed his flight to Dublin. He missed his flight to Ontario. He ate and slept, and dreamt of eating, sleeping and dreaming. *The Times* arrived each morning on his breakfast tray, each day devoting more and more space to proof of his success, but still lacking the special kind of headline he longed for: a black-and-white acknowledgement of the plague's divine purpose. Experts began declaring that all the signs pointed to a biological weapon run amok, with Libya and Iraq the prime suspects; sources in Israeli intelligence had confirmed that both countries had greatly expanded their research programs in recent years. If any epidemiologist had realised that only adulterers and homosexuals were dying, the idea had not yet filtered through to the press.

Eventually, Shawcross checked out of the hotel. There was no need for him to travel through Canada, the States, or Central and South America; all the news showed that other travellers had long since done his job for him. He booked a flight home, but had nine hours to kill.

'I will do no such thing! Now take your money and get out.'

'But—'

'*Straight sex*, it says in the foyer. Can't you read?'

'I don't want sex. I won't touch you. You don't understand. I want you to touch *yourself*. I only want to be *tempted*—'

'Well, walk down the street with both eyes open, that should be temptation enough.' The woman glared at him, but Shawcross didn't budge. There was an important principle at stake. 'I've *paid* you!' he whined.

She dropped the notes on his lap. 'And now you have your money back. Good night.'

He climbed to his feet. 'God's going to punish you. You're going to die a horrible death, blood leaking out of all your veins—'

'There'll be blood leaking out of *you* if I have to call the lads to assist you off the premises.'

'Haven't you read about the plague? Don't you realise what it is, what it means? It's God's punishment for fornicators—'

'Oh, get out, you blaspheming lunatic.'

'*Blaspheming?*' Shawcross was stunned. 'You don't know who you're talking to! I'm God's chosen instrument!'

She scowled at him. 'You're the devil's own arsehole, that's what you are. Now clear off.'

As Shawcross tried to stare her down, a peculiar

dizziness took hold of him. *She was going to die, and he would be responsible.* For several seconds, this simple realisation sat unchallenged in his brain, naked, awful, obscene in its clarity. He waited for the usual chorus of abstractions and rationalisations to rise up and conceal it.

And waited.

Finally he knew that he couldn't leave the room without doing his best to save her life.

'Listen to me! Take this money and let me talk, that's all. Let me talk for five minutes, then I'll go.'

'Talk about what?'

'The plague. *Listen!* I know more about the plague than anyone else on the planet.' The woman mimed disbelief and impatience. 'It's true! I'm an expert virologist, I work for, ah, I work for the Centres for Disease Control, in Atlanta, Georgia. Everything I'm going to tell you will be made public in a couple of days, but I'm telling you *now*, because you're at risk from this job, and in a couple of days it might be too late.'

He explained, in the simplest language he could manage, the four stages of the virus, the concept of a stored host fingerprint, the fatal consequences if a third person's SVM ever entered her blood. She sat through it all in silence.

'Do you understand what I've said?'

'Sure I do. That doesn't mean I believe it.'

He leapt to his feet and shook her. 'I'm deadly serious! I'm telling you the absolute truth! God is punishing adulterers! AIDS was just a warning; this time *no* sinner will escape! *No one!*'

She removed his hands. 'Your God and my God don't have a lot in common.'

'*Your God!*' he spat.

'Oh, and aren't I entitled to one? Excuse me. I thought they'd put it in some United Nations Charter: everyone's issued with their own God at birth, though if you break Him or lose Him along the way there's no free replacement.'

'Now who's blaspheming?'

She shrugged. 'Well, my God's still functioning, but yours sounds a bit of a disaster. Mine might not cure all the problems in the world, but at least he doesn't bend over backwards to make them worse.'

Shawcross was indignant. 'A few people will die. A few sinners, it can't be helped. But think of what the world will be like when *the message finally gets through*! No unfaithfulness, no rape; every marriage lasting until death—'

She grimaced with distaste. 'For all the wrong reasons.'

'No! It might start out that way. People are weak, they need a reason, a selfish reason, to be good. But given time it will grow to be more than that; a habit, then a tradition, then part of human nature. The virus won't matter any more. People will have *changed*.'

'Well, maybe; if monogamy is inheritable, I suppose natural selection would eventually—'

Shawcross stared at her, wondering if he was losing his mind, then screamed, '*Stop it!* There is *no such thing* as "natural selection"!' He'd never been lectured on Darwinism in any brothel back home, but then what could he expect in a country run by godless socialists? He calmed down slightly, and added, 'I *meant* a change in the spiritual values of the world culture.'

The woman shrugged, unmoved by the outburst. 'I know you don't give a damn what I think, but I'm going to tell you anyway. *You* are the saddest, most screwed-up man I've set eyes on all week. So, you've chosen a particular moral code to live by; that's your right, and good luck to you. But you have no real *faith* in what you're doing; you're so uncertain of your choice that you need God to pour down fire and brimstone on everyone who's chosen differently, just to prove to you that you're right. God fails to oblige, so you hunt through the natural disasters – earthquakes, floods, famines, epidemics – winnowing out examples of the "punishment of sinners". You think you're proving that God's on your side? All you're proving is your own insecurity.'

She glanced at her watch. 'Well, your five minutes are long gone, and I never talk theology for free. I've got one last question though, if you don't mind, since you're likely to be the last "expert virologist" I run into for a while.'

'Ask.' She was going to die. He'd done his best to save her, and he'd failed. Well, hundreds of thousands would die with her. He had no choice but to accept that; his faith would keep him sane.

'This virus that your God's designed is only supposed to harm adulterers and gays? Right?'

'Yes. Haven't you listened? That's the whole point! The mechanism is ingenious, the DNA fingerprint—'

She spoke very slowly, opening her mouth extra wide, as if addressing a deaf or demented person. 'Suppose some sweet, monogamous, married couple have sex. Suppose the woman becomes pregnant. The child won't have exactly the same set of genes as either parent. So what happens to it? What happens to the baby?'

Shawcross just stared at her. *What happens to the baby?* His mind was blank. He was tired, he was home-sick . . . all the pressure, all the worries . . . he'd been through an *ordeal* – how could she expect him to think straight, how could she expect him to explain every tiny detail? *What happens to the baby?* What happens to the innocent, newly made child? He struggled to concentrate, to organise his thoughts, but the absolute horror of what she was suggesting tugged at his attention, like a tiny, cold, insistent hand, dragging him, inch by inch, towards madness.

Suddenly, he burst into laughter; he almost wept with relief. He shook his head at the stupid whore, and said, 'You can't trick me like that! I thought of *babies* back in ninety-four! At little Joel's christening – he's my cousin's boy.' He grinned and shook his head again, giddy with happiness. 'I fixed the problem: I added genes to SVC and SVM, for surface receptors to half a dozen foetal blood proteins; if any of the receptors are activated, the next generation of the virus is *pure SVA*. It's even safe to breast-feed, for about a month, because the foetal proteins take a while to be replaced.'

'For about a month,' echoed the woman. Then, 'What do you mean, you *added* genes . . . ?'

Shawcross was already bolting from the room.

He ran, aimlessly, until he was breathless and stumbling, then he limped through the streets, clutching his head, ignoring the stares and insults of passers-by. A month wasn't long enough, he'd *known* that all along, but somehow he'd forgotten just what it was he'd intended to *do* about it. There'd been too many details, too many complications.

Already, children would be dying.

He came to a halt in a deserted side street, behind a row of tawdry nightclubs, and slumped to the ground. He sat against a cold brick wall, shivering and hugging himself. Muffled music reached him, thin and distorted.

Where had he gone wrong? Hadn't he taken his revelation of God's purpose in creating AIDS to its logical conclusion? Hadn't he devoted his whole life to perfecting a biological machine able to discern good from evil? If something so hideously complex, so painstakingly contrived as his virus still couldn't do the job . . .

Waves of blackness moved across his vision.

What if he'd been wrong, from the start?

What if none of his work had been God's will, after all?

Shawcross contemplated this idea with a shell-shocked kind of tranquillity. It was too late to halt the spread of the virus, but he could go to the authorities and arm them with the details that would otherwise take them years to discover. Once they knew about the foetal protein receptors, a protective drug exploiting that knowledge might be possible in a matter of months.

Such a drug would enable breast-feeding, blood transfusions and organ transplants. It would also allow adulterers to copulate, and homosexuals to practise their abominations. It would be utterly morally neutral, the negation of everything he'd lived for. He stared up at the blank sky, with a growing sense of panic. Could he do that? Tear himself down and start again? He had to! *Children were dying.* Somehow, he had to find the courage.

Then, it happened. Grace was restored. His faith flooded back like a tide of light, banishing his preposterous doubts. How could he have contemplated surrender, when the *real* solution was so obvious, so simple?

He staggered to his feet, then broke into a run again, reciting to himself, over and over, to be sure he'd get it right this time: 'ADULTERERS! SODOMITES! MOTHERS BREAST-FEEDING INFANTS OVER THE AGE OF FOUR WEEKS! REPENT AND BE SAVED . . .'

CLOSER

Nobody wants to spend eternity alone.

('Intimacy,' I once told Sian, after we'd made love, 'is the only cure for solipsism.'

She laughed and said, 'Don't get too ambitious, Michael. So far, it hasn't even cured me of masturbation.')

True solipsism, though, was never my problem. From the very first time I considered the question, I accepted that there could be no way of proving the reality of an external world, let alone the existence of other minds – but I also accepted that taking both on faith was the only practical way of dealing with everyday life.

The question which obsessed me was this: assuming that other people existed, how did they apprehend that existence? How did they experience *being*? Could I ever truly understand what consciousness was like for another person – any more than I could for an ape, or a cat, or an insect?

If not, I was alone.

I desperately wanted to believe that other people were somehow *knowable*, but it wasn't something I could bring myself to take for granted. I knew there could be no absolute proof, but I wanted to be persuaded, I needed to be compelled.

No literature, no poetry, no drama, however personally resonant I found it, could ever quite convince me that I'd glimpsed the author's soul. Language had evolved to facilitate cooperation in the conquest of the physical world, not to describe subjective reality. Love, anger, jealousy, resentment, grief – all were defined, ultimately, in terms of external circumstances and observable actions. When an image or metaphor rang true for me, it proved only that I shared with the author a set of definitions, a culturally sanctioned list of word associations. After all, many publishers used computer programs – highly specialised, but unsophisticated algorithms, without the remotest possibility of self-awareness – to routinely produce both literature, and literary criticism, indistinguishable from the human product. Not just formularised garbage, either; on several occasions, I'd been deeply affected by works which I'd later discovered had been cranked out by unthinking software. This didn't prove that human literature communicated nothing of the author's inner life, but it certainly made clear how much room there was for doubt.

Unlike many of my friends, I had no qualms what-soever when, at the age of eighteen, the time came for me to 'switch'. My organic brain was removed and discarded, and control of my body handed over to my 'jewel' – the Ndoli Device, a neural–net computer implanted shortly after birth, which had since learnt to imitate my brain, down to the level of individual neurons. I had no qualms, not because I was at all convinced that the jewel and the brain experienced consciousness identically, but because, from an early age, I'd identified myself solely with the jewel. My brain was a kind of bootstrap device, nothing more, and to mourn its loss would have been as absurd as mourning my emergence from some primitive stage of embryological neural development. Switching was simply what humans *did* now, an established part of the life cycle, even if it was mediated by our culture, and not by our genes.

Seeing each other die, and observing the gradual failure of their own bodies, may have helped convince pre-Ndoli humans of their common humanity; certainly, there were countless references in their literature to the equalising power of death. Perhaps concluding that the universe would go on without them produced a shared sense of hopelessness, or insignificance, which they viewed as their defining attribute.

Now that it's become an article of faith that, sometime in the next few billion years, physicists will find a way for *us* to go on without *the universe*, rather than vice versa, that route to spiritual equality has lost whatever dubious logic it might ever have possessed.

Sian was a communications engineer. I was a holovision news editor. We met during a live broadcast of the seeding of Venus with terraforming nanomachines – a matter of great public interest, since most of the planet's as yet uninhabitable surface had already been sold. There were several technical glitches with the broadcast which might have been disastrous, but together we managed to work around them, and even to hide the seams. It was nothing special, we were simply doing our jobs, but afterwards I was elated out of all proportion. It took me twenty-four hours to realise (or decide) that I'd fallen in love.

However, when I approached her the next day, she made it clear that she felt nothing for me; the chemistry I'd imagined 'between us' had all been in my head. I was dismayed, but not surprised. Work didn't bring us together again, but I called her occasionally, and six weeks later my persistence was rewarded. I took her to a performance of *Waiting for Godot* by augmented parrots, and *I* enjoyed myself immensely, but I didn't see her again for more than a month.

I'd almost given up hope, when she appeared at my door without warning one night and dragged me along to a 'concert' of interactive computerised improvisation. The 'audience' was assembled in what looked like a mock-up of a Berlin nightclub of the 2050s. A computer program, originally designed for creating movie scores, was fed with the image from a hover-camera which wandered about the set. People danced and sang, screamed and brawled, and engaged in all kinds of histrionics in the hope of attracting the camera and shaping the music. At first, I felt cowed and inhibited, but Sian gave me no choice but to join in.

It was chaotic, insane, at times even terrifying. One woman stabbed another to 'death' at the table beside us, which struck me as a sickening (and expensive) indulgence, but when a riot broke out at the end, and people started smashing the deliberately flimsy furniture, I followed Sian into the mêlée, cheering.

The music – the excuse for the whole event – was garbage, but I didn't really care. When we limped out into the night, bruised and aching and laughing, I knew that at least we'd shared something that had made us feel closer. She took me home and we went to bed together, too sore and tired to do more than sleep, but when we made love in the morning, I already felt so at ease with her that I could hardly believe it was our first time.

Soon we were inseparable. My tastes in entertainment were very different from hers, but I survived most of her favourite 'artforms', more or less intact. She moved into my apartment, at my suggestion, and casually destroyed the orderly rhythms of my carefully arranged domestic life.

I had to piece together details of her past from throwaway lines; she found it far too boring to sit down and give me a coherent account. Her life had been as unremarkable as mine: she'd grown up in a suburban, middle-class family, studied her profession, found a job. Like almost everyone, she'd switched at eighteen. She had no strong political convictions. She was good at her work, but put ten times more energy into her social life. She was intelligent, but hated anything overtly intellectual. She was impatient, aggressive, roughly affectionate.

And I could not, for one second, imagine what it was like inside her head.

For a start, I rarely had any idea what she was thinking – in the sense of knowing how she would have replied if asked, out of the blue, to describe her thoughts at the moment before they were interrupted by the question. On a longer timescale, I had no feeling for her motivation, her image of herself, her concept of who she was and what she did and why. Even in the laughably crude sense that a novelist pretends to 'explain' a character, I could not have explained Sian.

And if she'd provided me with a running commentary on her mental state, and a weekly assessment of the reasons for her actions in the latest psychodynamic jargon, it would all have come to nothing but a heap of useless words. If I could have pictured myself in her circumstances, imagined myself with her beliefs and obsessions, empathised until I could anticipate her every word, her every decision, then I still would not have understood so much as a single moment when she closed her eyes, forgot her past, wanted nothing, and simply *was*.

Of course, most of the time, nothing could have mattered less. We were happy enough together, whether or not we were strangers – and whether or not my 'happiness' and Sian's 'happiness' were in any real sense the same.

Over the years, she became less self-contained, more open. She had no great dark secrets to share, no

333

traumatic childhood ordeals to recount, but she let me in on her petty fears and her mundane neuroses. I did the same, and even, clumsily, explained my peculiar obsession. She wasn't at all offended. Just puzzled.

'What could it actually mean, though? To know what it's like to be someone else? You'd have to have their memories, their personality, their body – everything. And then you'd just *be* them, not yourself, and *you* wouldn't know anything. It's nonsense.'

I shrugged. 'Not necessarily. Of course, perfect knowledge would be impossible, but you can always get *closer*. Don't you think that the more things we do together, the more experiences we share, the closer we become?'

She scowled. 'Yes, but that's not what you were talking about five seconds ago. Two years, or two thousand years, of "shared experiences" *seen through different eyes* means nothing. However much time two people spent together, how could you know that there was even the briefest instant when they both experienced what they were going through "together" in the same way?'

'I know, but . . .'

'If you admit that what you want is impossible, maybe you'll stop fretting about it.'

I laughed. 'Whatever makes you think I'm as rational as that?'

When the technology became available, it was Sian's idea, not mine, for us to try out all the fashionable somatic permutations. Sian was always impatient to experience something new. 'If we really are going to live forever,' she said, 'we'd better stay curious if we want to stay sane.'

I was reluctant, but any resistance I put up seemed hypocritical. Clearly, this game wouldn't lead to the perfect knowledge I longed for (and knew I would

334

never achieve), but I couldn't deny the possibility that it might be one crude step in the right direction.

First, we exchanged bodies. I discovered what it was like to have breasts and a vagina – what it was like for me, that is, not what it had been like for Sian. True, we stayed swapped long enough for the shock, and even the novelty, to wear off, but I never felt that I'd gained much insight into *her* experience of the body she'd been born with. My jewel was modified only as much as was necessary to allow me to control this unfamiliar machine, which was scarcely more than would have been required to work another male body. The menstrual cycle had been abandoned decades before, and although I could have taken the necessary hormones to allow myself to have periods, and even to become pregnant (although the financial disincentives for reproduction had been drastically increased in recent years), that would have told me absolutely nothing about Sian, who had done neither.

As for sex, the pleasure of intercourse still felt very much the same – which was hardly surprising, since nerves from the vagina and clitoris were simply wired into my jewel as if they'd come from my penis. Even being penetrated made less difference than I'd expected; unless I made a special effort to remain aware of our respective geometries, I found it hard to care who was doing what to whom. Orgasms were better, though, I had to admit.

At work, no one raised an eyebrow when I turned up as Sian, since many of my colleagues had already been through exactly the same thing. The legal definition of identity had recently been shifted from the DNA fingerprint of the body, according to a standard set of markers, to the serial number of the jewel. When even *the law* can keep up with you, you know you can't be doing anything very radical or profound.

After three months, Sian had had enough. 'I never

realised how clumsy you were,' she said. 'Or that ejaculation was so *dull*.'

Next, she had a clone of herself made, so we could both be women. Brain-damaged replacement bodies – Extras – had once been incredibly expensive, when they'd needed to be grown at virtually the normal rate, and kept constantly active so they'd be healthy enough to use. However, the physiological effects of the passage of time, and of exercise, don't happen by magic; at a deep enough level, there's always a biochemical signal produced, which can ultimately be faked. Mature Extras, with sturdy bones and perfect muscle tone, could now be produced from scratch in a year – four months' gestation and eight months' coma – which also allowed them to be more thoroughly brain-dead than before, soothing the ethical qualms of those who'd always wondered just how much was going on inside the heads of the old, active versions.

In our first experiment, the hardest part for me had always been, not looking in the mirror and seeing Sian, but looking at Sian and seeing myself. I'd missed her, far more than I'd missed being myself. Now, I was almost happy for my body to be absent (in storage, kept alive by a jewel based on the minimal brain of an Extra). The symmetry of being her twin appealed to me; surely now we were closer than ever. Before, we'd merely swapped our physical differences. Now, we'd abolished them.

The symmetry was an illusion. I'd changed gender, and she hadn't. I was with the woman I loved; she lived with a walking parody of herself.

One morning she woke me, pummelling my breasts so hard that she left bruises. When I opened my eyes and shielded myself, she peered at me suspiciously. 'Are you in there? Michael? I'm going crazy. *I want you back*.'

For the sake of getting the whole bizarre episode over and done with for good – and perhaps also to discover for myself what Sian had just been through – I agreed to the third permutation. There was no need to wait a year; my Extra had been grown at the same time as hers.

Somehow, it was far more disorienting to be confronted by 'myself' without the camouflage of Sian's body. I found my own face unreadable; when we'd both been in disguise, that hadn't bothered me, but now it made me feel edgy, and at times almost paranoid, for no rational reason at all.

Sex took some getting used to. Eventually, I found it pleasurable, in a confusing and vaguely narcissistic way. The compelling sense of equality I'd felt, when we'd made love as women, never quite returned to me as we sucked each other's cocks – but then, when we'd both been women, Sian had never claimed to feel any such thing. It had all been my own invention.

The day after we returned to the way we'd begun (well, almost – in fact, we put our decrepit, twenty-six-year-old bodies in storage, and took up residence in our healthier Extras), I saw a story from Europe on an option we hadn't yet tried, tipped to become all the rage: hermaphroditic identical twins. Our new bodies could be our biological children (give or take the genetic tinkering required to ensure hermaphroditism), with an equal share of characteristics from both of us. We would *both* have changed gender, *both* have lost partners. We'd be equal in every way.

I took a copy of the file home to Sian. She watched it thoughtfully, then said, 'Slugs are hermaphrodites, aren't they? They hang in mid-air together on a thread of slime. I'm sure there's even something in Shakespeare, remarking on the glorious spectacle of copulating slugs. Imagine it: you and me, making slug love.'

I fell on the floor, laughing.

I stopped, suddenly. '*Where*, in Shakespeare? I didn't think you'd even *read* Shakespeare.'

★

337

Eventually, I came to believe that with each passing year, I knew Sian a little better – in the traditional sense, the sense that most couples seemed to find sufficient. I knew what she expected from me, I knew how not to hurt her. We had arguments, we had fights, but there must have been some kind of underlying stability, because in the end we always chose to stay together. Her happiness mattered to me, very much, and at times I could hardly believe that I'd ever thought it possible that all of her subjective experience might be fundamentally *alien* to me. It was true that every brain, and hence every jewel, was unique – but there was something extravagant in supposing that the nature of consciousness could be radically different between individuals, when the same basic hardware, and the same basic principles of neural topology, were involved.

Still. Sometimes, if I woke in the night, I'd turn to her and whisper, inaudibly, compulsively, 'I don't know you. I have no idea who, or what, you are.' I'd lie there, and think about packing and leaving. I was *alone*, and it was farcical to go through the charade of pretending otherwise.

Then again, sometimes I woke in the night, absolutely convinced that I was *dying*, or something else equally absurd. In the sway of some half-forgotten dream, all manner of confusion is possible. It never meant a thing, and by morning, I was always myself again.

When I saw the story on Craig Bentley's service – he called it 'research', but his 'volunteers' paid for the privilege of taking part in his experiments – I almost couldn't bring myself to include it in the bulletin, although all my professional judgement told me it was everything our viewers wanted in a thirty-second techno-shock piece: bizarre, even mildly disconcerting,

338

but not too hard to grasp.

Bentley was a cyberneurologist; he studied the Ndoli Device, in the way that neurologists had once studied the brain. Mimicking the brain with a neural-net computer had not required a profound understanding of its higher-level structures; research into these structures continued, in their new incarnation. The jewel, compared to the brain, was of course both easier to observe, and easier to manipulate.

In his latest project, Bentley was offering couples something slightly more up-market than an insight into the sex lives of slugs. He was offering them eight hours with identical minds.

I made a copy of the original, ten-minute piece that had come through on the fibre, then let my editing console select the most titillating thirty seconds possible, for broadcast. It did a good job; it had learnt from me.

I couldn't lie to Sian. I couldn't hide the story, I couldn't pretend to be disinterested. The only honest thing to do was to show her the file, tell her exactly how I felt, and ask her what *she* wanted.

I did just that. When the HV image faded out, she turned to me, shrugged, and said mildly, 'OK. It sounds like fun. Let's try it.'

Bentley wore a T-shirt with nine computer-drawn portraits on it, in a three-by-three grid. Top left was Elvis Presley. Bottom right was Marilyn Monroe. The rest were various stages in between.

'This is how it will work. The transition will take twenty minutes, during which time you'll be disembodied. Over the first ten minutes, you'll gain equal access to each other's memories. Over the second ten minutes, you'll both be moved, gradually, towards the compromise personality.

'Once that's done, your Ndoli Devices will be

identical – in the sense that both will have all the same neural connections with all the same weighting factors – but they'll almost certainly be in different states. I'll have to black you out, to correct that. Then you'll wake—'

Who'll wake?

'—in identical electromechanical bodies. Clones can't be made sufficiently alike.

'You'll spend the eight hours alone, in perfectly matched rooms. Rather like hotel suites, really. You'll have HV to keep you amused if you need it – *without* the videophone module, of course. You might think you'd both get an engaged signal, if you tried to call the same number simultaneously – but in fact, in such cases the switching equipment arbitrarily lets one call through, which would make your environments different.'

Sian asked, 'Why can't we phone each other? Or better still, meet each other? If we're exactly the same, we'd say the same things, do the same things – we'd be one more identical part of each other's environment.'

Bentley pursed his lips and shook his head. 'Perhaps I'll allow something of the kind in a future experiment, but for now I believe it would be too . . . potentially traumatic.'

Sian gave me a sideways glance, which meant: *This man is a killjoy*.

'The end will be like the beginning, in reverse. First, your personalities will be restored. Then, you'll lose access to each other's memories. Of course, your memories of *the experience itself* will be left untouched. Untouched by me, that is; I can't predict how your separate personalities, once restored, will act – filtering, suppressing, reinterpreting those memories. Within minutes, you may end up with very different ideas about what you've been through. All I can guarantee is this: for the eight hours in question, the two of you *will* be identical.'

We talked it over. Sian was enthusiastic, as always. She didn't much care what it would be *like*; all that really mattered to her was collecting one more novel experience.

'Whatever happens, we'll be ourselves again at the end of it,' she said. 'What's there to be afraid of? You know the old Ndoli joke.'

'What old Ndoli joke?'

'Anything's bearable – so long as it's finite.'

I couldn't decide how I felt. The sharing of memories notwithstanding, we'd both end up *knowing*, not each other, but merely a transient, artificial third person. Still, for the first time in our lives, we would have been through exactly the same experience, from exactly the same point of view – even if the experience was only spending eight hours locked in separate rooms, and the point of view was that of a genderless robot with an identity crisis.

It was a compromise – but I could think of no realistic way in which it could have been improved.

I called Bentley, and made a reservation.

In perfect sensory deprivation, my thoughts seemed to dissipate into the blackness around me before they were even half-formed. This isolation didn't last long, though; as our short-term memories merged, we achieved a kind of telepathy: one of us would think a message, and the other would 'remember' thinking it, and reply in the same way.

—I really can't wait to uncover all your grubby little secrets.

—I think you're going to be disappointed. Anything I haven't already told you, I've probably repressed.

—Ah, but *repressed* is not *erased*. Who knows what will turn up?

—*We'll* know, soon enough.

I tried to think of all the minor sins I must have

committed over the years, all the shameful, selfish, unworthy thoughts, but nothing came into my head but a vague white noise of guilt. I tried again, and achieved, of all things, an image of Sian as a child. A young boy slipping his hand between her legs, then squealing with fright and pulling away. But she'd described that incident to me, long ago. Was it her memory, or my reconstruction?

—My memory. I think. Or perhaps *my* reconstruction. You know, half the time when I've told you something that happened before we met, the memory of the telling has become far clearer to me than the memory itself. Almost replacing it.

—It's the same for me.

—Then in a way, our memories have already been moving towards a kind of symmetry, for years. We both remember what was *said*, as if we'd both heard it from someone else.

Agreement. Silence. A moment of confusion. Then:

—This neat division of 'memory' and 'personality' Bentley uses; is it really so clear? Jewels are neural-net computers, you can't talk about 'data' and 'program' in any absolute sense.

—Not in general, no. His classification must be arbitrary, to some extent. But who cares?

—It matters. If he restores 'personality', but allows 'memories' to persist, a misclassification could leave us . . .

—What?

—It depends, doesn't it? At one extreme, so thoroughly 'restored', so completely unaffected, that the whole experience might as well not have happened. And at the other extreme . . .

—Permanently . . .

—. . . closer.

—Isn't that the point?

—I don't know any more.

342

Silence. Hesitation.

Then I realised that I had no idea whether or not it was my turn to reply.

I woke, lying on a bed, mildly bemused, as if waiting for a mental hiatus to pass. My body felt slightly awkward, but less so than when I'd woken in someone else's Extra. I glanced down at the pale, smooth plastic of my torso and legs, then waved a hand in front of my face. I looked like a unisex shop-window dummy – but Bentley had shown us the bodies beforehand, it was no great shock. I sat up slowly, then stood and took a few steps. I felt a little numb and hollow, but my kinaesthetic sense, my proprioception, was fine; I felt *located* between my eyes, and I felt that this body was *mine*. As with any modern transplant, my jewel had been manipulated directly to accommodate the change, avoiding the need for months of physiotherapy.

I glanced around the room. It was sparsely furnished: one bed, one table, one chair, one clock, one HV set. On the wall, a framed reproduction of an Escher lithograph: *Bond of Union*, a portrait of the artist and, presumably, his wife, faces peeled like lemons into helices of rind, joined into a single, linked band. I traced the outer surface from start to finish, and was disappointed to find that it lacked the Möbius twist I was expecting.

No windows, one door without a handle. Set into the wall beside the bed, a full-length mirror. I stood a while and stared at my ridiculous form. It suddenly occurred to me that, if Bentley had a real love of symmetry games, he might have built one room as the mirror image of the other, modified the HV set accordingly, and altered one jewel, one copy of me, to exchange right for left. What looked like a mirror could then be nothing but a window between the rooms. I grinned awkwardly with my plastic face; my reflection looked

343

appropriately embarrassed by the sight. The idea appealed to me, however unlikely it was. Nothing short of an experiment in nuclear physics could reveal the difference. No, not true; a pendulum free to precess, like Foucault's, would twist the same way in both rooms, giving the game away. I walked up to the mirror and thumped it. It didn't seem to yield at all, but then, either a brick wall, or an equal and opposite thump from behind, could have been the explanation.

I shrugged and turned away. Bentley *might* have done anything – for all I knew, the whole set-up could have been a computer simulation. My body was irrelevant. The room was irrelevant. The point was . . .

I sat on the bed. I recalled someone – Michael, probably, wondering if I'd panic when I dwelt upon my nature, but I found no reason to do so. If I'd woken in this room with no recent memories, and tried to sort out who I was from my past(s), I'd no doubt have gone mad, but I knew *exactly* who I was, I had two long trails of anticipation leading to my present state. The prospect of being changed back into Sian or Michael didn't bother me at all; the wishes of both to regain their separate identities endured in me, strongly, and the desire for personal integrity manifested itself as relief at the thought of their re-emergence, not as fear of my own demise. In any case, my memories would not be expunged, and I had no sense of having goals which one or the other of them would not pursue. I felt more like their lowest common denominator than any kind of synergistic hypermind; I was less, not more, than the sum of my parts. My purpose was strictly limited: I was here to enjoy the strangeness for Sian, and to answer a question for Michael, and when the time came I'd be happy to bifurcate, and resume the two lives I remembered and valued.

So, how did I experience consciousness? The same way as Michael? The same way as Sian? So far as I could tell, I'd undergone no fundamental change – but even as I reached that conclusion, I began to wonder if I was in any position to judge. Did *memories* of being Michael, and *memories* of being Sian, contain so much more than the two of them could have put into words and exchanged verbally? Did I really *know* anything about the nature of their existence, or was my head just full of second-hand description – intimate, and detailed, but ultimately as opaque as language? If my mind *were* radically different, would that difference be something I could even perceive – or would all my memories, in the act of remembering, simply be recast into terms that seemed familiar?

The past, after all, was no more knowable than the external world. Its very existence also had to be taken on faith – and, granted existence, it too could be misleading.

I buried my head in my hands, dejected. I was the closest they could get, and what had come of me? Michael's hope remained precisely as reasonable – and as unproven – as ever.

After a while, my mood began to lighten. At least Michael's search was over, even if it had ended in failure. Now he'd have no choice but to accept that, and move on.

I paced around the room for a while, flicking the HV on and off. I was actually starting to get *bored*, but I wasn't going to waste eight hours and several thousand dollars by sitting down and watching soap operas.

I mused about possible ways of undermining the synchronisation of my two copies. It was inconceivable that Bentley could have matched the rooms and bodies to such a fine tolerance that an engineer worthy of the name couldn't find some way of breaking the symmetry. Even a coin toss might have done it, but I didn't have a coin. Throwing a paper plane? That sounded promising – highly sensitive to air currents – but the only paper in the room was the Escher, and I couldn't bring myself to vandalise it. I might have smashed the mirror, and observed the shapes and sizes of the fragments, which would have had the added bonus of proving or disproving my earlier speculations, but as I raised the chair over my head, I suddenly changed my mind. Two conflicting sets of short-term memories had been confusing enough during a few minutes of sensory deprivation; for several hours interacting with a physical environment, it could be completely disabling. Better to hold off until I was desperate for amusement.

So I lay down on the bed and did what most of Bentley's clients probably ended up doing.

As they coalesced, Sian and Michael had both had fears for their privacy – and both had issued compensatory, not to say defensive, mental declarations of frankness, not wanting the other to think that they had something to hide. Their curiosity, too, had been ambivalent; they'd wanted to *understand* each other, but, of course, not to *pry*.

All of these contradictions continued in me, but – staring at the ceiling, trying not to look at the clock again for at least another thirty seconds – I didn't really have to make a decision. It was the most natural thing in the world to let my mind wander back over the course of their relationship, from both points of view.

It was a very peculiar reminiscence. Almost everything seemed at once vaguely surprising and utterly familiar – like an extended attack of *déjà vu*. It's not that they'd often set out deliberately to deceive each other about anything substantial, but all the tiny white lies, all the concealed trivial resentments, all the necessary, laudable, essential, loving deceptions, that had kept them together in spite of their differences, filled my head with a strange haze of confusion and disillusionment.

It wasn't in any sense a conversation; I was no multiple personality. Sian and Michael simply weren't there – to justify, to explain, to deceive each other all over again, with the best intentions. Perhaps I should have attempted to do all this on their behalf, but I was constantly unsure of my role, unable to decide on a position. So I lay there, paralysed by symmetry, and let their memories flow.

After that, the time passed so quickly that I never had a chance to break the mirror.

We tried to stay together.

We lasted a week.

Bentley had made – as the law required – snapshots of our jewels prior to the experiment. We could have gone back to them – and then had him explain to us *why* – but self-deception is only an easy choice if you make it in time.

We couldn't forgive each other, because there was nothing to forgive. Neither of us had done a single thing that the other could fail to understand, and sympathise with, completely.

We knew each other too well, that's all. Detail after tiny fucking microscopic detail. It wasn't that the truth hurt; it didn't, any longer. It numbed us. It smothered us. We didn't know each other as we knew ourselves; it was worse than that. In the self, the details blur in the very processes of thought; mental self-dissection is possible, but it takes great effort to sustain. Our mutual dissection took no effort at all; it was the natural state into which we fell in each other's presence. Our surfaces *had* been stripped away, but not to reveal a glimpse of the soul. All we could see beneath the skin were the cogs, spinning.

And I knew, now, that what Sian had always wanted most in a lover was the alien, the unknowable, the mysterious, the opaque. The whole point, for her, of

347

being with someone else was the sense of confronting *otherness*. Without it, she believed, you might as well be talking to yourself.

I found that I now shared this view (a change whose precise origins I didn't much want to think about . . . but then, I'd always known she had the stronger personality, I should have guessed that *something* would rub off).

Together, we might as well have been alone, so we had no choice but to part.

Nobody wants to spend eternity alone.

UNSTABLE ORBITS IN
THE SPACE OF LIES

I always feel safest sleeping on the freeway – or at least, those stretches of it that happen to lie in regions of approximate equilibrium between the surrounding attractors. With our sleeping bags laid out carefully along the fading white lines between the northbound lanes (perhaps because of a faint hint of geomancy reaching up from Chinatown – not quite drowned out by the influence of scientific humanism from the east, liberal Judaism from the west, and some vehement anti-spiritual, anti-intellectual hedonism from the north), I can close my eyes safe in the knowledge that Maria and I are not going to wake up believing, wholeheartedly and irrevocably, in Papal infallibility, the sentience of Gaia, the delusions of insight induced by meditation, or the miraculous healing powers of tax reform.

So when I wake to find the sun already clear of the horizon – and Maria gone – I don't panic. No faith, no world view, no belief system, no culture, could have reached out in the night and claimed her. The borders of the basins of attraction *do* fluctuate, advancing and retreating by tens of metres daily – but it's highly unlikely that any of them could have penetrated this far into our precious wasteland of anomie and doubt. I can't think why she would have walked off and left me, without a word – but Maria does things, now and then, that I find wholly inexplicable. And vice versa. Even after a year together, we still have that.

I don't panic – but I don't linger, either. I don't want to get too far behind. I rise to my feet, stretching, and try to decide which way she would have headed; unless the local conditions have changed since she departed, that should be much the same as asking where I want to go, myself.

The attractors can't be fought, they can't be resisted – but it's possible to steer a course between them, to navigate the contradictions. The easiest way to start out is to make use of a strong, but moderately distant attractor to build up momentum – while taking care to arrange to be deflected at the last minute by a counter-vailing influence.

Choosing the first attractor – the belief to which surrender must be feigned – is always a strange business. Sometimes it feels, almost literally, like *sniffing the wind*, like following an external trail; some-times it seems like pure introspection, like trying to determine 'my own' true beliefs . . . and sometimes the whole idea of making a distinction between these apparent opposites seems misguided. Yeah, very fuck-ing Zen – and that's how it strikes me now . . . which in itself just about answers the question. The balance here is delicate, but one influence *is* marginally stronger: Eastern philosophies are definitely more compelling than the alternatives, from where I stand – and knowing the purely geographical reasons for this doesn't really make it any less true. I piss on the chain-link fence between the freeway and the railway line, to hasten its decay, then I roll up my sleeping bag, take a swig of water from my canteen, hoist my pack, and start walking.

A bakery's robot delivery van speeds past me, and I curse my solitude: without elaborate preparations, it takes at least two agile people to make use of them: one to block the vehicle's path, the other to steal the food. Losses through theft are small enough that the people of the attractors seem to tolerate them; presumably, greater security measures just aren't worth the cost – although no doubt the inhabitants of each ethical monoculture have their own unique 'reasons' for not starving us amoral tramps into submission. I take out a sickly carrot which I dug from one of my vegetable gardens when I passed by last night; it makes a pathetic breakfast, but as I chew on it, I think about the bread rolls that I'll steal when I'm back with Maria again, and my anticipation almost overshadows the bland, woody taste of the present.

The freeway curves gently south-east. I reach a section flanked by deserted factories and abandoned houses, and against this background of relative silence, the tug of Chinatown, straight ahead now, grows stronger and clearer. That glib label – 'Chinatown' – was always an oversimplification, of course; before Meltdown, the area contained at least a dozen distinct cultures besides Hong Kong and Malaysian Chinese, from Korean to Cambodian, from Thai to Timorese – and several varieties of every religion from Buddhism to Islam. All of that diversity has vanished now, and the homogeneous amalgam that finally stabilised would probably seem utterly bizarre to any individual pre-Meltdown inhabitant of the district. To the present-day citizens, of course, the strange hybrid feels exactly right; that's the definition of *stability*, the whole reason the attractors exist. If I marched right into Chinatown, not only would I find myself sharing the local values and beliefs, I'd be perfectly happy to stay that way for the rest of my life.

I don't expect that I'll march right in, though – any more than I expect the Earth to dive straight into the Sun. It's been almost four years since Meltdown, and no attractor has captured me yet.

I've heard dozens of 'explanations' for the events of that day, but I find most of them equally dubious – rooted as they are in the world-views of particular attractors. One way in which I sometimes think of it, on 12 January, 2018, the human race must have crossed some kind of unforeseen threshold – of global population, perhaps – and suffered a sudden, irreversible change of psychic state.

Telepathy is not the right word for it; after all, nobody found themself drowning in an ocean of babbling voices; nobody suffered the torment of empathic over-load. The mundane chatter of consciousness stayed locked inside our heads; our quotidian mental privacy remained unbreached. (Or perhaps, as some have suggested, everyone's mental privacy was *so thoroughly breached* that the sum of our transient thoughts forms a blanket of featureless white noise covering the planet, which the brain filters out effortlessly.)

In any case, for whatever reason, the second-by-second soap operas of other people's inner lives re-mained, mercifully, as inaccessible as ever . . . but our skulls became completely permeable to each other's values and beliefs, each other's deepest convictions.

At first, this meant pure chaos. My memories of the time are confused and nightmarish; I wandered the city for a day and a night (I think), finding God (or some equivalent) anew every six seconds – seeing no visions, hearing no voices, but wrenched from faith to faith by invisible forces of dream logic. People moved in a daze, cowed and staggering – while ideas moved between us like lightning. Revelation followed contradictory re-velation. I wanted it to stop, badly – I would have prayed for it to stop, if God had stayed the same long enough to be prayed to. I've heard other tramps compare these early mystical convulsions to drug rushes, to orgasms, to being picked up and dumped by ten-metre waves, ceaselessly, hour after hour – but looking back, I find myself reminded most of a bout of gastroenteritis I once suffered: a long, feverish night of interminable vomiting and diarrhoea. Every muscle, every joint in my body ached, my skin burned: I felt like I was dying. And every time I thought I lacked the strength to expel anything more from my body, another spasm took hold of me. By four in the morning, my helplessness seemed positively transcendantal: the peristaltic reflex possessed me like some harsh – but ultimately benevolent – deity. At the time, it was the most religious experience I'd ever been through.

All across the city, competing belief systems fought for allegiance, mutating and hybridising along the way . . . like those random populations of computer viruses they used to unleash against each other in experiments to demonstrate subtle points of evolutionary theory. Or perhaps like the historical clashes of the very same beliefs – with the length and timescales drastically shortened by the new mode of interaction, and a lot less bloodshed, now that the ideas themselves could do battle in a purely mental arena, rather than employing sword-wielding Crusaders or extermination camps. Or, like a swarm of demons set loose upon the Earth to possess all but the righteous . . .

The chaos didn't last long. In some places seeded by pre-Meltdown clustering of cultures and religions – and in other places, by pure chance – certain belief systems gained enough of an edge, enough of a foothold, to start spreading out from a core of believers into the surrounding random detritus, capturing adjacent, disordered populations where no dominant belief had yet emerged. The more territory these snowballing attractors conquered, the faster they grew. Fortunately – in this city, at least – no single attractor was able to expand unchecked: they all ended up hemmed in, sooner or later, by equally powerful neighbours – or confined by sheer lack of population at the city's outskirts, and near voids of non-residential land.

Within a week of Meltdown, the anarchy had crystallised into more or less the present configuration, with ninety-nine per cent of the population having moved – or changed – until they were content to be exactly where – and who – they were.

I happened to end up between attractors – affected by many, but captured by none – and I've managed to stay in orbit ever since. Whatever the knack is, I seem to have it; over the years, the ranks of the tramps have thinned, but a core of us remains free.

In the early years, the people of the attractors used to send up robot helicopters to scatter pamphlets over the city, putting the case for their respective metaphors for what had happened – as if a well-chosen analogy for the disaster might be enough to win them converts; it took a while for some of them to understand that the written word had been rendered obsolete as a vector for indoctrination. Ditto for audiovisual techniques – and that still hasn't sunk in everywhere. Not long ago, on a battery-powered TV set in an abandoned house, Maria and I picked up a broadcast from a network of rationalist enclaves, showing an alleged 'simulation' of Meltdown as a colour-coded dance of mutually carnivorous pixels, obeying a few simple mathematical rules. The commentator spouted jargon about self-organising systems – and lo, with the magic of hind-sight, the flickers of colour rapidly evolved into the familiar pattern of hexagonal cells, isolated by moats of darkness (unpopulated except for the barely visible presence of a few unimportant specks; we wondered which ones were meant to be *us*).

I don't know how things would have turned out if there hadn't been the pre-existing infrastructure of robots and telecommunications to allow people to live and work without travelling outside their own basins – the regions guaranteed to lead back to the central attractor – most of which are only a kilometre or two wide. (In fact, there must be many places where that infrastructure wasn't present, but I haven't been exactly plugged into the global village these last few years, so I don't know how they've fared.) Living on the margins of this society makes me even more dependent on its wealth than those who inhabit its multiple centres, so I suppose I should be glad that most people are content with the status quo – and I'm certainly delighted that they can co-exist in peace, that they can trade and prosper.

I'd rather die than join them, that's all.

(Or at least, that's true right here, right now.)

The trick is to keep moving, to maintain momentum. There are no regions of perfect neutrality – or if there are, they're too small to find, probably too small to inhabit, and they'd almost certainly drift as the conditions within the basins varied. *Near enough* is fine for a night, but if I tried to live in one place, day after day, week after week, then whichever attractor held even the slightest advantage would, eventually, begin to sway me.

Momentum, and confusion. Whether or not it's true that we're spared each other's inner voices because so much uncorrelated babbling simply cancels itself out, my aim is to do just that with the more enduring, more coherent, more pernicious parts of the signal. At the very centre of the Earth, no doubt, the sum of all human beliefs adds up to pure, harmless noise: here on the surface, though, where it's physically impossible to be equidistant from everyone, I'm forced to keep moving to average out the effects as best I can.

Sometimes I daydream about heading out into the

countryside, and living in glorious clear-headed solitude beside a robot-tended farm, stealing the equipment and supplies I need to grow all my own food.
With Maria? If she'll come; sometimes she says yes,
sometimes she says no. Half a dozen times, we've
told ourselves that we're setting out on such a
journey . . . but we've yet to discover a trajectory out
of the city, a route that would take us safely past all the
intervening attractors, without being gradually deflected back towards the urban centre. There must be a way
out, it's simply a matter of finding it – and if all the
rumours from other tramps have turned out to be dead
ends, that's hardly surprising: the only people who
could know for certain how to leave the city are those
who've stumbled on the right path and actually departed, leaving no hints or rumours behind.

Sometimes, though, I stop dead in the middle of the
road and ask myself what I 'really want':

To escape to the country, and lose myself in the
silence of my own mute soul?

To give up this pointless wandering and rejoin
civilisation? For the sake of prosperity, stability, certainty: to swallow, and be swallowed by, one elaborate
set of self-affirming lies?

Or, to keep orbiting this way until I die?

The answer, of course, depends on where I'm
standing.

More robot trucks pass me, but I no longer give them a
second glance. I picture my hunger as an object –
another weight to carry, not much heavier than my
pack – and it gradually recedes from my attention. I let
my mind grow blank, and I think of nothing but the
early-morning sunshine on my face, and the pleasure of
walking.

After a while, a startling clarity begins to wash over
me; a deep tranquillity, together with a powerful sense

of understanding. The odd part is, I have no idea what it is that I think I *understand*; I'm experiencing the pleasure of insight without any apparent cause, without the faintest hope of replying to the question: *insight into what?* The feeling persists, regardless.

I think: I've travelled in circles, all these years, and where has it brought me?

To this moment. To this chance to take my first real steps along the path to enlightenment.

And all I have to do is keep walking, straight ahead.

For four years, I've been following a false *tao* – pursuing an illusion of freedom, striving for no reason but the sake of striving – but now I see the way to transform that journey into—

Into what? A short cut to damnation?

'Damnation'? There's no such thing. Only *samsara*, the treadmill of desires. Only the futility of striving. My understanding is clouded, now – but I know that if I travelled a few steps further, the truth would soon become clear to me.

For several seconds, I'm paralysed by indecision – shot through with pure dread – but then, drawn by the possibility of redemption, I leave the freeway, clamber over the fence, and head due south.

These side streets are familiar. I pass a car yard full of sun-bleached wrecks melting in slow motion, their plastic chassis triggered by disuse into autodegradation; a video porn and sex-aids shop, façade intact, dark within, stinking of rotting carpet and mouse shit; an outboard motor showroom, the latest – four-year-old – fuel cell models proudly on display already looking like bizarre relics from another century.

Then the sight of the cathedral spire rising above all this squalor hits me with a giddy mixture of nostalgia and *déjà vu*. In spite of everything, part of me still feels like a true Prodigal Son, coming home for the first time – not passing through for the fiftieth. I mumble prayers

357

and phrases of dogma, strangely comforting formulae reawakened from memories of my last perihelion.

Soon, only one thing puzzles me: how could I have known God's perfect love – and then walked away? It's unthinkable. *How could I have turned my back on Him?*

I come to a row of pristine houses: I know they're uninhabited, but here in the border zone the diocesan robots keep the lawns trimmed, the leaves swept, the walls painted. A few blocks further, south-west, and I'll never turn my back on the truth again. I head that way, gladly.

Almost gladly.

The only trouble is . . . with each step south it grows harder to ignore the fact that the scriptures – let alone Catholic dogma – are full of the most grotesque errors of fact and logic. Why should a revelation from a perfect, loving God be such a dog's breakfast of threats and contradictions? Why should it offer such a flawed and confused view of humanity's place in the universe?

Errors of fact? The metaphors had to be chosen to suit the world-view of the day; should God have mystified the author of Genesis with details of the Big Bang, and primordial nucleosynthesis? *Contradictions?* Tests of faith – and humility. How can I be so arrogant as to set my wretched powers of reasoning against the Word of the Almighty? God transcends everything, logic included.

Logic especially.

It's no good. Virgin births? Miracles with loaves and fishes? Resurrection? Poetic fables only, not to be taken literally? If that's the case, though, what's left but a few well-intentioned homilies, and a lot of pompous theatrics? If God *did in fact* become man, suffer, die, and rise again to save me, then I owe Him everything . . . but if it's just a beautiful story, then I can love my neighbour with or without regular doses of bread and wine.

I veer south-east.

The truth about the universe (here) is infinitely stranger, and infinitely more grand: it lies in the Laws of Physics that have come to know Themselves through humanity. Our destiny and purpose are encoded in the fine structure constant, and the value of the density omega. The human race – in whatever form, robot or organic – will keep on advancing for the next ten billion years, until we can give rise to the hyperintelligence which will *cause* the finely tuned Big Bang required to bring us into existence.

If we don't die out in the next few millennia.

In which case, other intelligent creatures will perform the task. It doesn't matter who carries the torch.

Exactly. None of it matters. Why should I care what a civilisation of post-humans, robots, or aliens, might or might not do ten billion years from now? What does any of this grandiose shit have to do with me?

I finally catch sight of Maria, a few blocks ahead of me – and right on cue, the existentialist attractor to the west firmly steers me away from the suburbs of cosmic baroque. I increase my pace, but only slightly – it's too hot to run, but more to the point, sudden acceleration can have some peculiar side effects, bringing on unexpected philosophical swerves.

As I narrow the gap, she turns at the sound of my footsteps.

I say, 'Hi.'

'Hi.' She doesn't seem exactly thrilled to see me – but then, this isn't exactly the place for it.

I fall into step beside her. 'You left without me.'

She shrugs. 'I wanted to be on my own for a while. I wanted to think things over.'

I laugh. 'If you wanted to *think*, you should have stayed on the freeway.'

'There's another spot ahead. In the park. It's just as good.'

She's right – although now I'm here to spoil it for her.

I ask myself for the thousandth time: *Why do I want us to stay together?* Because of what we have in common? But we owe most of that to the very fact that we *are* together – travelling the same paths, corrupting each other with our proximity. Because of our differences, then? For the sake of occasional moments of mutual incomprehensibility? But the longer we're together, the more that vestige of mystery will be eroded; orbiting each other can only lead to a spiralling together, an end to all distinctions.

Why, then?

The honest answer (here and now) is: food and sex – although tomorrow, elsewhere, no doubt I'll look back and brand that conclusion a cynical lie.

I fall silent as we drift towards the equilibrium zone. The last few minutes' confusion still rings in my head, satisfyingly jumbled, the giddy succession of truncated epiphanies effectively cancelling each other out, leaving nothing behind but an amorphous sense of distrust. I remember a school of thought from pre-Meltdown days which proclaimed, with bovine good intentions – confusing laudable tolerance with sheer credulity – that there was something of value in *every human philosophy* . . . and what's more, when you got right down to it, they all really spoke the same 'universal truths', and were all, ultimately, *reconcilable.* Apparently, none of these supine ecumenicists have survived to witness the palpable disproof of their hypothesis; I expect they all converted, three seconds after Meltdown, to the faith of whoever was standing closest to them at the time.

Maria mutters angrily, 'Wonderful!' I look up at her, then follow her gaze. The park has come into view, and if it's time to herself she wanted, she has more than me to contend with. At least two dozen other tramps are gathered in the shade. That's rare, but it does happen; equilibrium zones are the slowest parts of everybody's orbits, so I suppose it's not surprising that occasionally a group of us ends up becalmed together.

As we come closer, I notice something stranger: everybody reclining on the grass is facing the same way. Watching something – or someone – hidden from view by the trees.

Someone. A woman's voice reaches us, the words indistinct at this distance, but the tone mellifluous. Confident. Gentle but persuasive.

Maria says nervously, 'Maybe we should stay back. Maybe the equilibrium's shifted.'

'Maybe.' I'm as worried as she is – but intrigued as well. I don't feel much of a tug from any of the familiar local attractors – but then, I can't be sure that my curiosity itself isn't a new hook for an old idea.

I say, 'Let's just . . . skirt around the rim of the park. We can't ignore this; we have to find out what's going on.' If a nearby basin has expanded and captured the park, then keeping our distance from the speaker is no guarantee of freedom; it's not her words, or her lone presence, that could harm us – but Maria (knowing all this, I'm sure) accepts my 'strategy' for warding off the danger, and nods assent.

We position ourselves in the middle of the road at the eastern edge of the park, without noticeable effect. The speaker, middle-aged I'd guess, looks every inch a tramp, from the dirt-stiff clothes to the crudely cut hair to the weathered skin and lean build of a half-starved perennial walker. Only the voice is wrong. She's set up a frame, like an easel, on which she's stretched a large map of the city; the roughly hexagonal cells of the basins are neatly marked in a variety of colours. People used to swap maps like this all the time, in the early years; maybe she's just showing off her prize possession, hoping to trade it for something worthwhile. I don't think much of her chances; by now, I'm sure, every tramp relies on his or her own mental picture of the ideological terrain.

Then she lifts a pointer and traces part of a feature I'd missed: a delicate web of blue lines, weaving through the gaps between the hexagons.

The woman says, 'But of course it's no accident. We haven't stayed out of the basins all these years by sheer good luck – or even skill.' She looks out across the crowd, notices us, pauses a moment, then says calmly, '*We've been captured by our own attractor*. It's nothing like the others – it's not a fixed set of beliefs, in a fixed location – but it's still an attractor, it's still drawn us to it from whatever unstable orbits we might have been on. I've mapped it – or part of it – and I've sketched it as well as I can. The true detail may be infinitely fine – but even from this crude representation, you should recognise paths that you've walked yourselves.'

I stare at the map. From this distance, the blue strands are impossible to follow individually; I can see that they cover the route that Maria and I have taken, over the last few days, but—

An old man calls out, 'You've scrawled a lot of lines between the basins. What does that prove?'

'Not between *all* the basins.' She touches a point on the map. 'Has anyone ever been here? Or here? Or here? No? Here? Or here? *Why not?* They're all wide corridors between attractors – they look as safe as any of the others. So why have we never been to these places? For the same reason nobody living in the fixed attractors has: they're not part of our territory; they're not part of *our own* attractor.'

I know she's talking nonsense, but the phrase alone is enough to make me feel panicky, claustrophobic. *Our own attractor*. We've been captured by *our own attractor*. I scan the rim of the city on the map; the blue line never comes close to it. In fact, the line gets about as far from the centre as I've ever travelled, myself . . .

Proving what? Only that this woman has had no better luck than I have. If she'd escaped the city, she wouldn't be here to claim that escape was impossible.

A woman in the crowd – visibly pregnant – says, 'You've drawn your own paths, that's all. You've stayed out of danger – I've stayed out of danger – we all know what places to avoid. That's all you're telling us. That's all we have in common.'

'No!' The speaker traces a stretch of the blue line again. 'This is *who we are*. We're not aimless wanderers; we're the people of this strange attractor. We have an identity – a unity – after all.'

There's laughter, and a few desultory insults from the crowd. I whisper to Maria, 'Do you know her? Have you see her before?'

'I'm not sure. I don't think so.'

'You wouldn't have. Isn't it obvious? She's some kind of robot evangelist—'

'She doesn't talk much like one.'

'*Rationalist* – not Christian or Mormon.'

'Rationalists don't send evangelists.'

'No? *Mapping strange attractors*; if that's not rationalist jargon, what is it?'

Maria shrugs. 'Basins, attractors – they're all rationalist words, but everybody uses them. You know what they say: the Devil has the best tunes, but the rationalists have the best jargon. Words have to come from somewhere.'

The woman says, 'I'll build my church on sand. And I'll ask no one to follow me – and yet, you will. You all will.'

I say, 'Let's go.' I take Maria's arm, but she pulls free angrily.

'Why are you so against her? Maybe she's right.'

'Are you crazy?'

'Everyone else has an attractor – why can't we have one of our own? Stranger than all the rest. Look at it: it's the most beautiful thing on the map.'

I shake my head, horrified. 'How can you say that?

we've stayed *free*. We've struggled so hard to stay free.'

She shrugs. 'Maybe. Or maybe we've been captured by what you call freedom. Maybe we don't need to struggle any more. Is that so bad? If we're doing what we want, either way, why should we care?'

Without any fuss, the woman starts packing up her easel, and the crowd of tramps begins to disperse. Nobody seems to have been much affected by the brief sermon; everyone heads off calmly on their own chosen orbits.

I say, 'The people in the basins are *doing what they want*. I don't want to be like them.'

Maria laughs. 'Believe me, you're not.'

'No, you're right, I'm not: they're rich, fat and complacent; I'm starving, tired, and confused. And for what? Why am I living this way? That robot's trying to take away the one thing that makes it all worthwhile.'

'Yeah? Well, I'm tired and hungry, too. And maybe an attractor of my own will *make it all worthwhile*.'

'*How?*' I laugh derisively. 'Will you worship it? Will you pray to it?'

'No. But I won't have to be afraid any more. If we really have been captured – if the way we live is stable, after all – then putting one foot wrong won't matter: we'll be drawn back to our own attractor. We won't have to worry that the smallest mistake will send us sliding into one of the basins. If that's true, aren't you glad?'

I shake my head angrily. 'That's bullshit – dangerous bullshit. Staying out of the basins is a skill, it's a gift. You know that. We navigate the channels, carefully, balancing the opposing forces—'

'Do we? I'm sick of feeling like a tightrope walker.'

'Being *sick of it* doesn't mean it isn't true! Don't you see? She *wants* us to be complacent! The more of us who start to think orbiting is easy, the more of us will end up captured by the basins—'

I'm distracted by the sight of the prophet hefting her possessions and setting off. I say, 'Look at her: she may be a perfect imitation – but she's a robot, she's a fake. They've finally understood that their pamphlets and their preaching machines won't work, so they've sent a machine to lie to us about our freedom.'

Maria says, 'Prove it.'

'What?'

'You've got a knife. If she's a robot, go after her, stop her, cut her open. Prove it.'

The woman, the robot, crosses the park, heading north-west, away from us. I say, 'You know me; I could never do that.'

'If she's a robot, she won't feel a thing.'

'But she looks human. I couldn't do it. I couldn't stick a knife into a perfect imitation of human flesh.'

'Because you know she's not a robot. You know she's telling the truth.'

Part of me is simply glad to be arguing with Maria, for the sake of proving our separateness – but part of me finds everything she's saying too painful to leave unchallenged.

I hesitate a moment, then put down my pack and sprint across the park towards the prophet.

She turns when she hears me, and stops walking. There's no one else nearby. I halt a few metres away from her, and catch my breath. She regards me with patient curiosity. I stare at her, feeling increasingly foolish. I can't pull a knife on her: she might not be a robot, after all – she might just be a tramp with strange ideas.

She says, 'Did you want to ask me something?'

Almost without thinking, I blurt out, 'How do you know nobody's ever left the city? How can you be so sure it's never happened?'

She shakes her head. 'I didn't say that. The attractor looks like a closed loop to me. Anyone who's been

365

captured by it could never leave. But other people may have escaped.'

'What *other people*?'

'People who weren't in the attractor's basin.'

I scowl, confused. 'What basin? I'm not talking about the people of the basins, I'm talking about us.'

She laughs. 'I'm sorry. I don't mean the basins that lead to the fixed attractors. Our strange attractor has a basin, too: all the points that lead to *it*. I don't know what this basin's shape is: like the attractor itself, the detail could be infinitely fine. Not every point in the gaps between the hexagons would be part of it: some points must lead to the fixed attractors – that's why some tramps have been captured by them. Other points would belong to the strange attractor's basin. But others—'

'What?'

'Other points might lead to infinity. To escape.'

'Which points?'

She shrugs. 'Who knows? There could be two points, side by side, one leading into the strange attractor, one leading – eventually – out of the city. The only way to find out which is which would be to start at each point, and see what happens.'

'But you said we'd all been captured, already—'

She nods. 'After so many orbits, the basins must have emptied into their respective attractors. The attractors are the stable part: the basins lead into the attractors, but the attractors lead into themselves. Anyone who was destined for a fixed attractor must be in it by now – and anyone who was destined to leave the city has already gone. Those of us who are still in orbit will stay that way. We have to understand that, accept that, learn to live with it . . . and if that means inventing our own faith, our own religion—'

I grab her arm, draw my knife, and quickly scrape the point across her forearm. She yelps and pulls free, then clasps her hand to the wound. A moment later, she takes it away to inspect the damage, and I see the thin red line on her arm, and a rough wet copy on her palm.

'You lunatic!' she yells, backing away.

Maria approaches us. The probably-flesh-and-blood prophet addresses her: 'He's mad! Get him off me!' Maria takes hold of my arm, then, inexplicably, leans towards me and puts her tongue in my ear. I burst out laughing. The woman steps back uncertainly, then turns and hurries away.

Maria says, 'Not much of a dissection – but as far as it went, it was in my favour. I win.'

I hesitate, then feign surrender.

'You win.'

By nightfall, we end up on the freeway again; this time, to the east of the city centre. We gaze at the sky above the black silhouette of abandoned office towers, our brains mildly scrambled by the residual effects of a nearby cluster of astrologers, as we eat the day's prize catch: a giant vegetarian pizza.

Finally, Maria says, 'Venus has set. I think I ought to sleep now.'

I nod. 'I'll wait up for Mars.'

Traces of the day's barrage drift through my mind, more or less at random – but I can still recall most of what the woman in the park told me.

After so many orbits, the basins must have emptied . . .

So by now, we've all ended up *captured*. But – how could she know that? How could she be sure?

And what if she's wrong? What if we haven't all, yet, arrived in our final resting place?

The astrologers say: None of her filthy, materialist, reductionist lies can be true. Except the ones about destiny. We like destiny. Destiny is fine.

I get up and walk a dozen metres south, neutralising

their contribution. Then I turn and watch Maria sleeping.

There could be two points, side by side, one leading into the strange attractor, one leading – eventually – out of the city. The only way to find out which is which would be to start at each point, and see what happens.

Right now, everything she said sounds to me like some heavily distorted and badly misunderstood rationalist model. And here I am, grasping at hope by seizing on half of her version, and throwing out the rest. *Metaphors mutating and hybridising, all over again . . .*

I walk over to Maria, crouch down and bend to kiss her, gently, upside down on the forehead. She doesn't even stir.

Then I lift my pack and set off down the freeway, believing for a moment that I can feel the emptiness beyond the city reach through, reach over, all the obstacles ahead, and claim me.

All Orion/Phoenix titles are available at your local bookshop or from the following address:

Littlehampton Book Services
Cash Sales Department L
14 Eldon Way, Lineside Industrial Estate
Littlehampton
West Sussex BN17 7HE

telephone 01903 721596, *facsimile* 01903 730914

Payment can either be made by credit card (Visa and Mastercard accepted) or by sending a cheque or postal order made payable to *Littlehampton Book Services.*

DO NOT SEND CASH OR CURRENCY

Please add the following to cover postage and packing

UK and BFPO:
£1.50 for the first book, and 50P for each additional book to a maximum of £3.50

Overseas and Eire:
£2.50 for the first book plus £1.00 for the second book and 50P for each additional book ordered.

BLOCK CAPITALS PLEASE

name of cardholder ....   *delivery address*
                      ....   *(if different from cardholder)*
address of cardholder ....
....
....
....
        postcode ....   *postcode* ....

☐ I enclose my remittance for   £..

☐ please debit my Mastercard/Visa (delete as appropriate)

card number ☐☐☐☐☐☐☐☐☐☐☐☐☐☐☐☐☐☐

expiry date ☐☐☐☐

signature ....